*USA TODAY* bestselling author **Janice Maynard** loved books and writing even as a child. After multiple rejections, she finally sold her first manuscript! Since then, she has written fifty-plus books and novellas. Janice lives in Tennessee with her husband, Charles. They love hiking, travelling and family time.

You can connect with Janice at www.janicemaynard.com
www. Twitter.com/janicemaynard
www. Facebook.com/janicemaynardreaderpage
www. Facebook.com/janices maynard
www. Instagram.com/therealjanicemaynard

**Yahrah St John** is the author of thirty-two books and one deliciously sinful anthology. When she's not at home crafting one of her spicy romances with compelling heroes and feisty heroines with a dash of family drama, she is gourmet cooking or travelling the globe seeking out her next adventure. St John is a member of Romance Writers of America. Visit www.yahrahstjohn.com for more information.

Discover more at millsandboon.co.uk

# AFTER HOURS SEDUCTION

JANICE MAYNARD

# SECRETS OF A FAKE FIANCÉE

YAHRAH ST JOHN

MILLS & BOON

First Published in Great Britain 2020
by Mills & Boon, an imprint of HarperCollinsPublishers,
1 London Bridge Street, London, SE1 9GF

*After Hours Seduction* © 2020 Janice Maynard
*Secrets of a Fake Fiancée* © 2020 Yahrah Yisrael

ISBN: 978-0-263-27924-5

0520

**MIX**
Paper from
responsible sources
**FSC™ C007454**

This book is produced from independently certified FSC™ paper to ensure responsible forest management.

For more information visit: www.harpercollins.co.uk/green

Printed and bound in Spain
by CPI, Barcelona

# AFTER HOURS SEDUCTION

## JANICE MAYNARD

For Anastasia—

You were the first to make me a nana! I love brainstorming book ideas with you... :)

# One

Quinten Stone's older brothers had been aggravating him all his life, but this time they'd gone too far. Thanks to their meddling, his ex-lover was on her way to his isolated house. To live and work with him for a month or more. He didn't know how he was going to survive.

As an old man of twenty-eight, he bore the weighty title of Chief Operating Officer at the outdoor gear company the siblings owned jointly. That was enough responsibility. The last thing he needed to add to his agenda was juggling unresolved feelings for the woman who had dumped him.

Now his frustration had reached the boiling point.

"Butt out, you two. I'll make my own decisions."

Except that it was far too late.

Katie had already agreed to come. He'd be damned if he'd let her think her presence would affect him. That her defection had wounded him.

The three brothers sat in oversize armchairs in front of

a massive stone fireplace. Had they been so inclined, they could have roasted a pig and had room to spare. But it was July in Maine, so the hearth was empty.

Farrell, the oldest of the Stone brothers—better known as the mad genius inventor when Quentin and Zachary were in the mood to tease him—leaned forward with a scowl on his face. "You've made some dumbass moves recently, Quin. According to the surgeon, you're in danger of injuring yourself permanently if you don't do what he says. You might never ski again if you don't give yourself time to heal."

*Never ski again...*

The knot in Quin's stomach clenched.

After his brothers, and their company, skiing was what he loved most in the world. And not so long ago he'd been one of the *best* in the world.

He stared at the angry red scar bisecting his knee. Eighteen months ago, in the car accident that had claimed their father's life, Quin's entire right leg had been mangled. He'd had three different surgeries, the latest of which was a complete knee replacement. Six weeks of grueling physical therapy had him back on his feet and walking fairly normally, but the surgeon insisted that ligaments and tendons needed time to recover.

Quinten wouldn't have been in such a mess now if he'd been appropriately cautious after the first two surgeries. He'd been desperate to prove he was still the same man he'd been before the accident. So on New Year's Day, Quin had strapped on his skis and tackled a punishing hill in Vermont.

Unfortunately for him, his not-quite-rehabbed knee had given out. He went down hard, slamming into a small clump of trees on the edge of the run. Help was with him immediately, but the damage was done. This time, the leg was so jacked up, it couldn't be repaired. Hence the new piece of metal in his now-bionic knee. With every painful step, he was hell-bent on getting his life back.

He was desperate to ski well again, to carry his part of the family business, and to enjoy recreational sex with no messy emotions involved. Was that so much to ask?

When Quin said nothing, Zachary continued the gentle harangue. "The doc wants you to take it easy for six more weeks. With Katie here to help you work remotely, you can rest *and* keep up with your responsibilities. It's an ideal solution, Quin. Give it a chance."

The Stone brothers shared a landing strip, a small private jet and a kick-ass helicopter. None of them spent more than two or three days a week at headquarters anyway. But it was the idea of having his wings clipped that made Quin feel like he was suffocating. Or maybe it was thinking about facing Katie that caused his chest to constrict…

"I don't like having strangers in my house," he muttered.

Farrell grinned. "You can hardly call Katie a stranger. We've all known her forever. I can do without my incredibly efficient admin for six weeks. Reluctantly."

Quin lurched to his feet and paced. The noose was growing tighter. He and Katie had been an under-the-radar item two years ago. Right up until the moment she dumped him with no good explanation.

Katie had been employed by Stone River Outdoors for six years, and Quin didn't feel comfortable pursuing her once she pulled the plug on their relationship. Not to mention that his pride had gotten in the way of asking for answers.

No one in his personal or business life had an inkling about the affair. Katie hadn't wanted gossip, and Quin agreed. Now he couldn't tell his brothers the truth. Katie was the *last* person he wanted under his roof. She'd made it clear they were over. Living together, alone in the Maine woods, would be incredibly awkward. They might have unresolved issues, but he had no doubt the chemistry was still there.

"What about *my* admin?" he asked. Quin had inherited the amiable employee after his father's death. The woman had been with the company since the first Bush was in office. She was set in her ways and flummoxed by new technology. But at least she was *not* Katie.

Farrell winced. "First of all, she's kind of a train wreck. We can either fire Mrs. B outright or find her something less taxing. Maybe give her a nice retirement offer. Katie will help you find a replacement."

Quin sucked in a sharp breath at the thought of Katie helping him with anything. He clenched his jaw. "What did Katie say when you asked her to come here?" He and Katie had managed to avoid each other for the most part since their breakup. But she *did* come to his father's funeral.

Despite everything, Quin had been oddly comforted by her presence.

Zachary stood as well and stretched. "She told Farrell and me she would do anything necessary to keep Stone River Outdoors up and running. A hell of a nice woman. It's asking a lot to put up with your sorry hide."

"So true." Farrell glanced at his watch. "I've gotta run. Meeting a contractor in twenty minutes."

The brothers had suspected for some time now that they were the victims of corporate espionage. Two of Farrell's designs had been scooped and rushed to market. The new products were inferior and not exactly what he had been working on, but they were close enough to raise red flags.

To handle the disturbing possibility, Farrell had decided to make some changes. He hoped to work exclusively at his vacation home here on the northern Maine coast during the coming months and not at his lab in the Portland headquarters. Hence the contractor.

Quin felt the raw taste of panic. "I can work remotely on my own. I don't need any help. Nor do I need a babysitter. I swear I'll take it easy."

His brothers stood shoulder to shoulder, their sympathetic expressions like acid poured on his screwed-up life. Farrell jingled his keys. "We know you, buddy. You push and push and push as if the sheer force of your will can do the healing. But it doesn't work that may. Maybe in endurance training, but not in this. Six weeks isn't long, Quin. And we're not deserting you. We'll be around more than you think. It's not a prison sentence."

Zachary sighed. "It sucks, Quin. All of it. Losing Dad. The accident. You being sidelined with medical crap. I get it. You're on the edge. I can tell. But follow the doctor's orders, and you'll be a new man."

Katie had boxed herself into a corner when she gave Farrell and Zachary her word. Farrell was her boss. Zachary signed her checks.

Though both men had emphasized multiple times that her participation in this unorthodox experiment was entirely voluntary, she couldn't in good conscience say no. Stone River Outdoors needed her.

*Quinten* needed her.

Her anxiety rose, even on a lush summer day with the sunshine beaming down from a brilliant blue sky.

At Ellsworth, just before the crowded tourist playground that included Acadia National Park, she turned onto a less traveled road for the last leg to Stone River. Here, nobody but locals traversed the winding rural highway. Nothing much to see but acres of forests and fields and peaceful ponds and lakes.

The looming confrontation with Quinten tightened her stomach and made her palms sweat as she clenched the steering wheel. Two years ago, he'd been her lover. Even now, the truth of that statement baffled her.

Quinten Stone, by any definition, was a wealthy, larger-than-life athlete and playboy. After missing a gold medal by half a second when he was a teenager, he had continued to compete on the world stage. Both Quinten *and* his brothers were accustomed to traveling the globe.

Despite the fiery attraction she and Quin had shared, their lives—and their values—had been too different. Katie thought money was for helping people. Quin had spent his fortune recklessly, including the many outrageous ways he'd tried to impress her.

Katie didn't care about trips and gifts, nice though they were. She had yearned for a deep, intimate relationship. But Quin was one of the most emotionally closed-off men she had ever met. A sad cliché, but true.

When her GPS lost a signal, she was forced to concentrate on the road rather than Quin.

At last, she found the turnoff. Katie had never been this far up in Maine, but she had seen aerial photographs. Three spectacular homes sat on rocky promontories overlooking the sea. Almost two centuries before, a Stone ancestor had acquired an enormous tract of pristine wilderness and had named the small river meandering through his property after himself. Subsequent generations sold off the bulk of the land, but the current Stone brothers still owned several hundred square miles. They liked their privacy.

She had been warned about the gate and was armed with an access code. The paved road must have been wildly expensive but necessary. In addition to Range Rovers, Jeeps and ATVs, the brothers each had various automotive passions that wouldn't take kindly to harsh treatment.

Quinten's indulgence of choice was a sin-black Ferrari. Sexy as hell. Once, during her short-lived relationship with him, he had taken her out on the open road in the sleek high-performance vehicle—at midnight. They'd been far from Portland on an obscure two-lane highway that was relatively straight. When Quin unleashed the beast beneath the hood of the car, the rush of speed had been exhilarating.

Even now, Katie could remember the sting of wind on her cheeks and the tug in her chest every time Quin accelerated. He'd been in his element, laughing and teasing her when she gasped and squealed.

Later, he had found a secluded lane and made love to her on the still-warm hood of the car.

Katie sucked in a breath and felt her breasts tighten. Everything about Quinten Stone had been perfect for her—as long as she ignored the zeros at the end of his bank balance and his inability to connect with a woman emotionally.

Slamming the door on those painful memories would not be easy. Actually, it might be impossible.

All around her, the forest created a lush, green tunnel. Ash and aspen, spruce and pine. Beech and butternut, juniper and fir. No wonder the Stone brothers came up here at every opportunity. Unfortunately, all roads came to an end, whether the traveler was prepared or not.

Katie parked her Honda Civic at the base of the steps and stared up at the house. Quinten's house.

It was magnificent. Made of cedar and stone, it nestled among a grove of evergreens. Enormous plate glass windows were meant to frame the wild expanse of ocean and horizon. Today the sea was placid.

No one came out to greet her, although she suspected

the aging Toyota sedan parked ahead of her belonged to an employee of some sort. Slowly, she climbed the stairs. She was ridiculously nervous.

Almost twenty-four months had passed since she broke up with Quinten. In the interim, she had made sure to know when he was in the building at headquarters, so she could avoid any awkward encounters. Though her office adjoined Farrell's, it was easy enough to duck out when she knew Quinten was likely to visit. That only happened when both men were in the Portland office at the same time.

Eighteen months ago—at the funeral for Mr. Stone Sr.— *of course* she had spoken to her former lover. Quinten had been tense and strained, still bandaged and on crutches in the midst of his grief. Her heart had broken for him. They exchanged a few words, and then Katie had moved away down the receiving line.

Knowing how close Quinten had come to death had shaken her badly.

Now here she was, more than a year later, about to step into the lion's den. She shook her head, though no one was there to see her dithering. The lion's den wasn't really a suitable metaphor for what she was feeling. People were scared of lions. Worried about being eaten alive.

When it came to Quinten and Katie, she *wanted* to see him. The scary part of the situation was her own abysmal lack of control.

Quinten Stone was the only man whose touch she had ever craved. Even knowing he was all wrong for her, it had taken every ounce of determination she possessed to break off the relationship.

Now she was about to undo all her brave, good work. Every sensible decision reduced to dust.

She tiptoed toward the nearest window and peeked

inside. The place looked deserted, though she knew the impression was false. The master of the house was in residence. That was why she had been summoned to work here instead of Portland.

Unfortunately, she had left her sunglasses in the car. She closed her eyes and squinted skyward, warming her face. That was a mistake. Behind her lids, images of Quin danced dizzyingly. Smiling. Laughing. He was six foot two to her five-eight. At one time, he'd told her he was glad she was tall, because it made *standing-up* sex easier. And then he had proceeded to demonstrate.

*Oh Lordy.* Her head ached. A band of tension wrapped her skull. What was she going to say when she saw him? His raven's-wing black hair and deep blue eyes were as familiar to her as her own.

Once more, she turned and looked through the glass. The furnishings inside intrigued her, though her line of sight was partially hampered by heavy, masculine drapes in navy and burgundy. Those thick window coverings were necessary insulation in the dead of winter.

Her pulse fluttered. She wasn't going to faint… Was she? She was scared and rattled and desperately anxious to see him. Pressing a hand to her stomach, she took one last look before she rang the bell.

As she lifted a finger to touch the buzzer, a sound at her back made her spin around. She tripped over her own feet and landed on her butt.

The tall, lanky man staring down at her managed a lopsided grin. "Are you casing the joint for a robbery?"

"Of course not," she muttered, her face flaming. "Hello, Quinten."

His brief nod acknowledged her greeting. "Katie…" He grimaced. "I would help you up, but I'm still working on keeping *myself* upright."

She scrambled to her feet, desperately glad she hadn't worn a skirt. "How are you doing?"

He shrugged, his expression guarded. "Depends on who you ask. I'm damned tired of people worrying about my health."

# Two

"Maybe you should quit feeling sorry for yourself and be glad you're not dead or paralyzed."

Quinten winced. Possibly *this* was the other reason his brothers had sicced Katie on him. She didn't suffer fools gladly, and she didn't tolerate whiners and slackers. She ran Farrell's department like a tight ship. Because she was both impeccably fair and incredibly compassionate, her coworkers loved and feared her in equal measure.

It dawned on him that he couldn't actually offer to carry her suitcase. Well, he could *offer*, but the outcome wouldn't be pretty.

Had his silence been as long as it seemed? Seeing her like this after so very long had him tongue-tied like a middle school boy. His heart pounded and his legs were weak, even more than they had been recently. "I didn't think you would agree to come here," he said bluntly, wondering if the memories of what they had once shared tempted her at all.

He sure as hell was tempted.

She wore her sunshiny blond hair up in a ponytail today, but he remembered far too well what it felt like to have that pale silk waterfall stream across his chest.

Big brown eyes surveyed him warily. "I didn't think you'd allow it," she said quietly. "So I guess we were both surprised."

He took a deep breath. "Maybe we should start over. Thanks for coming, Katie. I really appreciate it. So do Farrell and Zachary."

"You're welcome. Happy to do it," she said, shielding her eyes with one hand and staring out at the ocean. The surface glittered like a million diamonds flung beneath the sun. "Your home is lovely, Quin."

"Thank you." The stilted conversation was polite, but it covered a thousand unspoken memories. Katie wore a pink silk button-up top with the sleeves rolled to her elbows. Slim black pants hugged her legs. Simple silver sandals exposed feminine toenails painted shell pink. Was it bad that he wanted to nibble those toes? He cleared his throat. "Let's go inside."

"Of course." Katie was clearly nervous as they paused in the expansive foyer, though she was trying to hide it.

He gazed at her intently, trying to mask his frustration at not being able to bound up the stairs. "I've been bunking down here since the surgery. Mrs. Peterson will show you to the guest suite on the second floor. Let me know if there's anything you need. Anything at all. I want you to be comfortable."

Was it his imagination, or did Katie's eyes widen fractionally as a hint of pink matched her cheeks to her blouse. "Okay."

He cleared his throat. "Take your time settling in. We'll have dinner at seven. If you'd like a drink before that, I'll be in the library."

When Quinten disappeared down the hallway toward the back of the house, Katie exhaled forcefully. She hadn't realized she'd been holding her breath.

The housekeeper, possibly in her late fifties, was pleasant and welcoming as she led Katie up the massive rough wood stairs. She wore a khaki skirt and a white knit shirt. Almost a uniform, but not quite.

"Do you live nearby?" Katie asked.

"Call me Lydia if you like," the other woman said. "Yes. As the crow flies. My husband is a commercial fisherman. The work has its ups and downs. We have a house we love out in the woods, but jobs for me are few and far between. When Mr. Quinten built this house five years ago and advertised for a housekeeper/caretaker, it was the perfect solution."

"That's wonderful. I suppose you don't have to be here full-time since Quin travels frequently."

The housekeeper pointed out a luxurious bathroom and a sitting room with a mini fridge and microwave. "Not as a rule, but since this last surgery, much more often. We've had an in-house physical therapist until very recently. Mr. Quinten is determined to rehab his leg."

"Patience is not his strong suit."

The housekeeper grinned. "You could say that. Mr. Quin has a fully outfitted home gym and has been following the exercise regimen the therapist left behind."

"I see. Do you know where I'll be working?"

"Yes. I can show you in the morning, but not right now. Mr. Quinten was very insistent that you have time to get comfortable and settled. The three brothers worked together last week to rearrange things downstairs. You'll have your own work space. It's not huge, but I think you'll find they've set up everything as closely as possible to what you're used to in Portland."

"Sounds perfect."

"Do you need help with your bags?"

Katie stretched her arms over her head. "Thanks, but no. After all that driving, I could use the exercise."

"Very well. Please let me or Mr. Quinten know if there is anything you need, anything at all."

Katie followed the sturdy woman downstairs and thanked her again before heading out to the car. It took three trips to bring everything inside. She had her favorite pillow, one large suitcase and an assortment of tote bags. Six weeks was a long time. Her books had silently begged to come with her. A personal laptop. Toiletries. And last but not least, a stack of files from Quinten's office. Most everything she needed was online, but there were a few personnel and policy notes that would require Quin's attention.

The house was eerily quiet. Obviously, Mrs. Peterson was still there. She would be preparing dinner. Who knew where Quinten was? His stiff welcome had set Katie's nerves on edge. Neither of them had forgotten how it felt to be naked together. She could see it in his eyes.

She was impressed that Farrell and Zachary had convinced Quin to try this new setup. Quinten Stone was as stubborn and unmalleable as his last name. Sometimes she would swear he disagreed with people just for the heck of it.

When she was done unpacking, she walked out onto the second-floor porch. It ran the length of the house and was furnished with a row of beautiful stained hardwood rocking chairs. She picked her favorite and sat down with a sigh. It was the first time all day she had felt truly relaxed.

True, she still had to get through dinner, but she was working on her positive attitude. Quin was just a man. This was only a job—and a temporary one at that. A woman could cope with anything for six weeks.

The irony of these beautiful rocking chairs moving gently back and forth in the breeze on Quinten's porch wasn't lost on her. The only thing he ever slowed down for was sex. Now that she thought about it, even that was sometimes fast and furious.

Some would call it nervous energy, but Katie knew better. The man was driven. His ability to focus was legendary. He'd won national and international skiing championships so many times he'd been called an iron man on the slopes and in the air at ski jump competitions.

Did he still want to compete?

While they were dating, she had wanted so badly to know the man beneath the mask. She had been intrigued by the rare glimpses into his psyche, flattered by his interest in her. But as time passed, it became clearer and clearer that Quin didn't want anything beyond the physical relationship they shared.

He didn't really want to know her at all.

His indifference had hurt. Would it be the same now?

She dithered over what to wear to dinner. In the end, she didn't change clothes. No reason for him to get the wrong idea. Theirs was to be a working relationship, *not* a meeting of the minds, and especially not a stroll down memory lane.

She did, however, take the time to loosen her hair and brush it out. As soon as the sun went down, the evening would take on a slight chill. The ponytail either seemed too casual for dinner or bared too much of her neck.

All the careful self-lecturing didn't erase her anticipation about the evening to come. Her legs trembled as she descended the stairs and sought out the library. The small, intimate room was filled with floor-to-ceiling bookshelves that overflowed with history, biography and a broad range of fiction.

Quinten *had* changed clothes. He'd been casually dressed during their encounter when she arrived. Now he wore crisp navy trousers and a perfectly starched white button-down shirt. The tortoiseshell glasses that rested on the bridge of his masculine nose as he flipped through a leather-bound volume were new.

She bit down hard on her bottom lip. The man didn't need any help in the sex appeal department. Those studious spectacles were not at all fair to the female sex. "Were these your father's books?" she asked lightly, searching for an innocuous topic as she entered the room. Otherwise, she might simply pounce on him.

The small crease between Quin's masculine eyebrows told her the question puzzled him. "No," he said. "They're mine."

She wasn't quite able to hide her surprise. When did Quinten Stone *ever* sit down long enough to read? "Oh…"

He stared at her, obviously disgruntled. "Did you really think I was nothing but a dumb jock?"

"Of course not," she said. "But you…"

"What?" he demanded. "Spit it out."

What she wanted to say was that he seemed to have changed. That he was somehow more centered than the man she remembered. Perhaps her opinion wouldn't please him. "Nothing," she muttered. "May I have a drink?"

He poured a glass of her favorite champagne and handed it to her. "Cheers," he said gruffly.

Their fingers brushed briefly as he released the flute. How had he remembered this little detail about her preference? "I'm surprised you recalled how much I like this." He must have had a hundred dates since their breakup, been intimate with a dozen women. Isn't that what the Stone men did? Sample the smorgasbord?

Well, maybe not Farrell. As far as Katie could tell, her boss was still in love with his dead wife.

Quinten moved a step closer, though she didn't think he meant to crowd her. His eyes blazed with blue fire. "I remember every moment of our time together, Katie. All of them," he said gruffly. "You're the kind of woman who's hard to forget."

Something about the way he looked at her sucked every atom of oxygen out of the room. Her heartbeat grew sluggish. For one insane moment, she nearly stepped forward into his arms.

"I shouldn't have come, should I?" she whispered raggedly.

"It depends." His gaze settled on her mouth.

"On what?"

"On whether you want to walk back into the fire."

Half an hour later Quinten sat across the table from his new admin and cursed himself for his reckless stupidity. Katie's chocolate-brown eyes were hazy with arousal. That wasn't conceited conjecture on his part. He *knew* her. Intimately. He knew the way she looked when they had shared a night of passion and woke in each other's arms, ready to do it all over again.

Damn it. He hadn't even made it twenty-four hours without stepping over the line. "I'm sorry," he said, the apology both awkward and formal even to his own ears. "I shouldn't have spoken to you that way. You have my word it won't happen again."

Katie stared at him. She had barely touched her roast beef and mashed potatoes. And that was after picking at her Caesar salad. "How can you be so sure?" Her guarded gaze surprised him.

He jerked, physically disturbed by what was surely a teasing question. "Because I won't allow it."

"So pompous, so arrogant." Her gaze seemed to judge him. "We're both adults. And this situation is temporary. Surely we couldn't be faulted for enjoying a temporary liaison."

"I'm not falling for that. You're jerking my chain, aren't you?" Quinten shot a wild glance toward the doorway, expecting at any moment to be rescued from this surreal conversation by the imminently practical Mrs. Peterson.

Good help was hard to find.

"I couldn't resist."

He drained his wine and tried to clear his paper-dry throat. "Still a tease, I see."

Katie ran her thumb up and down the stem of her glass. The sensual gesture was so damned evocative he felt gooseflesh break out all over his body. "I like playing with you, Quin," she said. "Everyone at SRO walks on eggshells around the *boss*. But I know the truth. You're a pussycat when someone rubs your fur the right way." Her mocking smile reached inside his chest and squeezed his heart so hard he ached. But then again, that might be nothing more than raw lust.

"Perhaps we should discuss the work we'll be doing," he said, still trying to regain control of the situation.

Finally, Mrs. Peterson returned, this time bearing a silver tray with two perfectly torched crème brûlées. "I hope you saved room," she said cheerfully. "This was my grandma's recipe. The custard has been known to make grown men cry."

Katie dug into her dessert with such enthusiasm that

Quin felt his forehead bead with sweat. "Omigosh," she moaned. "This is better than sex."

The unflappable housekeeper chuckled. "I won't weigh in on that one, but you two enjoy. I'll clean up the kitchen and let myself out. See you tomorrow morning."

Quin had to force himself to eat the dessert. Not that it wasn't as amazing as Katie had said, but because he was suddenly, stunningly aware of the fact that he was going to be alone in this huge house with the woman he absolutely couldn't take into his bed.

He forced himself to swallow the last bite. "If you'll excuse me, I have to hit the gym and do some exercises." He stood up awkwardly. "Is everything upstairs to your liking?"

He was not running away. Not at all. But he couldn't breathe when he was this close to her.

She stared at him as if she could see inside his brain. "It's lovely," she said. "What time do you want to start in the morning?"

*Work, Quin. She's talking about work.*

"Mrs. Peterson will have breakfast ready at eight thirty," he said gruffly. "After we eat, you can bring me up to speed on whatever needs my attention."

"Is there an alarm set tonight?" she asked.

"No. But we're perfectly safe."

"That wasn't why I asked. I didn't want to disturb you if I took a walk later."

He frowned. "I'd rather you not do that alone."

"You just said I'm perfectly safe." She wiped her mouth, tossed her napkin on the table and stood, as well.

His jaw tightened. Other than his brothers, he was not accustomed to people arguing with him. "We get the occasional black bear, and of course, moose. Either or both can be unpredictable."

"I grew up camping out with my parents," Katie said. "I know all the right things to do during an animal encounter."

Quin had the oddest feeling this conversation was about more than any possible danger in the woods. "What if I join you?" he asked impulsively. "Give me an hour."

Her eyes widened. "Can you do that? With your leg?"

Her question piqued his pride. "I'm not an invalid," he snapped. "My leg is one hundred percent healed from the surgery. But soft tissue damage takes longer to get back to normal, at least another six weeks. The doc wants me to be cautious in the meantime."

Katie shook her head slowly, her expression hard to read. "I can't imagine it. The man who takes chances and flies through the air. Grounded."

He stared at her. "I thought I might get a little sympathy from you."

"Is that what you want from me? Sympathy?"

"I remember you as sweeter, kinder."

"Maybe you hit your head. I'm the same woman I've always been."

Something simmered between them. A sensual awareness that two long years hadn't managed to erase. "An hour," he said. "We'll go for a walk together."

She hesitated so long his stomach clenched.

Finally, she nodded. "Okay. I suppose that's best since I don't know my way around. Wouldn't want to fall into the ocean."

He exhaled. "Good. I'll meet you in the foyer at nine."

# Three

Katie changed into her boots and hiking pants and topped them with a thin fleece pullover. Although it was summer, the nights this far north were on the cool side. Since she and Quin weren't tackling a strenuous trail, the extra warmth would feel good.

Her nerves were jittery. Maybe this whole *work-from-Quin's-home* thing was a terrible idea. Had she mentioned the late-night walk in hopes he would want to join her? She couldn't trust her own motives. Her emotions were all over the map. She'd missed Quin. A lot.

From the beginning, being with him had been fun and exciting. One weekend when they were dating, he tried to fly her to Paris for dinner. Katie had declined politely, mildly horrified at the thought of spending all that money on a whim.

Her family was solidly blue-collar. No matter how hard she tried, she couldn't imagine herself assimilating into

Quin's jet-set lifestyle. It was possible she had a chip on her shoulder. About fitting in. Years ago, a friend had once called her a reverse snob for judging her wealthy bosses without really knowing them. The comment had stung, because it contained a grain of truth.

As pleasant as it had been to have a man like Quin shower her with attention and lavish her with gifts, she didn't need all those things to be happy. What she liked about Quin wasn't his money—it was *him*. But it seemed to her that he had used the expensive presents as a shield, a way to keep her at arm's length. She could never get through to him with a meaningful, genuine connection.

At five till nine she scooted down the stairs. He was waiting for her at the bottom looking darkly handsome and brooding. "Do you want to see the water?" he asked. "The moon is full. Should be a good view."

"Sounds wonderful."

Exiting the house was awkward. There was a moment when she was sure he was going to take her arm or link his fingers with hers. In the old days that would have been normal. Now, not so much.

Quin kept a hand resting on the stair rail as they descended. For a man who'd had his entire knee replaced six weeks ago, he moved with impressive grace. But she knew that an elite athlete wouldn't take kindly to the limitations of his current situation.

"We'll take a trail through the woods," he said. "It meanders a bit, but it's been cleared, and it's easy to follow even in the dark."

"Sounds good."

The path, strewn with pine needles and last autumn's leaves, was wide enough for two people to walk side by side. Here in the great outdoors—enveloped in the peace of a quiet summer evening—Katie felt a huge, poignant sadness for all she had lost. She couldn't *make* Quin be the man she wanted him to be.

As long as she reminded herself that he wasn't part of her future, perhaps she could get through this six weeks unscathed. Her heart clenched with regret. For a moment, she wasn't sure which she missed the most, the friend or the lover. Was it possible to resurrect the friendship and avoid the temptation to tumble back into his bed?

The fact that her pulse was all over the map said no.

Eventually, the trail led out of the woods into a clearing. "Watch your step," Quin said. "We're close to the edge."

Just ahead was nothing but darkness, although the moon was full and bright. The pitch-black ocean was an unknown expanse. A little tingle worked its way down Katie's spine.

She had a love/hate relationship with water. After almost drowning in a neighbor's pool when she was seven, she had always struggled to enjoy getting *in* the water. On the other hand, she was more than happy to sit and watch the tides go in and out.

Now that she and Quin were away from the trees, she could hear the crash of the sea on the shore below. This part of the coastline wasn't immensely high. Even so, the rocky promontory where Quin had built his house commanded a stunning view. She had glimpsed it on her arrival. She would enjoy the sea for as long as she was here.

Tonight, though, was different. Quinten had led her to the edge of certainty. The brink of safety. She shivered and wrapped her arms around her waist. Her stomach flipped and flopped with excitement or fear or a combination of both.

Their silent contemplation was not entirely comfortable. The rifts between them were gone but not forgotten. Quin was still an enigma. And Katie still wanted a man who would love her in a forever kind of way.

Since Quin wasn't likely to change, maybe this was a chance for Katie to find closure and learn how to relate to him in a new way.

She touched his arm briefly, barely making contact. "Will you tell me about the car accident?" she asked.

At her side, she felt his posture stiffen. His voice was low and gravelly when he responded. "I don't remember much. The doctors say I may never recover those moments. All I know is that Dad and I had a driver that day. We'd been visiting Farrell up here and were headed back to Portland. Somewhere east of Bangor, another vehicle crossed the center line and hit us head-on. My father was killed instantly when he was thrown from the car. No seat belt. My side of the car took the brunt of the collision. My right leg was crushed."

"Oh, Quin. I'm so sorry."

He shrugged. "I've had surgery, more than once actually. Pins. Reconstruction. You can imagine. Finally, they said they had done all they could."

"And then?"

"I convinced myself I had to get back out on the slopes. It was stupid, I know, but I was desperate. Skiing is my life."

"But you crashed."

He chuckled, though there was no real amusement in the sound. "Crashed and burned, you might say. I didn't go back to square one. Instead, I fell backward at least a hundred miles. The leg was so jacked up this time that a replacement was my only option."

"And the skiing?"

His profile was beautiful and remote in the moonlight. "No one knows."

They stood there, both contemplating those three awful words. She couldn't imagine Quin not being able to glide down a black diamond slope. "It must have been even harder grieving your father in the midst of all that," Katie said.

He moved restlessly, likely because his leg was hurting. "Surely you remember my father's reputation. He wasn't an easy man."

"I knew how people talked about him at work, but with his sons…" She trailed off, not quite knowing how to express what she wanted to say. *Mrs.* Stone had died when Quentin was born. The boys had been raised by their father and his drill sergeant brand of parenting.

Katie had her own issues with Quinten's stern parent, but now was not the time to rehash old wounds.

Quin shoved his hands in his pockets and kicked a small stone over the edge. "I loved my father, I suppose. I didn't want him to die. But the business is a lot easier now that it's just the three of us."

Katie had always been able to read people. It was one of her gifts, and one that wasn't always pleasant. Right now, she could tell that Quin was hurting, physically *and* mentally. She wanted to comfort him, to bring back his rakish smile and devil-may-care personality.

But any move on her part to initiate physical contact, no matter how innocent, would escalate rapidly. She and Quin shared a powerful attraction, even now, after two years apart. It shimmered in the air between them, almost tangible.

"We should go," she said, suddenly aware of the danger in this late-night walk. "I was up early this morning. I'm beat."

Quin nodded slowly. "Of course."

They didn't speak as they reversed their course. All her excitement about seeing Quin again had coalesced into a painful knot in her stomach, mostly because she had stood at this exact emotional precipice before.

It was like eating six cones of cotton candy at the county fair. The crazy choice was fun and deliciously indulgent at the time, but always ended up hurting you in the end.

Back at the house, they climbed the stairs. When Quin unlocked the door and stepped aside, Katie brushed past him, only to pause in the foyer. "Good night, Quin," she said.

For a fleeting moment, his guard slipped. She saw the hunger in his gaze. The intensity of it lodged a lump in her throat. Long seconds passed during which she was absolutely certain he was going to kiss her.

Instead, after breathless moments, he caressed her cheek with the back of his hand, his hard fingers warm against her chilled chin. "I'm glad you're here, Katie. Good night."

Then he turned his back and walked away.

Katie had trouble falling asleep, despite her fatigue. When she'd agreed to this unorthodox plan, it was under the misguided notion that she had mastered her infatuation with Quinten Stone. Apparently, she was as prone as her ex-lover to making dumb decisions.

She wanted to jump back in her car and escape to Portland.

The night was long and not particularly restful.

When morning came, she felt hungover and apprehensive. Was it possible that Quin read her as easily as she did him? Did he know how much she wanted him still?

Over breakfast, neither of them said much. Mrs. Peterson interrupted the uncomfortable silences, bustling in and out with fresh coffee, additional hot biscuits and second helpings of eggs and bacon.

At one point, Katie leaned forward and whispered to Quin. "I usually eat yogurt and granola at home."

He lifted an eyebrow. "Are you complaining?"

"Heavens, no."

The quick exchange lightened the mood.

Finally, the wonderful meal was over, and Quin showed her the makeshift office setup. All the amenities were there. The only eyebrow-raising moment was seeing how close his desk was to hers in the small converted downstairs bedroom.

Shoving aside a host of inappropriate emotions, Katie turned on the top-of-the-line laptop and uploaded the files she had brought via flash drive from Portland. "I'll email some things to you," she said. "A lot of it has to do with the first and second quarter financial reports. Zachary wants you to look over them, and then Farrell needs you to sign off on some preliminary designs."

After that, the morning settled into a routine. With both of them busy—independently but in the same close quarters—it might have been awkward. Fortunately, once Katie immersed herself in work, the hours flew rapidly.

She and Quinten were just getting ready to head to the dining room for lunch when Zachary showed up in the doorway.

Quin frowned. "I thought you were in Portland."

"I was. Now I'm here. I brought the chopper." He glanced at Katie. "Have you told her yet?"

"Haven't had a chance. She only arrived yesterday afternoon. We've spent this morning getting up to speed on everything I've missed."

Katie looked from one brother to the other. "Told me what? That sounds ominous."

Zachary perched on the corner of her desk, one leg swinging. "You could say that. We're starting to believe that Stone River Outdoors has been the target of corporate espionage."

Her eyes widened. "You can't be serious."

"Unfortunately, we are," Zachary said. "I've stumbled across irregularities in a few of our accounts. Farrell has seen a couple of his most promising ideas pop up in the marketplace. The first time, we wrote it off as coincidence. After all, two people can have the same idea at roughly the same moment. But then it happened again."

It was Katie's turn to frown. "Why didn't Farrell tell me any of this?"

"He's been trying to keep it under the radar to see if anyone at SRO tips his or her hand. Plus, we didn't want to place you in danger."

"Danger?" Katie laughed until she realized that Quentin and Zachary weren't the slightest bit amused.

Zachary spoke up again. "Farrell and I started to wonder if the crash that killed Dad and injured Quin was not an accident at all."

She sucked in a sharp breath, her gaze darting to Quinten. He'd barely said a word. "And what do *you* think?" she asked.

He ground his jaw. "That's the hell of it. I was recovering from the crash, so I wasn't dialed into what was happening. The guys didn't want to worry me when I was having my leg pieced back together. And then, of course, I pulled my dumbass stunt out on the ski slopes."

Zachary winced. "Yeah. A few weeks ago, we told Quin everything. It's true the doctor wants him to take it easy. A side benefit of having you here, though, is that you and Quin can take a look at all the departments remotely and see if you notice any unusual activity or red flags."

Katie gnawed her lip. "I understand how Farrell's department runs. That's my baby. Quinten controls a whole lot of stuff I know nothing about."

"I can teach you," Quinten said. "You're one of the smartest people I know."

Zachary nodded. "Quin is right. Plus, you're an outsider, so you might notice something the three of us have missed."

"I can't believe this," Katie said. "It sounds like a spy movie."

Quentin stood and waved them all toward lunch. "We hope we're wrong. We hope we're just being paranoid. The evidence is piling up, though. Somebody may be trying to take down Stone River Outdoors."

Over corned beef sandwiches and thick wedges of watermelon, Katie took a quieter role as the two brothers joked and laughed and eventually dedicated themselves to serious business. Zachary knew Mrs. Peterson, of course. When he teased her, the older woman's cheeks turned pink.

Even a stranger could see that Zachary and Quinten were clearly siblings. They shared the same broad shoulders and lanky build. But Zachary's eyes were brown, and his hair was chestnut. He probably inherited his coloring from his mother.

There were personality differences, too. Quinten was intense, competitive. Zachary climbed mountains and was also an incredibly athletic man, but he bounced from one activity to the next—whether it was racing sport cars in Abu Dhabi or navigating the Amazon in search of new experiences.

Zachary popped the top on his second beer. "This will be it for me. I still have to fly back to Portland later."

Quinten lifted an eyebrow. "I thought you'd be spending the night." He glanced at Katie. "My brother's house makes my place look like a shack in the woods."

"He exaggerates." Zach grinned. "But it is pretty damned awesome. I'll show you around sometime," he said to Katie.

A change in Quin's expression told Katie he didn't like that idea. Maybe because his middle brother had a reputation for playing the field—a *large* field. She smiled at Zachary. "I'd love to see your home when you have a chance. And what about Farrell's?"

Quin relaxed visibly. "Farrell has the biggest chunk of land…his choice. It starts at the ocean and runs inland, narrower than what Zach and I have, but long. From the air, our houses aren't that far apart along the coastline. When we're in the mood, we can even walk from one to the next."

Katie nodded. "And yours is the farthest south, because I didn't see the others as I drove in."

Zachary interrupted before Quin could respond. "Yep. It's the whole birth order thing. Farrell's is first, or northernmost if you like. Then me in the middle. And Quin, here, brings up the rear."

Quin made a rude gesture.

Katie laughed. "I thought middle children were supposed to be the peacemakers."

Zachary shrugged. "I never did like people telling me who I was expected to be, whether it was a book or my *dearly departed, God-rest-his-soul* father."

After a beat of silence following Zachary's unexpectedly revealing comment, Katie folded her napkin and scooted back in her chair and stood. "I want to help, any way I can."

The brothers rose to their feet in unison. "You already are," Quin said. "The three of us couldn't think of a single other person more capable of helping out with our situation than you."

Zachary shook her hand. "Thanks again, Katie." He grabbed his keys and phone from a nearby table. "Let me know if anything comes up."

# Four

*Let me know if anything comes up.*

Zachary's parting words echoed in Quentin's head for days. He knew Zachary was referring to possible clues about espionage, but where Quentin's mind went was a whole different ball game.

It was only the second week of Katie's intrusion into his routine, and already Quin felt out of sorts. His brothers had been extremely generous in not berating him for the time he'd been away from work. They had shouldered the burden of his responsibilities and had kept things running. That additional load meant his siblings had been tied down far more than usual.

Now it was Quin's turn to deal with important company issues and let Zach and Farrell get back to what they did best.

Unfortunately, that meant Quin had to utilize Katie's considerable talents. Now that she was here, under his roof, he wasn't sure he could handle it. Though he had no residual animosity about the way their relationship ended, it would be a foolish mistake—on several counts—to let personal feelings and urges creep back in.

Katie was an employee of Stone River Outdoors. An employee at the highest level. It didn't matter that he still responded to her physically. She was off-limits. Not only that, but she had made it very clear two years ago—he wasn't the kind of man she wanted in her life on a permanent basis.

He couldn't fault her logic. He was a selfish bastard. He'd put his desire to pit himself against the ski slopes ahead of what was good for his family. Now he had to deal with the consequences.

At this particular moment, he was taking a break from the claustrophobic in-home office on the pretext of stretching his muscles. Katie had worked quietly all morning, barely paying any attention to him at all. Didn't matter. All he could think about was dragging her down the hall and into his bed.

After a cycle of reps on the rowing machine that left him sweaty but still restless, he moved to the leg press. His range of motion improved daily. For any normal person, the speed and breadth of his recovery would be cause for celebration.

But Quin had never been satisfied with *normal* or ordinary. He'd spent years in search of *extraordinary*. Better, stronger, faster.

If he wasn't an award-winning skier, then who was he? The business didn't count. Heading up Stone River Outdoors was what he did, not who he was.

Unfortunately, the tenets that applied to being an elite athlete didn't translate to relationships. He'd never known his mother. Though he was tight with his siblings, he had no sisters. His father had governed their family life with authoritarian might. Any inkling of softer emotions had been beaten out of the Stone boys with a belt or a paddle.

Quin had suffered more than he needed to, because he was stubborn and wouldn't give his father the satisfaction of seeing him cry. Maybe he was screwed from the beginning when it came to understanding the female sex. He didn't have much to offer any woman in the way of emotional intimacy, which was why his romantic liaisons tended toward the brief and expedient. He couldn't *train* for the kind of closeness women wanted.

Katie had been the first female to make him wonder whether he had it in him to fall in love. And look how that had turned out.

He cursed as more sweat rolled into his eyes. This was nuts. He was letting her presence in his house disrupt his recovery. She was temporary. There was no going back to the past.

Only because he refused to be a coward did he shower and return to the office down the hall.

Katie looked up with a smile. "Oh good. I had a pile of questions and couldn't go much further without your input."

How could she be so damned *happy* all the time? Did she really feel none of the desperate need that was consuming him from the inside out?

Ten minutes later Quin found himself sitting elbow to elbow with his former lover, the two of them poring over reports and data that had to be reconciled and disseminated to the appropriate department heads.

Every time he leaned in to check a figure or answer a question, he inhaled her familiar scent. Like one of Pavlov's dogs, he salivated inwardly, his body on high alert. His enforced celibacy, combined with the advent of this extraordinary woman into his monastic existence, made him horny and desperate and despairing.

How was he going to survive an entire six weeks without pouncing on her? It wasn't a pretty picture.

Katie, on the other hand, barely seemed to notice he was around. She arose early in the mornings and went jogging through the forest. After that, he could hear her showering upstairs. Memories of what she looked like slick and wet tormented him.

When she arrived at the breakfast table every day, they made mundane conversation over their meal and then headed to the office and settled in to work. The teasing, flirtatious woman who sparred with him in the very beginning had disappeared. Perhaps, like Quinten, she had decided that the job at hand was more important than revisiting an old relationship.

By the beginning of week three, he'd had enough. If he didn't get out of this house soon, he was going to expire from cabin fever.

When he found his temporary admin, she was in the process of scanning and emailing quality control reports to an independent contractor who would be visiting their manufacturing plant in a couple of months.

Katie glanced up at him. "Farrell called the landline. He said you weren't answering your cell."

Guilt assailed Quin. He'd been ignoring his phone all morning. "Anything urgent?"

She wrinkled her nose. "I think they worry about you."

He felt his face heat. "I'm not a child. I'm in charge of the whole damn company."

"I know that, Quin. They do, too. But you almost died, and you've had to give up something you love, at least temporarily. That would be a lot for anyone to handle, plus you lost your dad, as well."

He scowled. "I won't be smothered. I won't do anything else stupid, I swear. But I won't be smothered."

She nodded slowly. "Okay. Would it be better if I gave you a break? I could go home and come back in a week."

The thought startled him. "God, no. You're not the problem. But I had an idea, and I was hoping you would agree."

Now her stance was wary. "What kind of an idea?"

"Zachary has Broadway tickets to see *Hamilton* in New York this weekend with one of his interchangeable girlfriends. His date is ill, and he says he doesn't want to look for a replacement on such short notice. Farrell mentioned to him that you're a history buff, so they thought you might like to see the musical. With me," Quin clarified.

"Oh." Her cheeks flushed. "I've never been to New York. Always wanted to. How would we get there?"

"I'm not cleared to fly the jet yet, but I can hire a pilot to take us down and back. We'd have two hotel rooms, of course. You'd need something fancy for both evenings, and then casual wear in case we decide to go walking in Central Park. We can do some shopping if you'd like."

She stared at him so long he had to fight the urge to fidget. "Quin?" she said.

"What?"

"Is this a ploy to seduce me?"

"Absolutely not." He bristled. "I do occasionally think of other people besides myself. I wanted you to have some fun."

"Calm down. I appreciate the sentiment, but you're not stupid. You have to know I still want you."

His jaw dropped before he caught himself and snapped it shut. "You do?" he said hoarsely.

"Of course I do. You're a handsome man. We share a past. We're here together in this enormous house with no distractions. Believe me, though, if we ever decide we want to end up in bed again, it will have *nothing* to do with work. Are we clear?" Her challenging stare made his spine tingle.

"Yes, ma'am. Does that mean you're up for a weekend in the big city?"

"I love the idea," she said. "Let's do it."

Katie was in big trouble. She'd been striving to maintain a business-as-usual attitude while working with Quin. If he was going to whisk her away to one of the most romantic cities in the world, she might forget to protect her heart. But still she'd said yes. She wanted to be with him too badly to say no.

For the first time, she seriously pondered the implications of sleeping with him again. She was older and wiser now than the last time they'd dated. But she still wanted something that was out of reach. She wanted him to *need* her. Desperately. Not for a momentary sexual encounter, but in every way that a man could need a woman.

She was clear that she had made the right choice before. He cared more about skiing than he did about Katie or any woman. The truth hurt. And then there was the money thing. She and Quinten Stone didn't come from different worlds; they came from opposite planets.

Breaking up with him two years ago had been the sensible thing to do.

Most people she knew worried about how often they could hit Starbucks each week without blowing their monthly food budgets. Quentin bought champagne like it was tap water.

His emotional distance and his careless attitude toward money bothered her still.

The big question was—could she let herself indulge in this once-in-a-lifetime trip and not end up sleeping with him? The temptation would be there, undoubtedly. Soon,

Quin would no longer require her professional assistance. On a finite day and time in the near future, her work in his home would be done.

When Quinten was cleared to return to Portland and resume his full roster of responsibilities, Katie would be free to go back to her role as second in command of the R & D department as Farrell's right-hand woman.

That day was still a few weeks away. What about all the lovely unpredictable moments in between?

For the remaining forty-eight hours until their departure, Quin made himself scarce. Katie buried herself in work. She was forced to email Quin her questions, because the frustrating man was tucked away somewhere in this big, lonely house.

By the time Friday morning rolled around, Katie's mix of anxiety and excitement rose to fever pitch. She had asked Quinten if they could stop in Portland and let her grab a few things she needed for the weekend. He had vehemently refused, insisting that she was on the company dime at the moment and that the CEO's expense account would more than cover the cost of a *couple of cocktail dresses*.

He said that last bit dismissively, as if couture clothing was little more expensive than the price of a yoga top and pants or a college T-shirt. To him, it probably was.

At last, they were on the plane and airborne. Katie tried not to gawk. Two years ago, she hadn't been Quin's girlfriend long enough to warrant a journey in this sleek, utterly luxurious Cirrus Vision Jet. It was light and fast and nimble, the perfect vehicle for a fantasy weekend.

Quin talked to the pilot for a few minutes before returning to his seat beside hers. From the tiny built-in fridge at his side, he extracted two mini bottles of wine and a cellophane-wrapped tray of cheese, fruit and crackers.

"Have some," he urged. "LaGuardia may be busy. Who knows how long it will be till lunch."

"We just ate breakfast," she protested. But still she took the glass he offered her, along with a selection of snacks.

The jet had large windows. The day was blue and bright. Nothing to fear, even for a novice traveler. It seemed as if they were gliding on clouds.

The wine must have given her Dutch courage. They'd been aloft less than an hour when she blurted out a question. "Is this how you feel when you're flying down a mountain?"

He actually winced. For a moment, she glimpsed his raw grief. "You could say that," he said, his shoulders hunched. "It's the quiet and the freedom. I've never found anything else like it."

After his painfully truthful answer, she was sorry she had brought it up. She didn't want him to be sad. And she didn't want to remind herself that skiing gave him something she couldn't.

Today, he looked every inch the successful billionaire. His sport coat and slacks were perfectly tailored, drawing attention to his fit, muscular body. He'd brought along those tortoiseshell reading glasses. The ones that made her all gooey inside with lust.

"I never knew you wore glasses," she said. "When did that happen?"

"During all those surgeries, it was too complicated to fool with contacts. I got these, and now it's a habit, I guess. I see fine at a distance, but farsightedness runs in the family. Or maybe it was all those years of squinting into snow glare—who knows?"

All Katie knew was that she had a burning desire to see him naked in bed reading the *Wall Street Journal* with nothing but those sexy frames perched on his masculine nose.

They landed in New York and handled the formalities

without issue. A private car met them as soon as they were done. Katie had a hard time not gawking. The traffic and the iconic yellow cabs and the tall buildings. Everywhere she looked, the city hummed and buzzed with activity.

The trip from the airport into the city was slow. She had plenty of time to drool over sidewalk flower shops, tiny art galleries, and eventually, on Madison Avenue, the glitzy storefronts of every high-end retail name in the world.

Quin had booked them rooms at the Carlyle on the Upper East Side. Katie adored the building on sight. She knew enough of the glamorous address to remember that Princess Diana had been known to stay here. The iconic hotel was only a block from the park and five blocks from the Met.

The bellman took them up to adjoining rooms on the thirty-second floor. With the drapes open wide, the view of Central Park was breathtaking. When the uniformed employee departed to deposit Quin's suitcase in his room, Katie threw her arms around her ex-lover and gave him a quick hug. "My first trip to New York. Thank you, Quin. This is incredible."

His pleased smile told her he was glad she was impressed. "Shopping next," he promised. "Or maybe lunch first."

"How about a hot dog vendor?" Katie asked. "I've always wanted to do that. And sit on a bench in the sun? What do you think?"

He gave her a wry look. "You won't find any hot dog vendors in this rarified neighborhood. But I might be able to dig up a gourmet pizza place. Would that do?"

Over thick, tomatoey slices of cheesy goodness, Katie relaxed. Maybe she and Quin would have sex during this trip, and maybe they wouldn't. She had a bad habit of overthinking things. As a self-confessed type A control freak, surely she could try to relax and see how the weekend unfolded.

It wouldn't hurt her to loosen up a little.

When she and Quin were dating, they had argued about money a lot. She thought he threw his fortune away too easily, and Quin said Katie let her relatives sponge off her to an alarming extent.

To Katie, money was something a person shared and spread around to do good. Her parents had struggled to get by, but they had helped their neighbors. In Katie's eyes, Quin—having the Stone fortune at his disposal—should have been a philanthropist.

In Quin's defense, though, Katie had to admit she didn't have healthy boundaries with the people she loved. As the only person of her extended family to have gone to college, she had ended up comfortably well off while her siblings and cousins lived paycheck to paycheck. Whenever she felt guilty for her blessings, she invariably let herself be manipulated into giving out loans that somehow were never repaid.

The hugest fight she and Quin ever had happened not long before she broke up with him. She had innocently asked his advice about rehab programs. When he questioned her, she admitted she was thinking about paying for her sister's boyfriend to go into a treatment facility.

Quin had been both furious and incredulous. He pointed out that the boyfriend—who had been in and out of jail— was never likely to agree, and if he did, he wouldn't last the course.

Katie called Quin callous. He'd told her she was naive and credulous. The bitter quarrel had colored what was left of their time together.

And then his father had intervened, and Katie's humiliation had been complete.

# Five

Quin had made the best of his *passenger* status on the jet, but he hated not being the one at the controls. It helped having Katie along.

He'd gotten a kick out of watching her face today as they traveled. She was bubbling over with excitement and not afraid to show it. Her enthusiasm for life was one of the qualities that had drawn him to her in the beginning. That and her limber, soft body.

The memories made him sweat.

Now, while he finished his pizza, he studied her again. She looked beautiful as always. Her pale blond hair was loose around her shoulders. Subtle eye shadow made her beautiful brown eyes sparkle. With her tailored black jacket and pants and a tangerine silk blouse, she looked as if she belonged among the throngs of Manhattan professional women out for lunch.

At the moment, Katie was chatting up their waiter. Quin watched as the handsome young man grew more animated.

Katie coaxed him to talk about his theatrical dreams and how he missed his family back in Kansas. After three trips to the table for drink refills, fresh parmesan and extra napkins, the kid was halfway in love with Quin's date.

It was nothing sexual that Katie did. She was simply Katie being Katie. The interest she showed in other people was genuine and authentic. Her sunny personality drew both men and women into her orbit. Everyone wanted to be her friend.

And Katie had said that *she* still wanted Quin.

The admission rocked him to the core. He was pretty sure she regretted saying it. If she still wanted him physically, why in the hell had they broken up? They had so much chemistry between them. Did she not realize that such an intense attraction was rare and wonderful?

Two years ago, she had wanted more from him. He knew it. And he resented the way she was always pressuring him to be a better man. What if the man he was didn't get any better? What if being selfish was his default setting?

He'd had his share of casual sex before Katie came along. Even a handful of what he would characterize as *serious* relationships. None of those women had kept him up nights wondering, wanting, wishing he could reset the clock and rewrite the past.

When Katie had given him the heave-ho, he'd been embarrassingly shocked. He'd thought they were doing great. How could he have been so blind to what was happening? He'd felt like a fool.

If it had been only his ego that had taken a hit, he probably would have brushed it off and taken his dismissal like a man. But he'd been so dazzled by Katie and drowning in raging lust, it had literally never occurred to him that the relationship was in danger.

Now, memories of the playful passion they once shared

made him itchy and horny and desperate. Katie said she still wanted him, but what did that mean? If they were to resume a physical relationship, it would be on his terms this time.

At last, his patience for seeing another man flirt with Katie ran out. "We should go," he said abruptly. "That is if you want time to pick up a few things for the weekend." He held out his platinum card to the waiter.

When the kid disappeared, Katie gave Quin a placating smile. "I wouldn't feel comfortable in any of these Madison Avenue stores. I brought several tops to swap out with what I have on now. And I threw in some running clothes and shoes. One of my friends at home came to a Broadway show recently. She told me you see people in jeans and sneakers all the way up to fancy stuff. I'll be fine without anything new."

Quin ground his teeth. The one sure thing he could offer Katie was pampering. He could wine and dine her and shower her with gifts. But the frustrating woman didn't want his money. She had told him so on more than one occasion. How could they connect if she continually dismissed his strengths? Extravagance was his strong suit—that and hot sex. Katie was honest about wanting him. The rest of it didn't seem to matter to her.

He debated his options. "I brought a tux for this evening," he said. "But I can buy a suit to wear if it would make you more comfortable."

Her eyes widened, aghast. "Don't buy a new suit. I'm sure you have half a dozen or more at home."

"Fine. I won't buy a suit. But let's dress up and have fun tonight," he cajoled. "It won't hurt, I promise. Stone River Outdoors can afford to buy a valuable employee a little black dress."

She chewed her lip. Hard. He could see the hesitation in her body language and in her eyes. "I don't know…"

"No strings attached. I swear."

When she swallowed, he saw the muscles in her delicate throat ripple. "I can't even imagine what a dress like that will cost," she said. "I don't like pushy, condescending salesclerks. They intimidate me."

Quin chuckled. "One of Zach's old girlfriend's works three blocks from here. I sent her a text earlier and told her we might drop by after lunch. She promised to pull a few things out of stock for you, so it won't take forever. Her name is Katiya. She's Bulgarian, I think. You'll like her."

Katie scowled. "Did you date her after Zach did? Is that why you're so chummy?"

He held up his hands. "Wow. Suspicious much? My brothers and I don't share lady friends. Zachary and Katiya spent a lot of time in Maine, so I know her pretty well."

"Fine. We'll go see her. But if she doesn't have anything appropriate, I don't want to spend the whole day shopping. It's my first time in New York. You promised me the Met."

"So I did." He nodded in surrender, wanting to laugh, but knowing it wasn't the moment. Just then, his phone dinged. The text made him smile. He showed it to Katie. "Zach and Farrell are in Midtown for a meeting. They want to know if we'd like to have dinner with them before they fly back to Portland. We don't have to," he added quickly. "We can wait until after the show." Truthfully, he wasn't entirely sure he wanted his aggravating brothers horning in on his night out with Katie. Still, having two chaperones might keep him from doing something recklessly stupid.

Katie hunched her shoulders and looked around her as if someone might be listening to their conversation. "I know it's probably incredibly unsophisticated," she whispered, "but I *hate* the idea of eating a big meal at ten thirty at night. Tell them yes. We'd love to."

"Even if it has to be early? Entering the theater after the lights go down is frowned upon."

"Whenever you say," she said. "It will be fun getting to know Zachary better."

Quin chewed on that unpleasant thought. Women loved Zachary. Come to think of it, Zach and Katie probably *would* hit it off. Katie never met a stranger, and Zach had been charming females since he was in kindergarten.

Before Quin could resolve his unease, someone held the door open for them and they stepped out onto the sidewalk, blinded by the July sunshine and a blast of heat. New York City in the summer could be rainy or brutally hot. Quin would take the heat any day, but he didn't know about his companion.

"Shall I get a cab?" he asked, moving toward the curb.

Katie grabbed his arm. "You said it was only three blocks. Let's walk." She paused, visibly stricken. "Unless your knee is bothering you. I'm sorry. I wasn't thinking."

Again, Quin ground his jaw. "Good Lord, Kat. I can stroll down the damned street. Come on. It's this way."

In his frustration, he had shortened her name without thinking. The affectionate *Kat* was what he had called her in the midst of their wild affair. Did she even notice his slip?

They headed off along the sunbaked sidewalk, dodging other pedestrians. Katie didn't say a word, her expression subdued. She had shed her jacket. Her bare arms were slender and defined with attractive muscles. Did she work out? It occurred to him that many aspects of her life were a mystery to him. Their time together had been relatively brief and more focused on sex than standard getting-to-know-you dates.

When they arrived at the well-known French fashion house, Katie almost balked again. "Couldn't we try something a little less pricey?"

He opened the plate glass door with the gold lettering and steered her inside. The cool air-conditioned air washed over them like a benediction. "Quit worrying. As thrifty as you are, you'll probably still be wearing this same dress a dozen years from now. Do the amortization. You're good at math. It will make you feel better."

Katiya sauntered up to greet them, her slender feet clad in five-inch heels that made Katie's eyes widen. "Quin," Katiya said, smiling broadly. She kissed him on both cheeks. "It's been too long. I was sorry to hear about your father. And your leg." She looked him over. "You seem to be doing well."

Quin returned the kisses. "I'm great. This is a friend of mine, Katie Duncan. We came to the city on short notice, and she needs a dress. Broadway show. Dinner with Farrell and Zachary. You know the deal."

Katiya kissed Katie on both cheeks, as well. "I have exactly the thing. Since dear Quin gave me a *heads*-up—I think that's the expression—I had time to pick and choose. The weather is hot as Hades this weekend. I thought perhaps plenty of bare skin."

Quin nodded soberly. "Bare skin. I like it already."

Katie punched his arm. "Go read your email."

"Yes, ma'am."

Katiya gave him an arch smile. "We'll be in the back. There's coffee and champagne and treats. Make yourself at home."

Katie trailed behind the gorgeous woman with the jet-black hair and felt her self-esteem plummet. *This* was the kind of female Stone men dated. Glamorous. Worldly. Fabulously dressed.

The jacket and pants Katie wore were from the clearance rack. With an extra coupon.

As Katiya swooshed open the thick damask curtain of a spacious fitting room, Katie couldn't contain her curiosity. "So how long were you and Zachary together?"

The woman who must have been a model at one point in her life shot a tiny smile over her elegant shoulder. "Not quite a year. It was a long time ago. We decided we were better off as friends." Katiya held up her left hand. "After that, I met the most wonderful history professor at NYU and married him six months later."

*A history professor?* "Congratulations," Katie said.

"Thank you. He is my soulmate. What can I say? True love is wonderful." The saleswoman waved Katie into the little nook. "Strip down to your undies. I'll grab what we need."

Back at the hotel, Katie had some kick-ass new underwear in her suitcase. Just in case. The fact that she had taken it to Maine meant her subconscious was more honest than she was.

Today, though, she wore solid white cotton. Too bad. She wished she had known that Quin meant for them to shop for a dress immediately. She would like to have worn something more upscale. Too late now.

Katiya returned with an armful of black. "I brought long and above-the-knee both. Either will be appropriate. It's your personal preference. Try this halter dress first, though. You have the figure to pull it off, and in the heat, you'll be glad you're mostly naked. I'll leave the rest of them on this hook just outside the cubicle. If you need me, press the button."

*Mostly naked?* Katie gulped. She took the dress the other woman handed her and examined it at arm's length. The black crepe fabric was light as air and had a lovely, subtle crinkle pattern. No bra with this one.

She was down to her bikini panties. Though she had

been hot before, now she shivered in the extremely efficient air-conditioning. Or maybe her tremors were the result of anticipation about the evening ahead. She was torn in two opposing directions. Throw caution to the wind and sleep with Quinten Stone? Or play it safe and not make the same mistake twice.

When she slipped the gown over her head, it fell like a whisper to her ankles. The design of the dress left her shoulders bare, as promised. But it also plunged to the base of her spine in back and halfway to her navel in the front. *Good grief.* Where was a sweater when you needed one?

Katiya appeared without warning. She peeked through the curtain. "How do you think?"

The odd expression was endearing. Katie inhaled and glanced at herself in the mirror. She wrinkled her nose. "I do like it. But this is a lot of bare skin. A. Lot."

The other woman chuckled. "You look stunning." She put her hands on Katie's waist. "See how it slides over your curves? This is one time when small breasts are a plus."

Katie loved her reflection in the mirror. The couture gown made her feel like the proverbial million bucks. But she didn't have the courage to wear this in front of Quin. How could she? He would take this sensual dress as an outright invitation.

"Let me try the others," she said.

Katiya shook her head vehemently. "I wouldn't be doing my job if I let you walk away from this choice. It's perfection. You know I'm right."

"I suppose." Katie smoothed her hands over her flat stomach, already imagining the expression on Quin's face when he saw her in this.

"Will you need shoes and a clutch?" Katiya asked.

Katie pondered the possibility of finding a discount store in this zip code. "I suppose so."

It took another half hour to select accessories and jewelry. Even the *costume* stuff was outrageously expensive. Some of the necklaces cost more than Katie's monthly rent.

Apparently, Katiya and Quin had been communicating via text. Before Katie could lodge a further protest, the steamroller saleswoman had swaddled the new dress in layers of tissue and tucked it into a glossy shopping bag—on top of the shoebox.

The jewelry, safely stowed in a mauve linen drawstring bag, nestled in a deep corner. Katiya had already arranged to have Katie's purchases delivered to the hotel.

Katie put on her own clothes again, feeling alarmingly out of her element. This fantasy shopping spree was delightful, but it gave her an odd feeling under the circumstances. The hour of decision was fast approaching.

Why had she told Quin she still wanted him? Was her subconscious trying to force the issue? Did she *want* Quin to play the role of seducer? It seemed more honest to simply admit she would like to sleep with him again. As he had said earlier—*no strings attached.*

Truthfully, she wanted strings. Lots of them. She wanted Quin to care about the things she cared about—to woo her in a way that said he understood her discomfort with his money. That said he understood her. Was that even possible?

Her time with Quin was half over already. Soon, she would be back in her pleasant condo in Portland, going about her ordinary routine. She might see him now and again in passing, but their day-to-day lives wouldn't intersect. Her six-week stint in the Maine woods would be only a memory.

If she said yes tonight, could she be satisfied with so much less than she yearned for?

Back at the front of the store, Quin and Katiya had their heads together, deep in conversation.

Quin looked up when Katie approached. "What? No fashion show?"

His lazy grin lit a spark in her belly. Her legs trembled. "Get over yourself," she said. "That's old-school cinema. You're not Richard Gere, and I'm not Julia Roberts."

His eyebrows raised in tandem. "I should hope not. We Stone men may have our faults, but doing the Pygmalion thing with charming hookers isn't one of them." Her comment had apparently insulted him.

"I was kidding," she said. "Chill out. Lighten up. I thought we were having fun."

Katiya giggled. "I like her, Quin." She gave Katie a charming smile. "I'm happy to meet you." Then she paused. "Our names are the same, you know? Katie. Katiya. Maybe we be friends."

Katie shook the other woman's hand, touched by the woman's apparent sincerity. "I'd like that. Thanks for your help."

"Enjoy the dress."

"Enjoy the history professor."

Out on the sidewalk, Quin shot her a puzzled look. "What was that all about?"

"After Katiya and Zachary called it quits, she found a history professor and married him. He's her soulmate. Her words. Not mine."

"Soulmate?"

"Some people think it's a real thing."

He pulled her beneath the shade of an awning. "And what about you, Katie Duncan. Are you looking for *your* soulmate?"

# Six

Katie sucked in a sharp breath, shocked to her core. She hadn't anticipated such a loaded question in the middle of the street in broad daylight. Weren't men supposed to lead up to this kind of thing?

Quin looked dead serious. His vivid sapphire eyes seemed to burn from within. In about three seconds she was going to melt into a puddle on the sidewalk. And not from the summer heat.

She swallowed hard. "What are you doing?" she asked, trying to breathe. Maybe it was the exhaust fumes from all those yellow cabs making her gulp for oxygen.

He touched her bottom lip with a single fingertip, barely stroking. "Weighing the odds. Gauging my chances."

"Chances of what?"

His mouth quirked at the corner. "You told me you still wanted me. Did you mean that?"

"I don't know *what* you're talking about."

"Liar…"

The intensity in his gaze made her shiver despite the temperature. "Maybe I was joking," she said. "I'm always sticking my foot in my mouth."

He cupped her face, his thumb caressing her cheekbone. "Don't be afraid, Kat. I can't explain what happened before. In fact, I've racked my brain trying to remember what dumbass thing I did to drive you away."

"It wasn't you," she muttered, suddenly near tears. "It was me."

He frowned. "You're not making sense."

She took a deep breath. This wasn't the time to fall apart. "You and I are *not* soulmates," she said firmly. "I never thought we were. That's the answer to your question. I suppose most women want to believe that their perfect match, their perfect man, is out there somewhere. You're wonderful, Quin, but you and me together…" She trailed off, searching for the exact words to make him understand. "We're *fun*. We're hot in the sack. But we're not soulmates. I walked away two years ago, because I didn't want to have my heart broken."

There. That was about as honest as she could be.

Something flickered in his eyes. Perhaps he hadn't expected her to be so blunt. "I see."

"I shouldn't have said I still wanted you."

"Because it's not true?" Now the set of his jaw was grim.

"Because it would be a mistake, and we're both old enough to learn from our mistakes."

He shook his head slowly. "I'm the guy who plunged down a mountain with a bum knee and almost killed myself. Because I was too stubborn and impatient to wait for the all clear. I'm not known for being levelheaded when it comes to things I want."

"Like skiing?"

"Like you."

His honesty deserved honesty in return. She tilted her face to his. "Then let's make our mistakes, Quin. Kiss me."

He slid his hand behind her neck, pulling her close. When his lips touched hers, she leaned into him with a mortifying whimper of pleasure and shock and delight. Eight million people in the big city, and all Katie could hear was the sound of labored breathing—Quin's and her own.

She had forgotten how good he tasted. A tiny hint of chocolate from the mini éclairs at the fancy salon lingered at the corner of his mouth. She kissed it away. Quin groaned and shuddered. It had always been like this whenever they touched. Raw insanity. Endless need.

"Quin…" She whispered his name, dizzy with wanting him. She had tried to be good and smart and careful with her emotions. But it all came down to this. The laser focus that had made him a champion raked her into his orbit.

He cursed under his breath and backed away. Streams of humanity ebbed and flowed around them. "We should head for the museum," he said gruffly. "If not, we won't make our dinner reservation. I'm sure you want time to shower and relax before we go."

She swallowed, nodding. "That would be nice." She reached out and squeezed his hand. "Truce?"

He nodded, his fingers warm and firm against hers. "Truce." Without asking, he hailed a cab. Katie would have been happy to walk, but Quin was right. If she was to see any of the Met at all and still have time to change, there was no opportunity to dawdle.

When the cabbie dropped them at the curb on Fifth Avenue, Katie stared up at the large flight of steps. "I had no idea the building was so big."

Quin curled an arm around her waist, guiding her among clumps of tourists. "In 1870, when the Met was founded, it owned not a single work of art. Now, some 150 years later, the permanent collection numbers around two million items, only a fraction of which are on display. And that begs the question—where do you want to start?"

Katie grinned, happy despite the simmering tension between them. "Van Gogh, Renoir and the Tiffany glass. That will do for today."

Quin blinked. "I didn't expect you to be quite so *prepared*."

"I'm a planner. Farrell can tell you that. There's a time and place for spontaneity, but my initial foray into the third most visited museum in the world is an occasion for careful attack."

He kissed her cheek and tucked a stray piece of hair behind her ear. "Your wish is my command."

Quin bought their tickets and grabbed several brochures. After studying the maps to refresh his memory, he nodded. "One level up." He steered her without hesitation to the second-floor gallery that included French Impressionists. When Quin took her hand, her heart turned over in her chest. They saw the Manets and the Monets. The Cézannes and the Cassatts. Van Gogh. Degas. Pissarro.

It was too much. Room after room of art. The color and light and passion that had survived through the centuries and across the miles. She felt overwhelmed. She and Quin turned a corner, and suddenly, she found what she was looking for. "Here it is," she said softly, speaking more to herself than to her companion. Standing in front of the large canvas, she felt her eyes burn.

"Why this one?" Quin asked quietly.

She shot him a watery smile. "When I was eight years old, I desperately wanted to take piano lessons. But my parents were barely getting by. I didn't even get a *maybe* from either one of them. A friend of our family, down the street, owned a piano. She let me peck around sometimes after school, but she didn't really know how to play. The instrument had belonged to her grandmother, so our friend kept it for sentimental reasons. It was scarred and out of tune, but to me it was magical."

"And the Renoir? *Two Young Girls at the Piano*?" He pulled her close.

Katie rested her head on his shoulder, inhaling his familiar scent. Was it possible for a man as wealthy as Quin to understand a child's vulnerability and yearning? Could a man who bought paintings or pianos as easily as a pack of gum recognize a woman's deep need to have dreams?

She sighed. "That same neighbor made a trip to New York one summer. She sent me a postcard of this painting. I still have it."

Quin often stared danger in the face. Every time he stood at the apex of a black diamond slope, his adrenaline surged and his heart raced. He was braced for any and all eventualities.

Today felt oddly the same but terrifyingly different. Spending so much time with Katie in a nonsexual setting these past three weeks had caused him to see her through a different lens. She was a beautiful, sexy woman. That, he had known before. Known it and been terribly disappointed when she walked away for reasons he still didn't quite understand.

Maybe that was the problem. He had been blinded by lust in the past—too hungry for her to see or understand that Katie was a woman of many facets. Because he hadn't known how to get close to her, he'd used his money to woo her.

But what he felt now was not as easily explained as lust. She had become more real and multidimensional to him.

Katie was a fascinating, complicated woman. He wanted her in his life, and he liked making her happy. Could one person even do that for another?

"We should go," he said gruffly. "If you want to see the Tiffany exhibit."

Katie glanced at her watch. "Oh gosh, yes."

Even though she agreed, he sensed her reluctance to leave the Renoir behind.

"We could stop by again tomorrow," he said.

"No." She shook her head as they returned to the main floor. "I knew I would only scratch the surface. I'll come back one day."

After a quick blitz through the incredible stained glass creations of Louis Tiffany, they grabbed a cab and rushed back to the hotel. In the elevator, Katie was subdued, her gaze downcast. He wanted to know what she was thinking. Memories of the kiss they had shared earlier kept him jittery and hungry. Would anything happen tonight?

He could press the issue. Katie wanted him.

But he was ruefully aware that she didn't *want* to want him. The distinction was tough on a man's ego.

In the hallway outside their rooms, he put a finger beneath her chin and locked his gaze with hers. "It's your decision," he said quietly. "But I want you tonight. Think about it. We're good together. Nothing that feels so damn fantastic could be wrong."

She didn't exactly answer him. And he hadn't exactly asked a question. They were each dancing around a conundrum.

Instead, she took her keycard from her purse. "What time do I need to be ready?"

"We're meeting the guys in the theater district at six. But it will be rush hour, so we need to allow forty-five minutes at least."

"So five fifteen?"

"That's about it."

She unlocked her door and bumped it open with one hip. "Today was fun. Thank you for taking me to the museum."

"And the shopping?" He couldn't resist teasing her.

Katie shook her head, her expression wry. "That was mostly for your benefit, I think. But yes, it was enjoyable."

"Lukewarm praise."

"I'll text you when I'm ready."

"I could wash your back," he offered. Even the light-hearted joke made his sex lift and swell.

Katie went up on her toes and kissed his cheek. "Behave yourself, Quinten Stone. Some itches are best left unscratched."

After her pointed dismissal, he sulked in his room for half an hour, and then had to take the quickest shower on record. That and shaving left him little time to wrestle with his tuxedo and bow tie. It was probably too hot to get geared up in this monkey suit, but he wanted to give Katie the whole night-on-the-town experience.

When he was ready, he glanced in the mirror. His customary tan was paler than most summers. The man in the reflection had spent far too much time indoors recently.

Three more weeks of *taking it easy*. The prospect frustrated the hell out of him. He was in New York. Three airports at his disposal. He could be on a flight to Chamonix or Megeve tomorrow afternoon.

If he was careful, he could fly under the radar when it came to the pro circuit. Try a few green and blue slopes. Test out his new hardware with no one watching.

Two things stopped him. Number one, he had promised Farrell and Zachary that he would follow the doctor's orders this time. And two, he didn't want to give up the next three weeks with Katie.

It was possible he was setting himself up for a second painful rejection. Taking Katie to bed was risky. Especially since he hadn't a clue what went on inside that fascinating brain of hers. But he had to take the chance.

When he knocked on her door a short while later, he shifted from one foot to the other, restless and unsettled. Why the hell had he agreed to meet his brothers for dinner? He should have locked Katie in his hotel room and kept her entertained until morning.

Without warning, the door swung inward, and suddenly he was staring at a vision. A sexy, mouthwatering vision.

"You look amazing," he said hoarsely. He was gobsmacked and trying hard not to show it.

"Thank you." Her smile was almost shy, as if she were on the way to prom and he was her high school date.

Her dress, however, was *not* prom material. It sizzled with sexual innuendo sewn into every thread. Hell, he was pretty sure Katie was naked underneath that dress Katiya had procured. In addition to being slashed to her navel in front and halfway down her back, the black gown was slit up one leg, tantalizingly high on her slender, toned thigh.

"We could stay in tonight," he said, deadly serious.

"I want to see the musical." Her brown eyes danced with humor. "And have dinner with your family. And enjoy Times Square after dark. Staying home would be boring."

He danced his mouth over hers, half-desperate, but waiting for a signal that she was receptive. "Not the way you and I would do it."

Katie blushed to her hairline and returned the kiss for a good thirty seconds, her lips soft beneath his. She broke free, panting. "I could be persuaded," she said. "But don't, Quin. Please. We're all dressed up, and I want to have fun. *Not* in bed," she said quickly.

"Spoilsport."

He tamped down his hunger and tried to think about something other than the shape of Katie's breasts beneath the silky black fabric. Her beaded nipples were easily visible. What was a man supposed to do? Look the other way? Wear a blindfold?

Oops. Bad choice. Now he was seeing Katie in his bed playing the dominatrix.

More than one male head turned as they made their way through the lobby to the car. The restaurant where they were meeting Farrell and Zachary was on the way to Midtown. It was old and filled with dark colors and leather seating and the heads of long-dead trophy animals high on the walls. Three decades ago, it would also have been filled with cigar smoke. In the twenty-first century, though, the ambience had changed. One of the city's finest chefs reigned over the award-winning kitchen.

Quin focused his gaze on the snarled traffic outside his window and tried not to fixate on the way Katie's cute knee and smooth thigh peeked through the slit in her dress. His throat was dry. His sex was hard as stone, aching. He'd always been a leg man.

A few moments ago, she had taken out a tiny cosmetic bag to repair her lipstick. The quick, feminine movements made him want to kiss her all over again.

What would it take to get her into his bed tonight? He knew Katie wanted him. He would kneel at her feet if he thought it would work. How could either of them resist this gnawing attraction any longer? It was like trying to ignore the tsunami rushing toward the beach.

At last, they pulled up in front of their destination. The doorman rushed to open Katie's side of the car and was rewarded with a sensual, unwittingly teasing dance as she exited. The poor man nearly swallowed his tongue.

Quin slid across the seat and followed her out. He started

to take her arm, but touching her right now would be courting disaster. His control was iffy. Instead, he turned to tip the driver and tried not to think about dragging Katie beneath him in a huge soft bed and taking her over and over until morning.

Fortunately for Quin, Farrell and Zachary beat them to the restaurant. Both men shook Katie's hand, and Farrell even gave her a quick little hug. He and Katie were tight.

The maître d' showed them to their reserved spot. Quin took a seat at Katie's right elbow. Their knees bumped underneath the table. She shot him a look that sent heat straight to his groin. "I'm starving," she said.

# Seven

Katie was enjoying herself, and the evening had barely started. Quin's mood was brooding and dangerous. Sexual need hovered just beneath the surface of his debonair exterior.

In his classic tux, he looked every inch the wealthy businessman. She wanted to gobble him up, though that was a clichéd way to describe her need to get naked with him.

His brothers were both impressive male specimens, but Katie couldn't take her eyes off Quin. He exuded confidence and a rakish virility that made her breath catch in her throat.

Was it something as simple as pheromones? She'd been telling the truth when she said he wasn't her soulmate. But Lord help her, he was gorgeous enough to make any woman reckless.

Moments later, Zachary and Quin spotted a mutual acquaintance at the bar. They excused themselves and strode across the crowded restaurant, their shoulders broad and eerily similar.

Farrell leaned forward, his expression harried. "I know I said six weeks, but *please* come back to work Monday. We're drowning without you."

"I'm pretty sure you're not serious," Katie said, laughing. "But your flattery is much appreciated."

"It's not flattery if it's true. You run the R & D department so well, I've always been able to concentrate on design. Now I'm having to put out fires, too. I swear I'm giving you a raise when you get back."

"It's nice to be needed. Job security and all that."

Farrell sat back in his chair, his amusement fading. "How's it going? You can tell me the truth. My brother can be a pain in the ass. Has he been kind to you? Considerate?"

She flashed back to that moment on a hot New York sidewalk earlier today. When she had felt the press of Quin's erection against her abdomen as they kissed. "Yes, of course," she insisted, her face heating. "Everything is going well. We'll be completely caught up when I come back to Portland."

"Any signs of possible espionage?"

"We've come across a few odd glitches in numbers. Nothing definitive. Most of it can be written off as random errors. So far, there's no proof that anything out of the ordinary is going on."

"Good. Maybe we're all being paranoid. And what about my baby brother's mental state? I know he's not chatty about his feelings, physical or otherwise, but I'm hoping he's climbed out of that dark place he wallowed in after the skiing accident. Quin thinks anyone can do anything if they only try hard enough. That's not always true."

"I know. He mentions skiing. Now and again. I'm not

a mind reader, though. A man that intense won't give up his dreams lightly."

"My brother is a good guy," Farrell said. "The car accident was a tragedy in more ways than one." He hesitated. "I know Quin can be blunt and stubborn and cantankerous. If you ever find yourself feeling uncomfortable or you simply decide you've had enough, call me and I'll get you out of there, no questions asked."

"Farrell—"

He stopped her. "No, I'm serious. I've felt guilty about you ever since Zachary and I cooked up the plan to make *our* lives easier. We dropped you in the middle of the woods with a man you barely know. You're far away from your friends and your family. I'm sorry about all of it."

"Farrell," she said quietly, glancing over her shoulder to make sure the other two brothers were still occupied.

"Yes?" He leaned forward, perhaps sensing her need for privacy.

"Quin and I dated two years ago. We were lovers," she clarified. No need to dance around the issue. "Neither of us wanted gossip at work, so we kept the relationship under wraps. It ended abruptly about six months before your father died."

Farrell's eyes widened as a look of discomfort washed over his face. "Oh hell. It's even worse than I thought. We sent you into exile with a man who dumped you? These last three weeks must have been terribly uncomfortable. I'm *so* sorry, Katie. You're a team player for sure, but I never would have asked this of you if I had known. Why didn't you say something?"

"Um, actually, I was the one to break it off, not Quin."

Farrell's jaw dropped. "*You* dumped *him*?"

Katie frowned. "Yes. Is that so hard to believe? I know

your brother is irresistible to the female sex, but you can't honestly tell me I'm the first one to walk away."

"I don't know," Farrell said slowly. "You might actually be."

"Oh, come on." Katie stared at him. "Quin's not great with opening up emotionally. I imagine other girlfriends have been frustrated by that."

"Those zeros in his bank account cover a multitude of sins."

She blinked. "Wow. That's a cold, cynical outlook."

Farrell shrugged. "It's true."

"So no one goes out with you and Zachary and Quin for your glowing personalities and sex appeal?"

"Let's just say it's not the first reason."

"Sucks to be you," she said. "Why don't you give it all away and see what happens?"

Farrell chuckled. "We're lonely, not stupid."

Just then, Quin and Zachary returned.

"Please don't tell your brothers what we talked about," Katie whispered urgently.

"What did we miss?" Zach asked, sitting down and flipping his napkin over his lap.

"I want to thank you again for the *Hamilton* tickets," Katie said. "I'm so excited I can hardly stand it, but I really am sorry your girlfriend couldn't go with you tonight."

Zach's quick smile was charming and carried a lot of voltage. "Not to worry. I've already seen the show twice, and the lady…" He paused and shrugged. "No great loss. You and my brother will love it."

The waiter arrived and took their orders. Shortly after, the same older gentleman returned to pour wine and deliver the appetizers. The conversation picked up again. Quin wanted to know about the day's meeting. While the three brothers discussed SRO business, Katie excused herself and went to the ladies' room.

The décor had been preserved as midcentury modern. Katie perched on a stool and repaired her lipstick. Being with the Stone men all at one time was certainly fun. But it kept a woman on her toes.

She stared at herself in the mirror. What did she really want? Quin had booked two rooms at the hotel. He wouldn't insist if she wanted to sleep alone. The conversation with Farrell had only solidified her doubts.

Two years ago, her breakup with Quin had been excruciating, even though it had been her decision. It had taken her months to get over the loss. Nothing she had seen in Quin recently told her he had changed. Was she being a fool?

This was like the time she'd tried to give up sugar, cold turkey. She'd made it an entire six weeks. Then, on a very difficult day when was feeling low, she had eaten a Hershey's bar, and the sugar cravings came rushing back.

Deciding to sleep with Quin would alter her life once again. She knew it deep in her gut. Did she want a brief, exhilarating physical affair if it meant more heartbreak in the near future?

Did she want a relationship with a man who was so besotted with skiing that he almost killed himself? The Quin who was her lover two years ago had been selfish in many ways. Driven. Unable to look beyond the moment. He'd been impulsive and wildly passionate.

Life with that Quin had been exhilarating to a point. But he had never understood her. Or maybe they had never understood each other.

She frowned at her reflection. Though it had taken patience and a few cusswords, she had finally gotten her hair to cooperate in an elegant French twist. With the expensive new dress and the more dramatic makeup, she didn't look out of place in this world.

But she was. *Her* menu at dinner tonight hadn't listed any prices. She'd heard of such a thing, but she'd never actually seen it in person.

This was a climate where money didn't matter. Well, it *mattered*, duh. But not in the way it mattered in Katie's world—where a broken washing machine or a flat tire or an unexpected car repair could send families into a serious downward financial spiral.

That was the world she had grown up in. Those were the people she knew and loved. With her extremely good job at Stone River Outdoors, she had gradually shifted away from her community in one way. She now had a savings account and a 401(k) and fantastic health insurance.

A single bump in the road wouldn't wipe her out. Even so, she understood her family and childhood friends in a way that Quin simply couldn't. If a man had never known hunger or desperation, it would be hard to empathize with those who had. She didn't blame the Stone brothers for being ridiculously wealthy. They were generous employers.

But there was a stark divide between their life experiences and hers.

She wanted Quin to *see* her. To honor her values and opinions. Otherwise, all they had was sex.

When she returned to the dinner table, all three men stood until she was seated. Their innate courtesy was as flawless as it was instinctive. Perhaps their father hadn't been the best parent, but he had raised his sons to be gentlemen. That much was clear.

When her phone dinged quietly, she slipped it from her clutch and read the text, sighing inwardly. Her face must have given her away.

Quin touched her hand. "Problem?"

She didn't really want to elaborate, but all three men were looking at her with varying levels of interest and concern. "My sister is trying to get her own apartment. She's been sleeping on the sofa at a friend's place. She has the rent covered, but she doesn't have any credit. I need to help her with utility deposits and a pet fee."

Quin made a weird sound beneath his breath and frowned. *"Need?"*

She glared at him. "This is none of your business, Quin."

Zachary seemed shocked, perhaps because he was now the only one ignorant of Quin and Katie's former relationship. "We all have to make those decisions at one time or another," he said. "When I turned twenty-five and inherited a large sum of money my grandparents left me, a lot of my old college buddies started crawling out of the woodwork. It's hard to say no."

Katie shook her head. "My sister isn't like that. She doesn't take advantage of me. But I've been luckier in life. I'm able to help, so I do."

Quin's jaw was tight. "I don't think you've been luckier in life. You've worked your ass off. In college you had *three* part-time jobs just to get through. That was your choice. You've worked your way up at SRO. All that is *you*, Katie. Your sister came from the same family."

In the uncomfortable silence that followed Quin's outburst, Farrell stepped into the breach. He gave his brother a warning stare. "That's a lot of information about a woman on such short acquaintance. Maybe we should talk about something else."

Zachary still looked mystified, as if he had missed part of the conversation. He had. Everyone else at the table knew Katie was far more than a temporary assistant during Quin's recovery.

Fortunately, their meals arrived. In the hustle and bustle

of making sure everyone was served, the awkward conversation fell by the wayside.

By the time dinner was finished, it was getting late.

"We should head for the theater," Quin said.

As they all stood, Zachary donned his jacket and picked up his credit card receipt. "You two need to keep an eye on the long-range weather outlook. The forecasters are thinking this latest hurricane may make its way up the coast eventually. Be careful."

"I hope they're wrong," Farrell said. "If we get too much damage, it will slow down the building project at my place. I want the new lab to be my sole work site until we figure out what's going on."

When they left the restaurant, the four adults parted ways. Another hired car was waiting for Katie and Quin. She didn't know what to say to him once they were alone. But she knew how she wanted the evening to end. Had their unexpected quarrel ruined the mood?

Suddenly, he reached across the seat and took her hand. "I'm sorry, Katie. I was out of line. What you do in your private life is none of my concern. Will you forgive me?"

He was genuinely sorry. She could see it in his eyes. A cynical person might think he was mending fences in order to coax her into sex tonight. Katie didn't believe that. Quin was not manipulative. Forceful and persuasive, but not manipulative. "I forgive you," she said.

His small smile was sheepish. "I'm not the easiest man to get along with," he confessed. "I wondered why you broke up with me, but it could have been any one of a dozen reasons."

She shifted on the seat. His forthright description of himself demanded equal honesty, but it would serve no useful purpose. "I think we can forget the past, Quin. We're not going back there. I'd prefer to live in the moment. It's safer that way."

"If that's what you want." The slight crease between his eyebrows told her he wasn't pleased with her answer.

The car slid into a momentarily empty space at the curb. The theater was half a block down the street. Quin and the driver exchanged quick words about a later pickup.

As Quin helped Katie out of the car, he explained, perhaps anticipating her question. "It's almost impossible to get a cab when the theaters let out. I don't want to waste any time getting back to the hotel."

It was a loaded statement. Her stomach flipped and her cheeks burned as his hand gripped hers.

Quin laughed. "You look like a scared rabbit. It's your choice, Kat. It always was."

His words stayed with her all through the fabulous musical. Though the story and the rap lyrics and the music were mesmerizing, she was hyperaware of the man at her side. Zachary's seats were box tickets, only eight chairs in the small balcony overlooking the stage. The two beside Quin and Katie were no-shows, so they had the second row to themselves.

As soon as the lights went down, Quin slid his arm around her. His fingers caressed her bare shoulder. He was warm and large and wonderfully *male* at her side. She wanted somehow to preserve this moment, this entire evening, but it was sand slipping though her fingers. A snowflake disappearing in a warm breath.

When the curtain fell for the final time, the enthusiastic crowd clapped and shouted. The sheer talent of the show's creator was awe-inspiring.

Out on the sidewalk, the heat remained, even after dark. Quin pulled her close, protecting her from the jostling crowd. "Coffee? Dessert?" he asked, his expression warm and happy.

"No, thank you," she said. "Let's go home."

It was a slip of the tongue. The Carlyle wasn't their home. But for tonight, it promised privacy and endless possibilities.

The car was waiting for them one street over. At another moment, Katie might have enjoyed riding the subway. That was a big-city rite of passage she had never experienced. But for now, she was content to be whisked away.

The hotel was quiet when they returned. In the elevator, Quin barely spoke. When they reached their floor and stepped out, Katie took his hand. "Give me half an hour," she said. "Then come to my room."

His eyes flared with shock, quickly followed by heat. "You're sure?" The two words were gruff and gravelly.

She slid her hand behind his neck and pulled his head down for a kiss. "Not really. But I won't change my mind, I promise."

# Eight

Quin felt like a condemned man faced with a reprieve. After his stupid stunt at dinner, he thought he'd ruined any chance of the two of them winding up together tonight.

His Katie had a kind heart. Either that, or she was as eager to re-create the magic as he was. He stripped off his tux, showered and changed into light knit pants and a T-shirt. Respectable enough for roaming the halls.

His prep took exactly eleven minutes. Which left him nineteen minutes to get antsy. He was second-guessing himself all over the place. Would Katie regret tonight? He didn't want that. Not at all.

But who was he kidding? No way in hell was he walking away from this chance to be with the woman who turned him inside out. He ached for her. In all the months since the accident that derailed his life, sexual needs had taken a back seat to pain and therapy and cumulative weeks in the hospital.

Now his libido had roared to life.

At twenty-nine and a half minutes, he grabbed up his keycard, deliberately left his phone behind and exited his room. The hallway was empty. At this point, he didn't care. He would have walked stark naked through the lobby for the chance to have sex with Katie again.

They'd had plenty of problems during their relationship, but sexual compatibility hadn't been one of them. When they were in bed together, the world stopped. Nothing mattered but the two of them connecting, skin to skin, shivering breath to ragged heartbeat.

He knocked softly at her door. Insanely long seconds passed before she opened it.

When he saw her, his mouth dried and his already semi-erect sex went on high alert. Either Katie had a thing for sexy sleepwear, or she had come prepared for this weekend with him. He hoped like hell it was the second.

She had showered as he had. Earlier tonight, her elegant hairstyle had bared her neck—sexy in a different way. Now, her silky blond hair, still damp in places, brushed her shoulders.

"You are so damn hot," he muttered. Her mostly sheer black nightgown did little to conceal her budded nipples or anything farther south. He ran a hand down her arm. "I want you, Kat. I know I should be cool about this, but I have to be honest. I haven't been with a woman since the accident. I may disappoint you this first time."

Eyes wide, she took his hand and pulled him inside, closing the door with a gentle shove. "I won't be disappointed, I swear."

He sifted his fingers through her hair, steadied her head in his hands and found her mouth with unerring desperation. "I've missed this," he groaned.

His instinct was to take what he wanted, what they both

wanted. But second chances were delicate and prone to collapse. Katie needed more from him than selfish lust. He saw that now. In hindsight, he could identify all the ways he had failed her. This time would be different.

He wasn't the same man.

Her lips were soft and eager. She leaned into him, signaling her readiness. With one arm, he dragged her close, molding their bodies from chest to knee. He could feel every inch of her warm, soft skin.

He was embarrassingly out of control. "I wanted to do this right," he panted.

Katie's laugh was low and knowing. The sound scraped his nerve endings and made the hunger worse. She nipped the shell of his ear with sharp teeth. "I believe you. Let's see what you've got, big guy."

He tugged her wrist, dragging her toward the lavish hotel bed, pausing only to throw back the covers and pillows and bolsters. He shoved them aside and laid Katie in the exact center of the bed. Her hair fanned out in a messy arc over the pillow. Her cheeks were flushed, her gaze soft.

With clenched fists, he forced himself to appreciate the picture she made. His chest heaved. He tried to control his driving need. He wasn't an animal. Still, something primitive stirred within him. Something possessive and determined and demanding.

The sleep pants that rode low on his hips had a single pocket. He had stuffed it with several condoms. Tossing the protection on the bedside table, he lifted his arms and ripped his T-shirt over his head. The stunned way she watched him was gratifying.

He hadn't planned a strip show. But when he dragged his pants down his legs and kicked them aside, Katie's eyes rounded.

Quin took his aching flesh in one hand and fisted it,

barely able to touch himself. "Is this what you want, Kat?" The skin was tight, almost painful.

"No." Her brown eyes heated. "I want more. I want it all."

Her words were like a physical blow. He flinched away from them, even as her bold pronouncement ratcheted his hunger upward. His breath sawed in and out of his lungs like a dying man's.

What more could he give her? He had laid his hunger and his fortune at her feet once before, and it hadn't been enough. What else was there?

Ignoring the nuances of her disturbingly ambiguous declaration, he joined her on the mattress. It barely dipped beneath his weight. A bed at the Carlyle wasn't a bad place to restart a sexual relationship that had lain dormant for two years.

He stroked her breast through her nightgown, pinching lightly. The curved mound fit his palm perfectly.

Katie's strangled moan urged him on. Her eyelids fluttered shut. He thought she was going to say something, but if her throat was as tight as his, the ability to speak had eroded rapidly.

Moving his hand to the other breast, he rested his head on her shoulder. She was warm, so warm. Her fingers sifted through his hair, massaging his scalp. This time he twisted the nipple with a firm grip. The raspberry nub was hard now. Puckered. Taut.

He couldn't resist. Shifting positions slightly, he bit down on her tender flesh, just enough to let her know he meant business. Katie's keening moan made the hair on the back of his neck stand up.

When she turned her cheek into his chest, his heart clenched. The gesture of trust affected him more strongly than he would ever admit. He knew that he had failed her somehow in the past. Hurt her.

Whatever it was that had dragged them apart didn't have to happen this time. He could fix it.

The bottom of Katie's gown had twisted around her legs. He tugged it loose and gathered it to her waist. Now his view was unimpeded. Her pink, moist sex was a thing of beauty. Katie was clean-shaven between her legs, but a tiny, heart-shaped fluff of pale hair covered her mons.

He started to shake as if fevered. His need for her scrambled his brain. When he stroked her center, Katie shook her head wildly. "I'm ready," she said, the words demanding. He might have smiled if he hadn't been out of his mind with lust.

Instead, he grabbed a condom, ripped it open and rolled it carefully over his aching erection. "Katie…" He wanted to say something tender and romantic. Words failed him.

She held out her arms, her eyes heavy-lidded. "I want you, Quin."

Straightforward. Impossible to misinterpret.

He spread her thighs and mounted her, sliding deep with one steady push. Katie whimpered. Her sex clenched around his, eager, ready.

The need to come was almost impossible to hold at bay. Embarrassingly so. In his head, he tried to list the slope gradients of his five favorite ski runs. It didn't work. He ground his pelvis against hers. Was she even close? They had barely started.

Again, he rubbed the base of his sex where it would make the most difference, trying to hit just the right spot.

Katie grabbed his shoulders, her fingernails scoring his hot skin. "I'm so close. Harder, Quin," she begged.

The desperation in her pleas galvanized him. He withdrew almost completely and slammed his body into hers.

The connection was messy and raw and inelegant. Any finesse he had once possessed was gone.

All he could see was her beautiful face. All he could feel was a rush of pleasure so intense, it burned to the point of pain.

Katie cried out and wrapped her legs around his waist, lifting into him and taking all he had to give. His own orgasm snapped like the sharp flick of a broken rubber band. He caught his breath and muffled his shout in her shoulder. His world ground to a halt.

It had never been like this. In the past, they had dented his bedroom wall a time or two with the headboard. One night they even broke Katie's bed. It was one of his fondest memories.

But the sex was different now.

Was it the two years of being apart, or had they each changed?

He rolled away from her, trying not to let her see how strung out he felt. His eyes stung.

Without thinking it through, he linked her fingers with his. Her touch was a lifeline in his spinning universe. "Katie?"

"Hmmm?"

"Did you see other men after we broke up?"

It wasn't a fair question. It wasn't his business. But the possessive need to stake a claim made him oblivious to the land mine he had planted.

"Yes."

His heart slugged once in his chest, as if someone had whacked him in the ribs with a baseball bat and cracked bone. Of course she had. The men in Portland weren't blind.

She raised up on one elbow, staring at him, her expression curiously blank. "Did you sleep with other women?"

He closed his eyes, not wanting her to see the truth. "At first. Several of them, actually. I was angry."

"About what?"

He sat up and raked his hands through his hair. "I was angry that you didn't give me a chance to undo whatever stupid thing I had done to make you walk out on us."

All the color drained from her face. Her expression was bleak, tormented. "It wasn't that simple, Quin."

"Nothing ever is…"

"We're better off being friends. Trust me."

"I think you're wrong."

She left him and went to the bathroom. When she returned, she had donned one of the plush hotel robes. Her jaw stuck out at a familiar angle. "I won't rehash the past, Quin." Her eyes were dark with misery. "We don't have a future. If you want this…" She waved a hand at the bed. "I'll be with you for three more weeks."

Fury flared in his gut. "So take it or leave it?"

She nodded slowly, her lips pressed tightly together. "Yes."

"Okay, then." He shut his mind to the *feelings* that bombarded him. He was a man who didn't trust feelings. Hell, he couldn't even trust his own body anymore. "In that case, come back to bed. I'm not through with you."

*He must think I'm a bitch.*

Katie's stomach curled. For the briefest of moments, she flashed back to that terrible day with Quin's father. He had made her feel she was less than nothing. If she'd had any inkling that Quin wanted more than sex, she might have fought for the chance to find out.

His father's cold, dispassionate summation of the truth had shattered her confidence and underscored every one of her doubts about her relationship with Quin.

Even back then, she had realized that Quin could *never* know what had happened. Now that his father was gone, the truth was even more dangerous. Quin had suffered so much. She couldn't add to his pain. But she also couldn't expect anything different from a relationship this time around. Not with the secret she carried.

She stared at her lover, his insolent smile chipping away at the happiness she had experienced only a few minutes ago. Even so, she couldn't look away. Sprawled in her bed, he was the epitome of erotic excess. Sin incarnate. The man with the tender grin and gentle touch had been replaced by a hard-edged billionaire bad boy.

This was the image she had run from two years ago. The hints of darkness inside him had both attracted and repelled her.

The Quin who made love to her tonight was a shock. In a good way. He had been passionate and demanding, though at the same time, protective. Warm. Affectionate.

In trying to guard herself, her words and actions had wrought a terrible change in him. He had withdrawn to a place that suited his lone-wolf personality—a place where he could be in control.

She shed the robe and approached the bed. Quin's unpleasant sneer faded. He blinked as a dark flush of red rode high on his cheekbones. "God, you're gorgeous, Katie Duncan." He reached for her without warning, grabbing her wrist and tumbling her onto the bed.

When she was breathless and pinned beneath his weight, his mood softened. "Hell," he muttered. "I can't stay mad at you. Women have always been a mystery to me. What they want. What they don't want."

"It's not so terribly complicated," she whispered. When she cupped his cheek, his skin was stubbly and warm. "All I want is for you to make love to me over and over again."

The planes of his face grew taut. His eyes glittered. "Lucky for both of us, we're finally on the same page."

She had expected harshness after their conflict. Instead, he gave her aching tenderness. It was like he was two different men. Carefully, he lifted her astride him, but didn't join their bodies. When her hair swung loose and shielded her face, he wound handfuls of it around his fingers and pulled her head down, so he could kiss her.

Her breasts pillowed against his hard chest. The contrast between their bodies, male and female, was both arousing and astonishing. How could two people so different in every way be so perfectly attuned in bed?

He smelled amazing. Warm male skin and the hotel's shower gel. It was a heady combination. She nipped his chin with her teeth. "How many condoms did you bring?" she asked, the question breathless.

"Not nearly enough." He sighed audibly, amusingly crestfallen. The kiss deepened. He slid his tongue between her lips, tasting, seducing.

Her bones turned to water. She wanted to climb inside his skin and occupy the same space, breathe the same air. Behind her, his considerable erection bumped her bottom. "You seem to have a problem, Mr. Stone. May I help you with that?"

He was panting now, his fingers bruising her skin where he clenched her ass. "Can't. Reach. Condoms."

"Hang on, Quin. I'll do it." Easier said than done. He was holding her so tightly, there wasn't much room to maneuver. When she bumped her elbow on the corner of the small bedside table, pain shot up her arm. Still, she persevered. At last, the small packet was in reach.

She held it up in triumph. "Got it!"

This reunion was still new enough that she didn't feel comfortable performing such an intimate task. Quin must have sensed her unease. He set her aside for a moment, dealt with the necessary protection and then rolled onto his hip to face her.

She felt the hot color that stained her cheeks.

Quin chuckled. "I can't believe you still blush."

"Not all of us are as world-weary as you are, Quin Stone." She sniffed. "And not all of us have a hundred notches on our belt."

One masculine eyebrow went up. He traced her nose with a delicate touch. "You're not wearing a belt, Kat. And for the record, your impressions of me are way off base. I told you I haven't been with a woman since the accident."

"But that's—"

He put a hand over her mouth, silencing her startled reaction. "I really don't want to waste this condom. Can we talk about this later? At a less *critical* juncture?"

She glanced down at his erection. Despite the momentary pause in the action, Quin was still locked and loaded. "My apologies. Carry on."

"So it's all up to me?" He rolled onto his back and slung one arm across his forehead. "Maybe I want you to take the lead."

She was skeptical. "Then maybe we put the condom on too soon," she said tartly.

"You're a creative woman. Oral sex isn't the only thing men like. Surprise me."

"But won't your…" She waved her hand in the general direction of his straining, swollen sex.

His grin was tight. "If you're concerned that I might *deflate* before I get inside you, don't be. The way I feel right now, I might be hard till Labor Day."

# Nine

Quin loved teasing Katie. She rose to the bait so beautifully.

Her eyes rounded. "Labor Day? That's a weird holiday to pick."

He took her hand and put it on his chest. "Please, Kat. I can't wait much longer."

It was true. His sex throbbed like a damned toothache. When she caressed his taut belly, his skin broke out in gooseflesh. This was a gamble on his part. Perhaps he had never let Katie feel the power she had over him.

"Do whatever you want," he croaked. "I'm all yours."

It was true he regretted donning the protection too soon. He'd been intent on penetration at all costs. At the last minute, he had backed off. Getting Katie to trust him meant letting her take the wheel now and then.

Her expression was endearingly intense. Her light caresses were almost as arousing as if she had taken him in her mouth. They would get to that. He hoped. For now, though, he was her willing subject.

Katie touched every part of his body. Almost. When she bent and kissed the arches of his feet, he almost came off the bed.

"Too much?" she asked, her expression guileless. Big brown eyes dared him to complain.

He shrugged. "You startled me. That's all. I'm ticklish."

"Ah." She worked her way back up his body. Shins. Knees. Thighs. Mostly kissing. Sometimes biting. His fingers clenched in the sheets. Sweat beaded his brow. Her scent filled his lungs.

When she bypassed the part of him that needed her most, he wanted to cry and curse. She had taken his challenge and run with it. Even if it killed him, he was determined not to crack.

She stroked his rib cage with two hands. Then she cupped his face between her palms and kissed him deeply. It was *her* tongue in *his* mouth this time. He would never have described Katie as a passive lover in the past. But unwittingly, he had unleashed a wild, sensual temptress tonight.

He couldn't decide which was worse. Eyes open, or eyes closed. He was breathing so fast the risk of hyperventilation was real.

"Katie," he said. The single word was all he could manage.

"Yes?"

He gulped air. "Enough, Kat. Please."

She had been leaning over him, her body pressed to his chest. Now she straightened and lifted up onto her knees. "I knew I could make you cry uncle," she said teasingly. But there was no smug triumph in her words. Her gaze was soft and affectionate.

He was enjoying himself. What red-blooded heterosexual man wouldn't? But some hazy discontent niggled at his composure. Something about the earlier conversation. Three weeks. Convenient. Temporary.

Maybe there was more. Maybe he *wanted* more.

He had lost his father and almost lost the use of his leg. He'd had to give up competitive skiing with no real possibility that he might ski again at all, thanks to his reckless behavior. Couldn't the Fates be kind? Couldn't Katie be his consolation prize? The one perfect, happy part of a screwed-up life?

She scooted backward and carefully lowered herself onto his erection. The slick friction and tight squeeze of her body on his was nirvana. Only the fact that he had come so recently allowed him to fully enjoy this next act. Watching Katie was almost as exhilarating as being inside her.

He deliberately maintained his passive role. When she hesitated, he urged her on. "Take what you want, Kat. Give us what we both need."

Her languid movements accelerated. She rode him well, though her technique was endearingly unpracticed. He lifted into her, thrusting upward to meet her descent. Suddenly, he was consumed with the need to know if she had done this exact ballet with another man.

An earthquake of fire burned jagged fault lines through his body without warning. He'd thought he had things under control. Apparently not.

"Sorry," he groaned, rolling her beneath him. He lost it. Completely.

The room disappeared. He locked eyes with the woman beneath him. "I don't want it to end, Kat." He meant the current frenzy, but he could have been talking about the big picture. Blindly, he drove into her. In some dim corner of his brain, he heard the echoes of Katie's climax.

He went deeper. Harder. He felt invincible. As if he were standing at the top of a mountain he'd wanted to scale for far too long. And then it happened, that intense, shattering moment of joy when he slipped over the edge and let himself fall.

Katie wrapped her arms around him. "Yes, Quin. Yes…"

After that, silence reigned but for the beating of his heart in his ears and the ragged unison of their breathing.

It might have been minutes or hours before he was himself again. He honestly couldn't say.

Katie had reached out at one point and awkwardly pulled the covers to their shoulders. The AC was highly efficient. Neither of them had thought to adjust it before now. Cool air bathed their damp bodies in currents of icy chill, drying the sweat on their skin. The quiet hum of the unit masked any noises outside.

With the drapes still open, the lights of the city shone red and gold and green and white and every color in between. Most people were home by now, but he knew the streets in some parts of town still teemed with activity on a Friday night. Around the Carlyle, the neighborhood was quiet.

At last, when he could function, he lifted himself off Katie and stumbled into the bathroom. When he returned, he found her sound asleep. As he stood in the doorway watching her, his heart clenched in his chest. She was right. By every metric, they were an unlikely couple.

He shut off the unpleasant thought, determined to live in the moment.

Katie was his for now. That would have to do.

When Katie woke up in the middle of the night needing to pee, she glanced at her phone. It was 5:00 a.m. Quin had made love to her again somewhere around two thirty.

Now he slept like the dead, one heavy arm slung over her waist as if trying to keep her prisoner.

Drowsy and sated, she lingered in bed, not wanting to give up such perfection. Outside the window, lights from tall buildings created a warm, comforting glow. If New York was the city that never slept, a person could feel safe knowing that somebody somewhere was keeping watch.

At last, she eased free of Quin's unconscious embrace and padded to the bathroom. Her muscles were stiff, and her sex was puffy and sore. When she pressed a cold washcloth between her legs, she sighed.

*This* was the memory she had tried so hard to suppress. *This* smugly happy feeling of repletion. She hadn't been a virgin when she and Quin first hooked up. But her few relationships hadn't prepared her for the hurricane that was sex with Quin. He was rough and wild and intensely arousing.

He never did anything to hurt her. He was endlessly tender. But that same tenderness was wrapped in masculine determination, carrying her to a place of physical bliss so deep and so wide, she nearly lost herself.

Sometimes she wondered if she broke up with him not because of the money squabbles, but because the feelings he invoked terrified her. She didn't want to always be teetering on the edge of insanity. It was a dangerous place to live.

When she slipped back into bed, the breath from his disgruntled muttering warmed her chilled skin. He wrapped two big muscular arms around her and pulled her close. The man's body radiated heat like a furnace. She burrowed into his side and soothed herself by listening to the steady, rhythmic beat of his heart.

He was so *alive*, so willing to tempt fate on the slopes, to live life on his terms.

As she drifted off to sleep, she prayed that she would have the strength to leave when it was time to go.

\* \* \*

When she woke again, it was morning. Clouds had rolled in. Though the day was gray, nothing could dent her euphoria. She rolled over to see if Quin was awake. Her heart stopped when she saw a pillow with only the indentation of his head. The sheets were cold.

Then she saw the tiny white note. He'd torn off half a sheet from the hotel notepad.

Katie—
Gone for coffee, condoms and croissants. Back soon...
Quin

Her smile grew. With no idea when her lover would return, she dashed into the bathroom and bundled her hair into a towel. Then she grabbed a quick shower to freshen up for whatever might come next.

She had just finished getting dressed and was gathering her hair into a ponytail when the door to the corridor opened without warning. Quin burst into the room, bringing with him the irresistible aroma of hot coffee and freshly baked pastries.

He tossed the smallest of the white paper bags on the dresser. Waving two large cups, he grinned at her. "Breakfast is served, madam."

She cocked her head and returned the smile. "You do know we're staying at the Carlyle? I'm fairly certain room service would have delivered anything and everything we wanted."

"Not condoms," he said, smirking. "Besides, I needed a walk. And I happened to remember a great little patisserie a few blocks over on Third Avenue. The real deal. Almost like being in Paris. You hungry?" He waved the bag in front of her face.

The scent of breakfast made her stomach flip. "Oh yeah."

Before she could claim her share, a discreet knock sounded at the door. Quin checked the peephole. "Ah. Reinforcements."

Apparently, as he had entered the hotel, he had paused to order fresh-squeezed orange juice, perfect strawberries and two extra pots of coffee. Along with a serving trolley draped in white linen and laden with heavy silverware and a single rose in a crystal vase.

*Wow.*

Quin tipped the uniformed hotel employee and shut the door. He pulled two small chairs to flank the table. "C'mon. I'm starving. I expended a lot of calories last night."

Her face heated. "On my way."

When Quin held out her chair, he bent to kiss the side of her neck just below her ear. The tantalizing caress sent shivers down her spine. He was so relaxed, so natural.

She felt vulnerable and unsure. How did a woman and a man follow a night like last night?

Apparently, Quin believed the answer was food. He ripped open the large paper bag and waved his hand, wafting the smell in her direction. "Croissants. Baked this morning. Chocolate-filled. Plain, with plenty of butter and orange marmalade. And my personal favorite—a lemon, raspberry and ricotta combo. We can cut them in half if you want to try them all."

Katie's stomach rumbled audibly. She tore off a piece of the chocolate-filled croissant and stuffed it in her mouth. "Oh. My. Gosh." The flavors exploded on her tongue. Like Mrs. Peterson's crème brûlée, almost better than sex. *Ha!* Not even close.

Quin poured their coffee, preparing Katie's the way she liked it without asking. Did it mean anything if a man remembered one sugar, no cream after two years apart?

Maybe not. In recent weeks she'd been drinking English breakfast tea at his house in Maine. So the memory was an old one.

She took a sip of coffee. The fabulous elixir was still surprisingly hot enough to make her tongue tingle. "How often are you in Paris?"

He had to chew and swallow before he could answer. "Three or four times a year. Stone River Outdoors owns a flat in Montmartre. We do a lot of business in Europe, so Paris is a great hub for us."

*A flat in Montmartre?* Good grief. He said it offhand, the same way she might refer to a Taco Bell in Portland. Again, her doubts surfaced. Of course, if all of this was only temporary, why was she worried at all?

They devoured the half dozen croissants in short order, Quin's four to her two. He reached across the table and caressed her chin. "Marmalade," he said soberly. But his eyes danced.

She grabbed his hand and held it to her cheek. "What's in the other bag, Quin?"

He shrugged. "Possibilities. For later. Right now, we're going to play tourist. That's why I brought you to New York."

She shook her head slowly. "No. The museums can wait. I want *you* for breakfast."

His eyes flared, those extraordinary irises sparking with heat. "Are you sure, Kat? This weekend is my gift to you."

"I thought this trip was about *your* cabin fever."

He shrugged, sheepish at being caught out in a lie. "I wanted to get away. That much is true. But when Zachary offered us the Broadway tickets, I thought it would make you happy. I like making Katie Duncan happy."

Those last six words were uttered with such raw sincerity it would be hard to fake. "This room is expensive," she said. "I think we should get our money's worth. You know how I like to be thrifty."

"I do know," he said wryly.

"Then come to bed with me. All that coffee has me hyped up. I need to work off some energy."

As it turned out, they didn't leave the suite until dinnertime. Quin was insatiable. So was she. If living in a fantasy was wrong, then her punishment would come later. For now, she was committed to enjoying the moment, a moment that was impossibly wonderful.

The sex ranged from playful to hungry to slow and sweet. In between, they napped, wrapped in each other's arms. She had thought she knew Quin. But he showed her new sides to him that their earlier affair had never revealed. It was as if he had dropped some unseen armor.

Katie's emotions were full. Happiness and peace. Fear and trembling. She was going to fall long and hard.

As she rested her cheek over Quin's heart, she knew the consequences would be worth every minute she spent in this bed.

Finally, he rolled over and yawned and glanced at the clock. "Good Lord, Kat. We're gonna need a redo of this weekend."

She lifted an eyebrow? "The sex? Count me in. But if you're talking about all the rest, I've seen plenty of movies set in New York. I swear I can fill in the blanks. Besides, you took me to see *Hamilton*. That was a great start. I'll save the Empire State Building for another day."

He yawned again. "Sorry," he muttered. He picked up his phone. "I know a couple of great restaurants you'd like. Let me see where I can get a reservation. I may have left it too late."

She snatched his phone and tossed it on the far side of

the huge bed. "I still haven't gotten my hot dog from a street vendor. Couldn't we find one and have a picnic in Central Park?"

"Half the benches have pigeon poop on them, and the park will be full of joggers and tourists."

She pinched his cheek. "*I'm* a tourist, remember? You said you wanted to make me happy." She batted her lashes dramatically.

"Unbelievable." He rolled his eyes, laughing. "We're surrounded by some of the finest haute cuisine in the world, and you want a meat stick of unknown origin?"

"Geez, Quin. Do you rich guys ever get down and dirty with the masses? Live a little. There's a good chance we *won't* get food poisoning."

"I wouldn't take bets on that," he grumbled. "But if I'm going to die later, I think I need a reason to live right now."

He pretended to roll on top of her. She shoved at his chest, knowing that for once, he was kidding about sex. "We skipped lunch, you maniac. You have to feed me. I'm pretty sure I read that in the fine print somewhere."

"You are such a diva," he complained. "First you want breakfast, then lunch. Now a hot dog? The things I do for you…"

She sat up, clutching the sheet to her chest. "I never *got* lunch," she reminded him. "Give me five minutes in the bathroom to get dressed. Then it's your turn."

"We could shower together," he said, looking hopeful.

"Put a pin in that. I could be persuaded. But not until I've had my hot dog."

# Ten

Quin helped Katie into the cab and slid in beside her. He was relaxed and mellow, definitely inclined to indulge the woman sitting near him. She had begged to walk to the corner and hail a cab the old-fashioned way, insisting that summoning a private car via phone was no fun at all.

Now he leaned forward to speak to the cabbie, feeling a bit ridiculous. "The lady wants to find a street vendor and buy a hot dog. I'm willing to double the fare. Can you help us out with that? But not too far, because we're taking it to the park afterward."

The cabbie nodded, though his dubious expression in the rearview mirror was a dead giveaway. Quin presumed the poor man probably dealt with crazy tourists on a regular basis. This impromptu hot dog trip might be the most boring part of his day.

Fortunately, they found what Katie wanted without driving across town. Maybe the driver had a relative in the food services industry. Whatever the explanation, soon the cab was idling at the curb while Katie and Quin bought bottled water and hot dogs with all the trimmings.

When they were back in the car, the cabbie swung around the block and headed toward the park. "Does it matter where I drop you?" he asked.

"Nope. Anywhere will do," Quin said.

Katie held the large bag in two arms. Quin had insisted on multiple hot dogs, bags of chips and some packaged oatmeal cookies. His companion stared into the bag lustfully, pausing to inhale now and then.

The cab rolled to a halt at a popular entrance not far from the hotel. The unadorned path led down a slope into the heart of the park. Quin paid the driver. "This way," he said to Katie. They found an unoccupied bench and put the food between them. "Happy now?" he asked, smiling. The humidity was down. Though the park was indeed crowded, the summer evening felt near perfect.

"Definitely." She handed him one of the all-the-way dogs. She had added only mustard and pickles to hers. She took a big bite and sighed.

"What's wrong?" he asked.

"Nothing. Not really. It's just not quite as good as the ones you get at a baseball stadium."

"I don't want to say I told you so."

"But you're gonna…"

He tucked her hair behind her ear. "Maybe."

"Well, I don't care. Even if the hot dog isn't the icon of culinary enjoyment I had hoped, the setting more than makes up for it. I had no idea Central Park was so big."

"It's two and a half miles long and half a mile wide."

"I'm impressed." She licked mustard off her fingers one at a time, which shouldn't have been particularly erotic to Quin, but it was. "Are we going to walk after this?"

"I thought we would. If you still want to."

"I'm game." Her neat khaki shorts bared legs that were slim and strong and capable. Her running shoes were turquoise and matched her nylon, scoop-necked top.

They finished everything but the cookies. Quin looked at the cellophane-wrapped sweets. The expiration date was eight months in the future. "Let's order dessert from room service when we get back," he said. "The hotel restaurant has a great pastry chef. Triple chocolate cake, bourbon pecan pie, gourmet banana pudding slathered with whipped cream. You name it." He dropped the two unopened packages in the trash.

Katie tried to stop him at the last second, but she was too late. The additive-laden snacks were down in the hole with melting ice cream, empty drink cans and already-chewed gum.

"Why did you toss them?" she cried. "That's so wasteful."

"It was a couple of bucks, Katie. No big deal."

"I could have given them to a street person."

Suddenly, there was tension back in the equation. And it wasn't the sizzling, nerve tingling kind. "I'm sorry," he said stiffly. "I'll ask next time. Let's go."

He walked swiftly, stretching his leg and his knee until the muscles burned. The doctor had said to take it easy for six more weeks. Didn't get much easier than a stroll through the park.

Katie walked beside him except for the moments when people passed them. Quin showed her the *Imagine* memorial to John Lennon, who had lived nearby and whose ashes had been scattered in the park almost four decades before.

Katie loved the Alice in Wonderland statue, the group of bears sculpture and also the small man-made lake, where adults and children sailed toy boats and made memories.

By the time they hit the pond, they had been walking rapidly for almost an hour. Katie plopped down on a concrete step, pressing the back of her hand to her forehead. "Let's take a break. This is a beautiful spot."

"One of my favorites," he said, sitting hip to hip with his charming but unpredictable companion. He almost curled his arm around her, but Katie had put up some kind of do-not-disturb thing between them. He didn't want to disrupt the momentary accord.

After a few moments, she shot him a sideways glance. "Why doesn't Stone River Outdoors have offices here?" she asked.

"Manhattan real estate is too damn expensive. Plus, it's not really necessary. We're so close timewise. We can easily fly down from Maine and back in a day trip...like Farrell and Zachary did yesterday."

"Ah."

"May I ask you another question?" she said softly, staring out across the water. "It's personal."

His stomach tightened. "Of course."

"I saw your knee—while we were having sex. I'm assuming the two longest, newest scars are from the recent knee replacement."

His hands fisted on his thighs. "Yes."

"I didn't know there were so many others. Scars, I mean."

He shrugged. "They worked hard to rebuild my knee after it was mangled in the car crash."

She touched his leg. "I'm so sorry that happened to you."

His stomach curled. He didn't like talking about the accident. "You said you had a question?"

"Will you be able to ski again competitively?"

He knew the answer, knew it well. But he could barely speak the words. "No. Not a chance," he said bluntly. "Even if I manage to get back out there on the slopes, I won't be able to ski aggressively enough to be a contender. When you're competing in the downhill events, you have to take chances. You have to snap those quick turns with precision, dig in your skis, gain every possible second. I can't do that anymore."

Admitting the truth to himself *and* to Katie was both cathartic and deeply painful.

She patted his leg, stroking it almost absentmindedly. "And skiing for pleasure?"

"The doc says yes. As long as I don't try too soon and screw things up like I did a few months ago. He thinks when everything heals properly, I should be able to do a nice downhill run on the bunny slopes."

"Seriously?" Her expression was aghast.

"No, not seriously. But it might as well be the bunny slopes. Nothing is going to be the same."

"You could find your joy in other places," she said. The sympathy in her dark eyes was a gift he wasn't willing to accept.

"Skiing is all I have, Katie. The sport has defined me for so long I don't know who I am without the wind and the mountain and the cold sting of snow in my face."

"A lot of wealthy people support charitable causes. They can even change the world. Maybe it's hard to see right now, because you've had so many disappointments. But helping people might be a way you can re-create the fulfillment skiing gave you."

He felt as if she was picking at a scab deep in his soul. "Let's change the subject," he said gruffly. Her slight flinch told him she recognized the *butt-out* subtext. To her credit, she didn't push.

"Okay," Katie said. "Then tell me about Farrell's wife.

I've heard snippets of gossip, but I'd like to know the truth. From you."

It was a definite relief to shift the focus away from the personal topics Quin hadn't even sorted out for himself yet. "Farrell married his high school sweetheart, but only after a long, horrible battle with our father."

"What do you mean?"

He rubbed three fingers in the center of his forehead. "I don't remember if you ever ran into my father at the office. Not likely. He didn't enjoy mingling with the *common* people." Quin snorted. "He didn't much like people at all. To be honest, he spent most of our lives warning us about the *leeches*—his words, not mine—who would try to use us."

Katie shuddered visibly. "What made him like that?"

"Our mother died when I was born. Apparently, a lot of women wanted to help the rich widower grieve. For a price. I think he really loved our mother. I don't know if he was always cynical and hard, but he surely was after she was gone."

"What does that have to do with Farrell?"

"Farrell and Sasha started dating when they were sixteen. Dad didn't like it, but he figured it was puppy love, so he mostly left them alone. Then somehow, Farrell graduated one day and bought Sasha a ring the next."

"Oh dear."

"Yeah. It was romantic as hell, but the old man was furious. He sent Farrell off to college on the West coast and, on the sly, told Sasha that she was ruining Farrell's life. I was still too young to pay much attention to what was going on, but Farrell has told me the stories. Farrell knew that what he and Sasha had was the real deal. But he didn't know what Dad had done to Sasha. Eventually he dragged the truth out of her. It killed him that she had been hurt so badly, especially by *our father*."

Katie trembled inside. "But you all still had relationships with your father. Was it only because of the business?"

Quin shook his head slowly. "It's a long story, more than you want to hear."

"Okay. Then finish the other one."

"Farrell and Sasha kept in touch by email and phone calls after he went off to college. Then when they both turned twenty-one, Farrell came home, told our father to go to hell and married his sweetheart."

Katie was spellbound. "That's such a beautiful story, at least Farrell's part."

"Not so much after Sasha got sick. Aggressive breast cancer. He lost her when they were both only twenty-five years old."

A single tear rolled down Katie's cheek. Quin caught it with the tip of his finger. "I didn't mean to make you sad."

"I know. I've worked for your brother a long time. I suppose I've always been curious. He never dates anybody that I can tell. Now I know why. I can't imagine losing the love of your life at such a young age. It must have been devastating."

"The tragedy affected all of us. I'd like to believe even the old man felt a shred of guilt, but I don't know. Zachary took the exact opposite road. He's had more females in his life than a cat has kittens. He keeps all his women at arm's length. Calls the shots. Walks away when the relationship reaches its expiration date. He's funny and smart and charming as hell, but he never lets anybody get too close."

"And you, Quin? How did Sasha's death affect you?"

Katie jumped to her feet, jolted by the expression on Quin's face. She wanted to know everything about his past, but not if it meant hurting him. He'd never offered her that kind of personal deep dive before.

"Forget I asked," she begged. "That's way too personal a question between you and me. Sex, yes. Unburdening soul-deep secrets, no."

In her defense, hearing that Mr. Stone Sr. had treated another woman as abysmally as he treated Katie rattled her. She had clung to her desperate humiliation and her injured pride for far too long. The man was dead. He couldn't hurt her anymore. The only person who could mess things up now was Katie herself.

Was she holding Quin to some impossible standard of perfection? God knows, she had plenty of faults of her own. She liked playing the role of savior. She could be too pushy at times. And she had a chip on her shoulder about Quin's money.

Still, her fear held her back, because she wanted him to connect with her intimately. And she wasn't sure such a thing was possible. Even if Quin wanted more than a few weeks of sexual excess, she was scared to think about what that might mean. It was easier and safer to micromanage other people's problems than to take a good, hard look at her own.

She held out her hand, smiling, pretending that she and Quin were nothing more than friends with benefits. "You ready to head back to the hotel? I see a shower in my future."

"*Our* future," Quin said waggling his eyebrows. "Remember?" He rolled to his feet. "I'll wash those spots you can't reach."

She knew he was teasing. Playing the goofball for her amusement. But the words gave her a thrill. Deep in the base of her abdomen, little firecrackers began to ignite.

"Can you run?" she asked.

He stared at her blankly, a crease between his eyebrows. "What do you mean?"

"The doctor. Your recovery. Taking it easy. Can you run?"

He stared at her intently. Suddenly, the wanting and the waiting were back and all mixed up with the emotional wringer he had put her through in telling his family's story.

Quin nodded slowly. "As long as it's not too far and not too fast."

"Excellent. See if you can catch me, Quinten Stone. If you do, maybe I'll wash a few spots for *you*." Katie took off jogging, no doubt taking Quin by surprise. But if she did surprise him, he didn't waste any time playing catch-up.

When she glanced over her shoulder, Quin was closing the distance she had put between them. The masculine scowl on his face sent a trickle of excitement down her spine. He looked predatory, determined.

Katie was running faster than she had planned. Suddenly, she remembered Farrell telling her about Quin's intensity, his laser focus. The way he pushed and pushed until he achieved his goals.

Only right now, Quin was supposed to be taking it easy. For a few more weeks. So his body could heal.

Katie stopped dead in the middle of the path. People went around her as if she were an island parting a river into two streams. She put her hands to her cheeks. "I am so sorry, Quin. I wasn't thinking. It was a game. But I don't want you to get hurt. Not again."

He pulled up short, right in front of her. Practically nose to nose. He slid his hands into her hair, tipped her head back, smashed his mouth over hers. "You make me crazy, Katie Duncan."

Frustration vibrated in his big frame. She could *feel* his turmoil.

Was that why she had run? Not a game at all, but a ploy to be chased? Captured? Subdued?

"Ditto, Quin." She wrapped her arms around his neck. "I don't even know what I'm doing anymore. We're supposed to be *working*."

He nuzzled her nose with his. "Not on the weekend. Everybody deserves a couple of days off."

"You're one of the big bosses. I suppose you could take off any day you want to… Isn't that where the term *playboy* comes from? A rich guy who can pilot a yacht or fly a helicopter or…" She trailed off, realizing she had backed herself into a corner.

Quin lifted a shoulder and let it fall, his expression wry. "Or ski down a mountain?"

# Eleven

Quin released Katie and took her hand, linking his fingers with hers. The quarter-mile walk back to the hotel was both silent and peaceful. He rarely spent a day as relaxed as this one. Even when he was skiing, he was setting goals and sailing past them.

At the Carlyle, he and Katie took the elevator up to their floor. Again, silence reigned. What was she thinking? What did she want?

He regretted not getting to know her better when they were dating two years ago. Instead, he had explored the mutual hunger that drew them like two strong magnets, one to the other.

In the suite, he touched her shoulder. "You ready for dessert?"

She put her hand over his, warm brown eyes signaling her intent. "I'd like a shower. With you."

She was direct. Not coy. Not making him guess. He

swallowed hard, his hands trembling. "I like the sound of that."

He couldn't put his finger on how things had changed, but they had. Their sojourn in the park had affected them both. The mood was more comfortable now, but no less sexually charged.

In the bathroom, Katie stripped off her clothes casually. Quin started the shower and adjusted the water. As she stepped into the roomy enclosure, Quin got naked as quickly as he could.

When he joined Katie, she averted her gaze, her posture wary. Pale blond hair turned rich gold as the water saturated the long strands. While he watched, Katie reached up with two hands and sluiced the water from her face, taming her soaked hair into a rich waterfall.

Though he wasn't sure, it seemed as if her hands trembled. "Are you nervous, Kat?" he asked. "We left the light on. It's still not dark outside. We can't blame this one on late-night debauchery."

"I know. And yes, I'm nervous. I'm always nervous around you. It's like throwing a baby doll into a moat with an alligator. You're always going to come out on top."

"Is that a loaded metaphor?"

"No. Just the truth. You and I are very different, Quin."

He opened a small bottle of shower gel. The heavy scent of jasmine filled the steamy enclosure. "Turn around," he said gruffly.

When she tugged her hair forward over her shoulder and gave him her back, he was struck by how vulnerable she looked. How beautifully feminine the nape of her neck was. How trim her waist. Softly rounded hips flared just enough for a man to grasp.

He'd been hard since she kicked off her running shoes and bared her narrow feminine feet with the high arches and perfectly polished toes. Instead of pouncing on her as his libido urged, he dug deep and found tenderness. Gentle care. The other was coming, but not yet.

Doing her back was tricky. He had lathered up a washcloth, but when he touched her, the practical aspects of the chore got derailed by the need to linger. Both shoulders demanded his attention. Then the shoulder blades. Before moving south, he remembered to wash her neck.

Katie stood perfectly still, almost as if she was holding her breath. He squatted and washed her round ass, her thighs, her legs. He was breathing hard now, his heart pounding against his rib cage.

"Turn around," he said hoarsely.

Now he was on eye level with her pink, perfect sex. He traced her center with one fingertip. Katie shifted restlessly.

He lurched to his feet and washed her breasts. One at a time. Trying not to lose focus when he saw how the soap bubbles glistened—then eventually slid—over her heated skin.

When he moved toward her navel, Katie grabbed his wrist. Hard. "Are we doing this right here?" she asked, the words barely audible. Tendrils of damp hair clung to her forehead. Her eyelashes were spiky.

He leaned down and kissed her nose. "Ladies' choice."

The tiniest of smiles tilted her lips. "And if I don't feel like being a lady tonight?"

His sex, already fully erect, tightened painfully. "Um…" His throat closed up and his legs threatened to wobble.

She put her hands on his wet shoulders and pushed. "Sit down, Quin."

He lost his balance and plopped down hard on the narrow shower bench. Katie straddled his legs.

"Wait," he said wheezing for breath. "We don't have a con—"

She put her hand over his mouth. "Relax. I'm just playing with you. Any objections?"

"None," he croaked.

Katie sat down carefully. Now his erection nestled between them. He wasn't at all sure this was a good idea, but he sure as hell wasn't going to stop her.

"You are a sexy guy, Quin," she said. "Did you know that?"

"Um…" Apparently this shower interlude was adversely affecting his vocabulary. And he was pretty sure this was a trick question. It seemed better not to answer.

She ran her thumbs across his eyelids, forcing him to shut them. Now his other senses were heightened. He felt the steam that moistened their skin. He smelled Katie's warm, wet closeness.

"Keep your eyes closed, Quin," she said.

"Yes, ma'am." Before he could guess what she was going to do next, she took his hands and put them on her breasts.

Damn that was good. He pushed both mounds together and buried his face in the fragrant valley.

Katie muttered something he couldn't decipher. She leaned into him. "I like that," she whispered. "A lot."

He was blind. Moving along in the darkness. The wanting in his gut became a living torment. Lust roiled in his belly. He tasted her nipples. She was sweet and tart and *exactly right for him.*

The random thought both shocked and terrified him. Katie was the kind of woman who would marry a regular guy, a man who would give her babies and a house in the suburbs. Quin would never be a good father, maybe no father at all. What did he know about kids or security?

His childhood had been crap. No home-baked cookies. No bedtime stories. No warm, loving hugs during a thunderstorm or a nightmare.

She had been right to walk away from him.

Katie bit his earlobe, pulling him back into the moment. He grabbed her ass. "You know I like your teasing, Kat, but I'm *not* made of stone. You're killing me. I need to be inside you."

"Soon. I want what you want, Quin." She stroked his hair with gentle repetitive motions that in another context would have been soothing. He was so wired and on edge, even the nonsexual touch was painfully arousing.

"We're done here," he groaned. He scooted her off his lap and stood, wrapping his arm around her waist. "Bed," he muttered.

Katie rebelled. "No, please. You'll get the sheets all wet."

"Fine." He grabbed a towel, dragged her with him into the bedroom, and despite his weak knee, scooped her up and dumped her on the settee. "Don't move."

Katie's eyes were huge. Had she really expected him to remain passive under such provocation? He rummaged for more of the protection he had bought that morning.

When he saw how she stared at him, he faltered. "Am I going too fast, Kat?"

She chewed her lip. "No. Your brothers told me how controlled you are. Seeing you snap is kind of flattering."

He ripped open a packet and rolled the condom onto his shaft. "You've made me lose control since the first day I bumped into you at the water cooler. Literally. You were wearing a pale pink sundress. Your hair was up. I think the earrings were sterling silver stars." Her look of incredulity amused him. "Why is that so surprising?"

"You're exaggerating about the control thing."

He came down beside her and lifted her leg to the back of the velvet-covered furniture, stroking her thigh. "No. Not even a little." Their bodies struggled in the awkward arrangement. No room to maneuver. Katie didn't seem to mind. He entered her slowly, holding her bottom in one hand and bracing himself with the other. "I'm glad you came to Maine, Kat. It's been pretty dark since the accident. You've dragged me out of the pit, I think."

"Don't talk," she begged. "Take me hard."

"Yes. Yes." It was an easy request to grant. He tried to make it last. He really did. But it had been hours since he'd made love to her. Her arms wrapped around his neck, threatening to choke him. She linked her ankles at his back, her heels digging into his waist.

"Ah, hell." He came in minutes, his mind blank with stunned pleasure. The end went on forever. Little aftershocks that left him dizzy and spent. He lifted away and pleasured her with his touch, groaning with relief when she came wildly, crying out his name.

When he could breathe, he surveyed the situation. "We're all dry now. Bed?"

She nodded, her eyes closed. "You're the boss."

Katie slept like the dead for hours. In fact, she would have happily slept longer if not for an annoying beep nearby. Grumbling and shifting to squint at her surroundings, she poked Quin. "Is that a smoke alarm?"

He lifted onto one elbow, bleary-eyed. "Phone alarm." His voice was hoarse with fatigue. That's what happened when two otherwise sane adults chose to fornicate like rabbits instead of getting the eight solid hours of sleep recommended by the American Medical Association.

"Why in God's name did you set an alarm?"

"We have to fly home," he muttered.

"You're a billionaire. It's a private plane. Tell him we'll be ready midafternoon."

"Can't. Flight plan's already been filed. Gotta go…"

She stumbled to the bathroom and did the best she

could. When they left the hotel forty-five minutes later, she pondered the inequities of life. Katie could barely look at herself in the mirror as they sailed through the lobby. Her hair was on top of her head in a messy knot. She still had pillow creases on her face, and the dark circles under her eyes were epic.

Quin, on the other hand, looked like the image of a wealthy, handsome bachelor enjoying a relaxing day off. He had topped his snug heather-gray T-shirt with a loose khaki linen jacket. His jeans were exactly the right amount of *worn*, and the shadow of dark stubble on his gorgeous chin made him look sexy and dangerous.

Their hired car waited at the curb. Quin tucked her in and ran around to the street side. Thank God it was Sunday. The usual morning traffic insanity was subdued.

All the way to the airport, through takeoff and during the brief flight north, Katie knew something had changed. It was possible that Quin's slightly aloof attitude was merely exhaustion. She might be reading too much into his silence. The fact that he was skimming the news on his iPad instead of flirting with her was nothing sinister.

Katie leaned her seat back and dozed during the relatively brief flight. Mrs. Peterson met them at the landing strip in a Jeep. The luggage was loaded in the back, and soon, Katie was climbing the front steps of Quin's house... Right where she had started.

Quin smiled at the housekeeper. "Thanks for coming in today. Why don't you go on home and take tomorrow off?"

"Thank you, Mr. Quin," she said. "There's plenty for lunch and dinner in the fridge. You can pick and choose. I left the cooking and warming instructions on the island."

"Sounds great."

The older woman paused. "I don't mean to be pushy,

but we may be in for a serious summer storm. I stocked the pantry just in case, and the generators have been serviced. You and Miss Katie should really take a look at the weather forecast."

Quin groaned. "Zachary said something similar on Friday. So it's taking shape?"

"Looks that way." Her matter-of-fact answer made Katie smile inwardly. Folks in Maine took bad weather in stride. Still, there had been a few very destructive storms over the years.

"In that case," Quin said, "Don't come back out here until you hear from me, one way or the other. You'll have preparations to make at your own home. Katie and I will be fine."

"Okay, then. Let me finish tidying the kitchen, and I'll be off."

When the older woman walked away, an awkward silence fell. Was Quin regretting the indulgent weekend he and Katie had spent in New York? Had too many barriers been crossed? Maybe he wanted to go back to the boss/employee relationship.

Hurt curled in Katie's stomach. The man with whom she had shared a bed—and various other real estate—was not the same man who stood before her now. Quin's gaze was shuttered, his jaw tight.

He hunched his shoulders, not quite meeting her gaze. "It's Sunday. We're not going to work today. Why don't you relax and get some fresh air? We may be cooped up in the house for a couple of days. You might as well enjoy yourself while the sun is shining."

She couldn't decide how to respond to that, and it didn't really matter, because Quin gave her a terse nod and walked in the direction of the makeshift office they shared.

Her eyes burned, and her throat was tight. Was he being

a jerk on purpose, or had something upset him? Did the reason matter? Clearly, their wonderful weekend was over.

She took her bags up to her room, dumped them on the bed and changed into comfortable clothes. Though she had been living at Quin's home for several weeks now, she had only surveyed the ocean from higher ground. Today she was in a mind to find the water's edge and drown her sorrows. The bad joke didn't even lift her mood.

The path down to the beach was not well marked. The jumble of boulders had been there for millennia, occasionally tossed about by rough seas. The narrow trail *existed*, but it was fairly treacherous. She was forced to pick her way carefully or risk breaking an ankle.

The challenge was worth it. By the time she made it onto the narrow strip of sand, her heart was racing, but her state of mind had lightened fractionally. She sat on a rock and removed her socks. The sand was cool beneath her feet.

It seemed impossible that a storm was in the offing. The sea today was a deep, placid turquoise, calm enough to soothe her fear of water. Small pools held sea creatures trapped by low tide. She examined each one, charmed by the diversity. Crabs and starfish, hot pink seaweed and deep red anemones. Even a sea urchin or two. Kneeling in the sand, she used her phone to snap a few pictures.

The creepiest thing she found was a slithery eel-like animal, which she absolutely *didn't* touch. There was even the tiniest of baby lobsters. Why that surprised her, she couldn't say. Obviously, lobsters weren't born being huge and meaty. They had to start small sometime.

She found a measure of peace in the rich beauty of nature. Even if things had soured with Quin, at least she could enjoy her time here. Though she had lived in Maine her entire life, Portland was a far cry from this wild northern coastline. Her parents had barely fed their family. Leisure trips to the shore, even for the day, were few and far between.

When she tired of exploring, she rolled up her pants legs to brave the water. The breeze had begun to pick up, whipping the surface of the ocean into frothy whitecaps. Her toes curled. Maybe this was a bad idea. Strong currents swept this part of the coast.

Not that she was going for a swim. She just wanted to be able to say she had waded in the Atlantic. And to prove that her long-standing fear of water hadn't crippled her.

The noise of the waves masked other sounds.

When a male voice spoke behind her, it was like that first day all over again. She whirled and nearly fell on her butt.

Quin chuckled. "I didn't mean to scare you. How long have you been down here?"

She shot him a wary glance over her shoulder, distrusting his whiplash mood changes. "I don't know. An hour… maybe two." Suddenly she looked up at the path to the house. "I don't think you're supposed to be doing something like this. The doctor said *gentle* exercise."

"I've climbed down this path a hundred times."

"Since the accident?"

# Twelve

Quin frowned. "I'm capable of monitoring my own fitness. I've been doing it since I was a teenager. If I had thought following you down to the ocean would negatively impact my knee, I wouldn't have come."

"That's not what your brothers say. They tell me you test your limits. Sometimes with painful results."

"That was the old Quin. I'm a reformed man." He said it lightly, but it was true in a way. He'd learned some hard lessons during the last two years.

Katie turned back to the ocean. "You're very lucky to live here," she said. "I was just about to stick my feet in the water. An homage to summer."

"It will be a shock," he said. "The water temperature is barely sixty degrees."

"I can handle it." She struck out immediately, halting when the water hit just below her knees. "Oh gosh."

"I warned you."

Katie wrapped her arms around her waist. Her hair began to come loose from its knot now that the wind had picked up.

She was guarded in her posture. No wonder. He'd been deliberately aloof earlier. Coming back to Maine had shocked him into a realization of what he was doing. Katie claimed to want only three weeks in his bed. But did he himself want more?

"Come sit on the rocks with me," he cajoled. "They're warm from the sun. You need to thaw out."

Thirty seconds passed. Then a whole minute. Finally, Katie turned around and slogged back to shore.

Her teeth were chattering. "I love the ocean," she said.

"But maybe Florida is more your speed?"

He was teasing. Katie took him seriously. "Oh no," she said, rolling down her pant legs and perching beside him. "I love the peace and the isolation here. I'm not a fan of crowded beaches. At least I don't think I would be. My family hasn't traveled much. My parents both had jobs where they didn't get paid if they didn't work, so no trips south for us. And to be honest, hot weather isn't really my thing."

"You said *had* jobs. Have they already retired?"

"Sort of…they sold their house in Portland and found a mobile home in Myrtle Beach. Not 'on' the beach, of course. They're just happy to be away from winters in Maine. They've found part-time work in South Carolina that helps pay the bills."

"Is their move why your sister is looking for an apartment? Didn't she live with them?"

"Yes."

"And what about the loser boyfriend? Is he still in the picture?"

Katie had one foot propped on a smaller rock. Her hands

were linked around her knee. "I'm not comfortable talking to you about Jimmy," she said. "Let's change the subject, please." The words were curt.

He deserved that. Katie's sister's boyfriend had sparked one of the biggest fights Quin and Katie ever had. He sighed inwardly. "I'm sorry."

"Did you check the forecast?" she asked, not acknowledging his apology.

"I did. They're expecting the storm to be a strong category three as it scrapes over the Outer Banks. Then it will track like Sandy did or Bob in '91. We'll get some damage for sure, but not catastrophic."

"I thought Maine was mostly hurricane-proof, because of the cold ocean waters."

"Technically true, but even a tropical storm can bring down trees."

"Are you worried?"

"No. If a hurricane makes it to Maine, it's usually downgraded rapidly." He put his arm around her shoulders and kissed her cheek. "You don't have to be afraid, Katie. I would never let anything happen to you, I swear."

"I'm not worried, Quin." Her body was stiff at first, but gradually, she relaxed. They sat in silence, enjoying the perfect afternoon. Trouble would come soon enough.

Being near her like this produced an odd mix of reactions in his gut. He wanted her. He was beginning to think he would never *not* want her. Even more than that—at least for now—he found himself surprisingly content. Almost alarmingly happy.

It had been a hell of a long time since he had experienced either of those emotions.

"I think I know why you broke up with me," he said.

"Oh?" Katie's reaction was hard to miss. He was holding her closely. Her body leaned into his. Right up until the moment he spoke those ten words. She jumped to her feet and went back to the water's edge. If he wasn't mistaken, the tide was about to turn.

When she didn't say anything else, he sighed inwardly. Maybe this was a bad idea. But he had started down this road and there was no room to turn around. "You wanted a family someday," he said. "And I was a guy with no roots. Just a passport and a determination to make it to the next city, the next tournament. Am I right?"

He joined her for a second time.

She nodded slowly. "That was part of it. But I wanted to know you. Really know you. And I wanted you to know me. You were so focused on your skiing that any woman who tried to fit into your life would always come in second place. Sometimes I think you were more emotionally connected to your stupid mountains than you were to me."

He grimaced. "You weren't wrong," he said quietly. "I was obsessed, determined to make it to that elusive first place podium before I hung up my skis. My plan was to continue competing until I was at least thirty-five, maybe longer. That seems laughable now."

"I'm sorry, Quin. I really am. You were so good at what you did and so buoyed by that dream. Is there even a tiny chance that you can go back to the World Cup alpine circuit, maybe as an experiment?"

"None. I would only embarrass myself. As I said before, if I'm lucky, and if I don't do anything else stupid, the docs think that skiing for pleasure can definitely be part of my future."

"Will that be enough for you?"

"It will have to be." He paused. "Things are different now, Katie. *I'm* different now. Perhaps you and I could try again."

Still, she stared straight out to sea. Her cheeks were

pink. It was hot in the full-on sun. Finally, she shot him a sideways glance, brown eyes judging him. "I don't think you realize how you sound, Quin. What you're saying is that I could be your consolation prize now that you've had to give up everything else you care about."

He winced. Was he really so clueless? "I didn't mean it like that," he muttered.

Katie laughed wryly. "I'm sure there are any number of women who would line up to take your mind off your troubles."

"You're the only one I want."

"At least for the moment. You told me you hadn't been with a woman since the accident. Was that true?"

His pride took a hit. "I am *not* a liar."

"Eighteen months. How is that possible? The Quin I knew could barely go eighteen *hours* without sex, much less eighteen months."

"I told you. I've changed."

"Why? How?"

Women always had to dig deeper. He didn't want to examine his inadequacies. Shoving his hands in his pockets, he squinted into the sun, looking for dolphins or the spume of a whale, anything to distract her.

"The car crash was bad. I was in and out of the hospital for weeks at a time. One of my incisions got infected. You saw me at the funeral home after Dad died. Those crutches? I was still using them months after the accident."

"Some women like nursing a wounded hero."

"I was surprised to see you at the service. For days afterward, I lay awake at night wondering what it meant."

She snorted softly. "It meant that I had sympathy for you and your brothers. Sorrow for your loss. It meant that the head of Stone River Outdoors was gone. It meant that I felt obligated to be there, *even though* I had to face you again."

"It had been six long months at that point," he said. "You avoided me at work. I wasn't stupid. I knew it."

"That's the downside of having an affair with the boss. When it ends, things get messy."

"And then—lucky for you—I was in a car crash, and you didn't have to worry anymore about bumping into me in the hallway."

Katie faced him, her expression stormy. "What a terrible thing to say. Maybe we weren't still together, but when I heard about the accident, it tore me up. It's true I didn't believe we had what it took to be a couple. I didn't hate you, though, Quin. I didn't want you to suffer."

"Gee, thanks."

"You didn't really answer my question. Why were there no women in your bed for a year and a half? I would have thought sex would take your mind off your troubles. A bit of oblivion occasionally."

"When life is reduced to its barest essentials, Kat, the truth becomes clear. I still wanted you."

Katie's heart jerked hard, then settled back into a boring rhythm. He was saying what he thought she wanted to hear. Surely, she wasn't going to be gullible enough to fall for his tempting exaggerations.

"It wasn't me," she insisted. "It's just that I represented a time *before* bad things happened to you. It was therapeutic to think about our affair."

"If you say so."

Goose bumps covered her bare arms. "I suppose we should go back to the house."

Quin stepped behind her and folded her in his arms. His big body radiated heat and a feeling of security. "You should gather your things and bring them down to my room. It will be safer to ride this thing out on the main floor. The wind will come off the water. My bedroom faces the forest."

"I bet you say that to all the girls," she teased.

He rested his chin on top of her head. His thumbs slipped under her shirt and caressed her belly. "There are two guest rooms on the first floor. You're welcome to the second one if you don't want to sleep with me."

Katie turned around and tipped back her head. Even then, she couldn't see the expression in his eyes. He wore expensive aviator sunglasses. "Don't play games with me, Quin. Admit it. You're not going to let me sleep in another room."

He shrugged. "I won't force the issue."

She cupped his sex through his pants. "Maybe I will."

Finally, the tension in his body relaxed. A sexy smile tilted his lips. "I like it when Kinky Kat comes out to play."

Beneath her fingers, his sex lifted and hardened. "I don't know about kinky," she said. "But I'm not dumb enough to give up having sex with you when we're living under the same roof. All our differences aside, we're good in bed, Quin. I can't deny that."

A tiny frown creased the space between his eyebrows. "Do you want to, Katie? Deny it, I mean?"

She chewed her lip. "It would be easier to walk away from you if there were no sparks. I'm as predictable as the next woman. When a hot guy wants to give me multiple orgasms, it's hard to say no."

"So you're using me?"

Was he serious? It was hard to tell. "I think we're using each other. And for the moment, I'm okay with that." She slid her hand into his and linked their fingers. "Come on. If I have to leave the guest suite and slum it downstairs, I'd better get to it. Besides, don't you have manly things to prepare? Generators and flashlights and all that disaster prep stuff guys like doing?"

He resisted her efforts to pull him toward the path. "Indeed, I do. But first things first." Before she could protest, he pulled every pin out of her lopsided topknot and tucked them in his pocket. Then he tunneled his fingers through her windblown hair and sighed. "New York was great, but I like having you under my roof."

He slanted his mouth over hers and took the kiss deep. Her toes curled into the sand. Her body heated from the inside out. The man was a fantastic kisser. *Really* good. Her hands clung to his shoulders.

When he released her, they were both breathing hard. He still wore those damned sunglasses. She reached up and removed them slowly. Brilliant blue eyes sizzled with heat.

"I'm a fan of good communication," she said. "For the record, I'm glad I'm here in Maine with you, Quinten."

He rubbed his thumb across her cheekbone. "Me, too, Kat. Me, too."

After she and Quin climbed back up from the beach, the remainder of the day passed uneventfully. They worked in tandem, making preparations for the storm to come. While Quin bungeed the outdoor rockers to the porch and secured other loose items, Katie moved her things downstairs.

The whole exercise felt oddly domestic, as if she was making the choice to move in with him. That wasn't exactly what was happening, but the situation was sexually charged, nevertheless. Sharing a hotel room with a lover was different than sharing a man's bedroom. Though she couldn't have explained why, it just *was*.

At dinnertime, Quin surprised her once again. She had assumed *she* would be the one in charge in the kitchen.

Instead, Quin took over and put together an impressive meal of beef Stroganoff and Caesar salad with homemade bread. Admittedly, Mrs. Peterson had begun the preparations, but Quin handled himself in the kitchen as if he was comfortable there.

When she teased him about it, he shook his head. "Don't be sexist, Kat. It's the twenty-first century. I'm a single man. Of course, I cook a little. Most guys my age can throw together at least one or two decent meals."

"I suppose I thought you would order takeout when your housekeeper was off duty."

"Takeout? In the middle of the Maine woods?"

"Well, I hadn't seen your house at that point, now, had I? My vision of you is changing. You're a chameleon. I can't decide if you're a Thoreau wannabe who loves the hermit life or the world-weary jet-setter looking for the next big thrill ride."

He tweaked her nose and reached for a bottle of merlot, removing the cork with impressive ease. "Can't I be both?"

As he poured the wine and handed her a glass, Katie pondered his question. The truth was, she hadn't known Quin at all when they started dating. He'd been nothing but a name and a face to her—the youngest Stone sibling who was, more often than not, somewhere on the other side of the world.

It was only after his father's death that Quin had been handed the CEO job. A year or so before that, he had begun to take a more active role in the company, but even then, Katie had never met him up close and personal. Though she worked for Farrell, her path and Quin's had not crossed in any kind of meaningful way. It was that weird quirk of fate at the communal water fountain that had thrown them together.

Now, here she was.

As they sat down to eat, she noted the flickering lights. "Do you think we'll lose power soon?"

"The generator is hardwired into the house…runs off propane. But even though I have a large tank, if we have severe storm damage, we could be stranded for days. We'll want to be cautious in the beginning."

# Thirteen

Quin could see on Katie's face that she hadn't thought through the implications of the upcoming storm. It was one thing to get clobbered in a city where fire and police and emergency responders would immediately start working to repair infrastructure. Where Quin and his brothers lived, they were miles from the nearest house.

Their needs would fall way down the list. As they should.

He paused to kiss his cute houseguest on the cheek before setting the salad bowls on the table and waving her to a seat. "Don't worry, Kat. We'll be fine. It's summer. If we have to, we can sleep outside when it gets too hot."

"Oh goody," she said, wrinkling her nose.

What struck him during the intimate dinner was how the conversation never lagged. Katie always referenced how good they were in bed, and damn, that was true, but Quin also knew that he'd met few women who challenged him on an intellectual and emotional level the way Katie did. He found himself wanting to be a better man when they were together.

"I have a surprise for you, Kat," he said, finishing off the last bite of apple pie.

"Oh?"

"Farrell and Zachary and I have been putting together a scholarship program for young people whose parents work for Stone River Outdoors. We want to make sure every kid who wants a college education can get one."

She beamed at him. "That's wonderful! Let me know if I can help with any of the paperwork."

"I might take you up on that. And we're also setting up a family relief fund. For the kinds of emergencies that drag people under. Any employee can apply and get help, depending upon the severity of the situation and how long they have worked for the company."

Katie came and wrapped her arms around his neck from behind. "I'm so proud of you," she said, brushing a kiss at his nape.

He shivered and caught her hands in his. "It's all because of you, Katie. When we were together, you kept ragging my butt about how my family's wealth was a great responsibility and how I needed to keep perspective about the world. You wanted me to always be aware of how much I have and how little others get by with. I heard you, Kat. Loud and clear."

She released him and sat down again, her gaze troubled. "Am I really such a sanctimonious prig? I'm sorry. I didn't mean to be. You should have told me to shut up. It wasn't my place to criticize."

He stood and began clearing the table. "It was a much-needed wake-up call for me. My father was not a generous man at all. *Charity* was never a word he taught us. But we're all grown men now, and I'm determined not to follow in his footsteps."

Katie's smile of approval warmed him. She began to help him with the dishes, but her cell phone rang. She glanced at the number, and her demeanor changed visibly. "Excuse me," she said, her face flushing. "I need to take this in the other room."

She didn't go far. Only out in the hallway. Quin didn't eavesdrop intentionally, but it was hard not to overhear.

Katie lowered her voice and answered the call. "Delanna. What's up?"

Her sister's voice had that squeaky note that always preceded a request. "I know you're helping me with all my utility deposits," Delanna said, "but I could really use a couple hundred more to get a few things I need. I'll pay you back, I swear. I'm just a little short right now."

"Delanna." Katie screwed up her courage. She hated these confrontations. "Are you giving part of my money to Jimmy?"

Long silence. "Why would you say that?"

"Because he always begs, and you roll over. I've helped him again and again. You know he's an addict. He's not going to change."

"He's trying, Katie, I swear he is. He just got out of jail this past weekend. He's been sober for three straight weeks."

"Until you hand over enough cash for him to hit up his dealer."

"Why are you being so mean?"

"I'm not mean, sis. But you're enabling him. You deserve better. I've done everything I can to help both of you, but I'm tired of being an ATM. You have a good job and a place to live. Please don't let Jimmy drag you down a dead-end road."

"I don't even know why I called," Delanna said, her tone indignant. "You think you're better than everybody else, don't you?"

The jab hurt, particularly after the recent conversation with Quin. Katie's throat tightened. "I'm sorry you feel that way. I have to go. Take care during the storm."

Katie tried blinking back the tears, but they spilled over. Lifting the hem of her shirt, she dried her face and took a deep breath. Had she done the right thing?

She leaned against the wall and thought about everything Quin had said. He really *was* changing. Was she the one who needed a wake-up call now?

When she was relatively calm, she returned to the kitchen.

Quin looked up when she entered. "Everything okay?"

She wanted desperately to bury her face in his chest and let him comfort her. But she was too embarrassed to talk about the current situation. Quin had been so vehement in the past about her penchant for rescuing her family and especially Jimmy.

Would the new Quin be any more receptive? His father's interference hung in the balance, as well. Katie wanted to unburden herself, but was it fair to dump the whole truth on Quin? It was bound to hurt him, or make him angry, or both.

She swallowed her desperation and her disappointment. "Everything is fine. I was thinking it would be fun to go outside for a bit. While we still can."

He dried his big masculine hands on a dish towel. "Whatever you want, Kat." How such a simple motion seemed so sexy, she couldn't say, but she melted inside.

They ended up sitting barefoot on the top step of the

front porch, looking for stars. Earlier, on the beach, the sky had been clear all the way to the horizon. Now clouds were already rolling in.

When Quin moved, it took Katie by surprise. He laid her back on the porch so gently she barely noticed the hard boards beneath her back. She cleared her throat. "What are you up to, Quin?"

It was hard to read his expression, but the amusement in his husky voice came through loud and clear. "If you have to ask, I'm probably not doing it right." He leaned over her and kissed her. "I'm all for modern conveniences, but the idea of making love to you by candlelight during a storm has a definite appeal, my Kat."

He pressed a second kiss to her throat, right where the shallow dip of her top bared her skin. Then he moved to the shell of her ear, his breath warm and scented with wine.

Katie's lungs struggled for oxygen. "The storm hasn't started yet," she muttered. The stars began moving in dizzying arcs. "Do you even own any candles?" That sound she heard was embarrassing. A cross between a ragged moan and a plea. Definitely her voice, not Quin's.

He chuckled, though he was breathing awfully hard for a man who was sitting still. Her activewear pants had an elastic waist. Quin's big hand trespassed beneath the band. His fingers splayed against her stomach. His thumb inched south.

"You can tell me to stop, Kat. I have several good beds inside the house. I could take you in every single one if you like."

She urged him lower—telepathically—but he didn't get the hint. "Do you have protection? Here? Outside?"

That frustrating thumb moved another millimeter in the right direction. With his free hand, he delved into his pocket. "Actually, I do." He waved the strip of packets in the air.

Katie wanted to laugh, but she could barely breathe. "Okay, then."

He tugged her to her feet. "I want you naked, Kat. There's no one here to see us but the coyotes and the raccoons."

Her nerve endings felt both numb and tingly at the same time. Quin wasted no time in dispensing with her shirt and bra. Her pants and undies met the same fate. Suddenly, she found herself bare-assed naked.

While Quin stripped off his own clothes, Katie wrapped her arms around her breasts. He possessed not one ounce of self-consciousness about being nude outdoors. She, on the other hand, felt exposed. As if at any moment a helicopter might hover overhead and pin them down with a giant spotlight.

Quin read her nervousness. "We're alone, Katie. Relax."

"I'm trying, believe me."

He sat down on the top step and patted his knees. "Come here, beautiful woman. Let me hold you."

At first, she wasn't exactly sure what he was suggesting. A sexy cuddle? Something more?

He didn't leave her in suspense. He tugged her ankle. "Straddle me. Before we get serious."

She gulped inwardly. *This* wasn't serious? Moments later, he moved her into position, his erect sex between them in the V of her legs.

Quin smoothed his hands over her bottom, squeezing.

Katie grimaced, though she doubted he noticed. "I could stand to lose a few pounds."

"Women are so dumb." He repeated that same motion, caressing her ass, stoking the fire in her abdomen until she squirmed.

"It's not nice to call me dumb."

"Then don't criticize your body again. I happen to like it exactly as it is. Soft and curvy and perfect."

The utter sincerity in his voice seduced her as surely as his magic touch. Did he really believe that? She was just an ordinary woman.

He leaned his forehead against hers. "What are you thinking about? I can tell when you zone out on me."

"Sorry." She slid her fingers through his silky hair, tracing the lines of his skull, playing with his ears. "I was wondering how long you were going to make me wait."

His breathless laugh held equal parts humor and male satisfaction. "Soon, Kat. Soon." He leaned back on his hands. "Touch your breasts."

"Excuse me?" Her sex tightened.

"You heard what I said. Touch your breasts. I want to watch."

Her mouth gaped. They had never played these kinds of games. Not two years ago, and certainly not since she had come to Maine. Did he think she was too inhibited to meet his challenge?

The night air was cool on her heated skin. The way she was sitting made her feel open. Exposed. Stingingly vulnerable. Already she was hungry for him. Damp. Needy.

Slowly, she lifted her arms and cupped her hands around her breasts. His muffled curse emboldened her. "Like this?"

There was enough ambient light from inside the house for him to see her every move, especially now that their eyes had grown accustomed to the dark. She squeezed and plumped her own curves, deepening the valley between them. With her thumbs, she fondled her own nipples.

Quin sat up abruptly. "That's enough," he said gruffly.

"Why? This feels so good."

He grabbed her wrists and held them away from her body, then leaned in and suckled her breasts one at a time. His teeth raked sensitive flesh. His tongue left her skin sheened with moisture. When the wind picked up, goose-flesh covered her body. The ache in her pelvis deepened to the point of pain.

She struggled. "I want you," she cried.

Quin cursed and reached for a condom, rolling it on with a single smooth movement that left her in awe of his grace. "You've got me, Kat." He lifted her with two strong arms and settled her onto his erection.

The slide of soft female sheath against hard male shaft was more than she had expected. Every time with Quin was different now. As if they were climbing a scale she couldn't see. Had it been this good before? Or was the long time they spent apart magnifying her reaction to him?

"Don't stop," she whispered. He felt huge inside her. The sensation was incredible.

"You're in this, too, Kat. Ride me, sweetheart."

She felt embarrassed at first. What did she know about pleasing a man like Quin? She was *not* sexually adventurous. But what if she concentrated on pleasing herself?

Slowly she slid upward until their bodies were barely joined. Her bare feet felt chilled on the wooden steps. Any residual heat from the day was gone. Her hands ended up on Quin's shoulders. For balance.

She could actually hear his labored breathing and feel the rigid strain in his arms. "Now?" she asked, teasing.

He nodded, mute. Palpably desperate.

When she pushed downward, Quin groaned softly.

With her thigh muscles protesting the unaccustomed exercise, she rode him slowly, torturing both of them with the exquisite pleasure. Up and down. Take and retreat.

Why didn't men and women have sex outdoors more

often? This was amazing. She felt free and wild. And though her climax rushed down the pike, she held it off, wanting more of this sweet, wanton experience.

Quin's hands were everywhere. Stroking her back. Gripping her butt. Sliding into her hair and dragging her close for hungry kisses.

If she listened hard enough, she could hear past the sounds of their bodies connecting forcefully. In the distance, an owl hooted a mournful cry. The rising wind bent the trees and made a song of branch and twig.

Quin buried his face between her breasts and kissed her curves, over and around, up and down. "Damn, woman. You're killing me."

She cupped his face in her hands, trying desperately to read his expression. "What a way to go," she whispered.

In that instant, she felt a sharp spike of grief. She loved him. Deeply. Irrevocably. What was she going to do with that information?

He shifted his hips and thrust upward, deliberately holding her against the base of his sex. The extra stimulation sent her reeling. Her cry of completion echoed on the breeze. The orgasm went on and on, both terrifying and electrifying. She had no defenses against this. Against him.

Whatever happened would happen. She no longer had the strength to fight the pull he exerted over her emotions, her life.

Quin held her close as she shuddered in his arms. "Will you be okay with me on top, Kat?"

She nodded, lax with pleasure. "What's a few butt splinters between friends?"

His chuckle was raspy. "That's my girl." Carefully, he disengaged their connection and laid her back on the porch once again. With her knees bent, her feet rested on the first step.

Quin moved over her and into her. His guttural moan when he shoved all the way to her cervix made the hair stand up on her arms. She wanted to say something, but her throat had closed, swollen with impossible, careening emotions.

As she held him tightly, he found his own release. His body was beautiful in its power and dominance.

She stroked his hair for hours, it seemed, listening as his galloping heartbeat finally settled back into an ordinary rhythm.

When he finally moved, it was to lift up onto one hand and swipe his face with the other. "Are you cold, Kat?"

She nodded slowly. "Yes. Let's go to your bed."

# Fourteen

When Quin thought his legs would support him, he stood and held out a hand to Katie. "No need to get dressed. We might as well shower and hit the sack. The next forty-eight hours may be challenging."

He winced inwardly. What kind of asshat lover discussed the weather after a cataclysm like that?

Despite his clumsy segue, Katie followed his lead. They each gathered up their own clothes. Once they were inside, he locked the front door and set the alarm. When he turned around, Katie was already halfway down the hall, her cute, naked, heart-shaped backside drawing his gaze.

When he entered the bedroom, she bent and took a T-shirt and underwear out of her suitcase. "I'll shower first," she said, not meeting his gaze.

Though he had a quip at the ready, his tongue wouldn't work. His lips couldn't form the words. He and Katie had moved into some new dimension he didn't recognize.

Maybe it was only the newness of the situation. Tonight was auspicious. His Kat was going to share *his* bed.

When she exited the bathroom, he strode past her, pretending he didn't notice the way her casual nightwear made her look like an innocent college girl ready to cuddle with her favorite teddy bear.

The thought of sleeping with her all night and again tomorrow and the next night and the next threw him off balance. What were these odd feelings assailing him? His beautiful home was possibly about to get pounded by a tropical storm. He had finally accepted that his professional skiing career was over. Someone might have tried to kill his father and Quin both.

As he examined his current life, there was damned little to be glad about. Yet here he was, grinning inside, because the woman he wanted was climbing into his king-size bed.

His shower was hot and quick. He toweled off, inhaling the scent of Katie in his bathroom. When he was dry, he wrapped another towel around his hips. No sense in tempting fate by waltzing out of the bathroom naked. He and Katie had been up early and had a very long day. He would let her sleep... If he could.

When he returned to the bedroom, all the lights were off except for the two small bedside lamps that cast a cozy but narrow glow. Katie was propped up against the headboard with a pile of pillows, reading a paperback novel. Mystery? Romance? Grisly police procedural? He couldn't be sure, because she slipped it under the sheet.

"That was fast," she said, her smile shy.

He shrugged, dropped the towel and climbed into bed. "I didn't want to waste any time getting back to my best girl."

She rolled her eyes. "Are we going to the sock hop after we stop at the soda fountain?"

"Don't make fun of me." He dragged her closer and kissed her slowly, smiling when she melted against him.

Her arms went around his neck. "Are we really having sex again?" Her yawn was either genuine or for effect. He couldn't tell.

"Fix your pillows, woman. We're going to sleep."

She gave him a mock salute. "Yes, sir."

When they were both settled under the covers, he spooned her. His yawn was definitely the real deal. "This is nice, Kat."

"Ditto, Quin."

The last thing he remembered was Katie lacing her fingers with his and sighing as they both crashed into unconsciousness.

Quin jerked awake at 5:00 a.m., sickly certain that something was wrong. He reached for his phone, rolled away from Katie so the screen wouldn't disturb her and checked the weather. His heart sank and fear dug claws into his gut. He wasn't worried about himself, but he couldn't let anything happen to Katie, not when she had come to Maine so cheerfully to be of service to the Stone family in general and Quin in particular.

Despite his careful silence, his movements in the bed must have disturbed her. She raised up on one elbow and shoved the hair out of her face. "What is it? What's wrong?"

He set the phone aside. "Go back to sleep. We'll deal with it in the morning."

Fortunately, Katie was too tired to argue. In moments, she was breathing deeply again. Quin wasn't so lucky.

Eventually, exhaustion claimed him, despite his unease.

When morning finally dawned, he slid out of bed, threw on sweatpants and padded to the living room. Might as well use the TV while they still had it. Soon, the outside world would be a mystery.

The news was about as bad as it could be for the Pine Tree State. Hurricanes always lost power over these colder waters, but Tropical Storm Figaro was bearing down on coastal Maine with a vengeance. It had picked up speed during the night, wreaking havoc all over the mid-Atlantic seaboard and getting ready to pound southern New England.

Katie appeared in the doorway. She crossed the room and curled up in his lap. "How long do we have?" she asked.

She still smelled like his bed, her body warm and cuddly in his embrace. His arm tightened around her. "Hard to say. We'll probably get hit with the worst of it around midnight, give or take."

"I hate having storms at night. It's not so scary in the daytime. I want to see what's coming for me."

He grinned. "Don't tell me you want to stand out on the rocky overlook and let the spray wash over you?"

"If I had a guarantee that I wouldn't get hurt, I would *love* to experience a storm like that. The power and the fury of Mother Nature. It has a certain appeal."

"You're a crazy woman. I like it." He picked up the remote and silenced the TV. "No sense in depressing ourselves. We might as well carry on as usual until dinnertime."

"I agree." She stood and stretched. "I'm very close to finishing two time-sensitive reports. I'd feel a lot better if I got those done."

"Sounds good. When you're finished, how about filling all the bathtubs with water. And the sinks, too. We can boil water later, but we'll need a supply. I'm going to make sure I haven't missed anything outside. All the vehicles are in the garage. I found a spot for yours, too. And don't forget to charge your devices."

Katie wrinkled her nose. "This is really happening, isn't it?"

When Katie disappeared to get dressed, Quin called Farrell. "Where are you, buddy?"

His older brother sounded stressed. "I'm still in Portland. Zach is, too. We shut down the plant and the office building this morning. Sent everyone home. It's too late for us to come north now. I hired a local guy to head up to my place and Zachary's and do basic storm prep."

Quin frowned, though Farrell couldn't see the grimace. "I'd have been happy to handle that for both of you."

"I know. But you're supposed to be taking it easy for a little bit longer. I'm sure you're tied up with taking care of your own place. Did Katie decide to go home?"

Quin felt his face heat. He'd never even contemplated that. "No," he said. "She's still here."

Long silence. Farrell sighed. "Tell her to call me, and I'll stop by her condo this afternoon."

"You and Zachary hunker down."

"You, too. I don't imagine cell service will survive. We'll check on you when we can. Love you, bro."

"Same here."

"Quin?"

"Yeah?"

"What's the story with Katie? I'd like to have my A.A. back sooner than later. Please don't screw with her."

"I'm guessing you don't mean that literally."

Farrell muttered a curse. "I didn't, but I do now. Be smart about this, man. Katie is important to Stone River Outdoors."

"She's important to me, too." Quin sat down hard on the arm of the sofa. Saying those words had him feeling a little dizzy and a lot queasy. He wasn't ill. But he sure as hell was confused.

"I've never heard you say that about *any* woman," Farrell said, his tone a combination of shock and concern.

"I *do* have feelings," Quin muttered. "I'm not a zombie."

"Who said zombies don't have feelings?"

"Oh my God. I think this conversation is over."

Farrell chuckled. "It's going to be a rough couple of days. Stay safe, Quin. And take care of Katie."

Quin decided to *avoid* Katie as much as possible for the next eight hours. His conversation with Farrell had upended the status quo to an alarming degree. Actually, it wasn't Farrell's fault at all. Quin was waking slowly, like a man who had been in a coma for weeks or months.

For the first time since he was ten years old, skiing was no longer the primary thing on his mind. Nor was he obsessing about his bum knee and how quickly—or not—it was healing.

Even though the storm was still hours away, the ocean was unsettled, the heavens above an angry gray. Clouds scudded across the sky so quickly it was clear that something ominous was just over the horizon.

He grabbed a handful of cashews for lunch and kept at his self-imposed list of chores. Though he didn't have storm shutters, he *did* have several sheets of plywood. They were Farrell's, actually. Picked up during a recent run to a building supply store. Farrell was planning to use them in his new lab. Now Quin conscripted them for a more urgent need.

He balanced them one at a time on a wheelbarrow and moved them around to the front of the house. It didn't take long to realize that he needed Katie's help. *Damn it.* Even if he didn't have a weak knee at the moment, the heavy plywood would have been awkward for one person to carry up the front stairs.

When he texted her, she came and found him right away. "Quin. Is it really going to be that bad?" She assessed his project immediately.

"Farrell says yes. I remembered this plywood. I need you to help me get it up the stairs and then steady it while I hammer the nails. I've already taken the stepladder up to the porch."

Her glare was full-on warrior Katie. "Farrell and Zachary sent me here to keep you from doing something stupid—remember?"

Quin ground his jaw. "I don't call protecting my property stupid."

She crossed her arms. "You are *not* climbing that ladder. *Capisce?*"

He wanted to argue. He really did. But his knee was already aching like hell from everything he had done yesterday and today. "Fine," he grumbled. "*You* can climb the ladder. But it's still going to take both of us to carry each piece of plywood up these stupid stairs."

She kissed his cheek and nuzzled his nose with hers. "The stairs are beautiful. Quit being grumpy."

He didn't have an answer for that. How could he tell her he'd had an epiphany that morning? And that it seemed like an eternity until they would both be in bed together again?

In the end, it took them half an hour to get all the plywood up to the porch. Katie got a splinter. Quin wrenched his good knee, because he was favoring the one that had had surgery.

They were both breathing hard and drenched with sweat.

He turned to glance at Katie. She was dressed as casually as he was, with her hair caught up in a ponytail, and long legs that were mostly bare thanks to tiny khaki shorts that made him drool. "Do you even know how to hammer?" he asked.

Katie lifted her nose and sniffed. Disdainfully. "I've hung pictures at your brother's office. Does that count?" She wiped beads of moisture from her forehead. "Come on. Let's get this done. I want to go back inside and bask in the air-conditioning before we lose power."

The oncoming storm had pushed thick humid air ahead of it. Maine summers were rarely this hot and sticky. The uncomfortable atmosphere was oppressive.

Quin set up the ladder. If Katie stood on the next-to-top step, she would be just tall enough to reach the highest part of the window. As much as it galled him to admit it, this was the only way. Aside from his recovering knee, if they reversed positions, he doubted whether Katie would be able to support the heavy piece of plywood long enough for him to get it nailed into place.

He handed her the hammer. "Put the nails in your pocket. I'll steady the ladder. Put a hand on my shoulder if you need to."

Katie climbed the ladder easily. Only now, he was on eye level with her shapely calves. If he looked upward…

He cleared his throat. "You okay up there?"

"Yep. Just tell me what to do."

"I'm going to pick up the first piece of wood. I'll slide it up the side of the house, and you'll have to tell me when it's in a good spot."

"Got it."

Lifting the plywood over his head was no piece of cake. Again, it struck him that his long convalescence had robbed him of his usual level of fitness. The strength of a skier's arms and shoulders was as integral to peak performance as thighs and knees. He needed to get back to the weight room soon.

In the meantime, he and Katie had to manage this somehow. Ignoring the slender legs in his peripheral vision, he inched the wood up the wall, completely covering the window.

"That's good," Katie said.

"Don't worry about messing up the window frame. It can be replaced. If you don't hit the right spot, get another nail and try again."

# Fifteen

Katie's entire body ached. She and Quin had been at this for over three hours. Now they were on the last window.

So far, she had smashed her finger twice and had to redo seven crooked nails. The chore was frustrating and difficult.

At last, she climbed down the ladder and groaned. "Please tell me we're done."

Quin collapsed the ladder. "Yeah. No more wood."

"What about the windows on the second-floor porch?"

"We'll just have to hope for the best. If we weren't so exposed here on this bluff, I wouldn't worry. The two big trees at the corner of the house will provide a little protection."

"Then that's it…right? We've done all we can do?"

He ruffled the ends of her hair. "Looks that way."

"Would you like me to fix spaghetti for dinner? Mrs. Peterson left us a container of homemade sauce."

"That's something we can cook on the propane stove if

we lose power. What if I grill steaks outside, and you bake some potatoes and do a salad and garlic bread? We might as well have a feast while we can."

"Okay. You want first shower?"

His grin made her stomach flip. "Don't be silly, Kat. I need you to wash my back."

In the end, the shower lasted far longer than was good for the water supply. Once they were done teasing each other with soap and water, they curled up in Quin's bed, made love and napped. If it weren't for the prospect of a tropical storm, it would have been the perfect afternoon.

Katie was the first one to wake up. She slid out of bed, found clean clothes and went to check the weather. Figaro had only now been downgraded from a hurricane to a tropical storm. The images of damage from Cape Cod were sobering. The storm had meandered out to sea at one point and was now headed west. Prepared to make a second landfall between Bar Harbor and the Stone brothers' property.

She shut off the TV, too unsettled to watch any more news. Might as well get the potatoes in the oven. Quin tracked her down in the kitchen. "You hungry?" he asked.

"Getting there." His jaw was shadowed with two days' growth of beard. He'd slept with damp hair, which now stuck out at weird angles. A plain white cotton T-shirt stretched across his impressive chest. The jeans that rode low on his body exposed tantalizing glimpses of hip bone.

He was the sexiest man she had ever seen.

Katie braced herself against the edge of the counter. "You sure you want to use the grill? It's getting dark outside…way too soon."

"It's the fastest way. Just tell me when you want the steaks ready and how you like yours."

She glanced at the clock. "Thirty minutes from now. Medium well."

Quin nodded. "Got it."

When he wandered away to prepare the grill, Katie began putting together the salad and spreading pieces of frozen bread on a cookie sheet. Suddenly, a gust of wind shook the house. It faded quickly, but she realized they were getting a taste of what was to come.

While she worked, she kept checking the weather app on her iPad. Quin was right. It looked as if the eye of the storm—or what was left of it—would pass almost directly over Stone River. Because of the way the brothers' houses were situated, all three would take a hit.

She couldn't deny that she was nervous. Still, with Quin around, she knew they would be okay. She trusted his intuition, and she felt safe when she was with him. Even so, as the wind began to blow with increasing force, her apprehension deepened.

All of the pieces of their *final* dinner came together right on time. Quin grabbed a platter for the steaks, and moments later brought them in to the table. He slammed the back door and locked it, shutting out the storm. His shirt was spattered with raindrops. He rubbed his hands together, surveying the food. "A condemned man's last meal."

She punched his arm. "Don't say that. We're still going to eat, even with no power."

"True." He held her chair until she was seated. "But it won't be this good. Canned food never is. We'll eat what's in the fridge as fast as we can before it spoils. After that, we'll be roughing it."

"Maybe we won't lose power."

As if on cue, the entire house went dark.

Quin chuckled. "Right on time." He stood and rummaged in a cabinet for candles and matches. Soon, quiet, flickering flames cast a cozy glow. He kissed the top of her head and sat back down. "Isn't this romantic..."

"Don't make fun of romance, Quin. That's a cheap shot." She scanned his face, searching for proof that he was being condescending.

He held up his hands. "I wasn't. I swear. This is nice."

He wasn't wrong. A scrumptious dinner with a handsome man. The rain beating at the windows. It was the perfect script for a rom-com. Except that Katie didn't feel like laughing. She had let herself get in way too deep with this relationship—with this fling that was supposed to be fun and temporary. Now the storm had cut off any escape.

Katie picked at her food. "I'm going to check the weather," she said.

"Do you still have a phone signal?"

She nodded. "One bar. For the moment." She clicked over to radar and showed the screen to Quin. The lopsided red and yellow spiral was almost on top of them.

He cursed beneath his breath. "Look how wide it is."

"And the rainfall totals…"

"Yes. The fact that it still has sustained winds over seventy miles an hour means it's barely below hurricane strength. This house is built to modern codes. We'll just have to hope for the best."

When dinner was done, Katie prowled from room to room, too nervous to sit. Quin settled back in the living room with a book and a candle and those sexy glasses. She loved to read, but she didn't see how he could concentrate with all the racket from outside.

The house actually shook. If this *wasn't* an actual hurricane, she couldn't imagine a Cat 4 or a Cat 5. That would be terrifying. Tropical Storm Figaro was bad enough.

Finally, she grabbed her yoga mat from Quin's bedroom, put it down on the runner in the hallway and ran through a familiar, comfortable sequence of poses. The more she stretched and tried to quiet her mind, the louder the storm became.

Now the wind howled. Like a banshee. It sounded as if every shingle was being ripped from the roof one at a time, though that was probably her imagination. By this point in her exercise routine, she had typically found her center, her breathing deep and restorative.

Tonight, she was toast. Her yoga teacher would be very disappointed.

Finally, she gave up. Her body was limber and warm, sweaty actually, but her anxiety was out of control. It was the not knowing that was the hardest. How could Quin sit there so calmly? Was this how he prepared for a huge downhill race? Was he so good at focusing his mind that he could shut out the storm entirely?

She poked her head into the room where he sat reading. "I'm going to take another shower."

Quin didn't look up from his book, but he waved a hand to acknowledge that he heard her. She grabbed a change of clothes and closed herself in the bathroom. At this rate, she'd soon be forced to do laundry in the sink. The house was still cool so far. That would change.

The hot, stinging spray on her bare skin actually helped. But when she shut off the shower, immediately the storm was in the room with her. How long did a tropical storm last? Two hours? Four?

She was surprised Quin hadn't suggested sex as a way to pass the time, but he probably realized they wouldn't be able to concentrate. Or at least Katie wouldn't. Men had a knack for shutting out the entire world when it came to sex.

It dawned on her suddenly that she was missing her contacts. She had probably forgotten to unload one of the drawers in the guest bath. In a minute, she would fetch them. But she couldn't resist the urge to join Quin on the sofa. He wrapped an arm around her shoulders and kept reading.

It was a biography. A book about a Swiss skiing legend.

She snuggled closer. "Is it good? The book, I mean."

He gave her a quick glance. "Actually, yes." He shut the book, but kept his finger in as a bookmark. "Are you okay, Katie?"

"Yes. No. I'm rattled."

His lips curled upward in one of those mouthwatering grins that made her stomach wobble. "Farrell always describes you as unflappable."

She snorted. "Your brother has never subjected me to a hurricane."

"Tropical storm. Don't exaggerate."

"ToMAYto, toMAHto."

"You can't blame me for this. I don't control the weather. Are you really scared?"

"Not so much scared as antsy." She shrugged. "It would help if I could take a walk or chop some wood."

His lips twitched. "Chop wood?"

"It's a metaphor. For somebody who reads so much, I'd think you would know about metaphors."

He put the book on the coffee table. "You're getting snippy now. Maybe we need a distraction."

"Oh no," she said, jumping to her feet. "No funny business from Mr. Sexy Stud. I have to make sure this storm is going to leave us."

"So you're tempted, but I have to sublimate my male desires so you can boss around a hurricane?"

"Tropical storm."

He threw back his head and chuckled. She loved making him laugh.

Quin tapped his fingers on the arm of the sofa. Maybe

he wasn't as calm as he seemed. "I thought *you* were reading a book in bed last night."

"I was. Can't concentrate on the words right now. Besides, I think I left my little case of contacts upstairs. I wear the disposable dailies. I'm going to run and get them. Be right back."

She was gone before Quin could stop her.

He was probably at least as concerned as Katie, but he knew if he confessed that the storm was more dangerous than he had expected, it would only make matters worse. He didn't like the idea of her being on the second floor without him. The roof might fly off. Who the hell knew?

This was his first tropical storm, too.

Suddenly, a ferocious crash echoed through the house accompanied by a female scream—a Katie scream. He shot down the hall and up the stairs, barely pausing to acknowledge the strain on his new knee.

Up here the storm was even louder. And then he saw the worst part. A huge limb had ripped loose from one of the nearby trees. The wind had hurled it through the window, a projectile that shattered glass and let in sheets of rain and the fury of Figaro.

Katie was kneeling just inside the door of the bedroom, holding her arm. It was too damn dark. He reached for her, crunching through large shards of glass. "Are you hurt?"

He didn't mean to shout, but he was terrified, and he could barely hear his own words over the cacophony of the gale.

She stood up. "I'm bleeding." Her voice wobbled.

Quin ripped off his T-shirt and tried to wrap her injury. Katie jerked backward. "Don't touch me, please. The glass is still in my arm."

Nausea heaved in his belly. "Stay calm, Kat. Let's get you downstairs so I can take a look."

"We have to cover the window," she said. "The water will ruin your floor."

"I don't give a rat's ass about the floor, crazy woman." He started to scoop her up into his arms and then groaned. If he tried to carry her down the stairs, they might both end up dead.

"We're going to walk down slowly," he said, moderating his tone. Yelling at Katie wasn't going to help a thing.

"Okay," she whispered.

It felt like a million hours before they made it to the bottom of the staircase. The only illumination came from the candle he had left burning in the living room.

Katie whimpered, the sound quiet and heartbreaking. He wasn't even sure she knew she was doing it.

On the bottom step, he stopped her. "We need to take off our shoes. So we don't track broken glass through the house."

She nodded. "Let me hold your shoulder."

Clumsily, she shed her slippers one at a time and stepped onto the floor below. Then it was Quin's turn. His deck shoes were not too bad to toe off. He left both of them on that same step and joined Katie.

"First things first," he said. "Let me get the flashlights. We don't want to drain our phone batteries." He felt like a fool for waiting until now. His only excuse was that Katie had seemed to enjoy the ambience of the candlelight. She'd obviously used her cell phone light when she ran upstairs.

He put her in a living room chair. "Don't move." She was still holding her arm, so he couldn't gauge the extent of her injury. "I'm only going to the kitchen. Won't take but a minute."

Fortunately, he and his brothers were very serious about

disaster preparedness. Quin had a stash of matches and flashlights and all sorts of other necessary gear, particularly for winter. Not that the latter was any help at the moment.

He grabbed two sturdy flashlights and went back to Katie. Her head rested against the back of the chair. Her eyes were closed. When he turned on the flashlight and pointed it in her direction, his heart lurched. There was blood everywhere. All down her shirt and onto her pants.

"My God, Kat. Where are you hurt?"

She moved her protective hand. At last, he could see what had happened. When the branch crashed through the window, a piece of shattered glass had embedded itself in Katie's forearm. Blood still oozed slowly. The shard extended outward half an inch.

He'd suffered plenty of injuries over the years. This was far worse. This was *Katie*.

Swallowing the lump in his throat, he sat on the coffee table. "Do you want me to bring the first aid stuff in here, or can you make it to the bathroom?" Her eyes didn't seem quite focused. He worried she was in shock.

She took a deep breath. Tried to smile. Failed. "I can walk," she said. With his help, she stood up slowly. "Is the room supposed to be spinning?" she asked, leaning into him heavily.

"Don't pass out on me, love."

"I won't."

He wouldn't place money on that bet. They made their way to his bedroom. Quin grabbed a small chair with his free hand and dragged it with them to the bathroom. He eased her into a seated position then folded a towel lengthwise. "Rest your head against the edge of the counter if you need to."

"Please don't touch my arm."

Hell, she hated splinters, and this was a splinter on steroids. "We have to clean it, at least," he said quietly, try-ing to make the tone of his voice as reassuring as possible. "I'll use hydrogen peroxide. It won't hurt at all. Shouldn't even sting." *He hoped...*

Katie sighed. "Okay."

While he rummaged under the sink for a plastic basin and everything else he would need, he snatched a surrep-titious glance at Katie's wound. The piece of glass looked obscene. As far as he could tell, the cut was an inch and a half long. Depending on how deep the glass had shoved beneath her skin, she might need stitches.

He set the rectangular bowl across her lap. "Rest your wrist and forearm on the edges of the plastic."

It was clear that she was dubious. It was also clear she was in pain. Her face was dead white, and the furrow be-tween her brows deepened every time she moved. Gingerly, she laid her arm where he had indicated.

Quin uncapped the bottle and removed the protective foil seal. Carefully, he poured a stream of liquid over the cut. Around the edges of the glass, the wound frothed and foamed.

Katie rested her head on the towel, her eyes closed. "That should do it," he said.

Her chin wobbled. "You have to remove the glass, don't you?"

He stroked her hair. "Yes."

Tears rolled down her cheeks. Quiet. Devastating. "I don't think I can do this," she whispered.

# Sixteen

Katie felt like such a baby. In her defense, she had never done well with blood.

Quin left her only long enough to return to the bedroom and find another small stool. Now he could sit beside her eye to eye. His gaze was confident and kind. "Do you trust me, Kat?"

She nodded. "Yes."

"I want you to know exactly what's going to happen. No surprises, I promise. When you're ready, I'm going to pull out the shard. Don't move at all, because we can't risk breaking the piece. The wound will start to bleed again, I'm sure. As soon as I finish…" He gulped, looking a little green around the gills himself. "As soon as I finish, I'm going to apply pressure for a few minutes. Then, I have some butterfly bandages that will hold the edges together until we can get you to a doctor."

"Which might be tomorrow or a week from now."

He scowled. "Whatever happens, we'll keep it clean and put antiseptic cream on it."

"I feel like I'm going to barf," she muttered.

Quin stood, found a clean washcloth, wet it and wrapped it around the back of her neck. "Better?" he asked.

She waited a few seconds, breathed shallowly and finally nodded. "I'm okay."

"The longer we wait, the more anxious you're going to be. But I'm not going to pull on it until you're ready. It's your call."

Katie wanted to burrow into a hole and never come out again. The storm still thundered on the roof. The eaves shrieked and groaned. "You could cover the broken window first," she said.

Quin's expression grew stern. "Procrastination is for weak-minded people. You're a warrior, Katie. A woman people depend on. You can do this."

He seemed so sure she was brave. But she wasn't. Not at all. "Can I hold your hand?" she begged. She had started to shake all over. And the nausea returned.

"No. I need both hands free to do this. Either close your eyes or turn your head."

Quin had been through so much physical trauma in his life. He'd been in a terrible car accident. He had endured multiple surgeries. Katie wasn't going to embarrass herself. If he thought she could handle this operation, maybe she could.

She turned over the washcloth on the back of her neck, tucking the cooler side against her skin. "In the old Westerns, they used to give the person a piece of leather to bite down on. Or whiskey to drink."

*"Katie."* He stared her down, forcing her to gnaw her lip. "Fine," she muttered. "Just do it."

"And you swear you won't move?"

"I'll do my best."

He stood and leaned over her, propping the flashlight at the correct angle with a towel and adjusting the beam. "I can't jerk it, Kat. But I'll be as quick as I can."

"Okay." Her eyes swam with tears. She looked away so he wouldn't see what a wimp she was.

What happened next was not something she ever wanted to repeat. Quin got a firm hold on the ragged edge of the glass and began to pull. *Damn it.* It hurt like hell. She counted to ten and then to fifty.

Suddenly it was over.

"It's out," Quin said. He sat down hard. Her arm gushed blood. Quin grabbed another clean washcloth—maybe she would have to buy him a dozen new ones—and held it against her arm tightly.

Even with the glass gone, the pressure hurt. She rested her forehead against his shoulder. "Thank you," she whispered. He cupped the back of her neck with his free hand and drew her closer. "Don't ever make me go through that again, Kat. Hurting you is harder than anything I've had to do in my life."

"It wasn't so bad."

"Liar."

They sat there in an awkward embrace for fifteen minutes. Finally, he eased the terry cotton aside. A trickle of blood continued, but not the heavy flow from before.

"Do you think you got it all?" she asked.

"I hope so. I'm going to rinse it one more time. Then I'll bandage it."

The hydrogen peroxide bubbled fiercely in the open wound, removing any tiny pieces of glass that remained, she hoped. Afterward, Quin patted her arm dry with a tissue. Next, he applied two butterfly bandages that pulled the edges of the cut together.

Finally, it was done.

He sighed deeply and stood to clean up the mess. "We should go to bed," he said. "Who knows what tomorrow will bring…"

"What about the window?"

His eyes widened. "Hell."

"You forgot?"

"Yes." He shook his head in disbelief. "I'll cover it. Once I have you tucked into bed."

"Oh no," Katie said. "I'm going to sit at the bottom of the stairs and make sure you're okay. I'd go back up there if I could, but my knees are wobbly."

"Join the club," he joked. He held her arm while they walked down the hall. When she was seated, he disappeared briefly and returned with a large blue tarp, sturdy electrical tape and some old rags.

He stepped into his shoes and steadily climbed the stairs. As he made it higher, she could hear glass crunch beneath his feet.

"How bad is it?" she yelled.

"Pretty bad. Maybe we'll install a pool up here."

The fact that he still retained his sense of humor buoyed her flagging spirits. As she listened intently, she heard him curse and mutter as he wrestled the tarp into place.

"Is it working?" she cried.

Quin's voice drifted down the stairs, even over the sound of the rain. "I think so. The windowsills are wet, so the tape doesn't want to stick."

"Don't cut yourself."

"Don't worry. I'm being careful."

At last, the sound of the rain was muffled. Thank God.

Quin came down the stairs, stepping gingerly. "I don't know if it will hold, but I did the best I could for tonight."

He took her hand and pulled her to her feet. "That arm

is going to ache pretty badly once the adrenaline wears off. Can you take hydrocodone?"

"As long as I have some food with it. Crackers, maybe?"

"How about a piece of Mrs. Peterson's famous pound cake? I was saving it for a breakfast surprise, but I think we could use a slice right now. With milk? How does that sound?"

"How fast does milk go bad?"

"Not this fast. We might as well drink it tonight."

She perched at the kitchen island while Quin prepared their snack. "I think the wind is not as loud as it was before," she said. "Is that wishful thinking on my part?"

He paused and cocked his head. "Maybe. But the rain will last longer, I think."

Katie swallowed the pain pill and yawned. "Can I help you clean up anything?"

"No. Go get your jammies on. Take this other flashlight. I'll be there in a minute."

After brushing her teeth and taking off her blood-soaked clothes, Katie washed up as best she could. She knew that getting in the shower was not a good idea with her wound still so new.

There was nothing comfy left to wear in her suitcase. Feeling both bold and guilty, she opened one of Quin's drawers and found a clean T-shirt. It fell to her knees and smelled of laundry detergent. She slid it over her head awkwardly. Her arm protested.

Suddenly, crippling exhaustion overtook her. It was all she could do to stumble toward the bed and fold back the covers.

Quin had to turn off Katie's flashlight. She was already asleep. He was so tired he could barely move. The day and night had taken on a surreal quality. After a few quick ablutions in the bathroom, he stripped off his clothes and slid naked beneath the sheets.

Though he was careful not to bump Katie's arm, he wanted to hold her while they slept. He dragged her close and spooned her, inhaling the scent of her hair. He loved her. The realization was no longer shocking.

Now all he wanted to do was get them out of this mess.

Surely, after all they had been through together these last weeks—surely Katie felt the same way. The fact that he still had doubts made his chest tight with uncertainty and dread.

His whole life had been turned upside down since the car accident. But one thing was becoming clear. Losing his skiing prowess had hurt him deeply. Losing Katie would destroy him.

The next morning, Quin faced a quandary. He wanted to stay in bed and cuddle with Katie. But the storm had passed, and he knew he had to assess the damage. He dressed rapidly and left the bedroom, hoping she would sleep longer. It was barely seven.

The sun shone down brightly, with benevolent warmth, as if nothing bad had happened. When Quin stepped out the back door, his spirits sank. As far as the eye could see, the forest was littered and crippled. The beautiful white pines had been most vulnerable, because they were the tallest and their canopies had little protection from surrounding trees.

Inland, it wouldn't have been so bad, but here on the beach, even without official hurricane winds, dozens of trees had fallen. The road out, the one to the main highway, was impassable without many hours of chain saw work. Going the mile and a half north to Zachary's place would be no better.

Though Quin couldn't see them from the house, the airstrip and helicopter pad were probably unusable, as well. He and Katie were well and truly stuck.

He decided to fire up the generator. Katie had said she needed to do laundry, and they could eat a big lunch to use up as much of the still-edible food as possible. When he finally went back inside, he found her in the bedroom. She had pulled on a pair of stretchy yoga pants, and if he wasn't mistaken, she was wearing one of his T-shirts. She greeted him with a smile. "The power's back on."

He shook his head. "Sorry to burst your bubble, but it's the generator."

Katie nodded. "Ah. Well, then, I'd better get busy."

"First things first." He took her wrist and reeled her in. The kiss was long and deep and left both of them struggling to breathe. He cleared his throat. "I need to check your arm."

"I think it's okay."

The cut looked raw but not infected. Hopefully, it would stay that way. "Let me know when you're going to shower," he said, "and I'll wrap your arm in plastic. Just today. It's a nasty cut. We need to be careful."

She nodded. "Laundry first. Once I have that going, I'll see about lunch. It will be on the early side."

"No problem. I don't want to run the generator too long, so that works. We'll make it our big meal and snack for dinner."

"How long do you think we'll be here?"

"Honestly? I don't know."

The mundane conversation covered a deep vein of subtext. Quin wanted to tell her he loved her, but because of the storm, he sensed the time was not right. Not only that, but he was still coming to terms with his feelings. *Love* was a big four-letter word. He had to be sure. Though it was hard to wait, he decided to use this quiet time together to savor the moment. Maybe even formulate a few hazy future plans.

Protecting Katie was his first priority. Quin knew the commentary that was running in *his* head. Katie was less easily understood. She had dealt with the crisis like a champ. But what was she *really* thinking?

For Katie, the day passed slowly. She now had her original suitcase full of clean clothes. At lunch, she and Quin had feasted on spaghetti and salad and the last vestiges of two cartons of ice cream from the now-useless freezer. Afterward, she had insisted on cleaning up the kitchen herself. Quin had plenty to do outside. She knew he was trying to clear the garage and driveway in order to get a vehicle out.

At eleven thirty when the generator shut off, she grimaced. It wouldn't be long until the house heated up again. Though Quin wouldn't like it, she found a broom and climbed the stairs. Sweeping up the glass and tiny bits of leaves and twigs from the smashed window at least made her feel useful.

Once that was done, she used bleach wipes to clean the blood spatters. The place looked like a crime scene. Reliving last night made her feel a little sick. Even so, she and Quin had come through the disaster relatively unscathed.

She was happy to see that the rockers on the porch had survived the storm. The bungee cords had held, but the chairs had taken a beating and would need to be repainted. She wouldn't be here to see that.

Acknowledging the coming break with Quin made her heart hurt worse than her arm. According to the original agreement with the Stone brothers, she had two weeks and change left to fulfill her obligation.

The truth was, though, she and Quin had worked through

the backlog of CEO paperwork efficiently. If she left today, Stone River Outdoors would be in good shape.

It was up to her to be smart. Athletes talked about wanting to go out on top. She and Quin were in a better place than they had ever been. He was affectionate and caring. And he had changed. He had let her in, let her get close.

But his father's words still haunted Katie. Part of her still believed them. Quin wasn't the kind of guy who settled down to marriage, even though he cared deeply about her. Maybe more than he had cared about any other woman.

What hurt so badly was knowing he might never reconcile himself to the huge loss he had suffered. It was one thing for Quin to decide to hang up his skis at a particular age. That wasn't what happened, though. He had been robbed of his future. Was he using Katie to assuage his pain and loss?

In the midst of her soul-searching, Quin came and found her. "I've got the Jeep out," he said. "And cleared the driveway. I'm going to see how far I can get toward the airstrip. The chain saw is gas powered. I'll try to drag smaller trees out of the way. The bigger ones I can cut into pieces. If we can get a wide enough space cleared off for the chopper, one of my brothers will find a way to help us. You want to ride along?"

"Definitely. It will go faster with two."

He frowned. "You're hurt. You'll stay in the Jeep."

"No, I won't." she said firmly. "I have one good arm. I'll do what I can to help."

Quin scowled. "I have never met a more stubborn woman."

"Pot. Kettle. So it's okay for you to run the show, but I'm not supposed to get involved? Think again, Quin. I'm going with you."

# Seventeen

Quin wiped sweat from his eyes and glared up at the sun. You'd think after a hell of a storm that Mother Nature would give them a break. Today's heat was likely record-breaking.

Katie never once complained. Their progress was painfully slow. They drove several hundred yards. Stopped. Dragged a tree out of the road. Back in the Jeep. Maybe only a few hundred feet the second time. Then another tree. Every third or fourth one had to be cut up because it was too heavy.

By five o'clock they had to call it quits.

Katie chewed her lip, her hair bedraggled and sticking to her forehead, big brown eyes wide with worry. "But what if they fly up here and can't land, because we didn't get finished?"

"Farrell and Zachary probably have plenty to do in Portland at the moment. They both know I have supplies. If phone and power haven't been restored by the weekend, *then* they might try to come north. We have time."

They drove back to the house and took turns in the shower. Again, Katie didn't complain. The water felt shockingly cold. Quin's fingernails were blue by the time he was done.

It felt good to be clean and dry, at least.

He fired up the small propane stove. They dined on baked beans and canned ham. It wasn't much, but it did the job. They still had enough pound cake for dessert.

Katie took her dishes to the sink and, on the way back, leaned over his shoulder from behind and nuzzled his neck. "Do you like card games? I'm pretty good."

He stood and scooped her up for a hard kiss. "Strip poker?" he asked hopefully.

She grinned. "I was thinking rummy."

"Bor-ing."

Quin happened to be pretty good at card games himself. In college, he'd played poker for money and kicks. Katie, on the other hand was a shark. With her innocent face, gorgeous eyes and distracting breasts, she beat him the first game.

His competitive instincts kicked in. "Rematch," he said, giving her his best intimidating stare.

She shrugged. "As long as you don't mind being humiliated. Again."

This time, he tried. He really did. The outcome was the same.

After four straight losses, he held up his hands in surrender. "I give up. Katie Duncan is queen bee of the rummy world."

"I warned you." Her amused smile caught something in his chest and twisted it. He still didn't know why she'd walked away from their relationship two years ago. She had insisted that this six-week stint in the Maine woods was strictly temporary. And truth be told, the first three weeks were a waste, because they hadn't been intimate. Had anything happened between them in the meantime to change her mind?

God, he hoped so. He loved her. That wasn't going to change. But was he any better equipped to be the man she wanted? He thought he could be. Katie was more real to him now. Not simply a woman to satisfy a momentary physical craving.

Every day they spent together revealed new facets of her personality. Things he'd been blind to before. And the more he knew about her, the more deeply he fell under her spell.

Whatever it took, however long he had to wait, he would make her understand. The stakes were too high to give up.

"I want to make love to you," he blurted out.

Her cheeks turned pink. Or at least he thought they did. Beyond the windows, the light was beginning to fade. "It's barely eight o'clock," she said, sounding both scandalized and interested.

He kissed the inside of her wrist. "We're both beat. Who cares what we do, Katie? The night is ours."

Half an hour later, Katie let him drag her toward the bedroom.

The way she wanted him was not entirely sane. She had lived by intellect her entire life. Until now. With Quin, all she wanted to do was wallow in her need for him, feel deeply and drown in the incredible pleasure he gave her.

Their evenings were governed by candlelight after the storm. It was a dangerous glow. Subtly arousing. Endlessly romantic.

They undressed in tandem and met in the center of the mattress. *I love you, Quin.* The words trembled on her lips. How would he react if she gave voice to them?

Never once had he given any indication that he felt anything deeper than lust. Tonight was the first time he had said "make love" instead of "have sex." Was the change in wording significant, or was she simply another pitiful woman desperate to believe?

They touched each other endlessly, drunk on the solitude and their gratitude for being alive. She was sleepy and her arm ached, and still she wanted him. When he slid inside her, it was like coming home after a long, hard journey. Quin promised protection and comfort and peace.

But more than that, enchanting sexual pleasure.

Her orgasm built to a warm, honeyed peak that flowed into deep relaxation. She heard and felt Quin find his own release.

They fell asleep instantly in a tangle of arms and legs.

The following morning, it rained. Hard. A steady deluge punctuated by lightning and thunder. They hadn't seen it coming, because they no longer had the luxury of forecasts and radar.

"We can't go out in this," Katie said. "It isn't safe."

Quin had smudges beneath his eyes. His jaw tightened. "I know."

He was like a caged tiger today. Sulky and vibrating with ill-concealed frustration.

She knew his bad mood had nothing to do with her, or at least she didn't think so, but telling him to chill out wouldn't help. Quin was a man who hated inaction. This waiting for the storm to be over was hard on both of them. She decided it was best to keep her distance. "I'll do some more cleaning upstairs. Just to keep busy. How about you?"

He drummed his fingers on the table. "I suppose I could go through my father's papers out in the garage. When the house was sold after he died, all the contents were listed and offloaded in an estate sale. My brothers boxed up the contents of four filing cabinets from Dad's office and sent them here for me to deal with. I assume the bulk of it is garbage. But there will be stuff pertaining to SRO that we should probably keep."

"I doubt I'd be any help with that."

"Probably not."

"Peanut butter sandwiches at noon?" Mrs. Peterson had left two fresh loaves of bread.

Quin nodded. "Sure." Then he paused. "I don't need you to look after my house, Kat. I can pay for a cleanup crew when the time comes."

"I know. But I can't go outside and climb down to the beach. Even if I wanted to walk in the woods, the trails are a mess. I have to do *something*, or I'll go crazy."

Finally, he gave her a reluctant grin. As if he had been enjoying his bad mood. "You and me both. But please be careful."

"I will. You, too."

"There's nothing dangerous in the garage."

"I hope not. I've had enough shocks for one week." She kissed his cheek. "See you at lunch."

Quin hated paperwork more than just about anything. Which was why he'd been putting off this unwelcome chore. But he needed something to occupy his thoughts. Some kind of distraction. Thinking about how to tell Katie he loved her and wondering about the fallout afterward was driving him nuts.

Months ago, Farrell had purchased an oversize shredding bin on wheels, but the electricity was out, so the shredder was useless. Quin found two empty boxes and set them beside a folding lawn chair.

His plan was to toss unimportant stuff in one box and shred it in the future. If he came across anything that seemed valuable, those pages would go in box number two. He and Farrell and Zachary could go through those items together. At a later date.

He grabbed a couple of water bottles and settled in for his boring morning. As he suspected, most of the reams of file folders were filled with minutiae. His father had saved everything.

Quin found a receipt for dry cleaning from 1991. And that was only the tip of the iceberg.

When he finished the first box, he stood and stretched the kinks out of his back, downing half a bottle of water at the same time. It was gratifying to realize that his knee was no worse for the wear after all he had put it through in the last few days.

Slow healing was hard to track. Today, though, it was clear to him that he was definitely better. Perhaps at some visceral level he had been afraid his knee would never again be reliable. But that wasn't so. He was on the mend for sure this time. Third surgery a charm.

As much as it galled him to admit it, his brothers and the doctor had been right. His leg as a whole had needed time to recover. Six weeks of taking it easy was a small price to pay for the prospect of normalcy.

And then there was Katie. What was he going to do about Katie?

Sighing deeply, he forced himself to sit down and get back to work.

The second box didn't have a million slips of paper like the first one. Here, he found his father's personal check-book registers and bank statements. Even with the advent of online everything, his dad had preferred the mental security of keeping everything under lock and key.

These were his personal transactions. Political contributions. Purchases large and small. Cars. Bespoke suits. Gold cuff links.

Quin couldn't imagine he would find anything relevant to the workings of Stone River Outdoors, but he continued to flip through the entries just in case. One name caught his eye.

Caught his eye and made his stomach clench.

*Katie Duncan.* $100,000.

In his father's distinctive handwriting. The entry was unmistakable, as was the date. The check had been written two years ago. In the same month Katie broke up with him.

His brain literally went numb. Thoughts floated in and out of his head, but nothing stuck. The feelings of hurt and disbelief crushed him as he tried to think back to that time. He and Katie had been arguing about money. As always. Katie had been about to drain her personal savings account in order to send her sister's loser boyfriend to rehab.

Quin had been vehemently opposed to the idea and furious that Katie's sister would take advantage of her that way. No drug addict was ever successfully rehabilitated unless the person in question *wanted* to change.

Katie had stood her ground. She told him he didn't know what it was like to have a dysfunctional family. She told her her choices were her own.

And a very short time later, she had ended their relationship.

She had never *asked* Quin for the money. Maybe she had been hoping he would offer. Hell, no. Not in that situation.

So what had Katie done? Gone to Quin's father and brazenly requested a loan? Surely the old man hadn't simply handed over the money.

Everyone at Stone River Outdoors loved Katie, so it was conceivable that his father might have had a soft spot for her. But an outright gift of that magnitude, no way. The old man was a tightfisted bastard. Not even for a pretty girl would he part with his hard-earned dollars.

But clearly, he had.

Quin felt hollow inside. Gutted. By all accounts, Katie had never wanted Quin's money. But maybe he had been so emotionally disconnected he hadn't recognized her need for help. Had she been in such a bad spot that Quin himself had forced her to borrow money from his father rather than ask her lover?

If he'd been that clueless, it was no wonder she broke up with him.

Even now, a tiny part of him felt betrayed. She had left him once before without a satisfactory explanation.

Had he earned her trust this time around? Did *he* trust *her*?

He stood and kicked the box with his good leg. The pain in his toes stoked his misery. Gripping the ledger, white-knuckled, he stalked into the house.

Katie hummed as she worked. It felt good to stretch her muscles and do something useful. She was careful not to bang her arm. After breakfast, Quin had cleaned the cut and put new butterfly strips on the ugly gash. The margins of the wound were a healthy pink. He had mentioned plastic surgery, but that seemed unnecessary.

She had run out of paper towels, so she scooted down the now-immaculate stairs to get more supplies from the kitchen. Just as she reached the foyer, Quin confronted her, his face dark, his expression frightening.

He stuck out his arm, waving some kind of diary in her face. "Would you like to explain this to me?"

Katie had never seen him so angry. She took a step backward. "I don't know. What is it?"

"Maybe you've never seen this particular ledger, but you sure as hell will remember this entry."

She took the leather-bound book from him, because she had no other choice.

Quin stabbed a finger at the left-hand page. "Recognize anything?"

She glanced down. There in neat printing was her name. And an amount. Her heart sank. "I was hoping you would never have to see this. I'm so sorry, Quin."

He gaped at her. His face went dead white. "You're not denying it?"

"How can I?" she asked, confused. "He wrote that check. I didn't want you to find out. I knew it would hurt you. So I kept the secret."

Quin scraped a hand through his hair, his eyes filled with some strong emotion. He was clearly distraught. "Why wouldn't you ask *me* for the money? Why ask my father? Did you think so little of me that you believed I wouldn't help you when you needed it?"

He stopped, stared, and gave her a stricken look. "And I suppose you thought when he died, you were off the hook. That you wouldn't have to pay the money back, because it was a *secret*."

In one blinding instant, Katie realized that he had misunderstood. Her legs trembled. Her stomach clenched and heaved. "Wait," she said. "You actually think I took money from your father without telling you?"

Her heart shattered, leaving fragments far more painful than the one that had lodged in her arm. She was too shocked to defend herself.

"Don't try to spin this, Katie. It's all out in the open now."

Before she could answer his sickening accusation, thunderous knocking sounded at the front door. Suddenly, Farrell and Zachary burst in, their faces painted in distress.

Quin's jaw dropped. "How did you get here? We haven't even been able to clear the helipad yet."

Both brothers enveloped him in a bear hug. Then they shook Katie's hand. "We were worried sick about both of you," Farrell said, "so I chartered a boat. Half the roads in the state are impassable. God knows how long it will be until basic utilities are restored this far north. We've come to take you back to Portland."

Zach zeroed in on Katie's bandaged arm. "Are you okay?"

She nodded. "I'm fine. Why don't all of you go to the kitchen and grab a sandwich. I'll pack my things. Honestly, I can't wait to get out of here."

Quin shot her a dark look as the three brothers disappeared down the hall. As if he was telling her, *this isn't over yet.*

In a matter of minutes, she had removed every trace of her presence from Quin's bedroom. She didn't want his brothers to know she and Quin had been sleeping together. She dragged it all upstairs so she could organize and pack for the trip home.

Which meant that half an hour later, the two older Stone brothers watched her descend the stairs from the guest suite as if she had been staying there all along. Zach met her halfway. "Here. Let me help you with those bags."

"Where's the boat?" she asked, feeling dead inside. That Quin could think she would go behind his back and betray him meant he still had no clue who she was. They hadn't connected at all. Not really. Not if Quin had jumped to such an appalling conclusion.

Farrell answered. "The captain is anchored just off-shore. No clearance for a big vessel on Quin's tiny, rocky beach. We waded in, but one of us will help you."

# Eighteen

Quin seethed during the long trip back to Portland. The rain stopped. The sun came out. Nothing could improve his mood. He told himself he was furious, but even he recognized his own lie. He was hurt. Slashed to the bone.

When Katie had ended the relationship two years ago, he had imagined any number of reasons why she had walked away from some of the best sex of his life. Maybe she hadn't felt the same way. Maybe she was squeamish about the work connection.

Never in a million years had he imagined anything like this.

He stayed in the front cabin of the boat, debriefing with his brothers. Katie sat out in the sunshine, her face turned toward the horizon. She hadn't spoken a word to him or vice versa since Farrell and Zachary arrived.

Surely his brothers had noticed the tension. If they had, neither of them commented. The trip back to Portland took forever. When they docked, a car was waiting for them.

"We'll drop Katie first," Farrell said. "Then the three of us can look over some damage reports from the warehouse and the office."

Twenty minutes later Katie said a general goodbye to the occupants of the car. Zach helped her with her bags. Katie looked at Farrell. "You'll let me know if you need me at the office before it opens?"

"I will," Farrell said.

Then she was gone.

Quin's chest was hollow.

Farrell had booked a reservation at one of their favorite seafood restaurants that had fortunately sustained only minimal damage. Quin ordered his usual crab cake meal, but tasted none of it. The three men sketched out a plan for repairs and the inevitable shipping backlogs. Finally, after an hour and a half, Farrell frowned at him. "You want to tell us what the hell is going on between you and Katie?"

Quin swallowed hard, feeling as if his dinner was in danger of coming back up. "I found out this morning that two years ago she took a hundred grand from Dad. A loan to send her sister's drug-addicted boyfriend to rehab. Since Dad died, I'm pretty sure she hasn't paid it back."

Farrell and Zach stared at him, dumbstruck. Then Farrell shook his head. "Nope," he said firmly. "That's impossible. I know Katie. She would be far too proud to accept help like that, even if it *was* for someone else. You've got it wrong, Quin. Dead wrong."

Quin explained about the boxes of papers, and the checking information he had found, and the entry with Katie's name. "I showed her the ledger," he said. "She didn't deny it. Didn't even pretend to be surprised. She said she had kept it a secret, because she knew it would hurt me."

"I'm lost," Zach said.

Farrell patted his hand. "Quin and Katie had a hot and heavy affair two years ago. Kept it under wraps. She broke it off. Try to keep up."

Zach shot him a rude gesture. "I still don't get it, Quin. If you and Katie were an item, why wouldn't she borrow the money from you?"

"That's just it," Quin said. "The thing we argued about the most was money. She always wanted to prop up various people in her family who—as far as I could tell—were all leeches. But she should have known I would help her if she had only asked."

Farrell ordered another round of beers. When the waitress nodded and disappeared, he drummed his fingers on the table. "So Katie never actually *asked you* for the money two years ago?"

"No," Quin said. "She told me she was going to clean out a chunk of her savings. I told her that would be stupid and naive."

"You always did have a way with the ladies," Zach said ruefully.

Farrell was like a dog with a bone. "None of this makes sense. If she was going to use her own money, why would she have gone to Dad, a man she barely knew?"

The pain in Quin's chest began to radiate throughout his body. Maybe he was having a heart attack. "The irony is I was crazy about her. I would have given her the moon if she had asked. Instead, she didn't trust me enough to help her. She told me I was selfish. Then she broke up with me and went behind my back to our father."

This time Zach was the one shaking his head. "That's ridiculous, Quin. Dad was a rat bastard half the time.

I can't imagine anyone getting money from him, especially not a woman like Katie. He would have chewed her to pieces."

"Then how do you explain him writing a hundred-thousand-dollar check to my ex-girlfriend? A check she knew about. She said so to my face."

The silence grew. Three men trying to find the answer to an unsolvable equation.

Suddenly, Farrell cursed. "Sasha…"

Quin and Zach stared at him blankly.

Zach leaned forward. "Gonna need more than that buddy."

Quin was too torn up to comment.

Farrell banged his fist on the table. "Think how Dad treated Sasha all those years. Belittling her. Chipping away at her confidence. Trying to keep us apart. What if Dad found out about Quin and Katie's affair somehow and offered her a hundred grand to break up with him? And what if she took the money, not for herself, but because the loser boyfriend needed rehab?"

Quin drained half his beer. "Does that make it any more palatable? She *lied* to me," he muttered. His head ached as if a railroad spike was drilling deep.

Zachary, the financial wunderkind who kept SRO in the black, waved a hand, an arrested look on his face. "What if you're half right, Farrell? What if Dad did exactly what you said? But what if Katie never accepted the money?" He speared Quin with an exasperated glance. "Do you have any proof the check was cashed?"

Quin felt queasy. "No."

Zach pulled out his phone. "Dad hated online banking, so I kept up with it for him. With probate dragging on, I haven't closed that account. What month did you say it was?"

"April." Quin's lips were numb now.

The three of them fell silent as Zach dug into the past. At last, he shot Quin and Farrell a triumphant grin. "I found it. The check never cleared. The money is still there."

Quin sucked in a painful breath. "So, Katie…"

Farrell's sympathetic gaze was almost more than Quin could bear. "Katie was protecting you," Farrell said.

Zachary nodded. "She didn't want you to know what a terrible thing your father, *our* father, had done."

"But she broke up with me anyway. Why?"

Farrell shrugged. "I suppose you'll have to ask her that yourself."

Zach nodded. "If she ever speaks to you again."

Katie had been scared during the tropical storm. But Quin had been with her.

Now she was physically safe, but her heart was breaking.

How could he believe she would take money from his father and not tell him?

All she had ever wanted was for Quin to understand what motivated her, but even now, he couldn't see the truth. She needed him to love her. To trust her. To let her into his heart. Instead, he had immediately jumped to the worst possible conclusion. Katie had thought they were beginning to build something more than a sexual relationship. Quin had gradually let her in to his head and his heart—or so she had thought.

Maybe he was right about her all along. She was too naive and too trusting. Glass half-full. Rosy-colored spectacles. Pollyanna. Pick your cliché.

Quin had been so tender with her, so caring. She had begun to believe, however stupidly, that the two of them might have a chance after all.

For a long time now, she'd thought that money would ultimately keep them apart. Her lack of it and his embarrassingly large surfeit.

In the end, money had turned out to be a peripheral, a tiny bump in the road. The real problem was that Quin didn't know her at all. And apparently, his tendency to keep his thoughts and feelings under wraps had made her blind to his arrogance and pride.

She could have pulled the covers over her head and wallowed in her misery. But there were people in Portland who had *actual* life-and-death problems. No place to live. No food. No water.

Katie threw herself into the recovery effort, shoving her own pain and loss into a dark place in her soul. She helped serve hot meals. She read to children at an evacuation shelter. She made sure her family and friends were okay. And when Farrell called two days after their return from northern Maine, Katie met her boss at the office to help him and a team of tech geeks get the phone lines and internet up and running again.

She had braced for an encounter with Quin, but he was nowhere in sight. Probably on a plane over the Atlantic looking for a high, snowcapped mountain in Europe where he could risk life and limb. Again.

During the daylight hours she kept herself so busy she could barely *think* about Quin. But at night, in bed, her heart ached so badly she wanted to run far away from Portland. From any reminder of what she had found and lost. Love. At least on her side.

Sleeping alone after being with Quin night after night was so lonely and so terrifyingly empty, she cried until there were no more tears. Curled up with her pillow and her heartbreak, she pondered her future bleakly.

How could she stay at Stone River Outdoors?

* * *

Quin had faced many tight races in his life, but none as critical as the one to win Katie's forgiveness. He'd done some painful soul-searching. What he realized was that there was precious little chance she *would* forgive him. Even so, he had to make his apology. And he had to make her understand that none of this was her fault.

He'd been the ass. The betrayer. The recklessly bad judge of character and motive. Even now, when he thought about that terrible morning just before his brothers showed up, his stomach tightened with nausea. Remembering Katie's face… God, she had looked as if he had struck her.

Now here he stood, ten days later, on Katie's front porch. Farrell had assured him she was home.

Quin had brought neither candy nor flowers nor even jewelry. Katie Duncan would not be swayed by empty gestures.

If he had come here too soon, there would have been no opportunity for him to cope with what he was feeling. To understand what he wanted. To make a plan for the future. So he had bided his time, examined his black heart and finally understood.

The important thing here was to make sure Katie heard his apology and recognized that it was true and sincere.

She deserved that much at least.

When he rang the doorbell, his hand was shaking.

He honestly hadn't expected her to answer. The door had a peephole. She had to know it was him.

But the door swung inward, and there she was.

Her gaze swept him from head to toe. "You look terrible," she said. No inflection at all in her voice.

"You don't, Kat. You look gorgeous."

It was true. Her casual shorts and Caribbean-print halter top framed her beauty in a whimsical summer theme. She was barefoot, blond hair loose and tousled.

When the nickname slipped out, she flinched. "Why are you here, Quin? Farrell said you arranged to have my car returned. I asked him to thank you."

"He did." Still she made no move to let him in to her home. "Katie…" His throat tightened. "I know there's no excuse for what I did, but you have to know how sorry I am."

She was stone-faced. "What exactly did you do Quin? Other than accuse the woman you were sleeping with of being a cheat and a liar and a user?"

When her voice broke on the last word, it was like a knife to his heart. "I won't rationalize my behavior. It was indefensible. But when you stood there so calmly and said you knew about the check, I went a little crazy."

"Yes, you did."

"I brought you this," he said desperately, holding out his hand.

She stared at the manila envelope. "Is it an arrest warrant?"

Her sarcasm was no more than he deserved. "Open the envelope. It's for you."

She looked at her neighbor's house where interested eyes were watching. "Oh, for heaven's sake. Come in. But don't get comfortable."

Quin eased past her and staked out a spot near the doorway to the kitchen. He shoved his hands in his pockets.

Katie sank into a chair and opened the envelope, extracting the contents slowly. After a few moments, she looked up at him with a frown. "What is this?"

He inhaled sharply, feeling like a fool. "I bought you a piano. It's being delivered tomorrow. The phone numbers are for two women here in Portland who give lessons to adults."

* * *

Katie shook her head slowly. Having Quin here in her house was painful and unsettling. Day after day she had worked to forget him. It was a stupid game she played. The aggravating man was imprinted on every cell in her body.

"I don't understand," she said.

His blue-eyed gaze seemed haunted, almost as badly bereft as the broken man she had met in northern Maine, the man who had lost everything that mattered to him.

Quin shrugged. "It's part of my apology. I don't know why you left me two years ago, and I know I've screwed things up royally this time. I love you, Katie. That's all."

The blood rushed to her head. "You love me?"

"I should have told you sooner, but I was waiting until after the storm. I wanted to take you to the Riviera or the Caribbean and propose with some big romantic gesture."

"Propose?" Her voice squeaked.

"Then I realized you don't like all the fuss. But before I could come up with plan B, everything went to hell, and it was too late."

She shuddered. "You were so angry, Quin. At me. You can't imagine how that made me feel."

He bowed his head, his posture dejected. "I know. I saw your face." He squared his shoulders. "I think I was afraid," he said simply, his gaze begging her to understand.

She frowned. "Afraid? Quinten Stone is not afraid of anything."

"Not true." He shrugged. "You left me two years ago with no real explanation. When I saw that check my father wrote, I was afraid you didn't trust me to take care of you. That you thought I was so selfish and shallow I wouldn't do everything in my power to help you."

"I don't understand why you're here now," she said softly. Faint sparkles of hope tried to ignite in her heart, but he had hurt her so badly. "What about your other mistress? What about skiing?"

His head came up. Now his eyes were clear. "I've made my peace with it, Kat. No more competing. That's in my past. I've talked to some people about opening a ski school next winter. Nurturing new talent. But whatever happens, skiing is never again going to come between me and the people I love."

"I see," she said softly, her brain spinning, trying to wrap her head around what he was saying.

Finally, Quin moved closer. Determination carved his features in sharp angles. "I'll say it again, because you probably don't believe me. *I love you, Katie Duncan.*" He didn't wait for her to respond. "So I tried to think of a way to make you understand how sorry I am for what happened. I remembered that day at the museum. And the Renoir, *Two Young Girls at the Piano*. And I remembered how you let me in to your bed that night." He paused and swallowed, the muscles working in his throat. "I would never ski another minute in my life if I could have you back."

She laid the envelope aside. "Do you know why I broke up with you two years ago?"

He winced. "I'm guessing my father made you feel like shit. Chased you away. Told you believable lies."

"No." She stood and went to him, face-to-face, toe-to-toe. "Your father had nothing to do with it. I had already decided to go before he spoke to me."

Quin paled. "So it was my fault all along. Something *I* did. Not my father."

Katie put her hand on his cheek, shaking her head. "You didn't *do* anything. That was the problem. I wanted you to be someone you weren't. I wanted a man who was open and self-aware. The problem was, I didn't know how to ask for what I wanted, and the future seemed hopeless."

"So you gave up on us." The words could have been heated, but his voice was low and steady.

She shrugged helplessly. "We had nothing in common, Quin. Recently, I decided we were in a better place now, but the fact that you believed I would take a large sum of money from your father and not tell you makes me wonder. How could it possibly work?"

He captured her hand with his, pressing her fingertips to his stubbly jaw. His skin was warm. "That's where you're wrong, Kat. We have *everything* in common. Every beat of your heart is mine. When you breathe, I breathe. I can't imagine my life without you in it." He stopped. Released her. Stepped back, as if he couldn't bear to touch her. "Do you love me, Kat?"

She was breaking apart inside, tumbled about by every lie she had told herself. "Yes." Tears she couldn't hold at bay spilled over. She hated feeling so emotional.

But Quin's gaze was suspiciously wet, as well. "Then I'll take that for now. Until you're sure. You'll see, my love. You're everything I need. And if you'll forgive me for my monumental stupidity and cruelty, I'll spend the rest of my life proving to you that we fit together well. As perfectly as two fragments of leaded glass in a Tiffany masterpiece. No one else will do for me, Kat. It's that simple. If you won't have me, I'll be a lonely bachelor."

Joy burst through the long hours and days of grief. "Don't overplay your hand." She threw herself at him and wrapped her arms around his neck, absorbing his strength and heat. "I do adore you," she whispered. "Say it again."

He found her lips with his, kissed her slow and deep, reduced her to mush. "I love you, my dearest Kat," he said, his words unsteady. "And just so you know, I'm going to buy you the biggest, gaudiest diamond I can find and make you wear it every day so the whole world will know you're my woman."

She rested her cheek against his firm, broad chest, inhaling the scent of him, soaking in the happiness that was almost too much to bear. "I think I can live with that, Quentin Stone. Now, if you aren't in too much of a hurry, I'd like to show you my new bed. The headboard is rated for restless sleepers."

He chuckled, his eyes bright. "Sounds like a challenge to me..."

*  *  *  *  *

# SECRETS OF A
# FAKE FIANCÉE

### YAHRAH ST JOHN

To my friend Kiara Ashanti for always
encouraging me to *write, write, write*.

# One

Morgan Young couldn't imagine a more perfect place for a wedding than this La Jolla beach on a spring evening. She was touched by the heartfelt vows her boss, Dane Stewart, had just shared with his new wife, Iris. The couple had pledged their undying devotion with their son, Jayden, standing by his father's side. The wedding was an especially happy occasion, considering Jayden was battling a rare form of acute lymphocytic leukemia, and finding the father he'd never met had provided him with the life-saving treatment he needed. Jayden had needed a bone marrow transplant and Dane's stem cells had been just what the doctor ordered. Morgan had played an instrumental part in bringing the boys' parents together.

Dane, however, had no idea of Morgan's true identity.

She was his baby sister.

Over the last year working as his assistant, she'd kept it hidden. Morgan hadn't intended to remain mum this long. On her deathbed, her mother, Crystal Young, had finally told Morgan her father was Henry Stewart. Crystal had had an affair with him decades ago. Morgan wanted to get to know him, but then she'd done her homework and learned of the man's previous infidelities and his estrangement from her half brother Ayden. Morgan wondered if Henry ever considered the consequences of his actions.

She was going to find out tonight.

"Can I get a whiskey?" Morgan asked the bartender from where she'd been perched watching Dane and Iris cut the cake and share their first dance.

"That's an awfully strong drink," a deep masculine voice said from Morgan's side.

She cocked her head and her breath was stolen from her chest. The voice belonged to the most handsome man she'd ever seen. He had skin the color of shortbread, stunning smooth bone structure, midnight eyes framed by bushy brows and a wide sensual mouth. His hair was short and his tuxedo fit his tall frame perfectly. He towered over her. Morgan was five-seven, so she figured he was over six feet.

"I can handle my liquor."

He regarded her. "Is that right?" When she didn't respond, he looked at the uniformed bartender. "I'll have what the lady is having."

"Coming right up."

"So, what brings you here?" the stranger asked, turning to Morgan. "Are you a friend of the bride or the groom?"

"Both." Morgan sipped her whiskey.

"Really? I'm surprised Dane would have let a beautiful woman like you get away."

Morgan chuckled. "Dane and I are more like brother and sister." The stranger had no idea how true that statement was. "And he couldn't have picked a better wife. Iris is an amazing mother. The way she's dealt with Jayden's condition is nothing short of heroic. Jayden's very fortunate to have a mother like her in his corner."

The bartender returned with another glass and slid it toward the stranger. He accepted and drank a generous swallow. "Sounds like you speak from personal experience."

Morgan glanced at Henry Stewart, who was dancing with Fallon Stewart, Dane's sister. An ache formed in Morgan's chest. "I do." She downed the rest of her whiskey and placed it on the bar. "If you'll excuse me, I have some urgent business to attend to."

It was time she finally told Henry she was his daughter. Now was her chance.

Jared Robinson stared after the stunning beauty as he sipped his whiskey. *Who was she?* She claimed to know Dane and Iris, but he had never seen her before. Of course, the last time he'd seen Dane had been on a pit stop Dane made to Austin last year. He'd indicated he'd met someone, but hadn't gone into much detail. Jared didn't have to wait long to find out; as an A-list movie star and America's Sexiest Man Alive, Dane's every movement was tracked by the media. The press caught wind that Dane had fathered a child via sperm donation. Who could have predicted Jared's former running buddy would fall hard and fast for the mother of his child? But fall Dane had.

Jared had no intention of going down the wedded-bliss path. He was merely here on sufferance, paying his respects to his friend. He and Dane had once been the screwups of their respective families. When they were younger, they'd been rabble-rousers, constantly getting into trouble. His father, Clay, had thought putting Jared in a boarding school would tame him, but that only gave Jared more access to females.

Jared had a way with the ladies and was unapologetic about it. He liked them in all colors, shapes and sizes. But today, there wasn't anyone at the wedding who could hold a candle to the woman he'd shared a drink with.

Straight jet-black hair hung gloriously down the woman's back. She had caramel brown skin, big expressive hazel eyes and a beautiful full mouth tinted with peach gloss that Jared wouldn't mind placing his lips on. She wore a blush gown with crisscross spaghetti straps that showed off her slender back. She was easily about five foot six or seven with a lithe body. Jared wanted to get to know her better, but she'd rushed off. He would remedy the situation before the night was over. After suffering through Dane's wedding, Jared was entitled to a little fun and she was it.

Morgan was determined. Tonight, she would reveal her true identity to Henry Stewart. She had no idea how he would take her revelation, but it was time to find out.

She was thwarted by the wedding planner, who was now ushering the guests toward the front driveway to send off the happy couple in a classic Rolls-Royce decked with streamers. Morgan was swept away in the melee. She now stood near the car and was handed a sparkler. From her vantage point, Morgan saw Dane and Iris kiss Jayden and hug their families.

Morgan's eyes welled with tears. *She* should be standing over there with them. She shouldn't have waited so long to tell the Stewarts the truth. Maybe then she wouldn't feel like an outsider with her own family only a few feet away. She was about to push people aside, when Dane stepped away and came toward her. To Morgan's surprise, he wrapped her in his arms.

"You're part of the reason this was all possible," Dane whispered in her ear. "You helped get us back together. Thank you."

Morgan couldn't stop a tear from escaping. "You're welcome."

Seconds later, Dane was gone, helping Iris into the Rolls-Royce. Morgan watched her half brother drive away to his happily-ever-after. She sighed and then glanced up to see the rest of the Stewarts watching the car wistfully.

Now was her time. She had to seize it.

Smoothing her hands down her dress, she made her way toward them. Morgan's legs felt wobbly as if she were a newborn foal. Dane's sister Fallon and her husband, Gage, were chasing after their son, Dylan, who was always on the move. Morgan didn't see where Ayden and Maya had gone, but Henry and his wife, Nora, were still there in all their finery. Henry wore a tuxedo and Nora was in a one-shoulder black gown. Neither of them acknowledged her presence until Morgan cleared her throat.

"May I help you?" Nora asked, raising a brow.

Morgan ignored the look of disdain Nora gave her. Whitney, Dane's publicist, had hooked Morgan up with a designer who loaned her the dress she was wearing, so she wasn't sure why Nora was finding fault. "I was hoping to have a word with Mr. Stewart."

"Tonight is a time for family," Nora responded. "If you want to talk business, it will have to be another time."

"It's okay, Nora." Henry smiled down at his wife. "I can be magnanimous. I mean, Dane got married tonight. That is worth celebrating."

Nora sighed. "All right, but don't be long." She picked up the sides of her gown and walked toward the reception area.

"Thank you," Morgan said as she and Henry stepped away from the crowd and headed toward the beach. When they stopped, Morgan allowed herself time to really look at her father.

She'd seen only pictures, and although she'd studied them religiously trying to see parts of herself in the man, it was different seeing him in person. Henry had more salt than pepper in his closely cropped hair and his eyes were just like hers, hazel gray. Morgan figured her father was slightly under six feet, but no less impressive in her mind.

"All right, young lady, the floor is yours," Henry stated. "What can I do for you?"

Morgan swallowed. Her mouth felt dry and full of cotton. "Yes… I."

"Well? Spit it out. I don't have all day."

Although she'd waited her whole life for this moment,

there was no easy way to say what she had to say. She just had to spit it out. "I'm your daughter."

Henry's eyes grew wide with alarm. "Excuse me?"

"You heard me," Morgan replied. "I'm your daughter."

"Like hell you are!" he bellowed. "I don't know what kind of game you're playing, young lady, but you're off the mark. My daughter *Fallon*—" he pointed across the lawn "—is standing over there."

"You have another," Morgan stated. "With Crystal Young. You met her in Las Vegas when she was performing as a showgirl at the Tropicana. You spent one night together and I'm the result."

"No, no!" Henry shook his head furiously. "You're wrong!" he yelled and then glanced around to see people were starting to watch their interaction, so he lowered his voice. "You don't know what you're talking about. I have never been unfaithful to my wife."

Morgan's ire rose. "C'mon, Henry. Nora wouldn't be the first wife you cheated on."

"So, what, you've done your research?" Henry huffed, "That means nothing. My first marriage with Lillian is public record."

Morgan noticed the crowd watching them had grown and Nora and Fallon were charging toward them. "So you're going to deny you spent the night with my mother at the Tropicana?

Henry glanced up at Nora, who was only a few feet away. "Yes. I don't know who you're talking about. You're mistaken."

"I'm not mistaken!" Morgan yelled. "You're my father."

A hush came over the crowd and suddenly even the reception music paused. All eyes were on the two of them. Nora had a look of utter shock on her face while Fallon's was more of disbelief.

Henry headed toward his wife. "Nora!" But she was running through the grass. He turned to his daughter. "Fallon?"

Fallon held up her hand and shook her head. "I don't want to hear it, Daddy. Not now. I'm going after Mom." Seconds later, Morgan was left alone with her father.

Henry spun around to face Morgan. "You!" He pointed at her. "You did this! On what should have been one of the happiest days for our family, you come here and cause discord. I don't know who you are and I will never claim you as my daughter. You should leave because your presence is no longer wanted." Without another word, he raced after Nora.

Morgan stared at Henry's back as he literally ran away from her. When she could no longer see him, she looked up and saw everyone at the reception was watching her.

*Everyone.*

*Waiting for her to do what?* Make more of an embarrassment out of herself than she already had? Well, they were in for a rude awakening. The party was over. Lowering her head, Morgan shuffled away as fast as she could and went straight for the bar. As she walked by, the crowd parted like the Red Sea. As if she carried some sort of plague. And maybe she did. She was glad she'd at least waited for Dane and Iris's departure before confronting Henry.

*Had she been hoping to be accepted with open arms?* Of course not. But she hadn't expected complete and utter rejection, either.

When she made it to the bar, she eyed the bartender and mouthed the word *whiskey* to him. He understood and immediately came over with the bottle. When he began pouring the requisite two thumbs she motioned for him to continue. Only when the tumbler was full did she tell him to stop.

Morgan took a swift mouthful. The liquid burned going

down and it felt good. She doubted it would wash away the stain of being humiliated, but it was a start.

"You didn't get the reaction you bargained for?"

Morgan glanced up at the stranger from earlier. Their exchange seemed like a lifetime ago even though it had been little more than a half hour since they'd shared a drink. She eyed him warily, noting he'd dispensed with his tie and undone several buttons on his shirt. "I'm in no mood for any commentary from the peanut gallery."

"Perhaps you should have had some earlier," he responded, his mouth quirking. "I could have told you you're timing for *that revelation* was lousy."

Morgan took another generous sip of her drink. "There was never going to be a right time. And I'd waited long enough."

"Apparently not long enough."

"Do you have to berate me? I've dealt with enough recriminations tonight."

He smiled. "Of course not. I'm sorry. How about we start over? My name is Jared."

"Jared." She turned to face him. It was hard to be angry at someone as good-looking as him. Morgan leaned over to clink her glass with his and saw it was empty. She motioned to the bartender. "Get Jared another drink. We're getting to know each other."

Jared was just the sort of distraction she needed to help her forget this terrible night.

# Two

"My name is Morgan." The beauty gave Jared only her first name. He was surprised Morgan wanted to stay, considering how her father's rejection must have hurt and Henry had asked her to leave. She was licking her wounds and looking for a distraction and that was fine with Jared. He could use some unadulterated fun without any pesky emotional attachments. He didn't do serious.

His longest relationship had lasted three months. His girlfriends were short-term with a shelf life of a month. After the thrill in the bedroom was gone, it was on to the next beautiful woman. And Morgan wasn't just beautiful. There was a fragility to her, which spoke to his masculine side. He was no hero, but he wouldn't mind being *hers* for the night.

Another whiskey appeared and Jared accepted without hesitation. "It's a pleasure to meet you, Morgan." He tipped his tumbler to hers.

Their eyes met and held for endless seconds over the rim and Jared could swear he felt his stomach turn upside down. He was the first to look away and put down his glass. "How about a dance?"

"So everyone can watch me?" Morgan inquired, taking a large gulp of whiskey. "No, thank you."

"I'm sorry to tell you, but everyone was watching you the moment you announced to the world you were Henry Stewart's daughter."

A hint of a smile touched Morgan's lips. "I can't argue with that." She swallowed the remainder of the whiskey and took his hand.

"You need to go easy on the whiskey," Jared replied. "Otherwise, you'll have a helluva hangover tomorrow."

"I know what I'm doing."

Jared wasn't sure, but for some reason he felt compelled to stick around and find out.

Jared's hand threaded through Morgan's and a riot of sensations shot right through her belly like a fire to dry tinder. Morgan glanced up to see if Jared felt it too and he had. His eyes were dark and cloudy. Nervously, Morgan followed him onto the temporary wooden dance floor on the grass.

Jared pulled her into the center, ignoring all the open-mouthed stares around them, placed his hands on her hips and began to move. Morgan wound her arms around his neck and joined in his sinuous rhythm. Jared was an excellent dancer.

"You're pretty good at this."

Jared flashed her a grin. "You're not bad yourself."

"I learned how to dance as a child."

He smiled as he thought of a young Morgan in ballet slippers. "Did you have a dance mom making you take ballet and tap? Or was it hip-hop?"

Morgan laughed. Her childhood was a far cry from what you saw on television. She didn't have Clair Huxtable from *The Cosby Show* as her mother. "Nothing as grandiose as that. I hung around backstage while my mom danced at the Tropicana in Vegas."

"Intriguing. I'm sure there's a story there." He used his thumb to push up her jaw and their eyes met. Attraction and lust were in those onyx depths.

"It's not one I plan on telling anytime soon."

"A woman with secrets," Jared surmised. "I like." He pressed forward until their bodies were flush.

Incendiary sexual heat slid up Morgan's spine. She wasn't used to this. Usually when things between her and a man heated up, she cooled off. But not tonight. Jared wasn't like other men she met. She dropped her nose to his chest and opened V of his tuxedo shirt. She inhaled his spicy scent. It was very intoxicating.

When he splayed his hand across her nearly bare back, Morgan stumbled, but Jared was right there, swaying them back and forth, pretending they were dancing. Morgan knew what this was—*it was seduction*. When his hands went lower and settled on her bottom, Morgan was shocked, but she didn't complain.

"You want to come to my room?" Morgan didn't know what possessed her to make such an outrageous proposition, but once it was out there, she couldn't take it back. With Jared, she didn't feel fearful like she did with other men. Maybe it would be okay to allow herself the one night. Maybe he could banish all the bad memories and she could finally be who she was meant to be.

Jared glanced down at her. "I don't know, Morgan. You've had a lot to drink and something tells me you don't normally operate this way."

Morgan glanced up at him in confusion. He could *tell* she was new at this? Was that why he wasn't rushing to take her up to her hotel room and have his wicked way with her? She'd already fumbled on revealing her true identity. Apparently, she couldn't even pick up a man, either.

She pushed away from him and Jared frowned. "Morgan, what's wrong?"

"I'm sorry to have bothered you. I was mistaken about your interest." She walked off the dance floor. She was grateful the crowd had begun to fade so no one witnessed her second rejection of the night. Morgan made her way back to the bar.

"Morgan, wait!" With his long strides, Jared caught up to her in no time. "It's not like that," he said when he finally met her back at the bar where she ordered another whiskey.

"Keep them coming until I tell you to stop," Morgan told the bartender, and slammed the entire glass down.

"Listen, Morgan. You've had a rough time tonight and I don't want to add to it by being a decision you regret in the morning."

"Then leave," Morgan replied. "I don't need a hero. I've been taking care of myself for a long time and tonight will be no different. So get lost, Jared."

Jared stared at her for several mind-churning seconds, turned on his heel and walked off. Good riddance, Morgan thought. He was probably too perfect to be her *first* anyway.

Jared wanted to ring Morgan's adorable neck. Drinking away her troubles wasn't going to solve anything, but was she willing to listen to the voice of reason? No.

And why was he being the voice of reason? *Because…* he'd never taken advantage of a woman in his life and he wasn't about to start now. Morgan was emotionally on the edge and well on her way to tying one on. Jared had been that way in his youth, but not anymore. And when he was *with* a woman, he wanted her to remember him when he was gone because he was nothing if not a giving lover.

He left her at the bar as she requested, but he didn't go far. Instead, he engaged in conversation with an acquaintance near the dance floor.

"So I hear you're working at Robinson Holdings," the older man said. Milton Brooks sat on the board of his family's company and often was in everyone's business.

"Yeah, in the marketing and public relations department."

"Your brother, Chris, has been making some big moves buying that La Shore development."

"Yes, well, Chris has an eye for such things," Jared said, keeping an eye on Morgan. He saw Pete Harris, an unscrupulous fellow from his and Dane's past, talking to Morgan, and Jared didn't like it one bit.

"He has a sharp eye, that brother of yours," the man said. "He's destined for big things."

His comment caught Jared's attention and rankled him. His older brother, Chris, was the favorite son, and it grated on Jared's nerves to hear the man's unabashed praise. Chris had been running Robinson Holdings since their father, Clay, unexpectedly stepped down due to a health crisis a year ago. Chris had doubled revenue and business was booming.

"Chris does seem to have the Midas touch," Jared replied. He turned in time to catch Pete putting his hand on Morgan's shoulder and her pushing him away. Pete wasn't taking no for answer and was getting handsy. "If you'll excuse me, I have some unfinished business to attend to," Jared said, taking his leave of the older man.

He quickly strode over to where Pete now had his hands wrapped around Morgan's waist. He caught the man by the collar and shoved him away.

"Hey…" Pete began, but stopped when he saw who it was. "Oh, hi, Jared." He held out his hand, but Jared glared at him, so he pulled it back. "Me and the little lady here were having a disagreement."

Jared turned to Morgan. Her face was flushed, and looking in her eyes he could see she was genuinely frightened. "Back off or I'll make you regret it."

Pete held up his hands. "I'm sorry." He quickly rushed off.

"Are you okay?" Jared asked, peering down at Morgan. Morgan sucked in a deep breath. "Yeah, I'm okay now."

She gave him a halfhearted smile, but he noticed her hand was shaking as she put her glass down on the bar. "Thanks for the assist."

"That's what heroes do." He offered her a wide grin.

"Well, thanks." She mussed with her hair for a few minutes, running her fingers through it, something Jared would sorely like to do. Then she turned back around and motioned to the bartender for another drink.

Jared stepped forward and put his hand over her empty glass. "You're done."

Her eyes flashed fire at him. "Just because you helped me out of a spot doesn't mean you get to tell me what to do."

"It does when you aren't capable of making good decisions. C'mon." He clasped her by the arm and started moving across the lawn toward the hotel entrance near the beach. "I'm going to walk you to your room and leave."

"Really?" Morgan asked mockingly as if she knew how much he wanted her and didn't believe for a second he'd walk away. "I doubt that." She stalked in front of him giving Jared a view of her delectable backside in her dress.

Damn her. She was not making it easy for him to walk away and do the right thing.

When they reached the bank of elevators, Morgan pressed the up button and they waited. The atmosphere was charged. When the elevator came, they both entered. It was empty and the air between them crackled with sexual tension. Morgan pressed the button for her floor and Jared went and stood on the other side of the car.

If he came any closer, he knew he would lose the control he was battling for. Need pulsed through every cell of his body. But he reminded himself Morgan wasn't like the other women he dated who knew the score. She was acting as if she did, but there was a certain naivete about her that told him he couldn't act on his desire.

The elevator bell chimed. They disembarked and walked

the short distance to her room. Morgan fished a key from her clutch and opened the door.

"This is where I take my…" Jared never got to finish because Morgan pulled him inside and shut the door.

Morgan didn't know what made her pull Jared into her room. She just knew she had to. She craved his touch and was desperate to know what he would taste like. And if anyone could make her forget tonight, it was Jared. When the door slammed, she suddenly found herself pushing him back against it and angling her head for a kiss. Her mouth covered his and she was surprised to find his lips were deceptively gentle, luring hers into a sensual whirlpool.

"You really shouldn't have done that," Jared rasped, lifting his head. Then he was drawing her closer until their lower bodies touched, pelvis to pelvis. His hands slid through the strands of her hair, then he lowered his head and took. His lips ravished hers with gentle pressure before his tongue glided into her mouth and discovered every secret she'd kept hidden with other men.

Something unraveled inside Morgan, something she'd long suppressed.

*Lust.*

She gave into the cascading shivers of desire by linking her arms around his neck and leaning into him. She loved the taste and feel of him. Jared's hands were already sliding down her hips and holding her tightly against his erection. Her breasts were pushed firmly against his chest and she could feel the ridge of his muscles underneath his tuxedo.

Jared groaned and his mouth engulfed Morgan's, further spinning her senses out of control and making her core contract with a need she'd never felt before. Whenever she got too close to a man, she clammed up, but not with Jared. First there was the dance and now this kiss. He had her under some sort of spell, so much so she was kissing him back with greedy fervor. Their tongues darted back and forth, dancing with each other in a brilliant tango Morgan never wanted to end. Jared had her entire body on fire. She wanted more, but like a cruel joke, her stomach churned.

She pushed away from Jared as quickly as she could and rushed toward the bathroom. Morgan made it in enough time to relieve her stomach of its contents. It was a horrible feeling knowing the sexy man of her dreams was on the other side of the door and she was retching because of the whiskey she'd imbibed earlier. He'd been right. She should have stopped while she was ahead and now she was going to pay the price.

Those were the last thoughts she remembered as she laid her head on the cold tile floor and passed out.

"Morgan?" Jared knocked on the bathroom door. She'd been in there a long time and there was no amount of exhaust fan noise to cover the sounds of her being sick. He'd tried to stop her from drinking too much her earlier, but she'd stubbornly refused to listen.

Jared ran his hands over his head. Fate had set the course of the night. When he'd walked Morgan to her room, he had every intention of leaving her at her door untouched. But when she'd pulled him in and kissed him, he'd lost all self-control. He wanted her with a burning ache that pulsed in his loins, even now. Jesus, he had to get the hell out of there, but first he had to make sure she was okay.

Easing the door open, he found Morgan on the floor.

"Morgan!" He rushed over and checked for a pulse.

She was okay. Just seriously inebriated. Lifting her in his arms, Jared carried her into the bedroom and laid her on the bed. She looked so youthful and innocent in that blush dress, with her jet-black hair spread out over the pillow. Since she'd just gotten sick, Jared suspected Morgan would prefer to be out of the dress as to not soil it further.

Decision made. Jared reached behind her, unzipped the dress and pulled it over her head. Morgan barely moved a muscle. She was out like a light. But Jared had to suck in a deep breath. *She wasn't wearing a bra.* Her breasts were small and round, but enough for a handful. She had a flat stomach and shapely legs. A tiny scrap of material covered her femininity but did little to staunch his hunger. Quickly, he reached for the comforter and slid it over her naked yet beautiful body.

She was going to be hurting tomorrow. So he called room service. When a waiter delivered the bottled water and aspirin, Jared placed them on the nightstand, ensuring they'd be waiting for her tomorrow. Then he left the room. Once in the corridor, Jared leaned against the door and closed his eyes. He was thankful it had been him and not Pete. When she awoke the next morning, she'd know her hero, although tempted, had done the right thing.

# Three

"Ugh!" Morgan clutched her pounding head as she rolled over in bed the next morning. "What time is it?" She glanced at the clock on the nightstand and saw it was nearly noon. She had slept the entire morning away. Memories from last night came flooding back. Henry's rejection at the reception. Her throwing back whiskey after whiskey. And then there was Jared.

Oh yes, she couldn't forget Jared.

The mysterious stranger who somehow made last night bearable. Morgan remembered their flirting, that first dance when they'd damn near dirty danced and then the amazing kiss up against her door. She glanced at the scene of the crime. When she closed her eyes, she could feel the pressure of his mouth, the glide of his lips against hers and then—the unthinkable.

She got sick. In the throes of her one and only make-out session with a hot guy, she'd ruined it by rushing off to the bathroom. But what happened afterward? She glanced at the space beside her; that side of the bed was untouched. Jared hadn't deigned to stay the night. Why would he? Sex was probably the last thing on his mind after witnessing her self-destruction. And she'd done it in epic proportion.

Glancing at the nightstand, she saw the bottled water and aspirin. She glanced upward and silently thanked Jared for his kindness. Swallowing two tablets, Morgan washed them down with water. He could have taken advantage in her weakened state, but he hadn't.

He'd been her hero.

Slowly, she sat up in bed and that's when she realized the state she was in. *Naked.* Lifting the covers, Morgan noted she still had on her underwear, but that didn't mean anything. Had she gotten it wrong? Had Jared done the unthinkable? She didn't feel any different. And wouldn't she? If they'd had sex, she would know. She was a virgin after all.

Yeah, the last of her kind, Morgan was sure. Most twenty-five-year-olds had had sex, but then again none of them had been raised by a mother like Crystal. But that was beside the point. If nothing happened between her and Jared, that meant he'd undressed her, seen her naked and left anyway. Morgan wanted to cheer in appreciation, but was also mortified to know after seeing her naked, it had done nothing for him. Then again, she doubted Jared wanted a corpse in bed.

Throwing back the covers, Morgan headed to the bathroom. As she brushed her teeth, she determined to look at the bright side. Jared was a good guy who'd saved her from a worse fate. Who knew what could have happened if he hadn't stepped in? When she was done, she wiped her mouth, turned on the taps for the shower and stepped in. She wanted the stench of last night off her.

She wasn't a heavy drinker. Or at least not usually. But yesterday was not ordinary. It wasn't every day the father you'd longed for your entire life rejected you. She had cause to drink, but Morgan vowed to never put herself in another situation like last night ever again.

When she was done, she turned off the shower and began toweling herself dry. In the closet, Morgan found her standard outfit of black jeans and a black T-shirt. She dressed like that every day to stay in the background as Dane's assistant. She was certain she wouldn't have a job for much longer once Dane found out what she'd done, but she was a college grad. Surely, she could find a new gig to pay the bills.

In the meantime, her role in Dane's life also gave her advantages because Morgan knew the Stewarts's schedule. They planned on leaving today to head back to Austin. She would have to go onto their turf to fight this battle. She wasn't going to cower and run off into the night like some poor relation. She was his *daughter* and Henry owed her. Owed her for all the missed birthday parties and Christmases. He owed her for not looking after her welfare and ensuring she had a happy, loving childhood.

And she was going to claim her due.

"Jared, are you listening to a word I've said?" his mother asked as he sat across the table where he and his parents were having Sunday brunch. It had been a weekly event ever since he was a kid. They hadn't stopped even after his father's heart attack and open-heart surgery a year ago.

"I'm sorry, Mom. What was that?" Jared asked. He'd been distracted the last week. He supposed it had something to do with a certain brunette he hadn't been able to forget. He'd been sleeping fitfully, tossing and turning thinking about the hazel-eyed beauty.

Jared wondered how she was faring. News of Morgan's relation to Dane had been leaked to the press and the story was splashed over the tabloids. Dane was on his honeymoon while Morgan had disappeared.

"I asked you if you knew where your brother, Chris was," Mary Robinson inquired. "It's not like him to miss Sunday brunch."

"No. I haven't talked to him," Jared answered. "His assistant said he took the week off for personal business."

"Chris is a workaholic, same as me," his father said. "I'm glad to see he's learned a lesson from me and is taking time for himself."

"What about Dane?" his mother asked. "I tried calling Nora about the tabloids' claim that Henry has an illegitimate daughter, but she didn't answer. Do you think it's true?"

"C'mon, Mary, you can't believe the gossips."

"It's not gossip, Dad," Jared replied.

His father frowned. "How would you know?"

"I met Morgan at the wedding. We talked and she's a lovely young woman."

"Who's no doubt after the Stewart wealth. She might be shocked to learn that not everything is what it seems. Henry hasn't been rolling in it for years," his father said. "If it wasn't for his son-in-law Gage and Fallon's business acumen, the company would have gone belly-up years ago."

"Not everything is about money," Jared said. "Morgan just wants to be recognized."

"So you're on a first name basis with her?" his mother asked, quirking a brow.

"You know our son can't resist a pretty face," his father responded. "She must be a looker."

Jared's spine stiffened at the affront and he wiped his mouth with his napkin. "I've lost my appetite, so I'll be on my way."

"Run away like you always do," his father countered.

"I'm sorry your favorite son couldn't be here for brunch, but don't take it out on me." Jared walked over to his mother and kissed her on the cheek. "Mom, I'll call you later."

Jared didn't bother saying goodbye to his father. They were never going to see eye to eye, so he'd stopped trying. He was curious about Morgan, but perhaps it was for the best he hadn't seen her since that night. He hadn't recognized himself around her and Jared suspected if he ever saw her again, he would be in trouble. He doubted he could walk away again.

\* \* \*

Morgan sat in her car outside the Stewart mansion that afternoon. It had taken a week to get her affairs in order, which included starting the paperwork to legally change her name from Morgan Young to Morgan Stewart. It was time she took her rightful name and place in the family. She'd also sent a letter of resignation to Dane. Within days of the wedding, news had broken that she was Dane Stewart's baby sister and the tabloids were staked outside of her small apartment in Culver City. Thankfully, she'd packed in advance and decided to drive to Austin. Flying would have drawn too much attention. She lived frugally and Dane paid her well, so she had savings to tide her over for a while.

And now here she was, waiting for security to approve her entry to the hallowed grounds. Morgan fumed in her car. She was a Stewart, after all, and was being treated like she was an outsider. *But wasn't she?*

She hadn't been raised on this estate like Dane or Fallon. They'd had everything. The best house. Clothes. Cars. Education. While she'd had nothing. She had a right to be here. Henry was going to own up to being her father. Morgan wasn't going to leave until he did.

The security guard placed the receiver of his phone down and leaned out of the guardhouse. "I'm sorry, ma'am. I'm told you don't have an appointment. You're going to have to turn around."

"You can't keep me out," Morgan insisted. "I need to talk to my father."

"I'm sorry, miss. But you're going to have to leave. If you don't, I'm going to have to call the cops on you for trespassing."

"Trespassing?" Morgan's voice rose. "Well that's rich. Imagine what the press will say when they find out Henry kicked his own daughter off the grounds."

A horn sounded from behind Morgan and startled her.

She turned as a red Audi pulled up beside her Honda Accord. The window rolled down and Fallon leaned out, but she wasn't alone. Ayden, their older brother, sat beside her. "It's all right, Drew. She's with me."

"Are you sure? Your father was insistent she not be let in."

"I'll handle my father," Fallon responded evenly. "Morgan—" Fallon glanced in her direction "—follow me in."

Morgan nodded mutely, put the car in gear and followed the Audi up the manicured road. When they finally stopped in front of the two-story mansion, Morgan sucked in a breath as she looked around.

After turning off the engine, Morgan exited the vehicle and found Fallon leaning against her car. She looked poised and sophisticated in jeans, a tank top, knee-high boots and a long duster. Morgan was sure the outfit was designer while her own was off-the-rack. Although Dane paid her well, living in Los Angeles was expensive and Morgan couldn't afford designer clothes.

Ayden, meanwhile, stood nearby, quietly assessing her. Morgan wished the situation was different and he would wrap her in a big brotherly hug. *Wasn't that what she'd always wanted?* A family of her own. Not just her and Crystal and the revolving door of men in her mother's life.

"Morgan, it seems we have a lot to talk about," Fallon said, her hazel eyes trained on Morgan. They were the same eyes Morgan saw every day when she looked in the mirror.

"No offense, Fallon, but *we* don't," Morgan said, folding her arms across her chest. "I need to talk to your father, I mean, *our* father."

"I disagree," Ayden said. "This involves all of us. Henry has a lot to answer for. It's why we both came. For answers."

"And I'm here to be a mediator," Fallon added. "I know neither of you is Daddy's biggest fan, but after your revelation last week, my mother was distraught. Inconsolable. She came home with me and Gage and has been there all week. She asked me to bring a few things, which is why I'm here."

"I'm sorry," Morgan said, "but that's not my fault. I didn't cheat on her. Henry did."

"It wouldn't be the first time," Ayden said underneath his breath.

Fallon gave Ayden a hard stare. "That might be true, but surely you could have revealed your existence in a less public way?"

Morgan sighed. Fallon had a point. "I—I didn't know another way, Fallon. He didn't know me from Adam. I knew he would stonewall me. And as you can see from today, I was right."

"That's because he's hurt and lashing out."

"Do you always make excuses for him?" Morgan asked.

"Yes." Ayden nodded.

Fallon laughed. "I know Daddy isn't perfect."

"He's my father, too," Morgan responded hotly. "And it's time he acknowledged that."

"Let's go inside and talk. But I warn you he's not in the best mood."

Morgan followed Ayden and Fallon through the gilded doors with gold-plated handles into the foyer. She was amazed at how beautiful the mansion was. The terrazzo floors gleamed and the two-story spiral staircase was breathtaking. Morgan could see the European influence in the decor. It resembled a French chateau with cathedral ceilings and baroque adornments throughout. Fallon led Morgan into a sitting room that had a massive two-story fireplace and a baby grand piano.

Fallon sat down on a chaise and Ayden took the spot beside her. Morgan envied the easy comfort they shared and hoped one day she could have the same.

"Why do you think he's your father?" Fallon asked.

Morgan sighed. She didn't care to explain herself, but

apparently she had to. "My mother met Henry when he was attending a tech convention in Las Vegas. They spent one night together. I'm the result. It's as simple as that."

"Why didn't she ever come forward? I mean, she could have gone to court and gotten my father to acknowledge you and pay child support. It's what I would've done."

"If you recall, my mother didn't fight to ensure Henry took care of me, either," Ayden interjected. "It's not easy coming forward."

"Thank you, Ayden." Morgan appreciated the backup considering their background was similar when it came to their father. "I doubt my mother knew how to find him. She said she didn't know who he was until a magazine article came out on Stewart Technologies, but she never told me until she was dying in the hospital."

"I'm so sorry," Fallon replied.

"It's all right. My mother and I didn't have a great relationship, which is why I wanted a father so badly."

"Then why didn't you tell us the truth sooner?" Fallon inquired. "You've been working for Dane for over a year."

"Fallon's right. We would have accepted you," Ayden said.

"I wanted to, but I was scared of how I would be received. Dane is a huge superstar. Considering his position, he might have thought I was trying to shake him down or something."

"Well, aren't you?" a harsh tenor voice sounded from behind them.

Morgan turned to see Henry. She didn't know how long he'd been standing there listening to their conversation.

Her father sauntered into the living room and Morgan felt his negativity from where she sat. It enshrouded him like a dark cloak. He looked foreboding even though he was dressed casually in navy trousers and a checkered button-down shirt. "You're here to claim what's yours? Isn't that right?"

"Daddy." Fallon rose to greet him. Morgan watched as Henry embraced his eldest daughter and accepted the kiss on her cheek, but his eyes never left Morgan's.

Morgan spoke quietly yet succinctly from the couch. "I'm here because it's time you acknowledge I'm your daughter."

"I don't know what lies your mama has been filling your head with, but I'm not your father."

"Prove it," Morgan stated. "Take a DNA test. If I'm wrong, which I don't think I am, I'll publicly admit I made the whole story up. But if I'm right—you have to claim me."

"*I* don't have to do a damn thing," Henry responded, moving toward her until he was inches away. "Who do you think you are? Steamrolling your way into our lives, into my home, and making demands?"

"Back off." Ayden jumped to his feet. Morgan appreciated that her big brother was ready to defend her from the big bad wolf, but she could fight her own battles.

"I'm—I'm your daughter." Morgan's voice broke. "How can you treat me this way?"

Fallon stepped between them and pushed her father backward. "Daddy, please...don't make this any worse. Do you have any idea how upset Mom is? I know you're no saint, but admit what you did. Maybe she can forgive you, but if you continue to act as if nothing happened—" she glanced at Morgan "—you're going to dig yourself deeper into a hole."

"Fallon, I appreciate what you're trying to do, but my relationship with Nora is mine alone. I don't need your interference."

"I think you do," Fallon responded hotly. "Look at her!" Once again, Fallon's gaze rested on Morgan. "She has our same eyes, Daddy. I'm surprised I never saw it before, but I suppose I wasn't looking."

"Admit it, Henry!" Ayden snarled. "You cheated on Nora. Just like you did my mother. Be a man about it and own up to what you've done!"

Henry walked up to Ayden. And Morgan thought if looks could kill, both men would have been struck dead in an instant. "Don't get in the middle of this, Ayden, and start stirring up the past. We've come to a truce. Let sleeping dogs lie, son."

Ayden shook his head. "I won't let you deny another child. Not this time and not on my watch."

"Why are you both ganging up on me?" Henry asked, looking at Ayden and Fallon. "Isn't it enough my marriage is in shambles because of this girl?"

*"This girl?"* Tears sprang to Morgan's eyes. "This girl grew up poor with nothing to call my own. No friends. We moved from pillar to post as my mother tried to find work, but it's not easy for an aging Vegas showgirl to find work. She turned to men, hoping they'd take care of her. There was an endless stream of them in and out of her life. In and out of *my* life. So I never had a father, much less a home. And when the men were gone, the drugs started—until eventually her body gave out from the drug use."

"I'm sorry for your childhood. Truly I am, but I owe you nothing. And if either of you—" Henry glanced at his other children "—are with her, then you can show yourselves out because I'm done with this conversation."

Morgan watched in astonishment as the father she'd hoped would acknowledge her walked out of the room. Morgan pulled the knife out of her heart and stood ramrod straight.

"Wow! I can't believe the nerve of that man." Ayden scrubbed the stubble on his jaw. "Just when I think he can't sink any lower, he proves me wrong."

"I have to go." Morgan started toward the exit.

"Wait!" Fallon reached for her arm. "Don't go. Give me some time to talk to him. I can get through to him."

Ayden nodded. "If anyone can, it's Fallon. She's his favorite."

"Ayden…" Fallon glared at him.

He held up his hands in mock surrender.

"Please stay," Fallon said softly. "We can figure this out. *As a family.*"

Morgan snorted. "Didn't you hear him?" She pointed at the empty doorway. "I'm not your family. I'm a nothing. A nobody. So leave me be. I want no part of any of you!" She wrenched her arm away and ran out.

When she got in the car, Morgan was hyperventilating and tears were streaming down her cheeks. She slammed her fists against the steering wheel.

*Damn him!*

*Why had she let him get to her?* She had been determined to be strong and demand what was rightfully hers, but instead Henry Stewart made it obvious he had no intention of recognizing her as his daughter. Instead, he was going to keep his head in the sand and act as if she didn't exist.

Morgan was done with being nice. She was going to the press with her story and give the press an exposé on the great Henry Stewart. She wouldn't allow him to ignore her ever again.

# Four

"I need to see you right away," Ruth Robinson told Jared later that evening.

Jared rarely received a summons from his grandmother. In fact, he tried to stay off her radar. Similar to his father, his grandmother wished he was more like his brother. Chris was the smart one with the brains and business acumen to run Robinson Holdings. Chris had never caused their parents a moment's worry. He did exactly what was expected of him. Attend Harvard. Check. Attain an MBA. Join Robinson Holdings. Check. Check.

Jared, on the other hand, was the screwup. He'd attained his bachelor's degree in marketing by the skin of his teeth. He'd been too busy partying it up with his fraternity brothers of Kappa Alpha Psi and taking the ladies to bed to bother with classes. After graduation, he'd taken a year off to travel Europe and then returned home to work at the family business.

After driving through the hills of Westlake overlooking Austin's skyline, Jared pulled his Porsche Cayman GTS through the gates of his grandmother's estate and parked. The grounds were kept immaculate by her staff and the house was nothing short of castle-like.

Stepping out of the car, he walked the short distance to the front door and rang the doorbell. A uniformed butler greeted him. "Hey, Antoine." He patted the older man's back as he entered the sprawling home. Antoine had been with his grandmother for years and was devoted to her. "Where's Grandmother?"

"In the library," Antoine replied. "Allow me to show you there."

"No need to stand on ceremony. Go back to whatever you were doing. I can find my way." Jared strolled down the Italian marble corridor until he found his grandmother in the mahogany-paneled library seated in a gold leaf armchair.

"Well, look who finally decided to make an appearance." She rose to her feet as he walked over and placed a kiss on her cheek.

Ruth Robinson was nothing short of regal with smooth café au lait skin and expert makeup. Even at seventy-five, she looked amazing in a crisp white shirt with billowing sleeves, black slacks and pearls. Her blondish gray hair was in an elegant coiffed bob that reached her shoulders.

"Grandma, it's good to see you too," Jared replied. "Would you care for a drink?"

"Would love one."

Jared crossed the room to a small bar tucked in the corner. He poured himself a Scotch and a sherry for her, then brought her the glass and settled on a plush tan leather sofa. He leaned back and took a swallow of his drink.

His grandmother sipped her sherry and looked him directly in the eye. "You're going to have to learn the value of time once this scandal hits."

Jared sat upright at her comment. "What are you talking about?"

"Mimi, a dear friend of mine who owns one of the Austin newspapers, gave me a call about an exclusive story hitting their paper tomorrow."

"Oh yeah? What's it about?" Jared brought his tumbler to his lips.

"Your brother knocking up an exotic dancer," Ruth stated unceremoniously.

Jared's drink sputtered from his lips. "Excuse me?"

"For Christ's sake, Jared." His grandmother rolled her eyes. "Clean yourself up."

Jared jumped to his feet, swiftly walked to the bar and grabbed several napkins, then dabbed at his shirt. When he was finished, he returned to stand in front of his grandmother.

"Sit."

Jared didn't argue and sat down. "I don't understand."

"What I've told you is as much as I know," she responded. "Chris has been MIA from Robinson Holdings the last week. He must have known the story was coming. But the worst part is he got the young woman pregnant. It's a travesty. I had such high hopes for your brother, but I guess that leaves you." Her eyes rested on him and Jared shifted uncomfortably in his seat.

"What's that supposed to mean?"

"Chris has shown poor judgment. If he can't manage his own love life, how can he be expected to run a billion-dollar real estate company? The answer is simple. He can't."

"Yes, he can," Jared replied. "So what he got a girl pregnant? It happens. It's not the end of the world. You're making too much of this."

"I disagree. Your grandfather and I worked too hard building up the business and our image as respectable stewards for our investors. We can't allow your brother's bad behavior to negatively impact the company. He's out. And you're in."

"Me?" Jared couldn't contain the disbelief in his tone. "You've got to be kidding. Chris has been groomed to run the company. He's your man. Furthermore, I'm not interested." He tipped back his glass, finished his drink and placed it on the cocktail table in front of him and stood.

"Sit down." His grandmother's voice rose.

"Grandma…"

"I said, sit down, Jared. I won't repeat myself."

Jared sighed, but did as she instructed. "I'm not cut out for this. I don't know the first thing about running the company. I'm in marketing."

"With the right people behind you, you'll learn."

"No." Jared shook his head and pursed his lips. "I can't do it."

"You can and you will." His grandmother stated unequivocally, dismissing his protest. "For too long, we've allowed you to monkey about, but no more. You will pick up the mantel like your father and brother before you."

Jared hated being pushed into a corner and he certainly didn't relish going up against the matriarch of their family, but what she was asking was ridiculous.

"You will start tomorrow." Ruth spoke as if Jared's taking Chris's place was a foregone conclusion. "I've taken the liberty of requesting the files on Chris's current acquisitions." She rose to her feet and went to a side table containing a stack of files. She handed them to Jared. "Read them over tonight and we'll talk in the morning."

He stared at her incredulously. "You're serious about this?"

"Of course. You should know me well enough to know when I make up my mind, it's done."

Jared did know and that was exactly what he was afraid of. He wasn't cut out to run Robinson Holdings. He was good at being a ladies' man and working when he felt like it, but *this*, *this* was too much. And he had no idea how to get out of it. God help them, because the business and their family were in for a bumpy ride.

When Jared made it to his penthouse after leaving his grandmother's, his first call was to Chris. But it went straight to voice mail.

*What was going on?*

Chris's silence was unusual. He never ignored Jared's calls—usually because he was bailing Jared out of a mess of his own creation. But this was different. On his way home, Jared stopped by Chris's usual spots—the gym, the office, a gentleman's club he sometimes frequented—but nothing. Chris didn't want to be found.

Jared couldn't understand his brother giving away everything he'd worked so hard to earn. For what? A woman? They were interchangeable at best or had always been for Jared. He had never met a woman who made him want to risk it all for love. Because that's exactly what Chris was doing. Their grandmother was ready to disinherit him for this stunt.

But this time, Jared was left holding the bag. Was this what it felt like when Jared went MIA after causing trouble? Now that the shoe was on the other foot, Jared was not pleased. He was used to Chris saving the day, but his grandmother was looking to *him*.

The responsibility she was putting on his shoulders was heavy and Jared felt the weight. He felt unsure. Unworthy. *How could he ever live up to Chris?* He couldn't. He would have to prove his worth until he earned his grandmother's respect, but it wouldn't be easy. The question was whether he was up to the task.

Morgan curled up on the sofa in her hotel room with a tub of Ben & Jerry's ice cream she'd picked up on her way back from the Stewart estate. She'd already consumed half a pizza and two beers and was doing her best to eat herself through her troubles.

The last week hadn't been stellar. The only bright spot had been seeing Dane and Iris get married and ride off into the sunset. Maybe she'd been wrong in approaching Henry after the reception, but she'd thought confronting him in public would force his hand. Make him own up to the truth that he'd cheated on Nora and had a child with another woman.

Morgan hadn't banked on Henry's temper. Or that he would completely shut her out and refuse to acknowledge her existence. Even when confronted by his own children, who begged for the truth, Henry refused to admit it.

*Maybe she was better off not having a father?*

None of the men her mother ever brought into her life had been father material. They were interested in using Crystal only for their own pleasure. Morgan hated seeing her mother dependent on them and so desperate for attention she'd take it from anyone. Including *him*.

Morgan sank her spoon into the chunky mixture and kept eating as she recalled one of those men. Troy Wilkins had been one of her mother's boyfriends. Often, he'd stay the night and when he did, Morgan locked her bedroom door. She'd hated him on sight. He was lean and wiry with ominous-looking eyes that were always roving over her. Morgan tried to steer clear, but one day when she'd come home from high school, he'd been at their apartment. Troy told her Crystal had gone to the grocery store.

Immediately Morgan invented an excuse and tried to make a quick exit, but Troy was faster than her. He'd slammed the front door and put the chain across, locking her inside with him. Morgan had been terrified and rightfully so. Troy told her it was time she was friendlier to him and had grabbed her by the arm and hauled Morgan into her bedroom.

He'd thrown her on the bed and covered her with his weight before she could move. She remembered the stale scent of cigarettes permeating his skin, the smell of alcohol on his breath. Then he was lifting her shirt up, palming her small breasts and rubbing his crotch against her. Morgan tried to fight him off, knowing if she didn't, he would assault her, but he was too strong. His hands were reaching for the snap on her jeans when they both heard the door. Her mother was calling out to them.

"If you tell your mother, I'll deny this ever happened. Who do you think she'll believe?"

Morgan would never forget the look in his eye. That was when she'd known she couldn't stay there. She'd had to get out. If she didn't, he'd come back and there would be no guarantee she'd be as lucky the next time. And so she'd run. She'd packed her meager belongings and left. She'd gone to her mom's friend Marilyn, another dancer, and begged to sleep on her couch. Even though Marilyn had two kids of her own, it was better than living in fear.

Marilyn allowed Morgan to stay on the sofa so long as she cooked, cleaned and tended her two kids while Marilyn worked nights as a dancer. Morgan happily agreed. The funny thing about it was—Crystal hadn't cared. She seemed happy to be rid of Morgan because she was cramping her style.

Somehow Morgan found a way to finish her senior year. Due to her good grades, she'd been able to attend the University of Southern California on a full scholarship.

When she thought about it, all her struggles were because both her parents refused to do right by her.

Morgan put down her ice cream on the cocktail table and reached for her iPad. Searching the web, she found the email for a local gossip blogger in Austin.

It was time one of her parents—Henry Stewart—paid the price.

# Five

*Jared, your father can't come back. His health is still too tenuous.*

Monday morning, as the elevator zoomed up to the top floor of the office building where Robinson Holdings was housed, Jared thought about his mother's words from last night.

*You're going to have to put on your big boy pants and do what needs to be done*, his father had said.

Jared rolled his eyes as he thought about his father's condescending tone. He knew what a huge task it would be stepping into Chris's shoes. But there didn't seem to be anyone else to fill the role.

When the elevator chimed on the top floor, Jared exited wearing one of the many custom suits in his wardrobe. This time, however, he looked at everyone with new eyes. Instead of traipsing to his office for a few hours, he would be the decision maker. Many of these people depended on him. It was a scary position.

When he opened his office door, he was surprised to find his grandmother. She was dressed elegantly in a blazer over a silk shirt and trousers. "Grandmother, I didn't expect you."

She smiled, which was a rarity. "Since Clay's health precludes him from being here and your wayward brother is off with some dancer, I'm here to give you some reinforcement."

"I thought you've been retired from the business for years."

"I'm still on the board and come in from time to time. Keeps the mind strong and a woman of my age young."

"You don't look a day over fifty."

"No need to charm me, Jared. Leave that to the ladies whose hearts you have strewn across Austin."

Jared clutched his chest with one hand. "Grandma, you wound me."

"There's a board of director's meeting in an hour," Ruth said sternly. "Let's get down to business."

Two hours later, Jared already wanted to throw in the towel. The board of directors meeting had been a free-for-all with many speculating about what would happen to the company now that their CEO had vanished for parts unknown. Then his grandmother dropped the bombshell that *Jared* was taking over as CEO in Chris's absence. Many of the directors revolted. Some outright laughed and thought it was a joke.

"Jared doesn't know the first thing about running this billion-dollar enterprise. He's about fast cars and women," one of the older board of directors scoffed.

"Jared may be green around the gills," Ruth responded evenly, "but listen when I say this. A *Robinson* will always run Robinson Holdings." Then she'd thrown them all for a loop when she'd said, "I'll be on-site in an advisory capacity to assist."

"You're putting the company at risk," another board member commented.

"I took a risk when I hired you, didn't I?" his grandmother replied.

After that, the meeting had continued smoothly with Ruth steering the ship. Now they were back in his office talking next steps over coffee.

"As head of the company, you'll need to keep your head low and avoid scandal. I don't want a repeat of what happened with your brother."

"I'm not Chris." Jared kept his affairs discreet.

"Good. Because as you can see, the board is looking for leadership. Your reputation as a ladies' man is well-known, which is why I think it's time you found a wife."

"I'm not ready for marriage, Grandmother. That's not in the cards for me. Maybe in the future, but not now."

She ignored him. "It would go a long way with the board embracing your leadership if you were settled."

"Don't you mean it would make you feel better?"

"Same difference."

"Well, you needn't worry because I already have a girlfriend." *Jeez. What possessed him to say that?* Jared knew why. He was sick and tired of being compared to Chris. Although he loved his brother, he wasn't incompetent.

His grandmother's large brown eyes grew wide in amazement. "Why is this the first I'm hearing about her?"

"Because it's new," Jared continued with the lie. *What choice did he have?* He'd already put his foot in his mouth. "And the press are always scrutinizing me, so we've kept our relationship private."

"I would like to meet her."

"It's too soon, Grandmother."

"Rubbish. You'll bring her over and introduce me." Ruth pulled a file out of the many stacked on his desk. "Let's get to work. You have a lunch meeting with a potential client Chris has been wooing and you need to be prepared."

His grandmother might consider the matter closed, but Jared certainly didn't. He didn't have a girlfriend. Nor did he have any prospects. Most of the women in his phone were of the affair variety. They were not the kind of women you brought home to meet your grandma. He was going to have to do some fancy footwork because he needed a fake girlfriend pronto!

Morgan felt confident as she drove to the posh restaurant where she was meeting the blogger Ally Peters. She told herself she was doing the right thing. By exposing Henry Stewart as her father, he would no longer be able to hide. He would be forced to face the truth and confront the allegations. *Could he ignore them?* There was always that possibility. But from the little she'd heard about Nora Stewart, she was *all* about reputation. She wouldn't abide having her family's name smeared in the mud. So one way or another the truth would come out and Morgan would be vindicated.

*But at what cost?* an inner voice asked. Last night, Morgan had received calls and texts from Fallon and Ayden respectively. Both of them had offered olive branches and wanted to talk, but the time for talking was over. It was time for action. The press was already speculating about whether her story was true. Since Morgan rarely had her picture taken and wasn't on social media, they couldn't find a recent photo. She was thankful for some anonymity.

Morgan pulled her Honda up to the valet and hopped out. She'd dressed smartly for her lunch in a sophisticated striped dress that hit at the thigh along with some knee-high boots and her favorite fedora hat.

"I have a reservation with Ally Peters?" Morgan told the hostess.

"Right this way." The statuesque blonde led her to a curved booth where the online gossip columnist was already seated. Her blog was extremely popular and had over two million followers.

"Morgan?" When she nodded, the redhead stood and air-kissed her. "Please have a seat. I already ordered some club soda. Hope you don't mind?"

"No, that's fine."

"I'm so excited to hear you dish." Ally rubbed her hands together with glee and a smile spread across her heart-shaped face. "You said you had a big reveal about a wealthy family here in Austin?"

"I do," Morgan said, but stopped herself as the waitress appeared. After ordering a peach sangria, Morgan continued. "I'm hoping you can get the truth out there because I feel as if I've been silenced."

"I hear you, girlfriend. And I've got an ear to listen."

Morgan was leaning her head toward Ally when a familiar voice from a table several feet away stopped her cold. *It couldn't be.* They'd met only once, but Morgan was certain she'd never forget the voice of the man she'd nearly gone to bed with. When he turned his head, Morgan caught sight of him.

Jared.

Morgan sucked in a deep breath. She would recognize that tall drink of water anywhere. Those bedroom eyes. The full, thick lips that had kissed her until sensations coursed through her, electrifying her entire being.

"Morgan, you were saying?" Ally interrupted her musings to bring her back to their conversation, but Morgan's brain was mush.

Morgan couldn't stop staring at Jared or pull her gaze away from his mouth, remembering how he'd plundered hers with it. Her mind was spinning. She never thought she'd see Jared again. *What were the odds they'd ever run into each other again?* It had to be fate or kismet or something.

Then Jared looked up and their eyes connected from across the room. His gaze held hers in a searing tether, causing a shiver to run down Morgan's spine. His pupils were black and bottomless pools of ink and Morgan felt her cheeks getting hot. She blinked and broke the stare.

"Who are you ogling?" Ally turned to look across the room. Then she spun back around with a wide grin on her mouth. "Is something going on between you and Jared? Omigod, it would be sooo delicious. This morning, the newspapers had a story about his brother, Chris, running off with some stripper. And now this…"

"*This* is nothing," Morgan said quickly—too quickly because Ally's brow rose. "I was merely looking at an attractive man."

"And he was staring right back at you. There's a story there."

"You're mistaken. My story is about the…"

Morgan didn't get to finish her statement because suddenly Jared was standing at their table. He looked as he had the night of the wedding, except today he was in a gray suit with a blue-and-white-striped tie. He was every bit the corporate tycoon, which she wouldn't have guessed him to be.

"Morgan." Jared looked at her, ignoring Ally, who was positively giddy.

"Jared."

"I see my timing is immaculate," he said, not taking his eyes off Morgan. "Mind if I sit down?" He didn't wait for an answer and immediately sat across from Morgan.

"No, not at all." Ally spoke since Morgan was tongue-tied at seeing the sexy stranger she'd fantasized about in the flesh.

"What are you doing, Morgan?" Jared inquired, staring at her.

"Ally and I were chatting about a big story I have."

His frown went deep as he peered at her intently. "Do you really think that's wise?"

"It's none of your business," Morgan stated hotly. "If I recall, you don't want to be a knight in shining armor."

His eyes darkened and sexual energy crackled in the air like static electricity. When Morgan ran her tongue over her suddenly dry lips, his eyes dropped to her mouth and then quickly jerked back to her eyes as if he were fighting some inner demon.

Jared looked at the other occupant of the booth. "Ally, would you mind if she rescheduled your meeting?"

"No, I…" Morgan tried in vain to talk, but one withering look from Jared cut her sentence short.

"Of course I don't mind." Ally slid out of the booth and gathered her purse and tablet. Morgan knew the gossip columnist was conjuring all sorts of juicy gossip about Jared and Morgan. Not Henry Stewart.

Jared was ruining everything. Why did *he* have to be here today?

Ally reached inside her purse and pulled out a business card, but instead of handing it to Morgan, who'd been the one to call her, Ally handed it to Jared. "Give me a call. I'd love to talk to you more." She gave him a wink and seconds later was walking out of the restaurant.

Morgan fumed in her seat. "How dare you?"

She didn't get another word out before Jared was beside her, sliding his hand behind her neck and bringing his mouth down on hers.

Jared had no self-control when it came to this woman. When he saw Morgan sitting with Ally, a notorious gossip blogger, his heart slammed against his chest. He'd known what she was about to do. Blow her life up. *He had to stop her.* Kissing her had been the last thing on his agenda, but now that he'd started, he didn't want the kiss to end. He could kiss her all day and all night.

He relished Morgan's fruity taste from the cocktail she'd been drinking. Her lips were soft and pillowy and clung to his. When his tongue darted inside to meet hers, they danced together, making his pulse throb. But they were in public, so Jared pulled back.

Morgan stared at him wide-eyed, her mouth slightly swollen and her cheeks flushed. "Did you kiss me to shut me up?"

Jared grinned. "Maybe. Did it work?"

Morgan chewed her lip and Jared could feel his erection press against his zipper. "You know it did, but stopping me from going after Ally won't prevent the inevitable. I intend to have my say."

"To what end?" Jared inquired. "It won't make Henry accept you. In fact, he and the other Stewarts might resent you for the negative press you're heaping on them. Did you think about that? And what about Dane, your brother?"

"When he gets back, he'll find I've tendered my resignation. I can't continue working for him after all that's happened."

"I think that's a mistake because Dane will want to get to know you, but regardless, don't you think he's been through enough in the media the last year without you dredging up more family secrets?"

Morgan was silent. He hoped she was listening to what he said. The press had been all over Dane when the story broke about him falling in love with Iris, the woman who'd used his anonymous sperm donation to become pregnant. Having their romance heavily televised had come at a price. He didn't want that for his friend or Morgan again.

"What do you expect me to do?" Morgan finally choked out.

"Be patient. And listen to me. I'm trying to save you from yourself."

"I don't need saving."

"Might I remind you of the stunts you pulled at the wedding? Your big revelation. Getting drunk. Attempting to spend the night with a complete stranger."

"You're not a stranger anymore," Morgan responded. "I know your full name now. Jared Robinson."

Jared couldn't resist smiling. "Yes, you do."

"So tell me, Mr. Robinson, why did you leave without...?"

"Without making love to you?" Jared offered. Because he'd wanted to. *Badly.* He'd wanted to caress every inch of her body and take her to heights of profound pleasure. Making love to Morgan would have been very satisfying. His loins had throbbed for days from unrequited lust, but he'd also wanted Morgan to remember him in the morning and not regret her actions.

Morgan flushed, clearly embarrassed at his directness. But then she surprised him, by glancing up at him underneath her lashes. "Why? Any other man might have taken advantage."

"I'm not any other man."

"No, you're not."

"I'm glad. And I'm going to continue being a man of mystery by offering you a deal you can't refuse."

"And what's that?"

"I need a girlfriend. A very public one and I've decided you're great for the role. So how about it?"

# Six

Morgan threw back her head and let out an uproarious laugh. It was a reflexive response because she didn't know what to make of Jared Robinson. Sometimes he was the sexy stranger she'd met at a wedding. Other times he was a white knight trying to save her. He kept her off-kilter and she couldn't figure him out.

Jared frowned. "What's so funny?"

"You were joking, right?" Morgan asked when her laughter subsided.

"No, I'm not."

Jared's expression was somber and Morgan realized she'd miscalculated. "You're serious? You want me to be your girlfriend? But why? According to Ally, you're quite the ladies' man. Stands to reason you don't need a girl like me."

"I may not *need* a girl like you, but you're the girl I *want*," Jared declared.

Morgan's heart went pitter pat. Wasn't it enough she felt as if he'd permanently branded her with his steaming-hot kiss? Her lips were still tingling from the searing heat of his mouth. His kiss had literally awakened her body to what was possible.

"Why?"

"I would think it's obvious. You're a beautiful woman and I'm attracted to you, Morgan. And if I'm not mistaken, the feeling is mutual. We could enjoy each other's company while you help me with my image problem."

"And why is your image important right now?"

"My brother, Chris, who was running the family business, has vanished with an exotic dancer. He left without a trace, causing a vacuum in leadership. My family and board of directors are looking to me to fill that void. Considering my dubious reputation, it might be an easier pill for them to swallow if I was a bit more…*settled*."

"In a committed relationship?"

He pointed with his index finger at her. "There you have it. Having a girlfriend would ease their concerns about my former status as a ladies' man."

"And what would be in it for me?"

A sexy grin spread across his full lips. "Time spent in my sparkling company and I'm a pretty good date if I do say so myself. And if you were my girlfriend, you'd want for nothing. And as a bonus, you can have the family you've always wanted—*mine*—for a limited period. Once the board is settled, we end our association."

"Your suggestion is a win-win for you," Morgan replied, reaching for her sangria and taking a sip. "As much as I love the offer of spending time with you and borrowing your family, I'm going to have to decline."

"Why? Do you have somewhere else pressing to be? Or perhaps a significant other I'm not aware of?"

Morgan laughed. As if. She'd never had a boyfriend because she'd never allowed anyone to get close enough to become one. Her near assault had frightened her from getting involved with men. In college, she'd watched her roommates and other friends falling in and out of love, but it hadn't happened for her. Morgan feared something was wrong with her. Until Jared. Until the night when she'd made out with a stranger.

"Well?"

Morgan realized he was still waiting for her to respond to his questions. "There's no one else."

*Did his shoulders visibly relax?* Morgan wondered. Or was she projecting? "Then why not?"

"Because I'm still trying to figure out my place in life. It may not be with the Stewarts, but it's not with you, either."

"Fair enough. But didn't you say you've given your notice to Dane? That means you're unemployed for the moment, so why not stay here in Austin for a spell. Afterward, when we go our separate ways I could help you. I have lots of connections. I can help you attain whatever future you desire. So tell me, what's it going to take to convince you to agree?"

Morgan allowed herself a swift glance underneath her lashes at Jared. She let her eyes linger on the sculpted planes of his face and his exceptionally firm and square chin. The impeccable cut of Jared's suit and his indefinable aura of wealth were entrancing. Morgan felt hypnotized. *Was that why she was starting to give his offer serious consideration?* Was she really going to throw all her common sense away and plunge herself into the thrill of the unknown?

No, she had to think logically. Tearing away her gaze from his for a moment, she looked down. It was easy for him to make her such an outrageous offer because in his world women were ornaments he could discard when he was done with them. If she did this, Morgan would have to ensure she was in a better position when it was over than when they began. Because there was no assurance Henry would ever accept her into the Stewart family, which meant she was on her own. Since she'd tendered her resignation to Dane, she would need a job and she didn't want any help from her brother.

"I want a job at a network or production company," Morgan stated. Film was in her blood. "I've been working for

Dane over the last year and I've learned a lot. Not to mention the degree I have. An MFA in screenwriting."

"I'll make it happen," Jared replied. "So can I consider you my girlfriend now?"

"Yes. Should we shake on it?"

"I have a better idea."

As he slid closer to her in the booth, understanding dawned on her. Morgan tilted her head back a little as he slowly came toward her. Lifting his hand to cup her face, he dipped his head and closed his mouth over hers.

Jared had to kiss her again. Morgan was so sweet and honest. He appreciated her directness. It was a huge turn-on. And so he kissed her with all the passion and longing he'd tried to clamp down but couldn't. Morgan clutched the lapels of his suit while she pressed her soft trembling lips to his, which told Jared she was as much a slave to their passion as he was. Slowly, he straightened and looked at her.

Her hazel-gray eyes shimmered with desire and made Jared's groin tighten in response. "It's settled then. You're mine."

His possessive tone must have snapped Morgan out of her passion-induced gaze because she replied, "I'm not yours or anybody's. I'm my own person. But I will help you and in return you'll help me get my dream job."

"Yes of course." Jared stared at her luminous eyes fringed with long black lashes and imagined her thick and lustrous black hair spread out on a pillow as he feasted on her.

Morgan may not have been his usual type. In the looks department, yes, but he found her too unguarded. She was unlike his typical lovers who were sleek and sophisticated. They welcomed him into their beds because of his name and rumored prowess. But she had an air of innocence, which told him that night in La Jolla was a fluke.

"So what do I need to do first?"

"Convince my grandmother Ruth that our relationship is legit."

Morgan smiled. "How hard can it be to convince a sweet old lady we're a couple?"

Jared snorted. "You don't know my grandmother. The woman is a force to be reckoned with. She helped my grandfather build the company."

"She sounds like an amazing woman."

"She is. And very astute," he responded. "We need to be on top of our game if we're going to convince her, which means we should probably spend some time getting to know each other. Otherwise, she'll sense something isn't right."

Morgan leaned back in the booth. "Considering I'm unemployed, my schedule is pretty open."

He reached inside his jacket pocket and produced his iPhone. "Good. What's your phone number?" She told him and he punched in her digits. "I have to get to a meeting, but I'll be in touch." He rose to his feet and buttoned his suit jacket. "We'll make a good team, you and me."

He turned away and strode out of the restaurant. He had to. Morgan was temptation personified and he could easily get distracted trying to seduce her. Jared would have to ensure they weren't alone together often. Otherwise, he was certain this arrangement of theirs would end with the two of them wrapped in each other's arms to the exclusion of everything else.

Had she really just agreed to be Jared's pretend girlfriend? Morgan thought as she walked through the revolving doors of her hotel that afternoon. *And exactly what did that entail?* They hadn't gone over the details or his expectations other than that he would take care of her. Did that mean he was going to take care of her hotel bill?

Not long after she'd settled in her room, she heard a

knock. She wasn't expecting anyone. Padding to the door barefoot, she glanced through the peephole and was surprised to see Ayden on the other side. "Please open up. I'd like to talk."

Morgan swung open the door. "Why would you want to talk to me when I've been ignoring you?"

Ayden swept past her into the room without an invitation. "Because you're my sister."

Morgan closed the door and turned around to face him. She folded her arms across her chest and regarded him. Her brother was handsome. In slacks and button-down shirt, he looked like their father. "So you believe me?"

Ayden's brow furrowed. "Of course I do. I don't doubt Henry was capable of cheating on Nora like he did my mother."

"Thank you." She walked over to the small sitting area and sat down. Ayden joined her.

"Years ago, I promised Fallon I'd be a better big brother," Ayden began. "I'm here today to be that brother. You got a raw deal."

Morgan couldn't resist a small smile. She didn't want to like him, but she did. "Ayden…"

"Regardless of whether our father says you're his daughter, you're my sister."

"Why won't he admit the truth?" Morgan asked softly.

Ayden shrugged. "Pride? I can tell you Henry isn't any easy man to like, let alone love."

"How did you forgive him after everything he did to you?" Morgan knew Ayden's story. Henry had divorced his mother, Lillian, to marry Nora, the woman he'd cheated on her with. He gave Lillian a small settlement and never acknowledged Ayden as his firstborn until recently.

"I haven't," Ayden responded. "I've learned to accept the things I cannot change and keep peace for the family, but I haven't forgotten. Because as he has with you, Henry has never admitted he did anything wrong."

"I don't know if I can let this go."

"And if Henry doesn't ever accept you, what then? You have to move on with your life, Morgan. No good can come from you spending your life waiting for something that may never happen. Trust me, I know."

"I appreciate that you came to offer your support. It means a lot to me."

"Fallon would have joined me, but Dylan has a stomach bug and she's at home with him. Both of us—and I'm sure Dane—will be by your side."

"Have you heard from him?"

Ayden shook his head. "I don't expect to, after such a harrowing six months. Dane and Iris wanted to be off the radar for a few weeks. Her parents are taking care of Jayden." He reached for her hand across the short distance. "Dane may be upset with you at first, but he'll accept you just like me and Fallon."

Morgan's mouth lifted in a smile. "You're pretty good at this big brother thing."

"I've had some practice." Ayden stood. "I'll get out of your hair, but if you need anything I'm here for you." He leaned down and enveloped her in a warm hug Morgan hadn't known she'd needed.

A lump formed in her throat when he moved away. It was nice to finally have someone in *her* corner. "We'll talk soon, okay, kid?" Ayden stroked her cheek and then he was gone.

Ayden knew what it was like to walk in her shoes. Yet, he'd gone on to become successful and start Stewart Investments. *Was he right?* Should she let the desire to be acknowledged by their father go? Morgan wasn't sure she could, but she would try.

# Seven

Jared surprised his grandmother and the board the rest of the week by working twelve-hour days and immersing himself in Robinson Holdings. He knew the business deals in progress or he wouldn't have been able to handle the marketing campaigns, but he'd never been involved in the development stage or seeing a project from beginning to end.

With Ruth's guidance, he was learning about everything firsthand. There was excitement blended with fear, but it bolstered his confidence when he saw respect in the eyes of his peers. Jared wasn't coasting like he usually did. He was digging in and finding he actually enjoyed what he was doing.

When the end of the day came on Friday, it shocked Jared to realize the week had gone by without him contacting Morgan. He felt like a heel for abandoning her when he'd been the one to suggest she become his pretend girlfriend. But he would make good on his promise.

Glancing at his Rolex, Jared saw it was almost dinnertime. It would be nice to spend the evening with a beautiful woman. His grandmother would notice if anything was amiss so he needed to ensure that he and Morgan were on solid footing. He reached for his phone and dialed her cell.

"So you didn't forget about me?" Morgan asked when she picked up.

"Forget you? As if that were possible," Jared said

smoothly. "But in all seriousness, it's been a busy week here. My brother had a lot of pans in the fire, so I've been getting up to speed. Are you free for dinner? I was hoping we could grab a bite at my favorite spot."

"Sure. What time?"

"I can pick you up in an hour."

"That's okay. I can meet you there. What's the address?"

*Why did she have to be obstinate?* "No woman of mine would drive herself," Jared responded. "I would be expected to pick you up, so I'll see you at seven."

"Fine."

He smiled after Morgan gave him her hotel information. Morgan was getting the hang of it. He always got his way.

When Morgan opened the door, she prayed her makeup and hair piled atop her head looked flawless because Jared stood in her doorway looking every bit the man of power. He was stylish and polished in a tailored suit that showed off the broadness of his shoulders. He smiled, and his dimples and deliciously full lips were irresistible.

*He was sexy. Too damn sexy.*

Morgan's heart swelled and her pulse quickened when his eyes roved over her figure. "I hope what I'm wearing is okay. You didn't tell me the attire."

"You, um…look good." His voice sounded strangled.

"Good?" She pouted. "I was hoping for a better adjective."

Jared cleared his throat and his eyes moved slowly over her curves in the sleek strapless black dress. A muscle tightened in his jaw. "How about hot."

She glanced up at him and their eyes locked, causing her belly to flutter. "I'll take that." She stepped into the corridor, closing the door behind her because no way was she allowing him inside. He was looking at her like she was dessert.

Jared walked beside her, his hand lightly resting on the small of her back as they made their way to the elevator. It wasn't anything untoward; instead, it caused Morgan to feel safe.

After a short elevator ride, they disembarked in the lobby. Morgan was surprised when Jared laced his fingers with hers. Only when he'd settled her in the passenger seat of his Porsche did Morgan exhale.

She reminded herself this date was pretend. It wasn't real. Jared didn't want her. He needed a girlfriend to convince his grandmother he was a reformed playboy, but that didn't stop her womanly bits from wanting it to mean more.

The restaurant and jazz bar Jared took Morgan to wasn't the flashy place she'd expected. She'd assumed he would take her someplace the local celebrities went to so they could be "seen."

"What's wrong?" Jared asked when they were seated at a secluded table for two by the owner. "Don't you like the restaurant? They have a great jazz quartet and singer."

Morgan smiled. "I love it. I just didn't think you would."

"You think I'm bourgie?"

She laughed. "There's nothing wrong with being used to the finer things in life. It's how you were raised."

"I also appreciate simple, good food," Jared countered, looking down at his menu.

"I've offended you," Morgan said, frowning. "I'm sorry if I made an assumption. It's just you're *you* and I thought you'd want us to be seen, which is why I wore this dress."

Jared's eyes roamed once more over her. "The dress is a keeper and as for our location, I wanted someplace where we could talk and be ourselves and not worry about prying ears."

"Thank you."

The owner came over with a bottle of red wine and poured them both glasses.

"A toast," Jared said. "To learning more about you."

"I can hardly wait." And Morgan couldn't. Something told her the evening was going to be very intriguing. She tapped her glass against his.

Jared watched Morgan over the rim of his wineglass. Tonight, her dark tresses were in a chic updo showing off her beautiful caramel-brown complexion, which was enhanced by dramatic smoky eye makeup and a nude lip. When she'd opened her hotel door earlier and he'd caught a glimpse of her cleavage, Jared had wanted to push her backward into the room and kiss and stroke her until they both forgot their names.

Instead, they were at his favorite restaurant pretending to act as if the chemistry between them wasn't burning red-hot. His eyes dipped down to her mouth as she spoke about growing up in Las Vegas. He liked the way she licked her lips every so often and his desire stirred. He was drawn to her. He had been from that first night when she stood across from him and he'd seen her warring with herself about confronting her father.

He wondered where her mother was in all this. "So, I know your father is Henry Stewart, but where's your mother? Is she here in Austin or Vegas?"

Morgan shook her head. "She passed away."

"I'm sorry for your loss. You must miss her."

"We weren't close," she continued. "She wasn't there for me growing up."

"Which is why you want your father in your life?"

"You can't miss something you've never had, right?" She reached for her wineglass.

Jared sensed Morgan was covering up her true feelings. She wouldn't be in Austin trying to connect with Henry if she didn't miss having a father. Because without her mother, she was alone. But he wouldn't pry. "My mother is the exact opposite. Mary Robinson is a homemaker and proud of it. Raising me and my brother was her great achievement."

"That's wonderful."

Morgan lowered her lashes and Jared could see the mood taking a downward spiral, so he pivoted. "Tell me about your first boyfriend."

"Great segue there." Morgan chuckled. "I never really had one unless you count Victor Nelson. He wasn't much to speak of. He was a nerd who loved movies. He used to try to sneak kisses in between study hall."

"Sounds mischievous. Did you ever sneak out of the house to go to a club with a fake ID?"

Morgan shook her head. "No, I was pretty tame because I was determined to have a better future than my mama. But something tells me you were the life of the party."

Jared shrugged. "What can I say? I like to have fun, but back then I had a wingman."

"Dane?"

He nodded. "He and I were hell-raisers. Skipping class, making out with girls, driving fast cars. Our parents were at their wits' end until they sent me away to boarding school."

"But that didn't stop you?"

"No." He pursed his lips. "I was just farther out of reach to my parents."

"C'mon, Jared, a guy as good-looking as you had to have been in love once, right?"

Jared looked across the table at Morgan. He hoped she wasn't getting some notion in her head about marriage, babies and white picket fences. Theirs was a mutually beneficial arrangement with an expiration date. "Never much cared for the notion. How about you? You have some great love that got away?"

Morgan shook her head. "No, can't say that I have."

"Then we're well matched." His eyes traveled to her cleavage. "Though I have to admit I have been in lust." He leaned across the table and placed his hand over hers. Sparks shot through his body and Jared had to work overtime to conceal the explosive desire he felt.

"L-lust."

"Yes," Jared murmured. "Tell me you feel it too."

"I feel like we should order," Morgan stated, cutting him down to size. He did as she asked and motioned the waiter over. The service was spot on and it didn't take long for their meals to arrive and for them to tuck in. As they ate, Jared pondered Morgan's reticence. He didn't understand why was she acting as if she didn't want him when he knew it was far from the truth? The kisses they'd shared thus far were electric. He still remembered the sweet erotic taste of her kiss and his body yearned for more. He would have to remind her how good it was.

Jared's dark intense eyes blazed into Morgan and she had trouble breathing. Her heart was already pounding in her chest and her pulse raced.

Heat. Desire. Want. All those emotions flared through Morgan. She could feel her nipples harden in her dress as she fought the sexual tension swelling between her and Jared. She didn't know what do with it. She was out of her element and didn't have liquor to hide behind.

"Is it wrong to want to explore the passion between us?" Jared inquired. "Because that night in your hotel room— you were prepared to go to bed with me."

Morgan swallowed the lump in her throat. "That was different."

"Please don't tell me you're going to use the cliché excuse you were drinking too much?"

"No, I wasn't going to do that, but I will admit I was emotional that night." Morgan couldn't help missing Jared eyeing her suspiciously as if he knew she was selling a load of hogwash. "Overwhelmed even, by Henry's rejection."

"Perhaps I wouldn't be confused if you weren't hot one minute and cold the next."

"I'm sorry if I'm giving you mixed signals," Morgan said. "So let me be clear. Although I might be your pretend girlfriend that doesn't mean it comes with fringe benefits. Perhaps it's best if we keep our arrangement strictly platonic so as to not complicate our relationship. Now, if you'll excuse me, I'm going to go powder my nose." She bolted upright and ran straight for the ladies' room.

Morgan knew she was running, running from an attraction that frightened her in its intensity. If she allowed herself, he could easily become her first lover.

*And would that be so bad?* her inner voice asked.

Perhaps it was time for her to stop living in fear and take a risk. If not for love, then for an undeniable passion.

Glancing in the bathroom mirror, Morgan saw her cheeks were flushed and there was a light bead of sweat on her forehead. That's what Jared did to her. He had her all hot and bothered.

*Pull it together.*

When she returned to their table, Jared was contemplative. "I'm sorry if I've offended you with my directness about intimacy. I will honor your wishes." He glanced behind her. "Ah, dessert is coming. Martin's crème brûlée is to die for."

Morgan gave him a half smile. Had she ruined the night with her past fears and insecurities? Because a guy like Jared wouldn't keep coming back if she kept brushing him off.

Jared backed off. Morgan was spooked and he didn't know why. The attraction between them was undeniable, palpable and inevitable, yet Morgan refused to acknowledge it.

Something was holding her back.

He doubted they'd scratched the surface on her past, but it made him curious to know more. Usually if a woman rebuffed his advances he was on to the next, but Morgan was different and it wasn't because she'd agreed to his arrangement.

It was more. *She* was more. Jared couldn't put his finger on it, but Morgan was intriguing. He would have to arrange their next date quickly in order not to lose momentum and to delve into what made Morgan Stewart tick.

He would have to approach her like a newborn foal. He would have to be delicate and tender. Listen to what she was and wasn't saying. Only then would he stand a chance of figuring out this incredibly complex woman.

After dessert, Jared drove Morgan home. A thick uncomfortable silence hung in the air. Morgan felt as if she'd ruined the evening by being such a prude. A handsome sexy man like Jared Robinson *wanted* her and wasn't afraid to show it. But instead, she'd pushed him away.

No wonder he was angry. Morgan wouldn't be surprised if he decided to end their arrangement altogether. No one wanted a stick-in-the-mud. *Why couldn't she be normal?*

When the car stopped, Morgan realized they'd pulled into the hotel driveway. A valet came to greet them, but Jared shook his head, so they sat with the car idling. Morgan was grateful when Jared spoke first.

"I'm sorry for coming on too strong. You want a purely platonic relationship for the duration of this arrangement, so I will keep my hands to myself." He turned to Morgan and held them up in mock surrender. "But I can't promise you I won't be tempted because you're a beautiful woman."

Morgan hazarded a glance in his direction. "Thank you."

"I took the liberty of paying your hotel bill," Jared continued. "I hope you don't mind. We didn't discuss how this was going to work. Since you're staying in Austin indefinitely, I figured you could stay in one of the apartments in the city we keep for executives. You might be more comfortable there."

"Jared, that sounds wonderful."

"Good. I'll have my assistant arrange everything and call you with the details." He hopped out of the car. Morgan wished they had more time, but instead he was holding her car door open and helping her out of the vehicle.

"We should hang out again before meeting my grandmother," Jared said, walking Morgan inside the hotel to the elevator bank. "Something more comfortable and less like a date."

The ding of the elevator made Morgan involuntarily step toward the doors.

"So what do you say?" Jared asked with a smirk.

"Sounds great. You really do know how to make a comeback."

Jared shrugged. "You ain't seen nothing yet." And with a wink, the door of the elevator closed.

Morgan leaned back against the panels and released a deep sigh. She hadn't messed it up. Jared was still willing to work with her and help her achieve her goals. *So why did it feel as if she'd lost out on something monumental?*

# Eight

"So when am I going to meet your girlfriend?" his grandmother asked when she unexpectedly came over for Sunday brunch at Jared's parents' house.

Since it was such a nice day, they were seated out on the lanai. "Soon, Grandmother. We've only known each other a short time and I don't want to frighten her away by taking her to meet the parents so soon."

His grandmother squashed the notion. "Nonsense. That's exactly why she should meet us to be sure she can keep up. We're not an easy bunch to love."

Jared knew that to be true. His grandmother, like his father, believed in the motto of tough love. There was no coddling or hugs in Jared's world. There was only winning and losing. He remembered a time when he was seven years old and had been on the soccer team. Their team had lost the tournament, but they'd each received participation trophies. When he'd gotten home, his father had taken his from Jared.

*Better you learn now, son, in life there's one winner. And you lost. Accept it and fight harder to win next time.* Jared had never forgotten that lesson.

"I'll bring Morgan over next weekend," Jared finally said.

"Excellent," his grandmother replied. "Let's hope you didn't pick this one up at a strip bar like your brother."

"Ruth, must you be so harsh?" his mother said. "I know you don't approve of Chris's actions, but we don't know the full story."

"I know enough. Chris turned his back on the company, on the family. What more is there to say?"

His mother glanced at his father. True to form, his father never stood up to his own mother, so Jared spoke. "Mom is right. We won't let you speak ill of Chris when he isn't here to defend himself."

His grandmother leaned back in her chair and regarded him. "So you're finally getting a backbone." She sipped her mimosa. "I like it, Jared."

Jared rolled his eyes upward and prayed for patience. How was he supposed to bring Morgan into this dysfunctional family when he could hardly stand it himself? He prayed the tough, fearless Morgan who'd stood up to Henry in front of a crowd of wedding guests was the one who came to dinner on Sunday. Otherwise, his grandmother would eat her for breakfast.

Morgan moved into the stunning corner unit located on the thirty-first floor of Residences at W Austin that afternoon.

Morgan was in awe as she walked through the condominium. The open plan apartment had white oak wood floors, a gourmet kitchen with quartz counters, ten-foot ceilings and floor-to-ceiling windows. The master suite held a large king-size bed and an impressive master bath with double vanity, walk-in shower and garden tub. The California closet would easily fit Morgan's meager clothing.

Morgan plopped herself on the buttery-soft leather couch and sighed. Was this the lifestyle she would have grown accustomed to if she'd been raised a Stewart? It was certainly something she could get used to, but she mustn't let herself. She was arm candy for Jared for a limited period, but that didn't stop her from having growing feelings for him.

Morgan found him charming, funny and sexy as hell. There was more to Jared than the playboy he portrayed. She wondered if he would show her more or continue to hide behind the facade. She hoped to find out on their next date. Morgan was excited at the prospect. Being with Jared connected her to the sensual side of her nature, but it also put all her senses on alert.

Troy's assault had made Morgan fear intimacy. But surely, a skilled man such as Jared could help her overcome those fears, couldn't he? *Could she allow more to transpire?* Morgan wasn't sure because losing control frightened her more than anything. On the other hand, when she was in Jared's arms, the world melted away and she felt completely alive.

*Was he worth the risk?*

Jared wanted to strangle the high-end client he'd been dealing with on Wednesday. As CEO, he didn't usually handle the sales side of Robinson Holdings, but apparently Chris already had this in the works. So Jared was playing real estate agent to an entitled multimillionaire, chauffeuring him around town when he had better ways to occupy his time. A certain dark-haired beauty came to mind.

While the client took another walk through the estate Jared was showing him, Jared stepped away to check in on his pseudo girlfriend.

"I'm surprised to hear from you in the middle of the day," Morgan commented when she picked up.

"Is that how you respond to your boyfriend?"

She chuckled on the other end of the line. "I'm sorry." She cleared her throat. "Let me try again." She paused for a beat. "Hi, honey, how's your day going?"

Jared smiled inwardly. "That's better. What are you up to?"

"Researching some positions I'm interested in in Los Angeles."

Jared's stomach sank. Why was the thought of Morgan going back home so distasteful? Was it because he was enjoying having her around? "Good for you. You'll let me know if there's anything I can do?"

"Of course. But I'm sure that's not why you called."

He laughed. "No, I was calling about this weekend. I thought we could get together on Saturday. I have someplace I'd like to take you. We'll need to get started a bit early in the afternoon if that's okay?"

"Should I wear anything special?"

"No need. It's our chill date, remember?"

"That's right. I can hardly wait to see you dressed down and looking like an everyday Joe."

"I doubt that's possible," Jared responded, "though you should consider enhancing your wardrobe while we're together. I'll have my assistant set up some accounts at the fashionable boutiques."

"Jared...that's not necessary. I'm not a charity case. I can dress myself."

"I know, but you're with me now and you'll be expected to be dressed in the latest designer clothing."

"Fine."

She was too quick to acquiesce to his request, but Jared let it go because his client was walking straight toward him. "I gotta go, but I'll see you on Saturday."

When Saturday arrived, Jared was happy. His date with Morgan was today. The rest of the workweek had gone by quickly. He'd sat through endless meetings about their next project in Lady Bird Lake and dealt with the board's reticence about his position as interim CEO. Jared was doing his best to show he was capable, but he wasn't used to the early mornings and long days.

Pulling into the Residences at the W, he saw Morgan waiting for him outside. She sashayed toward the door of his Porsche Cayman GTS and jumped in wearing inky-dark skinny jeans that hugged her curves and a ruffled one-shoulder top that raised the flirt factor.

She gave him a warm smile and Jared felt his heart kick in his chest. "Hey."

"Hey." She leaned over and to his surprise, brushed her lips across his.

"What was that for?" he asked when she lifted her head.

"I'm playing my role in case anyone—" she inclined her head toward the valets "—was looking."

She was right, but he wished she'd kissed him because she wanted to—because she missed him as he'd missed her all week—instead of out of necessity. "Of course."

"So where are you taking me?" Morgan asked, buckling her seat belt.

He gave her a quick glance as he pulled away from the curb. "You'll see."

As they drove, Morgan told him about her experience shopping in Austin's high-end boutiques. "I can't believe you didn't give me a limit. I have never spent so much money on clothes in my entire life."

Jared glanced at her in consternation. "My assistant told me you didn't spend that much. I was expecting a larger amount."

"I'm not spending all your money, Jared. Otherwise, I'd feel too much like my mother. She took money from her boyfriends all the time. I understand I have to dress the part, so I bought enough to get me by."

Jared sensed that the resentment Morgan had toward her deceased mother went deep and felt it best to let it rest. "All right, but if you ever need more, say the word."

Morgan glanced at him. "I appreciate that." He watched as her eyes traveled the length of him and back up to meet his gaze. "Jeans and a T-shirt look good on you."

"Why, thank you." Jared grinned from ear to ear.

Their conversation was light. Jared regaled her with stories about his week at the office. Eventually they drove through the gates of Avalon Memory Care. Morgan immediately turned to him. "What is this place?"

"It's a center to help those affected by Alzheimer's, dementia and other cognitive issues."

Her brow furrowed. "I don't understand."

Jared pulled his Porsche into a parking space and turned to face her. "My grandfather is here. He suffers from Alzheimer's. At first, the progression was slow. Sometimes he wouldn't remember me and Chris and would think we were our father. So he had a nurse at their home, but then it became worse. My grandmother couldn't—correction, *wouldn't*—deal with it, so she put him here." Jared didn't wait for more questions. Instead he bounded out of the door and Morgan did the same.

As he came toward her, Morgan touched his arm. "It has to be hard watching someone you love slip away bit by bit." Her voice caught. "I'm terribly sorry."

"It is, but let's hope today is a good day." Jared reached for her hand and Morgan allowed him to entwine their fingers together as they walked toward the entrance.

Sylvia, one of the many nurses on staff, greeted him. "Jared, it's so good to see you. Who'd you bring with you?"

"Sylvia, I'd like you to meet my girlfriend, Morgan."

Sylvia clasped Morgan's free hand in hers. "Great to meet you, honey." She turned to Jared. "I'm so happy you keep coming, Jared. I know it gets harder each time."

Jared swallowed the lump in his throat. "I can't leave him here and forget about him. He's my grandpa."

Sylvia smiled. "You're a good man. Follow me." She

led them down the hall, which although clean smelled like disinfectant. When they reached his grandfather's room, Sylvia knocked and then opened the door.

Jared went to walk inside, and Morgan squeezed his hand firmly. "I'm all right," he said.

His grandfather sat in a rocker watching television. He wore trousers and his favorite blue-and-white-checkered button-down shirt and loafers. When he glanced up and recognition crossed his face, Jared exhaled audibly.

"Anthony, look who's hear to see you!" Sylvia said.

"Jared! Come here ole boy." His grandfather opened his arms and Jared released Morgan's hand to rush into them. He squeezed his grandfather in a warm embrace.

"I'll leave you to your visit." Sylvia waved and left them alone.

His grandfather grasped both sides of Jared's face. "Let me have a look at you." He gave him the once-over. "You're a handsome young man and staying fit. It's how I kept Ruth interested in me."

"Grandpa." Jared went to Morgan, who stood immobilized near the door. "I'd like you to meet my girlfriend, Morgan."

She moved toward him and his grandfather wrapped her up in a big hug just like he used to do when he and Chris were little. Jared missed those days.

His grandfather kept his arm around Morgan and turned to Jared. "She's a real looker. I'm not surprised you fell. Bet you fell hard too."

Jared stared at Morgan. *Is that what happened?* No, Jared dismissed the notion. He was attracted to Morgan. It was nothing more than that.

"So tell me…" his grandfather said, sitting down in his rocker. "How did you and my grandson meet?"

"We met at a wedding," Morgan answered. "I made a big fool of myself and Jared rescued me."

His grandfather gave him a conspiratorial wink. "Is that right? I dare say it was because of your overwhelming beauty."

"That too," Jared responded with a smirk. And even Morgan laughed.

"I'm glad you were able to break through the barrier. Morgan, was it?"

"Yes, sir."

"Ever since he was a little kid, Jared's always been the guarded one. My other grandson, Chris—well, he's an open book, but Jared, you could never tell what he was feeling. He always kind of played it close to the vest. So I'm happy to see you're getting underneath those layers."

When Morgan looked at Jared, it felt as if she was peering into his very soul, so he looked away. *She* unnerved him because his grandfather was right—Jared never showed his hand because growing up his feelings had never mattered. Yet when he was with Morgan, Jared *felt* everything.

Was this how the other half lived? Because if so, Jared wanted no part of it. He would stay in his unfeeling world because it was safe there and didn't require him to be vulnerable.

Morgan was stunned Jared had brought her to meet his grandfather. He'd allowed her to see a different side she'd suspected existed, but he rarely showed. Jared wasn't some cookie-cutter playboy. He cared and was fiercely loyal to his family. During their visit to the facility, she'd learned that Jared came to see his grandfather often. He didn't merely pay lip service and come a handful of times a year like on birthdays or holidays.

After they had lunch on the terrace where several other families gathered with their loved ones, Morgan watched Jared and his grandfather play checkers. She noticed he could have easily won, but he allowed his grandfather to beat him because he didn't remember all the moves.

Morgan smiled as she watched the two men. Anthony Robinson was an older version of Jared with warm dark brown eyes, tawny skin and straight white teeth. But it was the mannerisms, the way they both cocked their head to one side or pondered their next move that made her see the real similarities.

Eventually, the senior Robinson tired and they walked him back to his room.

"Morgan," Anthony said when he finally sat back down in his rocker. "You take care of my boy."

"I will." She smiled because she intended to keep that promise. She leaned over and gave his hand a squeeze. Stepping away, she watched Jared with his grandfather.

When he looked her way, Morgan could have sworn there were tears in Jared's eyes, but he quickly recovered his composure. "You ready to go?"

"I am." She slid her hand inside Jared's as they walked to the car.

Jared's mood was somber as he pulled away. "Are you okay?"

"Hmmm…" He sounded distracted. "Yes, I'm fine."

"It's okay if you do want to talk."

"About my grandpa?" Jared asked. "What could I say? I hate having him there with strangers? Or maybe that I wish our family would take care of him? Is that what you're looking for?"

Morgan didn't take the bait. She knew Jared's underlying anger wasn't directed at her. "I understand it's hard seeing him there, but at least he has you."

Jared snorted. "He would be better off with Chris."

"Stop it!" Her raised voice caught his attention and he stared at her in shock. "Stop putting yourself down, Jared. You're the one who visits him regularly. You're the one who's busting your butt working night and day to cover for Chris because he chose to leave without letting anyone know. So I won't accept you demeaning yourself and saying your contribution to your family isn't as important."

The car came to a sudden stop and Morgan turned to him. Their eyes met and held, and that was all it took for him to lean forward and crush his mouth to hers. Morgan closed her eyes and embraced the kiss. It was gentle at first, but Jared quickly deepened it, sliding his hand through her hair as his tongue caressed hers. Morgan clung to him, returning his passion until he slowly released her.

She blinked up at him, dazed.

"No one has ever defended me like that," Jared said, his voice hoarse with lust. "I'm sorry for coming on so strong again. I promised I wasn't going to get handsy. Yet every time I'm around you, I can't seem to control myself."

"I can't explain what comes over me either," Morgan said honestly.

"What are we going to do about it?"

"I thought we agreed to remain platonic."

"It seems neither one of us is keeping that promise very well, but since we're back at square one, we should get a move on it to part two of the day." Moving back to his seat, Jared put the car in gear and drove them to the garage of a downtown high-rise.

"Is our date over?" Morgan inquired.

Jared chuckled. "No. We're having dinner at my place." He exited the vehicle and opened her door. There were several sports cars parked alongside Jared's Porsche including a Ferrari.

"Let me guess." She inclined her head. "These are yours?"

He grinned unabashedly. "What can I say, I like fast cars. C'mon, I'll take you upstairs."

The elevator zoomed to the fiftieth floor, taking them

straight to Jared's penthouse. The dark color palette was rich and masculine with cool neutral undertones that suited him. Unlike her apartment, the floors were a dark ebony hardwood and the kitchen had European-style cabinets with dark gray quartz countertops and a black hexagon backsplash. The penthouse had breathtaking views. Austin could be seen from every room and the balcony, which had a plunge pool and spa.

"This place is very you," Morgan said, looking out at the city. She turned and leaned against the railing. "I can see you bringing ladies up here to wow them with the view before you..." Her voice trailed off when Jared came to the balcony entrance and stood watching her.

Jared finished her sentence. "Before I take them to bed? I'm sorry to disappoint you, Morgan, but I don't bring women home. It's my retreat from the world. A safe haven if you will."

"So..."

"You're the only woman I've brought here," he replied. "Would you like a drink?"

"I'd love one." Morgan swallowed the lump in her throat. *She* was the only woman he'd brought here. *Did it mean he might like her more than he cared to admit?*

Minutes later, Jared returned carrying two glasses of a dark brown liquid. "Cheers!" He tapped his glass against hers.

She swallowed, if for nothing else than to ease the ache in her nether regions from the dark look in Jared's eyes. The alcohol burned going down but she welcomed it. "So what's for dinner?"

Jared chuckled. "Oh I'm no cook, but I'm excellent at ordering. Our dinner should be arriving any moment."

"Arriving?"

"A personal chef is delivering the food. I hope you don't mind."

Morgan drank more of her drink. "Not at all. But I could have cooked for us."

"Really?"

"Yes, I'm a pretty good cook. I had to learn how to at a young age. If I didn't, I would've been eating cereal and peanut butter and jelly sandwiches every day. My mother never remembered to shop so I had to fend for myself."

"Sounds like it was tough on you growing up."

"It was. I yearned for my father to come one day and take me away from it all. It was a silly wish." Morgan finished off the rest of her drink.

"Not silly," Jared replied. The doorbell rang and he glanced at the open doorway. "That would be our dinner."

Morgan followed him inside and watched as the chef removed the meals he'd brought. There were starters, entrées, even dessert; one for each of them. Once he'd gone, she and Jared helped themselves, piling chopped strawberry pecan salad and chicken piccata with capers on their plates.

"Looks delicious," Morgan said once they were seated at an enormous dining room table that could seat upward of eight.

"Yes, it does," Jared replied and somehow Morgan knew he wasn't talking about the food.

As they ate their meal, Jared tried his best not to think about their explosive kiss in the car. He'd intended to honor his word and keep their arrangement platonic, but Morgan had spoken up for him passionately. More than any person ever had.

This beautiful, feisty brunette was turning him inside out. He didn't quite recognize himself. The night they'd met, he'd been a gentleman, a protector ensuring no other man took advantage of her. Even when she'd brought him up to her room, he found himself taking care of her when she became ill.

And today, he'd wanted her to see a different side of him. To truly *know* him. She was special and he'd wanted his grandpa to meet her. And doggone it, if his grandpa hadn't hit the nail on the head when he'd commented on Morgan breaking through his reserve.

"Is there anything I should know to prepare for dinner with your grandmother tomorrow? Any deep dark family secrets?"

"Nothing so melodramatic," Jared replied. "My grandmother can smell a rat. So just be yourself. Honest. Direct. And she'll love you."

"I hope so. Our whole arrangement depends on my convincing her."

Jared eyed her. "Despite that, if you needed my help until you figured out your next step, I'd help you."

She stared at him in disbelief. "Why would you do that?"

"I like you, Morgan." Jared smiled. "A lot." He couldn't believe how forthcoming he was being.

"The feeling's mutual."

Her honesty was a breath of fresh air. There were no games or tricks. What you saw was what you got. And if he had his way, they'd get to know each other a whole lot better before their arrangement was over.

# Nine

"Stop fidgeting," Jared said when he and Morgan stood outside the door of his grandmother's estate the following evening.

"I'm not."

"Yes, you are." He grabbed her hand and Morgan felt the frisson of electricity go up her arm as it always did when Jared was near. Tonight was no different. He not only looked impeccably gorgeous, but he smelled divine, like citrus and spice.

He rang the doorbell and a uniformed butler greeted them. "Antoine, this is my girl, Morgan. Morgan, meet Antoine. He's been with my grandmother for years."

"Lovely to meet you." Morgan offered her hand and Antoine brought it to his lips.

"A pleasure, madam. Allow me to show you the way."

"You know I don't stand on ceremony, Antoine, even with my girlfriend here. Where's grandmother?"

"In the living room."

"C'mon," Jared said. "It's time to meet the queen."

Morgan walked on leaden feet down the marble corridor. She knew it was nothing for Jared to be around such opulence, but this home put Henry's estate to shame. Morgan could feel the history.

Jared led her to a room where a slender woman about five-foot-eight was sitting. Her blondish gray hair was in a sophisticated bob and she wore a killer designer sheath.

"Jared, you finally arrived. I was beginning to worry," she said, then her glance flickered to Morgan at his side. "And you must be Jared's girlfriend?"

"Grandmother, this is Morgan Stewart. Morgan, this is my grandmother, Ruth Robinson."

His grandmother's brow furrowed. "Stewart, did you say? Come over so I can have a look at you."

Jared released her hand and Morgan pasted a smile onto her face and moved closer. "Mrs. Robinson, it's a pleasure to meet you."

"And you, my dear, are definitely one of Henry's offspring. You have his trademark hazel eyes and his coloring. But why is this the first I'm hearing about you? If I recall, Henry only has one daughter. Fallon, I believe her name is."

"Grandmother, you're being indelicate," Jared admonished.

"I'm merely speaking the truth." She glanced at Morgan. She could tell the woman missed nothing. It was why Morgan had splurged and gone to the salon to have her hair and makeup expertly done. She couldn't afford any mistakes. "You can appreciate that, can't you, dear?"

"Honesty is always the best policy," Morgan stated with a tight smile. "And to answer your question, yes, Henry Stewart is my father, but you might want to remind him of that fact."

"Is he being difficult?" Ruth inquired.

"He downright refuses to acknowledge my existence," Morgan responded. "But that didn't stop me from taking Stewart as my rightful legal name."

Ruth smiled. "Good for you. I like a woman with chutzpah." She turned to Jared. "However did you find Morgan? She's not one of the usual bimbos you traipse about town with."

Morgan noticed Jared's jaw clench and she sensed he wanted to rebut, but he said, "Morgan and I met through Dane."

"Ah, the young man who used to be a troublemaker. I'm glad to see he's married and settled down with a family. Dare I hope you could do the same?"

"Don't push your luck," Jared responded.

"I beg to differ. Morgan is a breath of fresh air and I'm going to claim her," Ruth said, eyeing Morgan. "Come." She patted the seat beside her. "Sit beside me. Jared, be a dear and fix us a drink while we get to know one another."

They chatted about inconsequential topics until dinner. Jared was the consummate date. He drew Morgan's chair out and waited for her to sit down before lowering his tall frame into the seat across from her. She supposed he sat there on purpose so he could focus his full attention on her.

Over the next couple of hours, Ruth was direct, gently quizzing Morgan on her background—where she came from, where she went to school and where she worked. And just as Jared told her to do, Morgan was honest.

But nothing could stop the intangible spark of sexual attraction shooting back and forth across the table or the predatory hunger in Jared's gaze. Morgan wondered if he looked at every woman that way. *Did he make them all feel as if they were the most beautiful woman in the world?* His simple gesture of asking if she'd like more wine made Morgan feel the sizzle. Her eyes darted to his grandmother but she was none the wiser.

"I come from humble beginnings, Mrs. Robinson," Morgan said once they'd retired to the sitting room for coffee. Jared opted for something much stronger. "But I've prided myself in always being able to support myself."

Jared had been quiet for most of the night, content to let the two women dominate much of the conversation. Occasionally he put in an anecdote here or there. But all the while, he'd openly stared at her when he thought she wasn't looking.

An involuntary tremble went through Morgan at his searing gaze. What would it be like if she allowed herself to do more? If she ran her hands down his back, touched the corded muscles of his arms, felt the warmth of his skin? If she laced her fingers around his head and pulled him down to taste the sweetness of his mouth?

"Morgan?"

She blinked rapidly. Oh God, she'd been caught daydreaming. Morgan turned her gaze to Ruth and forced her expression not to betray where her thoughts had strayed.

"You were stating how you supported yourself," Ruth offered.

"Oh yes, I put myself through college, working two, sometimes three jobs to cover the books and expenses my scholarship didn't."

"See, Jared." His grandmother pointed to him. "This is what it's like when you've earned what you have."

"Thank you, ma'am." She'd rather enjoyed having someone older to talk to.

"You've impressed me, Morgan, and that's not easy to do."

"Believe her," Jared said. "I've stopped trying."

"No, you haven't," Morgan replied. "Right now, you've been working day and night at Robinson Holdings to show your grandmother and the board you're no slacker."

Ruth clapped her hands in glee. "Bravo, dear girl. You not only silenced him, but had my grandson's back." She looked at Jared. "You must do all you can to keep her."

The possessive look Jared bestowed on her caused a hard shiver to rock Morgan's body. "Oh, I intend to." He glanced down at his Rolex. "In the meantime, it's late. I should be getting Morgan home."

His grandmother rose to her feet and gave Morgan a

spontaneous hug. Morgan glanced at Jared and his eyes were wide with surprise. "I'm happy you came this evening," Ruth said. "My family and I are going to our compound next weekend. We usually go boating and ride horses, skeet shoot and picnic. It's rather bourgeois, but I would love for you to join us."

Morgan didn't have to worry because Jared answered. "Of course. We'll be there."

A broad smile spread across Ruth's lips. "I look forward to it."

As they walked to the car, Morgan felt like the evening was a resounding success. She'd convinced Ruth she was Jared's legitimate girlfriend, and she suspected the older woman had taken a liking to her. So why as he helped her into the Porsche did Morgan feel like she'd done something wrong?

Jared reflected on the night as he settled into the driver's seat. He couldn't put his finger on what made Morgan different from any of the other women he'd dated, only that she had charmed his grandmother of all people. Ruth had a genuine affection for Morgan and her ability to battle against the odds and come out on the other side. And she'd given Morgan a *hug*. She didn't even hug Jared.

"Jared?" Morgan touched his arm. "What's wrong?"

"Nothing."

"Tonight went great, don't you think?"

He sighed and hazarded a glance at her. Morgan had looked incredible tonight. Her makeup was flawless and she was more beautiful than ever. Her cheekbones were defined, her eyes smoky and sensual and that wide, pretty mouth of hers had captured his attention all night. White-hot desire gripped him when he allowed his gaze to linger on the soft mounds displayed in the low-cut neckline of the simple black jersey dress she wore. He'd tried hard not focus all evening on her décolletage.

"You're a charmer," Jared finally answered. "You won my grandmother over."

"That's good, right?"

"Yes, it is."

"Then why do I think I've failed you in some way?" she asked, her face twisted in consternation.

"You haven't, Morgan." Jared started the engine to effectively end the conversation. He would drive her home and go back to his place and take a long hot shower. The problem was, he didn't know how long he could keep dating Morgan and not ease the permanent sexual ache he had whenever they were together. *How was he going to survive a weekend at his family's compound?*

When they pulled into the W, Jared left the car idling and came around to Morgan's door. He helped her out, but when he made no move to go in, she looked at him expectantly.

"It's best we say good-night here," Jared said. He couldn't go up to her apartment, not when all he wanted to do was strip the dress from her body and sink deep inside her. He moved toward her and rubbed her arms, which felt chilled, then leaned forward placing his forehead against hers. "Thank you. I appreciate everything you did tonight."

"You do?" She sounded as if she was surprised.

"Absolutely, but you should go inside now so I can do the honorable thing."

"What if I don't want you to be honorable?"

"Morgan…" he murmured, but his resolve was gone, especially when she went on tippy toe to sweep her mouth over his, tantalizing him with a promise of sweeter delight. Jared cupped her neck and drew her to him. This time, he kissed her and when he felt a tremor run through her, he didn't stop. He continued moving his lips over hers, seeking, tasting and enticing. When she parted her lips, his tongue slipped inside and tangled with hers in an urgent frenzy.

It was only the sound of the valet clearing his throat that reminded Jared they were outside the hotel in a public place. "I have to go, Morgan. We'll talk soon."

With effort, considering the tightness of his groin, Jared made it back inside the car and pulled away. In his rearview, he saw Morgan still standing there, touching her lips.

# Ten

The last couple of days since the dinner with Jared and his grandmother had been marvelous. Was it because their relationship had taken a turn? Morgan had not only convinced Ruth of their blossoming romance, but Jared had taken her to meet his grandfather.

Yesterday, she'd surprised Jared at his office and whisked him away for lunch. Sure, it was a sandwich in the park, but it was something a girlfriend, someone who cared for him, would do. And Morgan cared. She was trying hard not to get carried away by this fake relationship, but she couldn't act as if she hadn't developed feelings for him.

The deeper they got into this arrangement, the harder it was to pull back. There was a palpable sexual attraction between them that could no longer be ignored, though they were giving their best impression it didn't exist.

Morgan was thankful when Fallon and Ayden invited her for coffee. Morgan hadn't seen Fallon since the day at the mansion when she'd told Fallon she didn't want anything to do with the Stewarts. It wasn't her finest moment, so Morgan was determined to make an effort.

When she arrived, however, another Stewart was waiting for her. Someone she'd been hoping not to face.

Dane.

She saw his two bodyguards chatting with each other as she went into the deserted coffee shop, where the workers stood mesmerized by her movie star big brother. She was unfazed by his good looks—smooth tapioca coloring, strong jawline, dark brown eyes and bushy eyebrows. Dane wore sunglasses and his usual dark jeans, T-shirt and old leather jacket. But when Morgan entered, he ripped the sunglasses off to glare at her. "You have a lot of explaining to do."

Morgan gulped as she walked toward him. "When did you and Iris get back?"

"Day before yesterday," Dane replied. "And we came back to a firestorm about my illegitimate baby sister. So I left Iris and Jayden and came straight here. What the hell, Morgan? You've been working for me for over a year. Why on God's green earth didn't you tell me we're related?"

"I'll explain, but I don't appreciate being ambushed."

"Fallon was worried you wouldn't show if she told you I was coming."

Morgan folded her arms across her chest. "What about her and Ayden? Are they coming? Or was this all an elaborate ruse so you can give me the business?"

"Sit down, Morgan," Dane ordered.

Morgan recognized his boss voice and rather than argue took a seat at the round table beside him.

"Of course they're coming, but we, you and me," he pointed between them, "need to clear the air."

Dane was right. She owed him an apology. "I'm sorry."

"Was that so hard?" Dane inquired, his brown eyes narrowing on her.

"No. I was wrong to keep my identity hidden from you."

"So why did you?"

Morgan shrugged. Why was it so hard to face Dane? She'd told this story several times since, but to him, the brother she idolized, she felt like she had cotton in her mouth.

"Morgan?"

She inhaled deeply. "I was afraid to tell you. What if you didn't believe me? Henry doesn't. I thought I'd get to know you first, but the more I did, the more I liked and respected you. How could I not? You accepted Jayden and Iris into your life when you could have lost everything. I was impressed by your valor."

"I'm no hero, Morgan," Dane replied. "I'm a man with flaws like everyone else. Don't go putting me on some pedestal. It's hard to meet folks' expectations from up there."

"That's what I love about you, Dane. You give it to me straight." Morgan covered her mouth. "I didn't mean *love*. I…" Her voice trailed off when she saw the amusement in his eyes.

He reached across the table and placed his rather large hand over hers. "It's okay, Morgan. I've always looked at you as the little sister I never had, so I have no problem accepting you into the family. I just wish you would have gone about this another way."

"I'm sorry for bringing you and Iris back into the spotlight after Jayden's illness," Morgan replied. "I didn't think ahead. I just wanted Henry to claim me as his own."

"My father is a stubborn man," Dane responded. "I'm not sure if he ever will, but I'll support you, kid."

Morgan beamed, and despite herself, happy tears slid down her cheeks. Dane leaned across to wipe them away with his thumbs.

"Oh, Lord," a female voice said from behind them, "please tell me you didn't make her cry, Dane."

Morgan knew that voice and spun around to see Fallon and Ayden at the door.

"Welcome back, bro." Ayden managed to lift Dane off his feet even though he was six feet tall, because Ayden had a few inches on him.

"How was the honeymoon?" Fallon asked, winking at Dane.

"Nothing I care to comment on with my big sis," Dane responded good-naturedly. "Come here." He wrapped his arms around Fallon. "How's Nora?"

"Still furious with Daddy," Fallon replied. "At least she's moved back home, though they are sleeping in separate rooms."

"He deserves it," Dane said. "He cheated on her. Though she shouldn't necessarily be surprised. He did the same to Ayden's mom."

"Don't be heartless, Dane. She should at least expect loyalty from her husband."

"I don't disagree, but this is our father we're talking about."

Morgan was overwhelmed watching their interaction. *These were her siblings.* She shrank back from the three of them. They were already a trio. *Where did she fit in?*

"And where do you think you're going?" Ayden asked. He quickly lifted her off her feet too and into his embrace.

Morgan couldn't resist releasing a big laugh. "Put me down, you big lug." She swatted him on the arm and he set her on her feet.

"It's nice to have the *four* of us together in one place," Fallon said, and her eyes went to Morgan. When her sister smiled, Morgan felt relieved Fallon wasn't holding a grudge.

"Let's have a coffee." Ayden looked around the room and noticed the store was empty. "What's the deal? Where is everybody?"

"My team paid the shop to close for the afternoon," Dane responded.

"Don't you think that's a bit extra?" Fallon replied.

"Nope. They even made everyone sign confidentiality agreements."

"It must suck to be you sometimes," Ayden commented.

"Hey, don't hate on my brother." Morgan didn't realize

she'd spoken aloud until three curious sets of eyes landed on her. "I mean…" she attempted to backpedal.

Fallon walked over to Morgan and wrapped her arm around Morgan's shoulders. "He's your brother too. You can defend him."

Morgan mouthed *Thank you*.

"Well, I'm going to have a frozen coffee concoction," Fallon stated and headed to the counter where an attendant waited silently at the register.

"I'll join you." Ayden stepped away to look at the menu.

"Please tell me you'll join me for a real coffee." Dane looked at Morgan. "Or are you going to have your usual, a café mocha?"

Morgan's brow furrowed. "You know what coffee I like?"

"Why wouldn't I?" Dane asked, peering at her. "You've worked for me for a while now."

"I never thought you paid any attention to me. I was your assistant, after all."

Dane stared at her incredulously. "You've been more than an assistant, Morgan. You helped make my life easier."

Morgan smiled at his heartfelt words. "That means a lot, thank you. And to answer your question, I will have a café mocha. Who drinks regular coffee anyway?"

Morgan shared how well the coffee meeting went later that evening on the phone with Jared. They'd stayed at the coffee shop for hours until Fallon and Ayden both commented they had to get home to their kids. Morgan was excited to have a niece and nephew. Dane was headed back to Los Angeles to Iris and Jayden. Seeing her siblings go home to their respective families made Morgan long to have a family of her own.

"That's wonderful, Morgan," Jared said. "I'm glad to see you bonding with your siblings. I wish I could do the same."

"Is Chris still MIA?"

"Yep. I've left countless messages for him and he hasn't answered a single one of them," Jared responded. "I wish he would just talk to me and tell me what's going on. Maybe I could help. And I could certainly use his advice when it comes to managing Robinson Holdings."

"I imagine it's been a trial by fire."

"You can say that again." Jared chuckled. "But I'll carry on. I don't have much choice. I'm the only Robinson left standing."

"True, but don't you find it rewarding to have your family need you?"

"Yeah, I suppose I do," Jared said. "They've never looked at me as anything other than a screwup, and suddenly I'm their salvation. It's a bit disconcerting. My grandmother is usually calling me about how I've embarrassed the family with my shenanigans, but now she's talking shop and asking my opinion."

"You've always had it in you, Jared," Morgan responded. "Perhaps you needed to be put to the test to realize your true potential."

"When did you become so wise, Morgan Stewart?"

"Maybe because I had to grow up early and take care of myself." Silence ensued on the other end and Morgan realized he'd meant it to be a rhetorical question.

"You're not alone now," Jared murmured softly. "You have your siblings and you have me."

"For a limited time," Morgan reminded him. The terms of their arrangement were never far from her mind. If she was honest, she would like to date Jared, *for real*, to see where their relationship would go, but he'd made it abundantly clear he was not in it for the long haul.

"Um…" Jared cleared his throat. "Yeah…that's right. So, are you ready for a weekend of fun with the Robinsons?"

"I am. After hearing about your parents, I'm eager to finally meet them."

"Good, I'll pick you up at three on Friday afternoon and we'll get an early jump on traffic. How's that sound?"

"Great, see you then." Morgan stared at her phone after he'd hung up. Was it her imagination or had their conversation ended on a sharp note after she'd brought up the short time they had remaining together? She wished it weren't so, but she had to keep telling herself not to get too attached to Jared before she got hurt.

Morgan inhaled deeply. *Who was she kidding?* She was already falling for the guy.

Jared rose from the sofa he'd been lounging on while talking to Morgan. She sounded so happy about connecting with her siblings. He was happy because he sensed deep down, she wanted to be part of something bigger. And now, as a Stewart, she would have in-laws, nieces and nephews.

He wanted that for her because it wasn't something *he* could give her. He could tell Morgan was growing attached to him. They were spending an awful lot of time together. He too was starting to feel a connection he'd never felt. Jared could talk to her about anything—work, family, it didn't matter—because Morgan offered good advice and positivity, something sorely missing in his life. She championed him and it was a heady feeling.

But it made Jared wary. He couldn't be her hero. He wasn't built that way. He was the lothario who knew how to show a woman a good time and please her in the bedroom. But offer more? He wasn't capable of it. Or at least he didn't think he was. He'd never stayed in a relationship long enough to find out.

Having been blessed with good looks, he been pursued by the opposite sex since he was a teenager. He'd relished the attention of the nubile women who'd flocked to him. Many had tried and been unsuccessful in their attempts to get Jared to want more during the affairs, until Morgan. *Was it because none of them could hold a candle up to her?*

She was the most innocent and guileless of the women he'd dated. Jared didn't want to hurt Morgan, yet he couldn't deny he wanted to make love to her. Whenever they were together, Jared felt not only his heart contract and expand, but his trousers get tighter. He was doing his best to keep his distance, but he suspected two days in the country was sure to either drive him crazy or Morgan into his bed. And if it was the latter, Jared wouldn't mind it one bit.

# Eleven

"Your family calls this a compound?" Morgan asked
that Friday afternoon. Jared had driven them about thirty
minutes outside the city toward Lake Austin and had slid
past two private wrought iron gates. The Porsche Cayman GTS was now on a tree-lined street with hundreds
of massive oaks.

"My grandpa bought this place because of the view, but
he also wanted to be surrounded by nature," Jared replied.
"There's a lot of white-tailed deer, spring-fed creeks and
limestone and granite outcroppings. When we were kids,
he used to take Chris and me out kayaking and fishing.
But if that's not your speed there's some local wineries,
boutique shopping and chef-owned restaurants. So there's
plenty to do."

Morgan absorbed Jared's words and thought about the
weekend ahead. She wasn't afraid of meeting Jared's parents or spending time with his grandmother again. She
liked Ruth. She was worried, however, about the sleeping arrangements. Morgan was certain everyone assumed
they'd want one room and it wasn't like she could request
a separate one. It would raise a red flag. So, she was going
to have sleep beside Jared for the next two nights. Given
how red-hot their kisses had been, Morgan was afraid of
what might happen.

Jared drove past a long white perimeter fence with

horses grazing in the field and Morgan had to ask, "You have horses? How many acres is this place?"

Jared shrugged. "I don't know. A couple hundred." The car curved around a winding paved driveway and stopped in front of a two-story brick-and-stone veneer mansion with medieval castle-style doors. Across from the house, there was an exceptionally large coy pond.

Morgan didn't wait for Jared to help her as she opened her door and got out, staring openmouthed at their beautifully serene surroundings.

"Want a tour?" Jared asked.

Morgan beamed with pleasure. "I'd love one."

Jared grabbed her hand and said, "We'll start outdoors."

The compound had not only the main house, but had smaller homes throughout the estate. It came complete with a theater, its own gym with indoor basketball court, game room, an entertaining pavilion, two pools with spas, a boat storage facility, a baseball field, a volleyball court and a chipping and putting green that overlooked the lake.

"I feel like I'm at a resort," Morgan said after the tour ended at the main house. She helped Jared with the bags and he procured a key and opened the front door.

"Hello!" Jared called out when they entered the foyer with a baby grand piano front and center. When no one answered, he turned to her. "We must be the first arrival."

"No, you're not." Antoine came rushing toward them down the hall. "I'm sorry I wasn't here to greet you. The staff and I are still getting ready for the weekend. We learned your brother, Chris, and his girlfriend are joining us."

"Chris is coming?" Jared's voice rose several octaves.

Antoine nodded. "Was it as much of a surprise to you as it was to your grandmother? Allow me to show you to your quarters."

As she walked up the winding staircase behind Jared,

Morgan surveyed her surroundings, noting the vaulted ceilings and elaborate chandeliers. Eventually, Antoine stopped in front of a large oak door and swung it open. The room contained a four poster bed covered in a steel-colored velvet duvet with tons of pillows, including one made of Mongolian fur. A beautiful stone fireplace sat across from the bed, giving the space a cozy atmosphere.

"Your en suite bath is to the right and has towels and toiletries," Antoine said. "Let me know if you need anything else."

"Sure thing." Jared closed the door behind him when he left.

"So." Morgan looked around the room, There were two accent chairs next to a table, but there was nowhere else for them to sleep but the bed.

"I can sleep on the floor," Jared offered, sensing her discomfort, "though I have to admit I'm not looking forward to the prospect. It can get pretty cool along the water at night."

Morgan offered a smile. "I wouldn't do that to you. This is your family's home. Plus, it's just two nights. I'm sure we can share a bed together. It'll be a piece of cake, right?"

Jared's pupils flared. "We should go," he said after several moments. "See who else has arrived."

"Like Chris?"

"Heck yeah. I have a major bone to pick with him."

Morgan was glad for the easy out, but she knew it was only a temporary reprieve. It wouldn't be long before they'd have to share that bed.

Jared was desperate to get out of the bedroom. If he stayed any longer, he wasn't going to be responsible for his actions. Sleeping beside Morgan night after night was going to be agony, *physically.* He wanted her badly. But she was like a skittish filly and he couldn't move fast or she'd run away. This weekend would test every ounce of his patience.

He supposed it was a good thing he had something—or should he say someone—else to focus on. Namely, his brother.

"C'mon." He led Morgan downstairs and found his grandmother and parents in the family room.

"Jared, darling." His mother rose and greeted them as they approached. "I'm so glad you're here. And I assume you must be Morgan."

"Yes, ma'am," Morgan answered.

"This is my husband, Clay." His mother motioned to his father on the couch.

His father stood and came over. "Good to see you, son." He gave Jared a handshake and rested his eyes on Morgan. He whispered. "She's a looker."

Jared grinned. "Yes, she is."

"We're so happy you could join us for a little respite," his mother gushed. "We all love it here."

"Morgan, come here." His grandmother patted the seat beside her. "Sit with me."

Jared frowned as he watched Morgan saunter over to his grandmother's side. "And what if I wanted her with me?"

"Our time with Morgan is limited, yours isn't," Ruth responded. "What do you think of the compound? My husband bought it for the family years ago."

"It's a beautiful property, Mrs. Robinson," Morgan replied. "Thank you for inviting me."

"Please call me Ruth. I still don't understand how my grandson—" Ruth glanced in his direction "—managed to catch someone as fine as you."

"Hey, hey," a deep masculine voice said from beyond the family room. Jared turned to see Chris, all six foot five inches of him, walking toward them with a petite woman with flaming red hair by his side. Jared doubted it was her natural hair color. He stood by the fireplace mantel and waited for the fireworks that were sure to come. He'd been on the receiving end of his family's discontent many times. This time the shoe was on the other foot.

"Chris! Where the hell have you been?" his father bellowed.

"Hello to you too, Dad." Chris's brown eyes rested on their father and swirled around the room. "Mama." He let go of the woman's hand long enough to bend down and brush his lips across his mother's cheek.

"It's good to see you, Chris." His mother smile was wan. Suddenly the tension in the room ramped up a notch.

Chris turned to the woman standing meekly in the doorway. She seemed afraid to enter. Had Chris told her she'd have an unwelcome audience? "Everybody? I'd like you to meet Kandi. My fiancée."

"Your what?" His mother sounded aghast.

"Have you lost your mind?" his father roared, charging at Chris. "You abandon your family and the company you've been head of—to what? Go off with and get engaged to this pop tart?"

"Clay, please," his mother said, clutching his arm. "Don't get overexcited."

"Mom's right," Chris said. "You need to calm down. We don't want you to have another heart attack."

"And who would be the cause?" his grandmother inquired. "You—for the shame you have brought to this family and our good name."

"Grandmother..." Jared said, a warning in his tone.

"No, let her go on," Chris responded. "It's exactly why I left to get away from all of this." He waved his hands in the air. "Your expectations were stifling. I couldn't breathe."

"So instead, you go to a strip club?" his father asked. "Then you get her—" he glanced at Kandi, who now stood teary eyed at Chris's side "—knocked up. For Christ's sake. And now you want to marry her?"

"I'm proud to marry Kandi. She's an incredible woman."

Ruth sighed wearily. "I had such high hopes for you, Chris. Thought you were destined to do great things. Clearly, I bet on the wrong horse. I mean, have you even looked at your brother, Jared? The one you left behind to clean up your mess."

For the first time, Chris glanced in Jared's direction.

"He's stepped up," Ruth continued. "Took over leadership at Robinson Holdings. Is dating this beautiful young woman." She motioned to Morgan at his side, who looked wide-eyed at Jared. He could see her uneasiness at having been caught in the middle of a family squabble. "I'm shocked to say this, but you could learn a thing or two from him. He's shown great resiliency these last few weeks."

Chris gave him a half smile. "If something good can come out of this, then I'm glad for it. But listen here, if any of you don't want to get to know Kandi—" he glanced around the room at their parents and grandmother "—then it's your loss. My family and I—" he placed his hand over the small swell of Kandi's stomach "—we can leave."

Jared quickly moved from the mantle and rushed to his brother's side. "Don't leave, Chris. Not like this," he murmured in his ear. "Tensions are high right now. Sleep on it."

"I don't know, bro."

"For me," Jared pleaded. "Don't go until we've talked. You owe me that much." He stared into Chris's eyes and saw him soften. At the same time, Morgan approached Kandi, and if he could have, Jared would have kissed her in front of everyone. He was so thankful for the gesture.

"Kandi, you have to see this place," Morgan said, beaming her megawatt smile. "It's an oasis. C'mon, I'll show you." He glanced over at his grandmother and saw the faint hint of a smile. Morgan had scored another goal in her favor.

But Morgan didn't need to try. She already had *him* wrapped around her little finger.

\* \* \*

After the women departed, Jared wrapped an arm around Chris's shoulder and said, "Why don't you and I have a talk."

"Please," his father stated gruffly, "perhaps you can talk some sense into him."

Chris rolled his eyes, but allowed Jared to lead him outside onto the terrace. They were hardly through the double doors when Chris went on a tirade.

"How dare they treat Kandi like that? They don't even *know* her." Chris began pacing on the travertine deck.

"Does it really surprise you?" Jared inquired, folding his arms across his chest as he faced his brother. "Chris, you've been MIA for weeks. We had to learn via the media that you'd gotten some woman pregnant, and now you just show up and announce she's your fiancée. You didn't even have the guts to tell us the news in person. Instead, you spring this on us? It's no wonder everyone's taken aback. I am too!"

"Are you done?"

"Not nearly," Jared replied. "You've been seeing Kandi for some time. You could have introduced her to the family months ago. You're the one who chose to keep your relationship a secret as if you've got something to hide."

Chris stared at him dumbfounded. "Since when are you the voice of reason?"

"Since you left, I had no choice but to step up."

"According to grandmother, you're doing a bang-up job."

"Yeah, well, for the record, I didn't ask for this."

"Neither did I, but maybe I've been a hindrance this whole time, always bailing you out of trouble. Who knew some good old-fashioned hard work was just what the doctor ordered."

"Don't patronize me, Chris. I've never wanted to be head of the family business. That was always your forte."

"But did you ever wonder if I wanted any of it?" Chris asked. "Perhaps all their lofty expectations were thrust upon me like they were on you."

Jared looked at his brother. He'd always assumed Chris enjoyed what he did. "No, I guess I never did. Dad and Grandmother were always grooming you as the chosen one. I got a free pass."

"Lucky you," Chris said, scrubbing his jaw. "You got to enjoy life and have fun. It wasn't until I met Kandi that I finally allowed myself to let loose."

"Considering Kandi's condition, seems you let loose a bit too much," Jared responded with a chuckle.

"Hey." Chris glared at him. "Although fatherhood wasn't necessarily on my radar, I'm happy about it. Kandi's a wonderful woman and I love her."

"Whom you haven't known very long."

"Don't get on my case. Everyone is freaking out because this is the first time I've ever done anything that wasn't planned," Chris replied, walking toward Jared. When he was within striking distance, he poked Jared in the chest. "But they should really be looking at you and figuring out who this impostor is that looks like my brother."

"Funny," Jared said without humor.

"It is. Everyone's favorite good-time guy is finally doing the right thing. Go figure!" Chris said. "Is it Morgan? Is she the reason you're finally behaving like an adult?"

"That's not fair," Jared replied. "You were happy being the big brother when it suited you. And when it didn't, you ran."

"Avoidance," Chris said, laughing, "Signature Jared. You like the girl and she's good for you. Admit it!"

"She's here, isn't she?" Jared answered.

Chris chuckled. "Yeah, she is. And making a big impression on our grandmother. Apparently Kandi needs some advice on how to cozy up."

"If that's possible," Jared said, laughing. He was happy to have Chris back. He'd missed the camaraderie they shared and didn't realize how much he looked forward to their bantering.

"Since you're not going to tell me what's really going on between you and the beautiful Morgan, I'll have to find out for myself," Chris said. "Shall we go join our women?"

"Lead the way." Jared motioned for Chris to walk ahead of him.

Jared wasn't ready to tell Chris or anyone his true feelings about Morgan. How this beautiful woman was starting to capture his heart.

# Twelve

Morgan had needed to do something. The Robinsons were crashing and burning around her. So she offered to show Kandi around the estate to keep the peace. Maybe Jared could smooth some ruffled feathers while they were gone. If they treated Kandi so harshly, Morgan hated to think how she would have been received if she and Ruth hadn't hit it off.

"Thank you for that," Kandi said, once they were walking back toward the house. "It was getting dicey in there."

"Ya think?" Morgan asked with a raised brow. She was surprised the woman could walk in the five-inch heels and form-fitting dress, but who was she to judge? "I'm hoping some time will help alleviate the tension."

"I doubt that's possible. Those people hate me," Kandi said, inclining her head toward the main house. "They're never going to accept me."

"You don't know that," Morgan said. "You can win them over." She opened the door to the sports pavilion, which housed the gym and basketball arena. "Check this out."

Kandi oohed and aahed like Morgan had earlier.

"It's pretty spectacular, huh?"

"Yes, and far removed from how I grew up," Kandi responded.

"Me too," Morgan murmured. "Not everyone was born with a silver spoon like Jared and Chris."

Kandi offered a small smile and Morgan hoped she was getting through to her. "So if you're not one of them, how did you win them over?"

Morgan shrugged. "I don't know. Ruth and I hit it off right away. I've never had grandparents and for some reason being around Ruth is comforting. And maybe vice versa."

"It's always been me and my mama. I was looking forward to being part of a family."

Morgan understood and wondered if that's why she felt a kinship to Kandi. She reached for Kandi's hand and gave it a gentle squeeze. "I'm new to the Robinsons too. All I can do is tell you to give it time. They'll come around."

"They won't have a choice," Chris said from behind them. He and Jared joined Morgan and Kandi on the trail. "We're getting married and having a baby."

Kandi rushed to Chris's side and encircled his waist with her arms. "True, but it would be nice if they liked me."

"All that matters is you and me," Chris murmured and bent his head to kiss her.

Morgan loved how affectionate they were. It was clear they were in love and Morgan wanted that for herself. *Someday.* What she had right now was Jared standing there watching her from a few feet away. The heat in his gaze was unmistakable. They might not have love, but one thing was for certain: they had lust in spades.

Jared opened his arms and Morgan felt compelled to stride toward him. When he wrapped his arms around her, Morgan felt as if she'd come home.

"What do you say we give this dinner thing another try?" Jared asked.

Morgan noticed the look of absolute terror on Kandi's face. "It's okay, you have allies." She glanced up at Jared and he gave her a wink.

"We'll do it," Chris said, "but if everyone can't be civil, we're leaving."

"Let's hope it doesn't come to that," Jared responded.

The four of them walked the short distance to the main house. When they did, Antoine met them in the foyer. "Your grandmother and parents are in the dining room. They were hoping you would join them for dinner."

"Thank you, Antoine." Jared led them all down the hall.

An hour apart had allowed the older Robinsons to realize alienating Chris wasn't productive. Dinner went smoothly. Ruth played the grand hostess, though Morgan saw the tight lines around her mouth. Clay was quiet, saying only a few syllables when the conversation required it. Mary was effusive. She seemed to be the only one who was genuinely happy about Chris and Kandi's news.

"I'm so excited to plan a wedding," Mary said with a smile when the petit fours arrived for dessert. "It's going to be so much fun."

Morgan was about to tuck into hers when Chris coughed and Morgan sensed the family wasn't going to like what came next. She put her fork down on the table and waited for the fallout.

"Umm, we were thinking about just going down to the courthouse. We don't want a big fuss," Chris said.

Ruth sucked in a loud breath. "Robinsons have always been married in a church before God and family. It's a *tradition*."

"Surely a small gathering could be held at a church for the family." Morgan knew she was speaking out of turn and glanced across the table at Kandi, silently pleading for her to reconsider.

"Morgan, I appreciate…" Chris started speaking, but Kandi patted Chris's hand on the table.

"Yes, I'm sure we can work out something."

"Excellent," Ruth stated and gave Morgan a conspiratorial wink.

Morgan released a sigh, which Jared heard because he

bent his head and said, "What do you say we get out of here?"

She glanced up into his dark eyes and whispered, "Are you sure?"

Jared nodded. "If you'll excuse us." He stood. "Morgan and I are going to turn in."

Morgan flushed as several sets of eyes looked at her. Were they all assuming she and Jared were going upstairs to have sex? She was sure that was the expectation, given Jared's reputation and the fact they were dating.

She allowed Jared to lead her away from the dining room, but instead of going upstairs as she'd anticipated, he said, "Walk with me for a minute."

The sky was dark but a dusting of stars could be seen as Jared took her to the outdoor living area. They walked over to a high-end wicker sectional with a large round ottoman. Jared sank down, taking Morgan with him. She settled beside him in the crook of his arm.

"Thank you for tonight," he finally said. "You were a lifesaver."

"It was nothing."

Jared peered down at her. "You and I both know it was more than that. Chris's announcement caused a mutiny in the Robinson clan. You defused the situation by taking Kandi aside so cooler heads could prevail. And I heard what you told her. You were a friend and made her feel welcome."

"Being confrontational wasn't going to solve anything," Morgan responded. "I learned from my stunt at the wedding. All it did was alienate Henry."

"You still want a relationship with him, don't you?"

Morgan's mouth ran dry and she couldn't speak; she merely nodded. "I just want to belong."

Jared turned her until she was facing him. Then he placed his hands on either side of her face. Morgan could see the heat in his gaze and something flared inside her.

"You belong here with me," he murmured and then he pulled her toward him. Jared captured her mouth with his own. She kissed him back with a fervor that drew a low groan from him.

This time, they didn't pull back, and the kiss became hot and urgent as passion exploded between them. Morgan sensed a wildness in Jared he'd been holding back. This time he didn't. He gathered her close, crushing his body against hers, and the divine fragrance of his aftershave mixed with his own uniquely male scent shot Morgan's senses into overdrive.

Jared broke the kiss and trailed kisses down her cheeks, throat and over to her neck. He lingered there and suckled. Morgan couldn't suppress the moan that escaped her lips. And she didn't stop Jared's hands when they began sliding under her sweater to cup her breasts. He teased her nipples with his thumbs until they turned into hard pebbles at his touch and Morgan wanted more.

"I'll give you more," Jared said in an amused voice. Color flared on Morgan's cheeks when she realized she'd verbalized her plea. So it was no surprise when he lifted the sweater higher and pushed aside her bra cups. Morgan felt a cool breeze against her skin seconds before he flicked his tongue back and forth across her nipple.

"Oh!" Morgan let out a cry when he continued by closing his mouth around the peak and sucking hard. Morgan sighed with pleasure as he drew her nipple even deeper into his mouth. She wasn't thinking about denying the moment. Instead, she was powerless against the tide of desire and need swelling inside her.

Jared's hands skimmed lower to her leggings and reached the apex of her thighs. She sucked in a harsh breath when he slid inside, touching her abdomen. When he came to the waistband of her panties, Morgan could feel herself blush as he brushed his hands across her. She'd never allowed another man to touch her this way, but Jared was different, so when he pushed the damp fabric to one side and touched her intimate flesh, she quivered.

"Easy, I've got you," he murmured.

His fingers teased and explored her crease and Morgan ached—for what, she didn't know. She soon found out, when he slid one finger inside and she bucked off the sectional. Jared kissed her again, this time hard and fierce, and Morgan gave herself over to the invasion of not one, but yet another digit. She writhed against his fingers as they began thrusting in and out, and lost the battle. Hot, sharp barbs of pleasure took over and her orgasm was so intense, she screamed.

Jared covered her mouth with his, absorbing her cries as his fingers continued to caress her through the waves. Morgan panted out a breath and was coming back down to earth when Jared said, "I want you, Morgan." To prove it, he brought her hand to the large swell of his erection. There was no denying how turned on he was.

But it also caused Morgan to flash back to the event in her bedroom when her mother's boyfriend Troy made her *touch* him.

"I can't!" Morgan straightened her clothes and jumped up from the sectional. "I just can't," she cried and ran as fast as she could away.

Morgan knew she was being irrational after the intimacy they'd shared, but she wasn't sure she was capable of getting over her fears, not even for Jared.

For a moment, Jared shrank backward in stunned silence. He'd never had a woman run away from him. Usually women were lining up to be with him because of his sexual prowess. But Morgan was pushing him away, and if he wasn't mistaken, tonight had been her first orgasm. She'd seemed surprised by her body's reaction to their lovemaking, but how was that possible? She was an attractive twenty-five-year-old woman. Were the men she was with incapable of pleasing her? Or was it more? He did sense a fear in her. *Had she been hurt previously in a sexual relationship?*

*Was that why she was running away?*

He had to know. If for no other reason than to show Morgan he could make her body hum with pleasure. Jared knew they would be spectacular together. He'd known it the minute he'd seen her at the bar at Dane's reception. He only needed Morgan to let down her guard long enough for him to show her how good it could be. She had for a moment and she'd felt so good. Tight, but good, and he couldn't wait to make love to her.

Rising to his feet, Jared gave chase.

Instead of going back to the main house as he'd anticipated, he saw Morgan skirt into one of the guest cottages on the estate. Was that a sign she wanted to be alone? Yet he couldn't let this go.

He knocked and when Morgan didn't answer, he tried the door and found it unlocked. She was sitting on a sofa in the enormous room in the gathering dark. Jared turned on the lamp on the cocktail table, giving the room a subtle glow. Morgan was squeezed onto one side of the couch as if she were going to bolt any minute. Jared sat in the chair across from her so she knew he would keep his hands off if that's what she wanted.

"What's going on, Morgan?" Jared searched her face for an answer, but all he saw were tears streaking her cheeks. "I'd like to understand what's got you so rattled. If I'm not mistaken, you enjoyed what just happened. Am I wrong?"

Morgan shook her head.

"Then was is it?" Jared asked. "Sweetheart, whatever it is, you can tell me."

Morgan sniffed and wiped away her tears with the back

of her hand. When she finally looked up at him, her lashes were wet. "When I was sixteen, one of my mother's boyfriend's assaulted me."

"What!" Jared's eyes grew hard as ice. "You were raped?"

"No…" Morgan shook her head furiously. "It didn't come to that. My mother came home before—before he could."

"Morgan, I'm so sorry. You don't have to talk about this anymore."

"I have to. Don't you see?" She looked at him with beseeching eyes. "If I don't, he'll always win and keep me from having a fulfilling life."

"All right, then talk to me. What happened?"

"I came home from band practice and Troy was waiting for me. From the empty beer bottles, I could see and smell he'd been drinking."

"Go on."

"I rushed to my bedroom. He chased after me, slamming the door shut. I was terrified. He threw me on the bed and climbed on top of me. Then he was ripping my blouse open and fondling my breasts." Morgan wrung her hands and Jared's heart broke for her and all she'd been through. "He started rubbing against me. I could feel how aroused he was even though I was fighting him every step of the way. He made me touch him and told me in vivid detail what he was going to do to me. Thankfully, he heard the apartment door and jumped off me."

"What did your mother do?"

More tears fell down Morgan's cheeks. "She took his side. He told her I'd thrown myself at him and she believed him. My own mother took the word of a would-be rapist over mine!"

Jared rushed to her side and wrapped Morgan in the cocoon of his arms. "I'm so sorry, sweetheart. She was wrong. She should have believed you, *her child*."

"I always wondered if I did anything to lead him on."

"You did nothing wrong," Jared said, clutching her face in his palms. "Please tell me you know that." He wiped away her tears with the pads of his thumbs. "You didn't *deserve* what happened to you. It was your mother's job to protect you and she failed. You were the victim."

"I don't want to be a victim anymore," Morgan responded softly. "He robbed me of the joy and thrill of intimacy with a man. It's why I'm still a virgin."

Jared wasn't surprised at Morgan's bold statement. Given how skittish she was whenever things heated up between them, Jared had expected as much, but in this day and age, she was a bit of an anomaly.

"I want to take back what he stole from me and you can help me."

"I don't understand."

"Make love to me," Morgan murmured, looking up at him with her mercurial hazel-gray eyes. "Help me wash away the bad memories so all I can think about is you and how good you make me feel."

Jared shook his head. "No, I—I can't. You've been through too much. I'm glad you were able to tell me about what happened, but I won't take advantage of you. If I did, I'd be as bad as he was."

"You're *not* taking advantage of me," Morgan replied, her tone defiant. "Back out there—" she pointed to the door "—I wanted you. Like I did that first night when I asked you up to my hotel room. I want you still. It's *my choice* to be with you."

She launched herself at him until she straddled his hips, then leaned forward and covered his mouth with hers.

For heart-stopping seconds, Jared didn't know how to respond. Morgan had been through so much and her opening up was a breakthrough. To take what she was offering tonight would be wrong, reckless even, but Morgan was pressing hot kisses all over his face and moving against him, causing his length to swell.

But she was right. It was all about choices.

And tonight, his choice was to have her.

His arms came around Morgan like steel bands and he opened his mouth to the fierce demands of her kiss.

# Thirteen

A thrill rushed through Morgan when Jared responded to the passion in her kiss. Throwing herself at him was all sorts of stupid, but she hadn't known what else to do to convince Jared she was ready. He made her feel safe and cared for. She was tired of living with regrets. Desire was pulsing through her veins and she wanted to forget about anything and everything but the exquisite havoc Jared was wreaking.

His lips moved with an increasing urgency over hers, and her body came alive at the determined thrusts of his tongue. No one had ever made Morgan feel this level of excitement. When Jared crushed her against his broad chest, Morgan was left with little doubt of how strong and muscular he was. She arched into his embrace and as a result, felt the hard points of her nipples pebble against him. Jared shuddered. It gave Morgan a burst of self-confidence knowing she could stir the same emotions in him that she felt.

Suddenly Jared was lifting her off the sofa and walking. She didn't know where he was going because she was greedily kissing him. Seconds passed, then she felt the softness of the mattress as Jared laid her down and joined her on the bed. But instead of climbing astride her, he lay beside her.

"Don't stop," Morgan whispered fiercely, looking over at him.

"I have no intention of stopping. I want you, Morgan. I want to touch, taste and discover every part of your body."

Morgan's stomach dipped at his intimate words and she blushed.

"But I want you to be sure," Jared said, his dark glittering eyes laser focused on her, "so we're going to take this slow."

"I don't want slow."

Jared laughed—the low, husky sound caused every cell of her body to be acutely aware of him. "How about we undress first?"

Morgan sat up on her haunches and leaned over to start unbuttoning Jared's shirt. He smiled at her enthusiasm and seemed content to let her take over. When she was done with the buttons, he shrugged off his shirt, then deftly removed his shoes and socks and returned to the bed.

Morgan's eyes roamed over Jared's gorgeous body. He was so magnificent with his powerfully hard masculine chest and impressive six-pack. She stroked her hand down the length of his chest. Feeling the sprinkling of hair set her nerve endings on fire so she kept going until she reached the waistband of his jeans. She'd felt his lust during their kisses, but now she would feast her eyes on *him*. She unzipped his jeans, working them down his slim hips until he was able to step out of them.

Morgan's gaze dropped to his black boxer shorts, which in no way concealed his arousal. She licked her lips and slipped her hand inside the waistband to curl her fingers around him. She explored the shape of him and could feel moisture at the tip.

"Morgan." She heard the warning in Jared's tone and then his mouth was on hers in a blistering kiss sending a bolt of lightning straight through her. And when his tongue came in search of hers, she joined him in a dueling tango of lips and tongues. Jared splayed his fingers into her hair and

Morgan's scalp tingled with the sensation. He was making her feel desired and every part of her wanted him.

*Every part.*

Jared lifted his head long enough to pull off his boxer shorts and kick them aside. Now he stood naked at the foot of the bed while she was still fully clothed. Morgan knew there was something wrong with this picture, but sensed Jared was okay with the dynamic. He was comfortable in his own skin while she was burning up.

She reached for the hem of her tunic and lifted the offending garment over her head until she was wearing only a bra. His gaze went to her breasts. Morgan reached behind her back, unclipped the bra and let the cups fall away from her breasts.

Jared swallowed audibly. "You're beautiful," he said, his voice strained. Then he moved toward her and laid her gently back down on the bed. Morgan hooked her fingers in the waistband of her leggings and glided them along with her panties down her thighs and legs, finally throwing them in a heap on the floor with the rest of their clothes.

Morgan had never gone this far with a man, never been this vulnerable. She wasn't frightened, though, because the look in Jared's eyes was naked hunger. He came down beside her and his lips found hers once more. Morgan wanted to feel his lips everywhere, tasting her and tantalizing her with sensual promise only he could fulfill. When he lifted his head at last, he was breathing hard. "You can tell me to stop at any time."

"I know, but I don't want you to."

Jared began slowly caressing her breasts. Then he lowered his head and circled his tongue around a tight nipple, teasing it. He drew the bud into his mouth with gentle sucks that sent riotous pleasure surging through Morgan. He moved his attention to the other breast and her desire ratcheted up a notch when he added teeth and gentle pressure to his ministrations.

He didn't stop at her breasts; he continued upending her with soft kisses and flicks of his tongue along her stomach and belly button. Morgan knew what came next—she'd read Harlequin romances—but she'd always she'd been too shy or embarrassed to allow what was coming next to happen.

But as Jared's mouth traveled lower, nipping the back of her knees and kissing her thighs, he stopped shy of what she really wanted. What she *needed*.

With a boldness she didn't know she had, Morgan begged. "Please…"

Jared listened.

He softly kissed her mound, allowing her time to get used to him in such an intimate part of her body. When she didn't balk, Jared gently began lapping at her with soft strokes of his tongue. The intimate caress caused powerful sensations to cascade down her body, but Morgan didn't pull away. So Jared went deeper still and when his lips and tongue came to that swollen nub, he sucked hard.

Morgan closed her eyes as Jared tantalized, licked and teased her wet core. Her heart hammered in her chest and she ached deep inside, wanting to be filled, wanting to have him inside her, but unable to voice it. Pleasure was building so hard and fast and spreading through her like wildfire and she began to shake uncontrollably.

"That's it," Jared whispered softly as her body grew tense. "Let go, so I can taste you." He continued worshiping and exploring her with his mouth. Morgan dug her nails into the tousled sheets, desperate for something to anchor her for what was coming, but there was nothing. Her orgasm was intense and she screamed out her release.

As she drifted out of the pleasure cloud, Jared was right beside her. "You okay?" he murmured.

She nodded. Blushing furiously, she tried to cover her face with her hand, but he wouldn't let her.

He framed her cheeks with his palms, his gaze searching. "Don't hide from me during our lovemaking. I need to know if you like everything we're doing or if you want me to stop. At any time, you can say no, okay?"

Tears bit at the back of her eyes. How had she found a man so giving in the bedroom? All Morgan could do was nod.

"Good," he grinned, "because that was just the appetizer. It's time for the entrée."

Jared was doing his best to slow down—to fight his body's instinctive need to dominate and control. But he had to. Jared had never made love to a virgin, so he would have to take his time and be sure Morgan could handle each step. But it was hard on his libido—and he was hard as a rock.

He reached in the pocket of his jeans for a condom. He always carried protection though lately he'd wondered if he'd ever get the opportunity to use it. But now he knew why Morgan had been guarded. She'd been traumatized by the act of sex. It was a privilege and honor she'd chosen him to be her first partner and he didn't take it lightly. He wanted to show her how pleasurable it could be between two consenting *adults*.

He unwrapped the condom and put it on and then came back to settle between Morgan's legs, his weight propped up on his arms. "Are you sure you want to do this?"

Morgan took his face in her hands and kissed him. She wasn't tentative or scared. She deepened the kiss, entwining her tongue with his, and he tasted everything sweet and somewhat forbidden about this woman. He let her set the rhythm and pace, let her lead.

Then he reached between them and parted her with his

fingers. He gently inserted one finger. When she accepted him without flinching, he inserted another, moving them ever so lightly. Morgan undulated against his hands, all the while keeping her mouth locked tightly against his. Jared loved every minute of it.

"You still okay?" he murmured, removing his hand.

"Hmm…" Morgan released a low moan.

Jared moved over her, positioned himself and slowly began to enter her, stretching her wide so she could fully accept him. He took his time so she could get used to his length.

"Oh…" Her eyes opened in wonder, locking with his.

"Am I hurting you?" Jared felt his brow crease in alarm. It was taking tremendous restraint to hold back and not thrust deep to the hilt inside her.

"No, d-don't stop…"

Jared slowly inched further inside her, inch by delicious inch. There was a moment when he reached a barrier and Morgan cried out and clutched his shoulders as she sensed the shock of his final penetration. He apologized in advance before he pushed through the last breach and was fully seated inside her.

He rose on his elbows. "Please tell me you're okay?"

"I'm fine, better than fine." Her lashes were wet, but she wasn't crying. She reached behind him and clutched his behind. "I told you don't stop."

Jared released a sigh and began thrusting, slowly and gently. He kissed her breasts and throat, taking his time on the way back to her mouth. Then he pushed his tongue between her teeth as he drove deeper inside her. Morgan arched her hips to meet his stroke.

"Yes, like that," he growled when she circled her hips, clenching her muscles around his shaft.

It felt unbelievably good to finally be with Morgan. Jared almost forgot to breathe. It was the culmination of weeks of getting to know this incredible woman who made him laugh and smile more than any woman ever had. His body screamed for him to go faster, harder. He gritted his teeth, ignoring his body's demands. Jared doubted Morgan could accept the wild untamed version of him. He had to make her first night of lovemaking one she'd never forget.

Gripping her hips, he lowered his head to suckle her breasts, first one, then the other. His body moved in circular motions and her sweet innocent body pulled him tighter and tighter. Jared didn't know how this woman could make him feel so much, but she had. He could feel his heart tightening in his chest. *What did it mean?*

Morgan sensed Jared holding back from her. She didn't know how she knew, but he was and she didn't want him to. He was her first lover and she was enjoying every minute of it, the way he felt, smelled and tasted. She was wrapping this moment up in her memory in case she never felt this way again.

"I'm not made of glass," she murmured, gripping his backside. "You don't have to be gentle."

He laughed softly and then pounded deeper, *harder*. Her hips lifted as the pressure inside her built to a crescendo. Morgan clawed her nails down Jared's back as he continued pumping. She couldn't hold anything back and suddenly let out a low, keening cry as a maelstrom of intense pleasure struck her.

Jared continued to move with an urgency and tempo that took her breath away until eventually Morgan saw stars and climaxed yet again. Then Jared emitted a low groan as shudders racked his body. *Had he experienced the same earth-shattering sensations she'd felt?*

Afterward, they collapsed in each other's arms. Morgan loved the feel of Jared's big, strong body lying on top of her and the skin-on-skin contact. His arms held her close as if he never wanted to let her go. And in this moment, Morgan didn't want him to. Because she was in love with him.

Sex wasn't clouding her brain. She'd known she was going down the rabbit hole and she'd tried valiantly to fight it, but it was too late. She was a lost cause, in love with a man who didn't believe in happily-ever-after. Yet despite knowing Jared could never return her feelings, Morgan would never regret her first time was with the man she loved.

# Fourteen

Morgan slowly awoke to see dawn breaking over the clouds. She was naked, cradled against Jared's chest. She could hear his even breathing, which told her he was still asleep and she could reminisce about the previous evening.

She wasn't a virgin anymore. She was no longer the frigid woman every man told her she was. Jared had brought her alive with his kiss and his touch. She embraced the fiery attraction she'd felt. She'd never felt anything like the tumultuous fever in her flesh. Her every nerve had been activated by the act of his body becoming one with hers. She'd felt his possession deep in her inner core, and remembering it, Morgan clenched in a spasm of desire.

She felt movement beside her and realized it was the swell of Jared's morning erection. Last night, Jared had been solely focused on her; he hadn't allowed her to pleasure him. Glancing at him now, she saw his eyes were still closed, so Morgan felt a little daring. Wiggling down the sheets, she came to his engorged length. She stroked and massaged him before bringing her tongue to him and lapping with soft licks. He stirred, but didn't yet open his eyes. If he thought it was a dream, she was going to make it a good one.

Opening her mouth, she took his shaft fully inside and began moving up and down. Jared's eyes popped open and he stared down at her in stunned disbelief, but Morgan didn't let that stop her. She continued sucking him using various degrees of suction. He watched her and it gave Morgan a thrill knowing she could make him feel as good as he'd made her feel last night. But he was still fighting to stay in control, so she went to the tip and teased it with her tongue.

Jared threw his head back against the pillows and let out a guttural groan as his orgasm struck. His whole body shuddered in pleasure and Morgan continued pleasing him through the shocks.

When she was done, she glanced up at him. "So how was I?"

Jared grinned at Morgan's playfulness. When he awoke and saw himself inside her mouth, he'd nearly come right then. He'd thought he was dreaming because he'd felt hands moving over his body in an almost worshipful manner, but then those same hands grew less shy and they'd reached for his erection. She'd stroked him with confidence, making his senses go haywire. When the licks and sucks had become increasingly urgent, Jared had known it was no dream.

Who would have imagined his innocent Morgan would be pleasing him in such a way? He took her hand and kissed each one of her fingertips. "You were amazing." He knew she needed to hear it to bolster her self-confidence because he was certain she'd never done *that* to another man.

She smiled broadly. "Happy to be of service."

Jared stroked a wayward strand of hair from her face and tucked it behind her ear as he stared at her. He was usually a master at blocking any sort of feelings from getting in the way of casual sex. Being with Morgan felt much different from his no-strings flings. He'd never been involved with anyone longer than a few months, but Morgan had him crossing all sorts of boundaries. Sex with Morgan had been extremely satisfying. His attraction to her wasn't solely physical and that terrified him.

*She* unnerved him because she awakened something in him that up until now had been dormant. He didn't know if it was her body that had triggered something inside him, but it was there, lurking deep—the need to be close to someone and not just physically, but to tell that other person all your goals and the fears weighing you down and have them buoy you up. Morgan did that. She understood him in a way none of his casual flings ever had.

Determined to take back control, he reached for a condom and after donning it, eased Morgan back down. He brought his mouth down to hers and kissed her long and deep.

He bent his head and sent his tongue to work on her breasts. His teeth grazed one nipple in a gentle bite before soothing it with a wet flick of his tongue. He did the same with the other, pushing it up to meet his tongue. Morgan moaned softly and he used the opportunity to move down her body with his hands until he came to her core. He gently parted her folds and used his fingertips to open her like a flower and slide inside. She gave a breathless gasp; she was still extremely tight.

He teased and tormented and when he found her sweet spot, Morgan climaxed instantly. Spreading her legs, he slid inside her with a groan. Morgan welcomed him, wrapping her legs around his hips.

"Yes, that's it," he encouraged, going deeper with his thrust. And then he moved to nibble on her neck and find the spot between her neck and ear that had her writhing underneath him.

He recognized the tension in her body and knew she was getting close. When he reached between their joined bodies and caressed her clitoris, Morgan soared, clenching around him. A pulse of pure energy went through Jared and he increased the pace with faster, deeper thrusts, which triggered his own release. He let out a ragged groan and collapsed over her.

\* \* \*

Eventually Morgan and Jared made it out of their sex-induced coma to leave the cottage and head back to the main house. They'd fallen asleep after their dawn lovemaking session, so it was after 9:00 a.m. when they marched up the spiral staircase. Chris was descending at the same time.

"Well, well," he said with a knowing smirk. "Look who the cat dragged in. Hope you enjoyed your night." He laughed on his way down the stairs.

Morgan blushed down to the roots of her hair and immediately rushed up the steps to their bedroom. She hoped she didn't run into anyone else who would notice they were still in yesterday's clothes. Morgan let out a deep breath when Jared closed the door behind him.

"Don't be embarrassed, Morgan," Jared said. "What happened last night is natural. My family know we're together."

"I know, but…"

Jared walked toward her, circling his arms around her. "No buts. You're my woman. Everyone expects that we're sleeping together."

Morgan laughed, looking into his gleaming dark eyes. "We weren't until last night."

"But we will be going forward," Jared said with confidence. "Because now that I've had you, I can't get enough." He bent his head and swept his mouth across hers.

Morgan pushed away from him. "Don't start something we can't finish. We probably already missed breakfast and I'm hungry."

"All right," Jared said as if he were a chastised child. "How about a shower?"

A half hour later, Morgan was embarrassed as she made her way to the dining room. She hadn't known a shower could be such a sensual experience. Jared had soaped every inch of her with a sponge, including in between her thighs, where it was a bit sore from the previous evening. Then he'd stunned her by dropping to his knees, taking one of her legs over his shoulder and pleasuring her with his mouth.

When they arrived at the dining room, it was empty and the remnants of breakfast were being cleared by staff. They were about to leave when Antoine came in.

"Good morning." He smiled at them. "You're finally up. Would you care for some breakfast? I can have the cook whip something up."

"An omelet would be great," Morgan said, "with some veggies and whatever protein you might have. And I'd love a cup of coffee."

"Right away. Jared?" Antoine waited for a response.

"I'll have the same," Jared said, helping Morgan into her chair.

Jared sat across from her. The predatory gleam in his eye made Morgan realize he was having naughty thoughts about her. She was about to comment when Ruth stepped into the room. She was in a stylish white tennis dress and sneakers, holding a tennis racket.

"You're awake," Ruth said. "I was beginning to think you'd rather spend more time with each other than us."

Morgan was mortified and couldn't muster a response, but Jared was quick to react. "Of course not. We were just tired. If you recall I worked yesterday."

"You were tired?" Ruth smirked. "Sure, dear." She turned to Morgan. "Mary and I were about to play some tennis. Would you care to join us?"

"Um, my breakfast is coming," Morgan replied as Antoine walked in carrying a carafe of coffee. He poured Morgan a cup and moved to Jared. "Can we meet up later?"

"Of course. Get some rest." Ruth winked at Jared. "Antoine, is the court ready?" she asked on their way out, leaving Morgan and Jared alone.

Morgan's eyes were wide as she stared across the table at her lover. "She knows."

"Grandmother wasn't born yesterday. She's aware of what happens between a man and a woman who are as attracted to each other as we are."

"Is it always this—this intense?" Morgan whispered, reaching for her cup and sipping her coffee that she'd left black. She felt like she needed straight caffeine after the night they'd shared.

Jared watched her over the rim of his mug and Morgan felt a tug in her core. "Not always, but we're very compatible *sexually*."

She blinked several times, trying to escape the trance he seemed to have her in. "So what are you in the mood to do today?"

"Do I really have to answer that?" he asked with a hungry gaze.

"Jared…"

"Oh, you were talking about other than having you naked in my bed?" He placed his index finger on his chin, "Hmm, we could go hiking, canoeing on the creek or riding some horses. Whatever you want?"

"Care for some company?"

They both turned to find Chris in jeans and a polo shirt. Kandi was beside him in a denim jumpsuit looking like she was going to the club rather than a day out in the country.

"Sure." Jared eyed his brother.

"How about canoeing? You and I can race and see which of us has the biceps to win," Chris said boastfully.

"I'm game," Jared responded. "It's been a few years since I've given you a proper whipping."

"Ha, ha, we'll see who's laughing at the finish line."

Jared laughed. "Morgan and I'll meet you at the dock in about an hour after we finish up breakfast."

"See you then." Chris waved and left with Kandi.

Morgan liked seeing the brothers together. She knew the strain of not hearing from Chris had taken a toll on Jared.

She was hoping this weekend would heal the rift in their family. The Robinsons weren't bad people, but they needed to be kinder to one another. Morgan supposed it was easy to see that from the outside looking in.

She could envision herself as a part of this family, but Jared didn't want a relationship with her. Once their agreement was over, they'd go their separate ways. It would be difficult because Jared was her first lover. He would always hold a special place in her heart because he'd taught her how to give and receive pleasure.

Making love with him wasn't simply about two bodies joining in mutual release. There was so much more to it than that. They'd shared an intimacy Morgan had never shared with another human being. Each kiss, each stroke, each caress had bonded her to him. She was now closer to Jared than anyone. She'd confided in him and told him all about her past. *How could she not love him?*

"Morgan?"

She glanced up and noticed Jared was frowning at her. "Is everything okay? I'd lost you for a moment."

"I'm fine."

"Fine is never good when a woman says it," Jared commented. "Are you regretting last night?"

Morgan didn't answer because Antoine came in with two steaming-hot omelets. "Thank you so much. We won't be late tomorrow and make you go through the extra work," she said.

"No worries." Antoine nodded at Jared on his way out.

Morgan was about to tuck into her food when she realized Jared was waiting on a response to his question. "No, I don't regret making love with you. It was the most wondrous, exciting experience of my life."

Jared grinned. "I'm glad. And trust me, it only gets better."

# Fifteen

Jared laughed more that afternoon than he had in years. He and Morgan met Chris and Kandi at the dock as planned. After picking their respective canoes and paddles, he and Chris had helped the ladies inside. One of the grounds-keepers was going to keep time and confirm the winner.

The race was challenging. Chris took off like a bat out of hell while Jared set a steady pace, conserving his energy for the long haul back. He let Chris pass him. When Morgan cried for him to move faster he said, "I've got this. Trust me."

And he did. On the return to the dock, when Chris's arms were tired and starting to fail, Jared kicked into high gear and surpassed his brother, finishing a full ten minutes ahead. He helped Morgan out of the boat, while they waited for Chris and Kandi to arrive.

"That was awesome!" Morgan yelled, wrapping her soft curves around his body and pulling him into a kiss. Jared accepted the congratulatory kiss, but he hungered for more. He had been since Morgan had cut short their shower fun earlier.

Their kiss was getting steamy so it was good thing Chris and Kandi came surging forward. "I want a recount," Chris said as the groundskeeper helped Kandi and him out of the canoe.

"I won fair and square." Jared released Morgan, but only long enough to circle his arm around her waist.

Chris rolled his eyes. "Yeah, yeah. You have youth on your side."

"Anytime you want a rematch, you need only say the word," Jared responded good-naturedly. "I'll even give you a five-minute head start."

Everyone laughed.

"How about a drink?" Chris asked wearily. "I could sure use one." He turned to Kandi and rubbed her belly. "I'm sorry, babe, it'll have to be sparkling fruit juice for you."

The group returned to the main house and found Jared's parents had returned from playing tennis. Or rather his grandmother and mother had played, while his father watched.

"There you kids are," Ruth exclaimed as she lounged on the sofa. "I was wondering if you'd abandoned us old fogies."

"Never, Grandmother." Chris pressed a kiss on her cheek and Jared was glad when she didn't pull away.

"Antoine has the chef preparing some lunch."

"I'd love some," Jared replied, joining them in the spacious living room. He and Morgan sat on one couch, while Chris and Kandi took the larger sofa with his grandmother.

"So what were you kids up to?" Ruth inquired.

"I was reminding Chris how old he is," Jared responded with a smirk.

Chris glared at him.

"They raced canoes," Kandi explained. "It was so much fun, but my pooh bear lost." She looked adoringly up at Chris.

Jared wanted to gag. He couldn't take the lovey-dovey thing. He liked Morgan a helluva lot, but he doubted he would be giving her pet names anytime soon. Even so, if he had his way, he'd have her naked for the duration of their weekend getaway. There was so much more he wanted to show her.

"I'm so glad you're enjoying your visit," his mother responded. "Ruth and I wanted to go into town and do a little shopping while the men did some fishing. We would love for you to join us so we can get to know you better."

"We would?" His grandmother raised a brow and Chris sent her a warning look.

Kandi beamed with a smile. "I would like that. I'm afraid I didn't know what to bring for a weekend retreat."

"You look great, babe," Chris said.

It was true that love was blind, Jared thought, because her denim jumper was the epitome of tacky. He was glad Morgan was a notch above the rest. She had been from the moment they'd met.

"You're coming, Morgan?" His grandmother's question was more of a statement.

Morgan didn't bother looking at Jared for reassurance. She was comfortable holding her own against Ruth. "Of course."

"Excellent."

After enjoying a leisurely lunch of seafood salad, crusty bread and pinot grigio, the women left for town while the men stayed back to go fishing. It had been a long time since Jared, Chris and their father spent any significant amount of time together. And so, after gathering their chairs, poles, tackle boxes with fishing lines hooks and baits, water bottles and much-needed insect repellant, the Robinson men headed to the creek.

Once they had their lines baited and in the water, they sat along the creek bank and waited. Fortunately, Chris was smart enough to bring a cooler full of beer, so Jared reached inside, screwed off the top and took a swig.

"I'm glad we're alone," their father began. "Perhaps now

you could enlighten Jared and I how you came to be en-gaged to Kandi."

Chris's expression sharpened. "If you're both going to gang up on me, I'm going to head back to the house."

"Far from it," Jared said. "We just want to understand where you're coming from. How did you meet?"

Chris sighed and the tension in his shoulders slowly began to lapse. "I met Kandi after one of our clients wanted to go to a strip club. I admit it wasn't my thing, but when I saw Kandi on that stage, it was love at first sight."

"I think you're confusing lust with love, son," their fa-ther replied. "It's easy to do."

"C'mon, Jared. Don't leave me hanging. You said you met Morgan and were instantly intrigued. Am I right?" Chris asked.

"I was but that's different," Jared objected. He thought about how Chris and Kandi were already engaged. What if Morgan were his fiancée? His *fake* fiancée, he quickly amended. He couldn't offer her more than that. So why did the idea cause his heart to speed up? "Finish your story."

"After I took the client home, I came back to the club. At first, Kandi didn't want to spend time with me be-cause I was a customer, but I convinced her to come out for breakfast. And well, the rest, as they say, is history." Chris shrugged.

"And you're sure she's not after your money?" their fa-ther inquired.

"Dad…" Jared intervened, but Clay held up his hand.

"I'm not done," he said sternly. "A young woman who's found herself on that stage may see you as her meal ticket. You're worth millions."

"Kandi isn't with me for my money. And to prove it, she's agreed to sign a prenup."

Their father rubbed his jaw. "I'm pleasantly surprised, but I'll believe it when I see it. All I'm saying, Chris, is I don't want you led around by the wrong body part. I'm shocked to say it, but perhaps you need to be more like Jared. It appears he's found a class act in Morgan. She's poised, educated and not bad on the eyes."

Jared felt proud his father thought so highly of the woman on his arm. "Thanks, Dad."

"But she is the type of girl you marry." His father wasn't short on advice. "Are you ready to handle that?"

Both Chris and his father stared at Jared, but he wasn't ready to answer their questions any more than he could the ones running through his mind since he'd met Morgan.

"How did this fishing expedition get serious all of a sudden?" Jared finally asked, lightening the mood. "I thought we were here to catch fish."

Jared thankfully got a reprieve because one of their poles moved, indicating they'd caught something. Just like Morgan had caught his heart.

Morgan had no idea part of her weekend included being mediator between the Robinsons and Kandi, but that's exactly what she was. After changing out of her active wear, Morgan donned a straight skirt, tank and her favorite jean jacket and joined the women for a jaunt into the town that was a few miles from the compound.

Ruth's version of getting to know Kandi included loaded questions destined to trip up the poor girl and have her walk into a minefield. Morgan did her best to help, but it wasn't easy. Her mind was still in the cottage with Jared where he'd introduced her to all the ways he could make her body sing.

The maelstrom of need he'd created in her after years of being frigid had Morgan feeling out of sorts. A kaleidoscope of butterflies was swirling though her insides as she anticipated the night to come with the man she loved. *But what did he feel for her?*

Kindness?

Affection?

*Or was it simply about lust pure and simple.*

"Morgan, darling," Ruth called to her from one of the racks in the upscale boutique where they were shopping. "You must come here. I've found the most divine dress for you."

Morgan smiled and walked over. She'd never had a grandmother. Heck, she hadn't had much of a mother, either, so being fawned over by Ruth was heartwarming. Ruth held up a stunning silk green dress, but the price tag was outrageous.

"It matches your eyes," Mary concurred.

"I'm getting it for you." Ruth handed the garment to a saleswoman who had seemed to hover nearby ever since they'd walked in.

Morgan shook her head. "I can't let you do that. It's too much."

"Of course you can," Ruth said, nodding at the clerk. "We'll take it. And you, my dear," she looked at Kandi, who'd been quiet since they'd arrived in the store, "we need to find you something."

Kandi shrugged, glancing around. "This isn't really my style."

"You mean wearing clothes with decorum?" Ruth asked.

"Ruth!" Mary called her out.

"I'm sorry," Ruth replied, "but, my dear—" she sauntered over to Kandi "—if you intend to be with my grandson, you're going to have to change your look. Because this—" Ruth motioned to Kandi's zebra-striped pants, bustier and leather jacket "—simply will not do. You will be an embarrassment to Chris and the entire family."

"Oh!" Kandi clutched her mouth and rushed out of the store.

"Ruth, did you have to be so harsh?" Morgan asked. "She's new to this world."

"So are you," Ruth responded, "but you've acclimated like fish to water. She *has* to learn proper decorum."

"And she will in time," Mary said. "I'm going to talk to her and let her know not everyone in the family shares *your* opinion."

Ruth sighed as Mary left the store. She walked over to the clerk and handed her her credit card and then turned to Morgan. "Was I harsh?"

Morgan knew Ruth respected directness so she gave it to her. "Yes, you were. Kandi doesn't have to be your enemy. In fact, you want her as your ally. Otherwise, Chris could leave again. You don't want that, do you?"

"No, of course not." She reached out and caressed Morgan's cheek with her palm. "You are a marvel. I don't know how my grandson was lucky enough to find you, but I'm so glad you're a part of this family."

Her words were like a knife to Morgan's heart, because she wasn't a part of their clan. She was only Jared's *pretend* girlfriend, but somewhere along the way it had become real. Not just for her, but for his family too. *How would they feel when they learned it was all a lie? Would they hate Morgan like they did Kandi?*

When they returned to the compound, the Robinson men were feeling very full of themselves, having caught striped and largemouth bass in the creek. While the chef was preparing their catches for the night's meal, everyone went to their respective rooms to change for dinner.

It didn't take long once the door closed to their room for Jared to reach for Morgan, but she pulled away and walked to the French doors leading to the terrace. The air outside had turned crisp and that was fine with her. She was still thinking about Ruth's comment from earlier about how

Morgan had seamlessly integrated into their family. She hated lying to them, but at the time when he'd presented the offer, it had given Morgan some breathing room to figure out what came next. Because she had to face it. Henry wanted nothing to do with her. Only her siblings were interested in getting to know Morgan.

"What's wrong?" Jared asked, coming to join her outside on the terrace outside their bedroom window. He placed his arms on either side of the railing, caging her in. Morgan tried to ignore his presence behind her, but she couldn't.

It was Jared. His scent was like an aphrodisiac to her.

"I'm thinking about when this all ends."

"Don't," Jared whispered, nuzzling her neck. "Think about right now." He pulled her against him and Morgan felt the hard press of his arousal against her bottom. He lowered his head and began sucking the skin between her neck and ear he'd found was her sweet spot.

"Jared…"

"The only thing I want you thinking about—" Jared's fingers reached for the waistband of her skirt and he slipped his finger inside past the barrier of her panties until he came to her damp core "—is me inside you." He moved his hand deeper, plundering her, and Morgan felt her control slipping.

Morgan shook her head, trying to ignore the sensations coursing through her. "No, we can't. Not now. Everyone is waiting." *Were they really going to do this outside?*

"Oh we can." He shifted Morgan away from the railing and backed her up against the wall of the terrace. Before she could stop him, Jared had her plastered against his chest and was yanking her skirt up over her waist while he masterfully palmed her butt. Then he shoved his hand into her hair and gave her a no-holds-barred kiss. He literally devoured her mouth and Morgan gave up thinking about anything else except this moment.

Emboldened, she opened the button of his jeans and then the zip, until they were loose enough around his hips for her to shove them and his briefs down. Jared's erection sprang free and Morgan licked her lips. She couldn't wait to have him inside her again. Jared was quicker than she was and pulled a condom out of his pocket.

He rolled it over himself and said, "I'm sorry, Morgan, but I've been dying for you all day, so this is going to be fast and hard. I'll give you slow and sexy later."

He hooked his hand over her thigh and when he came to the thong she wore, he pushed it aside. Pinning her against the wall, Jared slid into her with one long, sure stroke. Morgan felt not only herself dissolve, but their surroundings fade away as Jared began pumping inside her.

Morgan entwined her arms around his neck and kissed him fiercely as she clutched at his shoulders. Jared continued moving his hips upward until he touched something inside her, causing her to rocket up and down against his length.

"Ride me, Morgan," Jared encouraged. "Use me."

Morgan felt her orgasm build until eventually her entire body shattered into a million pieces. Jared shouted her name as she screamed out her release into the evening sky.

Eventually, Jared let go of her thigh, but still kept her pinned against the wall. And Morgan was thankful he did because she had no strength left. Never had she felt so free and utterly abandoned.

"Was it good for you?" Jared asked with a wide grin.

"What do you think?" She smirked.

# Sixteen

When Sunday afternoon arrived, Morgan was sad for the weekend to end. She'd enjoyed spending time with Jared and his family. They'd gone horseback riding that morning. It was her first time, but Ruth had insisted on buying Morgan riding breeches, a long sleeve shirt and knee-high boots during their shopping trip. Jared had barely been able to keep his hands off her in the stables as he'd helped her into the saddle.

The ride had been scenic. Even Kandi, who'd never ridden a horse either, had managed to stay upright. They'd stopped to enjoy a delicious picnic lunch of wine, chilled tiger prawns, poached lobster with tarragon, brie, baguettes and fresh fruit with Grand Marnier cream. The mood had been light and easy.

When they returned to the compound, they cooled off the horses, then everyone packed their cars to return home for the workweek ahead. Morgan hated to leave. She'd felt such a sense of belonging with the Robinsons. And it hurt, knowing it wasn't going to last.

"What's on your mind?" Jared asked as he drove her back to her apartment.

"Our arrangement will be coming to an end soon," Morgan answered.

He turned and glanced at her for a moment. "I thought

I'd squashed these thoughts on the balcony. Are you that eager to be rid of me?"

Morgan frowned. "Of course not," she answered a little too quickly. When she should have been thinking of self-preservation, she'd blurted out her real feelings. The truth of the matter was, the longer they were together, the harder it would be to walk away.

"Good. Because I'm not ready for this to be over." She noticed him grip the wheel a little too tightly as he spoke.

"You're not the only one who gets a say," Morgan answered defensively.

"I know that," he murmured. "You need only the say the word and we can end it at any time."

Morgan folded her arms across her chest and stared out the window. *Was that really how Jared felt? Was she so easily expendable he'd let her go without a fight?* She knew Jared didn't do commitment, but she'd thought he felt some affection for her, if for no other reason than he'd been her first lover. Her *only* lover. She didn't want anyone else, but apparently he could take her or leave her.

And it hurt because she loved him. It was plain and simple as that, but she couldn't show her love. He would only scorn it. She had to keep her feelings hidden.

Glancing around, Morgan noticed that Jared had missed the turn to the Residences at the W. "Where are we going?"

"To my place," he said, looking straight ahead.

She couldn't go home with him. If she did, Morgan was afraid of what she might reveal. "Jared, it's been a long weekend and you have to work in the morning. I think it's best if I go home."

He glanced at her, but his eyes were hooded. "I'd rather you came home with me, but if you want me to turn the car around, I will."

Morgan swallowed. He was putting the decision in her hands. Or was he really? *Was this some sort of manipula-*

*tion to get her to do what he wanted?* Whatever the reason, deep down Morgan wanted to be with him. "Fine."

Conversation was nonexistent for the remainder of the drive and on the elevator ride up to his penthouse. Once inside, Jared placed their luggage on the floor and turned to her. "I'm sorry."

Morgan stared at him in disbelief. Jared wasn't a man who apologized. He was cocky, arrogant at times, but always self-assured. But when she looked at him his expression was uncertain. *Had he never told someone sorry before?*

"Why are you sorry?"

"For what I said earlier," Jared explained, shifting from one foot to the other. "Or should I say the callous way I said it. We have something good and I don't want it to end. There, are you happy now?"

Morgan smiled. "That you apologized?" she asked, coming toward him. Despite her brain screaming to run for the hills, she wound her arms around his neck.

"No. That you got me to admit my feelings," he responded.

"A little humble pie never hurt," Morgan said, looking at him from under her lashes. "So why don't you get to apologizing." She grabbed him by the head and planted her lips on his.

The next morning, Jared sat in his office at Robinson Holdings staring at his laptop. He'd been looking at the same set of figures for an hour and they still made no sense. His mind kept wandering to when he'd kissed Morgan awake near dawn. He'd ignored her protests for sleep and nudged her legs apart with his shoulders.

Pressing his mouth against her feminine core, he'd feasted on her sweetness until he heard her moans of pleasure. He hadn't been satisfied with just a taste. Instead, he'd turned her over onto her stomach and taken her from behind. He'd fondled her breasts while thrusting inside her and teasing her wet sex until she'd screamed his name. Only then had Jared been sated enough to drift off to sleep.

The problem was that sex wasn't just sex with Morgan. It was a discovery of all the secret ways he could pleasure her. Jared was toying with the idea of extending their relationship even though he'd already convinced his grandmother of his committed status but the board was still skeptical, so he needed to keep up appearances. He kept telling himself it was all about sex.

Great sex.

He didn't want or need the fairy tale Morgan undoubtedly wanted. He didn't do commitment of any kind. So why was he doubting everything he'd ever told himself?

"It's really strange seeing you behind that desk," Chris said from the doorway.

Jared was surprised to see his brother in a gray suit and tie standing on the threshold of his office. *Chris's former office.*

"It feels strange for me too," Jared responded. "What brings you by?"

A disconcerted look came across his brother's features. "Well, I…"

"You thought now that you've returned, Jared would step aside?" their grandmother inquired from behind him.

Chris instantly jumped at the sound of her voice. "To be honest," Chris replied, "yes. I thought Jared would relish the opportunity to get back to his former lifestyle of laid back days and fast nights."

"Those days are over now that he's met Morgan," Ruth answered. "He wouldn't ruin that by reverting to his former playboy ways."

Jared noted the look of disbelief on his brother's face.

"It might surprise you, Chris, but I have enjoyed learning more about Robinson Holdings and I don't intend on leaving." Jared shocked himself by agreeing with their grandmother.

"What am I supposed to do?" Chris asked.

Jared rose to his feet and buttoned his suit jacket. "We can share the responsibilities. As you said, one person handling all the weight is *too* much. We can share."

"I don't think I agreed to that," their grandmother interjected, folding her arms across her chest. "And neither did the board. You've begun to gain their grudging respect, Jared. Why stop now?"

"Because I want to have a life, Grandmother." Jared didn't know if that included or didn't include Morgan, but he would never find out if he walked the same path as Chris. "I don't want to burn out like Chris did. No offense." He glanced at his older brother. "You must see this is the best solution. And I need your help in convincing the board."

She stared at him. "I have to say, Jared, you've impressed me these past weeks and I'm really proud of you."

Jared grinned. "Thank you."

"So am I." Chris faked a sniff and they both laughed. "I would be honored to work with you, brother." He offered his hand and Jared shook it.

"It was so nice of you to join me," Kandi said when she and Morgan met up midweek at a baby boutique frequented by upper class moms. Morgan had been surprised to receive the invite, but suspected Kandi needed a friendly ear.

"No problem," Morgan replied. "I'm happy to help."

"I'm nervous," Kandi said as she ran her fingers over the blankets. "Not about having the baby, about fitting into Chris's family. You seem to be such a hit with his parents and grandmother. I was hoping you could give me some pointers."

"Be yourself," Morgan said evenly. "Ruth is all fire,

but once you get to know her, there's a warm individual underneath."

Kandi gave her an incredulous look and Morgan couldn't resist a chuckle. "Okay, maybe warm is pushing it, but I don't know…we sort of hit it off. She's like the grandmother I never had."

"A cranky one. She criticized everything I wore this weekend."

Morgan lowered her head.

"What?" Kandi asked, putting her hands on her expanding hips. She was in leopard print pants, a bodysuit and bomber jacket.

"If you want to fit in, you have to dress the part. I'm not saying you have to lose your individuality. Just tone it down a notch. Not so many low-cut tops, skintight jeans or leopard prints."

"That's how I got Chris," Kandi said with a smirk.

"But it won't be how you'll keep him. I can help you find a few things that you can sprinkle in with your own clothes. How's that sound?"

Kandi shrugged. "If you say so, but I think I look fabulous."

Morgan smiled. Kandi would think that, but the mirror was lying to her.

Later that evening, after enjoying takeout over a bottle of wine, Morgan regaled Jared with stories of her day with Kandi. Morgan liked that they could sit in their comfy clothes on the sofa like a real couple and have a night at home. She was in a tank top and yoga pants while Jared wore a T-shirt and sweatpants.

"You don't have to hang out with her if you don't want to," Jared responded. "It's not a condition of being my girlfriend."

Morgan frowned, feeling a bit annoyed. "I know that,

but I like Kandi. She reminds me in many ways of my mother. Misguided. I thought I could help her win over your grandmother." Then she paused to stare at him for a moment. Did he realize he'd called her his girlfriend? Not his pretend one?

Jared looked at her incredulously. "That's not likely, Morgan. Don't go giving Kandi false hope."

"C'mon, she's not that bad."

"No, but once my grandmother forms an opinion, it's hard to convince her otherwise."

"You did," Morgan responded, poking him in the chest. "In a short time, you've been able to convince Ruth of your willingness and ability to lead Robinson Holdings. Surely, Kandi can change her mind, too?"

"I'm her grandson. I'm family."

"I refuse to believe that's all it's about," Morgan replied. "With a little grooming and maybe some etiquette classes, Kandi can overcome…" She searched for the right words.

"Her lack of class?" Jared offered.

"That's harsh."

"But true. Don't go changing Kandi. Chris fell in love with her exactly as she is. They'll have to muddle their way through this."

Morgan lowered her lashes. "I'm sorry. I was only trying to help."

"Aw, come here," he murmured, reaching over to pull her into his lap. "You didn't do anything wrong. It was a really nice thing to do. And I…" He stopped midsentence and without another word, lifted her away from him and rushed out of the room, leaving Morgan wondering exactly what he'd been about to say.

Jared splashed water over his face in the master bath. *What the hell?* He'd almost said, "And I love that about you." *Love*. That word wasn't in his vocabulary when it came to any other woman. So why now?

It was Morgan.

*She made him feel.*

For the first time, a woman had stumbled into his life and he'd forgotten to put up barriers to keep her out and his emotions in. With Morgan, Jared's feelings were allowed free reign and he didn't know how to coral them back in.

A knock sounded on the door.

"You okay?" Morgan inquired from the other side. "The way you got up so fast—I hope it wasn't something we ate?"

Of course she would think it was food poisoning rather than him running away because he was scared of the emotions she was bringing to the surface.

"I'm fine. I'll be out in a second."

"Okay." He heard her retreating footsteps and sucked in a deep breath.

He'd thought he could have it both ways, that he could keep Morgan and not get caught up. But he was wrong. He wasn't the settling down kind. Never had been. Never would be. Morgan deserved a man who could give her his whole heart and who knew how to love. He wasn't that man. He had to let her go.

His hands gripped the countertop. But how could he deny the attraction they shared? He'd never met a woman he'd wanted so much. When Morgan was in his arms, his entire body felt electric. It had been that way from the start when he'd noticed her at the wedding reception. He'd instantly wanted to claim her as his own as he did now. Thinking about her made him want to get them both naked.

Jared stood straight.

One more night. That was all he would give himself. Maybe then, he could find a way for them both to move on.

But the minute he came out of the bathroom, Jared found Morgan sprawled across his bed, naked, wearing nothing but a smile. All thoughts of saying goodbye to this gorgeous woman flew out the window as hot, molten lust drove him to fling off his T-shirt, drop his sweats and briefs and charge toward the bed.

He allowed himself enough time to don a condom before slanting his lips over hers in a demanding kiss that sent his pulse racing. Morgan responded by teasing her tongue with his own. Jared reacted by covering her body with his and smoothly thrusting inside her.

Incredible pleasure coursed through Jared and he wanted to close his eyes, but he couldn't. He wanted to look up at Morgan because who knew if this might be the last time they were together. Their eyes locked and Morgan lifted her hips to move with him in unison until a tidal wave of passion swept over them and they both exploded. Jared saw stars as he continued pumping the last of his release. With their sweaty bodies entwined together, Jared fell asleep in Morgan's arms.

# Seventeen

"Thank you so much for agreeing to meet me, Fallon," Morgan said when her sister joined her at the downtown wine bar the following evening. She'd dressed casually in black jeans, ruffled shirt and ankle booties. Fallon was equally relaxed in gray slacks, a lavender silk shirt and flats after coming straight from the Stewart Technologies offices.

Morgan needed someone to confide in about her feelings for Jared. Although she liked Kandi, their relationship was still so new. Morgan didn't feel like she could pour her heart out to Kandi.

"I was happy to get the call." Fallon leaned back against one of the sofas in the corner of the room and sipped from her wineglass. "I was hoping one day you'd feel comfortable enough to consider me not just a sister, but a friend."

"I feel like I need one."

Ever since she and Jared had shared takeout and acted domestic like a real couple a few nights ago, he'd been acting distant. She hadn't seen him all week. He'd told her he had to work, but Morgan felt like it was an excuse.

*Had she done something wrong?*

*Had the novelty of being with a virgin her first time worn off?*

She wouldn't have thought so, because it appeared he'd

been satisfied after they'd made love, but what did she know?

"Talk to me," Fallon said, leaning in. "What's going on?"

"I'm sure you've heard I've been seeing Jared Robinson." Morgan took a sip of her crisp Riesling.

Fallon nodded. "I was surprised anyone would be 'seeing Jared.'" Fallon made air quotes with her fingers. "He's always been a sly one with the ladies."

"I know." Morgan offered a small smile. "His reputation precedes him."

"That's an understatement." Fallon chuckled. "You have no idea the amount of mayhem he and Dane used to get into."

"He told me before he asked me to be his pretend girlfriend."

Fallon sat up straight. "Pretend girlfriend?" She frowned. "Explain."

Morgan filled Fallon in on the details of their deal, explaining Jared's predicament with the board, his grandmother's demands and Chris's absence.

"Morgan, honey." Fallon reached for her hand, "You didn't have to do this. Ayden and I, even Dane would have helped you find a job or given you whatever you need."

"After Henry's rejection, I was determined to make it under my own steam without any help from the Stewarts. That's why I accepted the offer. But then Jared and I started spending time together and I realized I liked him."

Fallon raised a brow.

"I think I love him, Fallon," Morgan said quietly, glancing at her sister. "And if I'm honest, it might have been love at first sight when he rescued me at the wedding after I'd humiliated myself in front of our father. I drank too much and threw myself at him, but he didn't take me up on it. Instead, he put me to bed when I got sick."

"As he should have done," Fallon responded hotly.

"Hey, it's not his fault," Morgan said. "He was very clear about our arrangement. Except somewhere along the line, our relationship became more intimate."

"And you slept with him?"

Morgan nodded. "You see—it was the first time I'd ever..." She couldn't go on. It was too embarrassing at her age to reveal she'd still been a virgin.

"Been with a man?" Fallon picked up on what Morgan hadn't been able to say aloud. "Did Jared take advantage of you? If he did, I'll sic Dane on him."

Morgan shook her head fiercely. "No, I wanted him and it was wonderful. He was patient and gentle. And since then, well, it's been nothing short of amazing. Or at least I thought it was. But the last few days, I can feel Jared pulling away."

"And you're worried he's lost interest?"

"Yes."

"Oh, sweetie, these things happen. Sometimes we're not always meant to be with our *firsts*. Sometimes they're only meant for right now. And considering Jared's background, distance could be his way of trying to end your relationship without coming right out and telling you."

"I don't want it to end." Tears seeped out of Morgan's eyes and she wiped them away with her fingertips. "I love him."

"Have you told him?"

She shook her head.

"Has he said those three little words to you?"

"No."

"I don't want to hurt you, but a guy like Jared isn't meant for the long haul. He's not the marrying kind."

Morgan knew Fallon spoke the truth, but to hear it out loud still hurt. Perhaps she'd needed someone to sound the alarm and snap her out of this fantasy she'd been living in where she and Jared had a happy ending.

"Come here." Fallon wrapped Morgan in her embrace and Morgan softly sobbed in her big sister's arms. "I know it seems like the end of the word now, but I promise you, you'll get through this."

Morgan wasn't sure. *How did you get over your first love?*

Morgan heard from Jared later that evening. She was at her apartment getting ready for bed and was curled under the cover with a good book when he finally called.

"Hello."

"Morgan, I'm sorry I've been MIA this week," Jared said.

"I understand. You've been busy." She didn't understand, not after the intimacies they'd shared, but what else could she say? She wasn't about to embarrass herself by appearing needy and desperate for his company.

"I know it's short notice, but I forgot to tell you about a charity event on Saturday my grandmother throws every year. It's for Alzheimer's research. It would mean a lot if you could come with me."

*Damn him.*

Right when she was ready to write him off, Jared sprang this on her. She wanted to say hell no, she wouldn't go. A girl had to have some pride. Yet despite his lack of interest in her over the past week, he had to know she wouldn't turn him down knowing how dear this cause was to him.

"Morgan?"

She blinked and realized it had been several moments since he'd asked the question. "Yes?"

"Will you go?"

She paused again. Her head told her to end this now while she still could, but her heart told her to be there for the man she loved even knowing how much it might cost her in the end. "Yes, I'll attend."

She heard his audible sigh of relief on the other end. "Thank you. It's black tie, so buy whatever you need."

"I'll do that."

"All right, well, I'll pick you up on Saturday night around six. Sound good?" His voice was stilted as if he was finding the conversation as difficult as she was. *How could two people be so close one moment and so far apart the next?*

"Fine."

"Okay. Well…have a good night." Seconds later, he'd hung up.

Morgan's heart sank when Jared ended the call so quickly. He couldn't bear to talk to her when barely a week ago, he couldn't keep his hands off her? *Was she really so terrible he no longer wanted her?*

Morgan threw the phone down and flung herself on bed. This mess was of her own making. She'd agreed to this arrangement, which was supposed to be strictly platonic. Instead, she'd let herself be drawn into Jared's family life and into his bed and now she was in too deep to see a way out.

Jared stared at the handset on his desk in his office. He felt horrible. He'd been cold and distant with Morgan and she didn't deserve it. She hadn't done anything wrong. She'd done everything he'd asked of her. No, she'd done more. She'd endeared herself to his grandmother and his entire family loved her. She'd befriended Kandi when she didn't have to.

As for him, she'd brought a happiness into his life he hadn't known before. He smiled. Laughed. And it was all because of Morgan. *She* was turning him into a better man. He was more engaged in his life than he'd ever been. It was no longer about the women, fancy cars and extravagant trips.

Having Robinson Holdings thrown into his lap had forced him to grow up and take stock of his life. He'd been going through the motions for years, aimlessly rushing from one thing to the next with no real direction. Becoming CEO had shown Jared he was not a useless member of the family. He had value and brought something to the table other than a bad boy reputation.

Meeting Morgan was the other catalyst. Seeing her at Dane's wedding had revealed a protective side of his nature. He'd never considered himself a knight in shining armor by any stretch of the imagination, but somehow because of Morgan he'd become one. Saving her from the leech who'd been manhandling her at the wedding. Taking care of her when she'd become ill in her hotel room and putting her to bed. Stopping her from blowing up her family's reputation with the gossip blogger. He'd done all of those things because *she* brought out the best in him.

Then their relationship took a turn at his family's compound as he'd always known it would. The attraction between them was too strong to be denied. She'd opened up to him about her past and allowed him the special gift of being the first man to make love to her. And it had been epic. Beyond his wildest dreams or anything he could ever have imagined.

She'd *touched* him.

Now he was acutely aware of her—whether it was the inflection in her voice, the scent of her hair or the fit of those skinny jeans she loved to wear. He had spent every night of the last week lying awake, recalling their passionate unions, and he'd literally ached. All of it disarmed him and he didn't know how to deal with it. He knew how to be the man he'd been, but Jared wasn't sure he could give her the white picket fence she inevitably wanted. This week he'd pushed her away in hope of getting her out of his head. Or was it his *heart* he was afraid of?

Avoidance had worked until Ruth reminded him of the charity event she held every year in his grandfather's honor to raise awareness about Alzheimer's and find a cure. He was ashamed to say it, given how he'd treated Morgan all week, pretty much ignoring her, but he *needed* her there. Not just for his grandmother, but for *him*. Every year, the event got harder and harder because his grandfather was slipping further and further away. Jared couldn't stop it or control the outcome.

Morgan's presence would be a balm; a comfort on a night when he needed it most. Jared knew he was being unfair. He should end it so Morgan could find someone worthy of her love and affection. He suspected she had feelings for him and it gutted him because he *couldn't* return them.

Somehow, he would get through the night. And when it was over, he would release her from their arrangement. *What choice did he have if he wasn't willing to commit?*

# Eighteen

The night of the charity event, Morgan reminded herself to be calm, cool and collected. She mustn't get carried away by the grandeur of being on Jared's arm because after all it was a mirage.

When Jared arrived to pick her up from her apartment, he'd been distant. He'd remarked on how beautiful she looked in the shimmery metallic Dior gown with spaghetti straps she'd purchased earlier that day. The top was a bustier style, and the skirt, covered with thousands of silver sequins, flowed all the way to the floor. Morgan had loved the dress instantly despite the outrageous price tag.

She'd chosen to wear her hair down tonight and it now hung in luxurious waves down her back. Between the salon and the store, she'd had little time to get ready so she'd had to apply her own makeup. She was pleased with her appearance until she encountered Jared's lackluster reception. He, on the other hand, looked dashing in a tuxedo, and it made Morgan's heart clench in her chest.

She sat as far from Jared as she could in the limousine he'd hired. She couldn't bear to look at him, let alone touch him, because deep in her gut, Morgan knew what they had was over.

The event was being held at the Hotel Ella, a beautiful historic hotel with a large wraparound veranda, circular staircase and expansive front lawn. Morgan half expected Scarlett O'Hara to descend the steps as they entered the foyer.

Scarlett didn't, but Ruth Robinson greeted them in a floor-length gown and swept her up in a hug. "My darling, you look stunning." She stroked Morgan's cheek and turned to her grandson. "Doesn't she, Jared?"

He looked at Morgan and the arresting expression in his eyes caused her to nearly stop breathing. She hadn't seen that look all week and she hated that it still mattered to her. Morgan accepted a glass of champagne from a passing waiter, swigged it and set it back on the tray.

"Yes, she does," Jared responded.

Jared's parents came forward to greet Morgan as did Chris and Kandi. Chris looked handsome in a navy tuxedo while shockingly Kandi wore a simple strapless gown with a side slit. It was tasteful and elegant. She was finally listening to Morgan's advice and it brought a smile to her face. It reminded Morgan of how in a short time, these people had come to mean a lot to her.

"C'mon, I'd like to introduce you around." Ruth looped her arm through Morgan's and led her away. Morgan was thankful for a reprieve to get her mask back in place. She couldn't let Jared know how much he was hurting her with his coldness.

"Is everything all right, my dear?" Ruth asked, once they were some distance away.

Morgan offered a small smile. "Everything's fine."

Ruth raised a brow. "What's going on? Has my grandson done something wrong I need to give him a kick in the shins over?"

"No." It wasn't Ruth's business what went on between her and Jared. She couldn't put her in the middle and certainly wouldn't cause dissension in the family now that their relationships were on better footing.

"All right, well, if you need me. I'm here," Ruth said and

walked over to a small group in the corner. "Everyone, I'd like to introduce you to Morgan Stewart. She's my grandson's girlfriend and very dear to me."

Several pairs of eyes landed on Morgan. What she hadn't been expected was to see her father and Nora in the group. Morgan swallowed the lump in her throat. She prayed neither of them would make a scene.

She needn't have worried because Henry looked through her as if she wasn't there and Nora, well, she x-rayed Morgan as if she was a specimen on a slab. She stared incessantly for what seemed like an eternity. Nora must have found her wanting, because she immediately excused herself. Henry glared at Morgan and quickly moved away to follow his wife.

Morgan tensed. Henry didn't need to speak to relay the message. He hated her. "If you'll excuse me, I'm going to go powder my nose." She extricated her arm from Ruth's and quickly walked away. She was moving through the ballroom, trying to keep the tears at bay when a figure moved into her path.

"Morgan, are you all right?"

She heard Jared's voice, but she wanted nothing to do with him. Not now. She needed air. Morgan rushed out and through a haze of tears she saw the sign for the restroom. She passed a varied collection of contemporary art until she arrived at a luxuriously appointed ladies' room complete with a sitting room.

Morgan sank into one of the chairs and reached for a Kleenex sitting on the nearby table. Why did *he* have to be here? Morgan wondered. She could have gotten through the night and Jared's coldness toward her, but to see the father who refused to acknowledge her was too much. Even hearing she'd taken his name hadn't elicited a reaction from Henry. Just fury.

Tears flowed down her cheeks. *Why was she here and putting herself through this abuse?* She should have left

Austin as soon as Henry rejected her. Instead, she'd allowed herself to get caught up in Jared's life. And now that he'd gotten what he wanted, Jared was done with her.

"Really? You're going to cry now after everything you've done?"

Morgan glanced up into the stormy brown eyes of Nora Stewart. She wore a long red gown with a V neckline and a billowing skirt. She looked regal and every bit the queen of the ball. Morgan sat up straight. "What do you want?"

"I want you to go back to whatever rock you crawled out from under and leave my family alone. You have no place here."

Morgan stared at Nora and that's when she realized it. Nora knew she was Henry's daughter because tonight, for the first time, she'd *really* looked at Morgan and seen the same eyes staring back at her. "I have every right to be here. I'm Henry's daughter."

"You're a mistake," Nora said. "A moment of weakness on Henry's part."

Nora admitted the truth! "And you've forgiven him for cheating on you?" Morgan asked incredulously. "Why?"

"Despite what everyone might think of me, I love Henry and we've spent a lifetime together. I won't let an interloper come in and cause friction in my family."

Morgan rose to her feet. She wasn't going to let Nora intimidate her. "They're my family too. I didn't ask for any of this."

"Yet, here you are making pronouncements at Dane's wedding. Showing up on our doorstep with your hand out," Nora responded, folding her arms across her chest. "What else am I supposed to think?"

Morgan sighed. "I admit I could have waited for a more opportune time, but I didn't know if Henry would see me, let alone believe me. And guess what? He didn't. He hates me as much as he hates Ayden."

Nora sighed. "Henry doesn't hate you, but seeing you is like seeing his failure, his mistakes all over again."

"I'm not a mistake," Morgan said fiercely.

"You must see you're not going to get the result you're looking for. Henry will never accept you. Isn't it better that you move on from this town? Hooking yourself up with Jared Robinson, a notorious playboy, will only bring you heartache."

"Leave my relationship with Jared out of this."

"How can I? When you've flaunted it to all of Austin," Nora said, sweeping her hand wide. "He'll never marry you. I've known that young man since he was a child and he's easily bored, moving on to the next thing before he's put down the first. You're merely a distraction, nothing more."

Morgan's eyes narrowed. Even if Nora's words struck a chord, she would never let her see it. "You can keep your observations to yourself."

Nora shrugged. "Don't say I didn't warn you." Lifting her skirts, she swept out of the room, leaving Morgan staring after her.

Once she was gone, Morgan crumbled into the chair and placed both her hands over her face. Tonight was an epic fail. Not only had Jared rejected her, but so had her father. And according to Nora, that wasn't ever going to change. She was a "mistake." Whenever he saw her, Henry was reminded he'd cheated on his wife and she was the result. She was unwanted by every man in her life.

She had to leave now with as much dignity as she could muster. Rising to her feet, she rushed over to the sink and tried to repair the damage her crying jag had done to her makeup. She managed to obscure it, but her eyes were still red and rimmed with pain. Breathing deeply, Morgan pulled out her cell and called for an Uber. The car was nearby and would be there in minutes. She intended to slip out quietly before anyone else saw her.

Morgan prepared to move swiftly down the corridor but Jared was leaning on the wall outside the restroom. He stood upright when he saw her.

"Morgan?" He rushed to her side and tried to touch her cheek, but she moved away.

"Don't touch me!"

"What happened in there?" Jared didn't let her harsh tone deter him. "What did Nora say to you?"

Morgan didn't answer. She started down the hall. As she did, a young woman stepped in front of her to block her way. Morgan recognized the redhead. It was Ally, the journalist Morgan had tried to sell her story to.

"Morgan Stewart?" she said. "We meet again."

"Excuse me." Morgan tried to step away, but Ally moved in front of her.

"Not so fast," Ally replied. "I wish I had stuck around. You had a story to tell me and I should have listened. How was I to know you were Dane Stewart's baby sister? But it doesn't matter. I've got the local scoop. You've been seeing Jared Robinson, Austin's most notorious bachelor."

"I have no comment." Once again, Morgan tried to leave, but Ally wasn't budging. "Please step aside."

"You might not want to confirm your relationship with Jared, but perhaps you might want to comment on my latest story. Seems Jared here has a love child with his former fling Samantha Russell whom he's left to languish in poverty. Do you have a comment on that?"

"A child?" Jared roared from behind Morgan. "You must be out of your mind, Ally. I knew you liked to make up stories, but that's utter rubbish."

Morgan's stomach lurched. "Is it?" she asked, spinning around to face him.

Ally smirked at seeing her handiwork. "Jared has a child, Morgan. Didn't he tell you? Do you have a comment *now*?"

"I have to go." This time, Morgan shouldered past the

woman and rushed down the corridor. She didn't stop until she reached the outside and had run down the steps. Glancing around, she saw the car with an Uber sign in the window. Rushing toward it, she was nearly to the door when Jared caught up with her.

Jared grabbed her arm and spun her around. "Morgan, please, don't leave like this."

The desperation in his eyes was evident, but Morgan didn't care. "Please, let me go."

"I can't do that," Jared said. Concern was etched across his handsome features. "Not like this. I can't let you leave thinking the worst of me."

"Why should that matter to you, Jared?" She tugged on her arm and he released her. "You've ignored me all week. And tonight, I came here for *you*. Yet you treat me like something on the bottom of your shoe. Just like my father. I won't take it. Not anymore. I deserve better."

"Morgan…"

"Don't apologize. I agreed to this arrangement. It was temporary and I accept that. But a child? For Christ's sake, how could you abandon your own child?" Shaking her head in disbelief, she reached for the door handle and slid inside the car, but Jared blocked her from closing it.

"She's lying, Morgan. I would never abandon any child of mine, ever. If you believe nothing else from our time together, believe that."

He let go of the door and Morgan slammed it shut. "You can go to hell!"

The driver drove away and Morgan's last view was of Jared staring after the car with sadness in his eyes. It was over between them and finding out Jared abandoned his child was further confirmation that Morgan walking away was the best decision she'd ever made.

# Nineteen

He let her go.

He shouldn't have. The despair in Morgan's eyes destroyed Jared. He'd been keeping her at a distance all week, including tonight. In his mind, he'd done it for her own good, but he hadn't wanted to hurt her. Yet he didn't think he was good for her either. On the other hand, he wasn't the monster Ally was claiming he was.

Hearing the car door click shut was like a vault slamming, shutting him out of something so precious, Jared knew he'd never get it back.

"Jared, what is this I hear about you fathering a child? My God what's happening in this family? First Chris and now you?" His grandmother confronted him once he returned to the ballroom. The look on her face wasn't embarrassment, it was disappointment. He hadn't seen her expression of chagrin aimed at him in weeks and realized he never wanted to see it return.

"It isn't true."

"Are you sure about that?" His parents came over and his father was the first to jump on the bandwagon. "Up until Morgan, you were quite the playboy."

Chris and Kandi joined their circle and his brother defended him. "Jared would never be that negligent. There's one thing Jared has always practiced and that's safe sex."

"Must you be so crude, Chris?" his mother scolded.

"I will repeat. I don't have a child," Jared said, rather loudly so that several people standing nearby glanced up at his raised voice. "And I certainly wouldn't leave one I'd fathered to be raised without me. I'll prove it to all of you. To the entire world if I have to."

His mother breathed a sigh of relief, but his father still looked skeptical. Jared glanced at his grandmother. "Please tell me you believe me, Grandma?" He'd never called her that, but the endearment came to his mind given how close they'd become in recent weeks.

She didn't reply. Instead, she glanced around the room. "Where's Morgan?"

Jared lowered his head.

"Where is she?"

"She's gone," he answered.

"Because she believes this story?" his grandmother asked. "If your girlfriend believes this is true, how can we not?"

"She's not my girlfriend," Jared blurted out.

His grandmother frowned. Jared glanced around; his entire family looked perplexed. "What do you mean, son?" his father inquired.

*It was time to come clean. He was tired of the secret.* "I asked Morgan to pretend to be my girlfriend to help win over grandmother and the board."

Several looks of disbelief came his way. Even Chris rolled his eyes upward and spoke quietly to Kandi, who stepped away from the group so the Robinsons could have some privacy. "What the hell did you do, Jared?"

"I don't believe it." His grandmother shook her head. "What I saw between you wasn't make-believe. Morgan cares for you. I would bet my life on it."

Jared lowered his head. "She probably does, but I don't deserve her. She's too good for me."

"Why would you deceive us?" his mother asked. He could see that for once, he'd exasperated even her.

Jared sighed. "I didn't set out to lie to you. I just wanted to prove to everyone I could be like Chris and run the business." He motioned to his brother, who was scraping his jaw with his hand. "That I could step into his shoes. Grandmother said the board would prefer someone settled so I…" His voice trailed off.

"Roped Morgan into your lies," his grandmother finished. "How typical. And now she has feelings for you, but you've gotten yourself caught up in a scandal. My God, Jared, when will you ever learn?" Turning on her heel, she stormed away.

She wasn't the only one. His parents expressed their disappointment in him once more before heading off, leaving Jared and Chris alone. Jared was glad his brother didn't leave him and was still at his side as he'd been so many times.

"Well, you've really done it this time," Chris said.

Jared glared at him. "Yeah, I know. I've mucked it up bad. What am I going to do?"

Chris wrapped an arm around his shoulder. "The first thing you're going to do is clear your name of this slander about the baby. And then, you're going to get your woman back."

"Morgan?" Jared shook his head. "I can't. That ship has sailed. She thinks I fathered a child and abandoned it like her father did her. We're done."

Except Jared didn't feel like they were over.

"You have to talk to her," Chris said. "Convince her of the truth. I've seen you with Morgan, Jared. You're a different man—dare I say, a better man—because of her. You need Morgan. You have to make this right."

Jared nodded. He doubted Morgan would open the door to him, let alone listen to a word he had to say. He may have hurt her so bad that there was no coming back from it, but he wouldn't know unless he tried.

Morgan was on autopilot. She had been since last night when somehow she'd made it from the Uber to her apartment. Once the door shut, however, she'd fallen to the floor in a heap, where she'd stayed until she was all cried out. Eventually, she went to her bedroom, where she'd drawn the shades, curled into bed and turned off her phone. She needed sleep.

Except her sleep wasn't peaceful. She dreamed of Jared's smile. His laugh. His sinful abs. His tight butt, which she'd grasped as he'd driven her to the brink of pleasure. But that was over. It had been an illusion. A lie.

Jared wasn't the man she thought he was. He'd turned his back on her like he'd done his own child. He was no better than Henry. And she'd fallen head over heels in love with him. What a fool she'd been to fall for his lies hook, line and sinker.

She drifted off to sleep near dawn. When she woke up, Morgan had a plan: get out of Austin. She would go someplace remote to clear her head so she could figure out her next steps. Given that their relationship was over, Morgan didn't want anything from Jared, including his help finding a job. She realized now that wasn't the reason she'd stayed in Austin to begin with. It was because she'd fallen for him.

And now she would have to swallow her pride and ask Dane for help. Morgan would have preferred to be self-sufficient, but beggars couldn't be choosers.

She was finished packing by noon and planned to leave the key with the concierge on her way out. They'd already seen to her luggage so Morgan was giving the apartment one final look and was picking up her carry-on when the doorbell sounded. Morgan didn't need to look through the peephole to know who it was. She just knew.

Jared.

When she'd finally turned on her phone this morning, there had been endless texts and voice mails from Ruth and Morgan's siblings, who'd all read the story and wanted to know if she was okay. And then there were half a dozen voice mails from Jared. She didn't want to talk to him then and didn't intend to now.

But she had to face him one last time. Morgan swung open the door. Jared was leaning against the door frame in faded jeans and a pullover sweater with a bleak look in his eyes.

"Whatever you have to say, I'm not interested."

"We need to talk."

"*We* don't have to do anything." Morgan walked inside her apartment and to her despair, Jared followed. She smelled his spicy scent and it caused a fissure in her chest. But she refused to let her emotions bleed out and make a mess on the floor. "And I was just leaving."

Jared glanced at her small carry-on. "Are you going somewhere?"

"Yes."

"Where?"

"Does it really matter?" Morgan asked. "You have bigger fish to fry, like taking care of your child."

Jared's eyes turned stormy dark. "I don't have a child, Morgan. That's what I came to explain. Ally spewed lies last night. I don't have a child with Samantha. This is all some elaborate media ruse they've concocted, which is why I went to Samantha and told her I want a paternity test."

"Good for you." Morgan grasped her handbag and carry-on and moved to open the door. "I'm sure your family will appreciate that, but I have a flight to catch."

Jared pushed the door closed with the palm of his hand. "You can't leave like this, with so much unfinished between us."

Morgan shook her head. "You've made it pretty clear you're no longer interested in continuing our arrangement or in being my lover. I'm sure it must have been a strain dealing with my lack of knowledge for someone so experienced as yourself, but I got the hint, okay? So please, let me leave gracefully and with a shred of dignity."

She passed underneath his arm, walked to the elevator bank and pressed the down button. Jared followed her.

"You're not even going to give me the benefit of the doubt?" he asked, his expression watchful. "After everything…"

The elevator chimed and Morgan stepped inside. Jared did the same. She couldn't look at him. She didn't dare because Morgan knew if she did, she'd be lost, caught up in his world again where she'd lose herself. Jared was never going to be her Prince Charming. He'd told her from the start and she'd foolishly built him up in her heart to be more.

*She'd been wrong.*

When the elevator made it to the ground floor, Jared surprised Morgan by taking her carry-on and walking with her through the lobby. But when they reached the French doors he stopped.

"Don't go," he pleaded, halting her steps. "Stay with me. We can figure this out."

"I can't. I can't see you ever again, Jared. It hurts too much." Morgan couldn't take it anymore. She wrenched her bag from his grasp and rushed out the doors. She knew if she didn't leave now she would never leave because Jared had a hold on her.

Morgan wasn't looking where she was going and ran out into the circular driveway just as a car drove up to the entrance. Morgan caught a glimpse of it, but not in time to stop. Her last image as the car struck her was of soaring through the air and Jared's horrified expression before everything went black.

* * *

Jared was frozen for several seconds on the sidewalk as he watched Morgan fly through the air and hit the pavement. Then, he sprang into action, rushing to her side. She was unconscious, sprawled out in the driveway, with blood gushing from her head.

He was terrified. He knew enough not to move her with a head injury. "Call an ambulance!" he screamed.

The valet was on his phone immediately while the driver of the car got out and started toward Jared. "Stay away!" He held his hand up.

"I'm so sorry," the man cried. "I didn't see her. She jumped out in front of my car. I tried to…"

"Shut up! I don't give a damn about your excuses." Jared responded. He just prayed Morgan would survive this, but she wasn't moving. He looked down at her and whispered, "Please, baby, please don't leave me."

He lowered his head and rested it against her bosom. It was inconceivable to him that Morgan could leave this earth and he would never see her again. And tell her what he'd only just discovered as she'd hurtled through the air.

"I love you," he said softly against her chest. But feared it was too late.

# Twenty

"Jared, what the hell happened?" His grandmother ran toward him in the waiting room of St. David's Medical Center with his parents, Chris and Kandi close behind her. It was the first time in his life he'd ever seen his grandmother disheveled. She was usually so put together, but today, her hair was ruffled and she wore jeans and a tunic. He doubted she'd ever worn jeans a day in her life. "How's Morgan?"

"I—I don't know…" Jared shook his head. "They've been running lots of tests—X-rays, CAT scans and some sort of EEG to record the electrical activity in her brain."

"Omigod!" His grandmother clasped her hand to her mouth, fell into a chair and began sobbing.

"It's okay." His mother rushed to her side. "She's going to pull through."

"Is there anything we can do?" Chris asked and Kandi nodded.

"Morgan's been so great to me," she said, tears in her eyes. "This is so awful." She turned into Chris's arms and wept.

Jared moved away from them to the window and stared blankly outside. He felt a presence behind him and saw his father's reflection in the glass. "I'm sorry, son. I know I was hard on you the other night. And I can see I was wrong. You've changed. You care for this girl."

"It's more than that, Dad," Jared said, turning to face

him. "I love her. And I never thought I could feel that way about anybody. But when I saw that car hit her and she went flying through the air—" he shook his head trying to rid himself of the images "—I swear to God, I... I thought..."

His father clutched his shoulders, bringing him into a hug. "Don't say it. Let alone think it." He grasped both sides of Jared's face. "Morgan's a strong woman, okay?"

Jared nodded. "I feel so guilty. She was leaving because of me."

"Perhaps you should feel guilty," a sharp female voice said from behind his father. Jared glanced up and saw Fallon standing there. Her husband Gage, Ayden and his wife, Maya, were by her side. Jared had met them all at Dane's wedding.

On his way in the ambulance, he'd called his parents and then he'd called Dane. When he'd reached him, his friend had been beside himself, but promised to be there as soon as he could. Dane told Jared he'd call the rest of Morgan's siblings.

"Fallon." Chris came toward them. They'd all grown up together, but Chris and Fallon were close in age, like Dane and Jared. "That's not fair. Jared wasn't driving the car that hit Morgan."

"But you hurt her." Fallon's hazel-gray eyes—*Morgan's eyes*—stared back at him accusingly.

"The rumors about Jared fathering a child are a blatant lie," Chris said. Jared appreciated his brother defending him, but Fallon was right. It was because of him Morgan was in this predicament. Maybe if he'd stayed away, she wouldn't be hurt.

Tears sprang to his eyes. "I'm sorry." Jared spun on his heel and walked out of the waiting room and down the hall. He didn't have a particular destination in mind. He just needed breathing room. Everyone in that waiting room knew Morgan was a good woman and wondered why she'd been with a schmuck like him. She'd been leaving because she had cause to believe the rumors were true. He wasn't a good guy.

Or at least he hadn't been.

Until Morgan.

Jared walked aimlessly and found himself at the doors of the small hospital chapel. He didn't know how he got there, but he pushed the doors open and walked inside. It was empty. There were several pews with a cross in the center of the room.

Jared wasn't a religious man, but he sat in one of the pews anyway. If he closed his eyes, he could feel Morgan's lips on his. Picture her smile. She'd imprinted on his heart and he couldn't imagine his life without her.

Clasping his hands together, Jared lowered his head and prayed. He prayed that Morgan would pull through this. There was so much left unsaid between them. He loved her. He'd been afraid to see it. He'd tried to deny and ignore it, but he couldn't deny the truth any longer. She was everything he'd ever wanted and hadn't known he needed. And although he didn't know Morgan's exact feelings, Jared was certain she felt something. If not love, then genuine affection for him. They had a foundation to build on.

He heard the doors of the chapel open, but he didn't look up. He was too caught up in his own guilt. When he turned, it was his brother. Chris sat beside him and wrapped an arm around him. And for the first time in his life, Jared cried. Tears gushed out of his eyes and he let them. If anything happened to Morgan, he'd never forgive himself.

"I've got you, bro," Chris whispered. "I've got you."

Jared didn't know how long they stayed that way, but eventually his tears subsided and he pulled himself together and rose to his feet. He had to get an update on Morgan's condition.

But first he turned to Chris and pointed at him. "If you tell anyone I cried, I'll deny it."

"I would expect nothing less," Chris said. "C'mon." They walked out of the chapel together.

When Jared arrived back at the waiting room he was shocked to see Henry and Nora Stewart there.

"What the hell?"

"Easy, Jared," Chris whispered beside him.

Jared pushed Chris's warning aside. "I'm not going to stay calm. What are you doing here?" He looked at Henry. "You've consistently denied Morgan was your child and rebuffed her attempts to get to know you. If I recall correctly, you told her you would never accept her as your daughter, would never claim her. So I ask again, why are you here?"

He saw Fallon stand up, but her husband, Gage, gently pushed her back in her chair. Jared didn't care if Fallon was upset. Morgan couldn't speak up for herself, so he would.

Henry lowered his lashes for several moments. "You're right, Jared. I may not have known of her existence before, but once I did, I treated Morgan horribly. I've been a terrible father to her and not just to her, but to my oldest son, Ayden." Henry glanced at Ayden, who was sitting nearby with Maya, glaring at him. "I've never liked admitting I was wrong, that I could make a mistake, but I'm doing it now. I'm truly sorry, and if Morgan pulls through, I'll be a better father."

"That's a little too late," Jared said. "What if…"

"Jared Robinson." His grandmother came up beside him and spun him around. "You will not say such a thing. My girl—" at his raised brow, she amended "—*our* girl will make it. All of us will accept nothing else." She looked sternly at Henry as she said those last words.

Jared nodded and took a seat beside her. Morgan had a lot of people praying for her recovery. Jared hoped it was enough.

Morgan fought to open her eyes, but it was so hard. Her vision was hazy. She couldn't hear, either, except for a low buzzing noise and her entire body throbbed with pain, especially her head. She felt lost and unsure of her surroundings.

Slowly her sight became clear and she saw Dane sitting in a chair beside her with a blanket thrown over him. *What was he doing here? Shouldn't he be in Los Angeles with Iris and Jayden?*

She tried to speak, but realized something was in her mouth and she couldn't talk. Panicking, Morgan tapped the bed to get his attention.

Dane started when he heard the noise. "Morgan?" His brown eyes rested on hers and a large smile spread across his face. "Oh, thank God." He rushed toward her and began kissing her furiously on the forehead. "I'm going to call the nurse to get that tube out of your throat."

*There was a tube in her throat? Why?*

*What happened to her?*

Dane ran out of the room and Morgan heard him calling for help. She tried to calm down. Soon nurses and a team of doctors flooded the room. First they removed the breathing tube, then checked her vitals and examined her. They explained she'd been in a coma for a few days. She suffered a brain injury when she'd been hit by a car.

*Hit by a car?*

Morgan vaguely remembered being in her apartment with Jared and then nothing. Despite her spotty memory, Morgan noticed one thing. Her family had come into the room.

All of them.

It wasn't just Dane. Fallon and Ayden were present with

their spouses, but most surprising of all, her father was here with Nora. Morgan stared as the medical team worked around her. *Why was Henry here?* He'd told her he'd never acknowledge her and she'd believed him. It was one of the reasons she'd finally decided to leave Austin. *That much she remembered.*

And then there were the Robinsons. Ruth was beaming at her from the other side of the bed, while Jared's parents, Chris and Kandi enthusiastically smiled at her.

But one person was missing.

The one person she wanted to see more than anyone else, even though she'd told him she was leaving Austin and never wanted to see him again. Even though he may have fathered another woman's baby. Morgan still loved him and wanted to see him.

Jared.

*Why were his parents here and not him?*

*Where was he?*

Eventually the doctor turned to the large group assembled. "All right folks, I let you all come in so you could see for yourself Morgan is on the mend, but we're going to need to limit visitors. Morgan's been through quite an ordeal."

"Of course," Ruth said with a small smile. "We'll wait outside." She walked over to Morgan and squeezed her hand. She could see Ruth trying to keep it together, but the old bird had a soft spot because a tear leaked from her eyelid. "We're just so thankful to see you awake."

Morgan nodded because she too was overcome with emotion to speak. She watched as the Robinsons filed out of the room. Now only the Stewarts remained.

Her father came toward her bed. "I'd like to speak to Morgan alone if I may?" He glanced back at his children and their spouses. Ayden, Dane and Fallon looked back and forth at each other, clearly uneasy with their father's request.

Fallon spoke up. "I don't know, Dad. Perhaps this re-union can wait?"

Henry shook his head. "I'm sorry. It can't wait another minute."

Fallon looked at Morgan, asking an unspoken question.

"It's okay," Morgan croaked. "I'll hear him out."

"We'll be right outside the door if you need us," Dane said. Several moments later, her siblings and their spouses all exited the room, leaving Morgan alone with Henry and Nora.

Surprisingly, Henry turned to his wife, who stood wood-enly at his side. Nora looked no worse for wear in jeans and a white button-down shirt, though Morgan did notice she wasn't as made up as she'd seen Nora in the past.

"That includes you too, darling," Henry stated softly. "I need to talk to my daughter alone."

"Henry…"

He gave Nora a look that said the topic wasn't up for dis-cussion. Begrudgingly, Nora left the room. Henry pulled up the chair Dane had vacated to Morgan's beside.

Morgan didn't know how to feel having Henry here. After all the years of wanting and dreaming of a father, when she'd finally revealed herself, he'd cast her aside. He'd made her feel less than, as if she wasn't good enough to have his blood running through her veins.

"Morgan, I'm sorry."

"Exactly what are you sorry for?" A couple of instances came to mind such as his cold words when she'd confronted him at Stewart Manor and he'd told her, "I owe you noth-ing." Or perhaps it was the angry glare he'd given her at the Alzheimer's charity event. She may have forgotten some things, but not his hostility toward her.

"For everything. I've treated you abominably."

Morgan's hearted contracted and the machines hooked

up to her began to beat erratically as her blood pressure spiked. "Yeah, you did."

Henry touched her hand and Morgan flinched, so he pulled away. "Please calm down. I don't want you upset."

"Your being here is upsetting."

His features contracted and Morgan knew she'd hurt him. "I was hoping for the opposite effect. I know I was wrong. I pushed you away when I should have been pulling you closer."

Tears sprang to her eyes and she only had one thing to say. "Why?"

Henry rubbed his hands together and she could see he was mulling over his words. He was silent for several beats and then he spoke. "Because I thought I was a better man with Nora. Or at least I was going to try to be after my marriage to Lillian ended badly. But one night in Vegas I messed up. Nora and I had been going through a rough patch in our marriage and I was feeling lonely. Neglected. There's no excuse, but I met a beautiful showgirl and we became intimate. I regretted it soon after it happened and I went back to Nora more determined than ever to make our marriage work. And I did. We got through it."

Morgan stared back at Henry. She was finally getting an explanation for his behavior, but she suspected it wasn't going to bring her the comfort she thought it would.

"I'd put that evening with your mother behind me and never thought of it again," Henry said. "It was as if it never happened. But then you showed up at Dane's wedding and told me you were a result of that night when I was at my lowest. I wasn't just angry. I was embarrassed at being faced with my greatest failure as a man, *as a husband.*"

So Nora was right, Morgan thought. He thought of Morgan as a mistake. "Please stop. I don't want to hear any more." He was nailing the coffin shut on their ever having a relationship.

"Morgan, please. Let me say this. You deserve an explanation."

Morgan shook her head. "It hurts too much."

"And I'm sorry for that," Henry said. "I lashed out at you when the person I was angry at most with was myself because you were the next best target. It wasn't your fault I cheated on Nora. *I* did that. You were an innocent child who deserved to have a father, but I swear to you, I had no idea you'd been conceived. Your mother never reached out to me after that night, but then again we hadn't exchanged much info. Had I known…"

"You would have acknowledged me?" Morgan snorted with derision. "Like you did Ayden? You were married to his mother, for Christ's sake. Please don't lie."

Henry rose to his feet and began to pace, then stopped and turned back to her. "You're right. I've been a selfish bastard trying to hold on to my wealth and my young wife. I've treated you and Ayden horribly and I can't take those moments back, Morgan. All I can tell you is that I want to try to make it right. I want to heal the divide between me and my children. I intend to embrace all of my heirs, including you. If you still want that."

Morgan was speechless. She'd waited a lifetime to hear a father say he wanted to be part of her life, but she was scared to reach for the brass ring. *What if he pulled the rug out from under her because she didn't measure up?* Morgan wasn't sure she could trust him with her heart.

"I don't know if I can believe you," Morgan responded. "You talk a good game, but actions speak louder than words."

"I know I don't deserve it and you have every right to tell me to take a hike after the way I've treated you, but I'm asking if you will give me a chance to be a father." Henry's eyes were watering. "I will work on making it up to you. I promise. I just need to know if you'll give me another shot."

Tears slid down Morgan's cheek. Out of spite, she wanted to tell him no. To be as mean and hateful as he'd been to her. But deep down all she'd ever wanted was to have a dad. To have someone save her from the awful life she'd endured with her mother and all those men. To have a father to kiss away the boo-boos and make it all better.

Being angry with Henry wouldn't hurt just him. It would hurt her too. If she didn't forgive him, she'd never really heal and be able to move on with her life. Or have a good relationship with a man because didn't a women's first relationship start with her father?

Morgan nodded. "All right."

Henry's hazel-gray eyes became cloudy as he reached for Morgan and she reluctantly allowed him to hold her in his embrace. "Oh, thank God. I'm not too late." He leaned back and kissed the top of her head. "I'm sorry, baby girl. I'm so sorry, but Daddy's got you."

Henry held Morgan in his arms and it was wonderful knowing she was finally accepted. She belonged.

# Twenty-One

Jared ran through the corridors of St. David's Medical Center after Chris texted him Morgan was awake. Of course it happened when he'd left the hospital for an hour. He'd gotten a call from the lab that the results of the paternity test were in. While he'd waited for Morgan to wake up, he and Samantha's daughter had had blood drawn. Jared had to know the truth, so he'd gone personally to get the results. When Morgan awoke—and he'd believed she would—he wanted to have the paternity results to show her the truth. To show her he wasn't like Henry and would never abandon his child.

And he was right.

The results said with one hundred percent certainty that he couldn't have fathered Samantha's child. He'd already called Ally's boss and threatened him with a lawsuit over slandering Jared's name. The blog had a retraction being prepared, which would go live that afternoon. In time, the brouhaha would die down, but Jared was furious because he could have lost Morgan because of it.

Jared was relieved as he'd driven back to the hospital. Then Chris had given him the good news Morgan was awake, but he wasn't there. Jared felt terrible. He'd wanted to be the first person Morgan saw when she awoke. Hopefully, seeing the Stewarts there would help salve the

wound. Because if he was honest, would she really want
to see him?

*Would she remember she'd told him they were over and
she never wanted to see him again?*

He hoped not, but even if she did, Jared planned on convincing Morgan he would never leave her side. He couldn't
wait to tell her just how much he loved her.

On his way to Morgan's room, he stopped by the waiting room. His family and the Stewarts were all assembled.

"Jared! Thank heavens you're here." His grandmother
smiled when she saw him. "Morgan is awake."

Jared grinned. "I know, and I'm headed to see her, but
I wanted to share some news." He held up the envelope in
his hands. "Results of the paternity test showing I *didn't*
father a child."

He noticed Fallon raise her hands up to the sky in silent thanks.

"I never doubted you," Chris said, coming to Jared and
giving him a hug.

"We may have." Ayden glanced at Fallon and Dane. "I'm
glad that we were wrong." He came forward and offered
his hand. Jared shook it. He knew Morgan's siblings only
wanted the best for her. But he was that man and it was
time their sister knew it.

"Thank you," Jared said. "Now, if you'll excuse me. I
need to see someone."

"Go get her, tiger!" Kandi yelled from the sidelines as
Jared quickly walked down the corridor to Morgan's room.
When he arrived, the door was partially open and to his
surprise, Henry had Morgan wrapped in his arms. He didn't
want to interrupt the reunion, but Henry caught sight of
him and motioned him forward.

"Come in, Jared. I think someone might like to see you."
He pulled away and Jared's eyes connected with Morgan's.

His heart expanded at finally seeing her awake after so many days of praying for her recovery.

Henry glanced at Jared and back at Morgan. "I'm going to give you both some privacy."

Jared was speechless and merely nodded. Henry patted him on the shoulder as he left and whispered, "Don't give up on her."

Jared stood by the doorway after he left, afraid to step forward.

"Are you just going to stand there?" Morgan asked.

At her words, Jared sprang into action, walking toward the bed and sitting in the chair beside her. "Morgan, I... I'm so thankful you're okay," he barely managed to get out.

She nodded.

"How much do you remember? Of the accident?"

"Not much," Morgan answered. "The doctors said, my memory could come back today, in pieces or not at all. And I don't much care if it does. I don't want to remember being hit by a car." She gave a half laugh. "But I do recall telling you I was leaving Austin for good."

Her words hit Jared's ears like the crash that had almost taken her from him and his heart sank. "I was hoping you'd forget that part."

Morgan sighed. "Not likely." She stared at him. "I know we need to talk, but I have to say this first. Thank you."

"For what?"

"For calling my family," Morgan replied. "It's because of you they're all here. Henry—I mean, my father—told me you called Dane and he rallied everyone. And as you can see—" she motioned to the door and he could see tears glistening in her eyelids "—I'm going to have the family I always wanted. So thank you."

Jared swallowed the lump in his throat, but it remained lodged in his chest. "You already have a family, Morgan. Me and all the Robinsons. Please tell me you know that."

\* \* \*

Morgan stared into Jared's beautiful dark eyes, eyes she'd come to know so well. It appeared as if he hadn't gotten much sleep. Instead of his usual tidy appearance, Jared looked haggard with several days' stubble on his chiseled jaw. He was wearing a simple T-shirt and dark stonewashed jeans. But in her opinion, he'd never looked sexier. Handsome didn't come close to describing his lethal good looks.

She'd been disappointed when she hadn't seen him among all her visitors, but he was here now and she wanted to weep with gratitude. "When I woke up and you weren't here…"

"Sweetheart." Jared jumped out of the chair and onto the edge of Morgan's bed. "I've been by your side day and night driving the doctors and nurses crazy. The only reason I left was for this." He pulled out the manila envelope from his back pocket.

Morgan frowned. "What's that?"

"The results of the paternity test," Jared replied. "Showing I'm not a father."

Morgan lowered her lashes. "I know."

His eyes widened in surprise and a faint smile touched his mouth. "You do? But you said…"

"I was hurt and in my feelings." She glanced up and felt her eyes swim with tears while her mouth trembled "I—I thought you didn't want me and I latched on to the first thing I heard that validated that premise. But I know you, Jared." Morgan reached out and pressed her hand to his cheek, smiling when he closed his eyes and let her caress him. "I know you're not the kind of man who would abandon his child. I *know* that."

She heard his audible sigh of relief. "Thank you. So if you can believe that much about me, can you believe one more thing?"

She shrugged. "Maybe?"

"I love you, Morgan."

Joy careened through her, but Morgan had to be sure she wasn't hearing things. "What did you say?"

"I love you." Jared gazed into her eyes for a long, lingering moment.

Astonished and struck speechless by his confession, Morgan looked back at him.

"I'm *in love* with you. You're the first thing I think about in the morning and the last thing I think about at night. And it scared me to feel that much, never mind admitting to it. So I kept my distance because I was afraid I couldn't be the Prince Charming you'd built me up to be. I thought I wasn't good enough for someone as beautiful, sweet and kind as you."

"Oh Jared…"

"I've never been in love, Morgan. I made a mess of things last week with you, but I know what I feel now. Seeing you nearly die in front of me, everything in my world went gray and I knew I couldn't live a day without you. I realized how precious life was and that I didn't want to waste another minute. I promised myself if you pulled through that I would confess my love. Because when I'm with you, Morgan, my whole world is brighter, lighter and filled with love."

Morgan had dreamed of this moment, but never thought it was possible Jared could feel the same way about her as she felt about him. "I feel the same way, Jared."

"You do?" His mouth curved into a smile.

Morgan smiled through her tears. "I love you too." And she loved the way his gleaming dark eyes pulsed as she said the words. "I think I have from the moment we met. If you had told me you could fall in love at first sight, I would have told you, you watched too many Dane Stewart romantic comedies, but it's true. I love you."

Jared framed her face with his hands, bringing her closer

to him so her forehead rested on his. They stayed that way for several moments, neither of them speaking, just soaking in the emotion of what they'd revealed to one another. A deep happiness Morgan hadn't known was possible spread through her.

Jared lifted his head and stared deeply into her eyes, allowing her to see the depth of his soul. "Is spending the rest of your life with me something you would consider?"

Morgan tried to hold it together, but her emotions were all over the place after her reunion with her father.

"I want to be with you now and always, Morgan, and that's not ever going to change. So let me try this again." Jared slid out of her grasp and onto one knee by her hospital bed. "Morgan Stewart, would you do me the honor of becoming my wife?"

"Yes, yes, yes," Morgan bent down to lift him up and the machines beside her bed went haywire. She didn't care— she cupped Jared's face and kissed him with breathless, urgent kisses. When they finally parted, she murmured. "You're my beginning and my ending, Jared. You're my everything."

# Epilogue

*Three months later*

"To Jared and Morgan!" Henry raised a glass to toast Morgan and Jared after their wedding at Stewart Manor.

"To Jared and Morgan." Everyone's voices rang out in the backyard near the terrace. Jared clinked his glass against Morgan's and she beamed up at him.

He hoped the day had been everything Morgan dreamed of. It was a small intimate gathering: the Stewarts, the Robinsons and a few close friends. Morgan had looked spectacular in her designer gown. The crystal bodice sheath with the silk tulle skirt had fit her figure like a glove and Jared couldn't wait to take it off later.

Fallon was Morgan's maid of honor while her friend Whitney and Dane's wife, Iris, served as her bridesmaids. Morgan had wanted Kandi too, but at eight months, his sister-in-law was very pregnant with his brother's child and not inclined to stand on her feet all day. Jared had been proud to have Dane and Ayden as his groomsmen standing alongside Chris, his best man. He couldn't have asked for a better entourage. As married men, Chris and Dane had both offered him some sage advice.

*Happy wife, happy life.*

Jared planned on ensuring that, which was why he had a special surprise in store for Morgan for their wedding night.

He ambled close to her. "Have I told you lately how incredibly happy you've made me?"

"Not lately," she said, flirting. "How about you start."

He lowered his head and pressed his lips to hers and knew he'd finally come home.

Morgan enjoyed Jared's kiss, but they were interrupted by her nephew Dylan tugging on Jared's tuxedo.

Morgan watched Jared lift him in his arms. He was going to make a great father someday.

Thinking of fathers had Morgan reflecting on the highlight of her day: Henry walking her down the aisle. They had come a long way in their relationship since her accident. Henry hadn't lied when he told her he'd be there and wanted to heal the rift with all his children. It had been a toss-up between him and Jared as to whom she was going to stay with after her recovery. In the end, she decided to be with her man, but she visited Henry often and they were slowly getting to know each other.

"What are you thinking about?" Jared asked from her side after Dylan went off to play with his cousin Jayden.

Morgan glanced up at Jared and saw love shining in his eyes. "I was thinking about how perfect our wedding was."

"It was perfect, because you finally became mine, all mine. And I can't wait to get you alone," he growled.

Jared's appetite for Morgan hadn't waned. In fact, it was stronger than it had ever been and she was ready for their honeymoon to begin. "What do you say we get out of here?" she murmured.

"Gladly."

They were nearly to the terrace doors when Ruth came forward to kiss Morgan on each cheek. "I'm so happy to officially have you as part of our family. I knew from day one Jared had a keeper."

"So did I," Jared said with a wide grin. "Now, if you'll excuse us…"

"Are you two sneaking off?" she whispered.

Jared nodded.

"All right then, I've got you covered." She winked at them conspiratorially.

Morgan and Jared slipped away without anyone else noticing their departure. They slid into a Bentley minutes later and let it take them the thirty-minute ride to the Robinson family compound. They'd decided to honeymoon there because it was the place they'd fallen for each other.

Jared carried Morgan over the threshold of the cottage where they'd first made love and placed her on her feet. Dozens of candles adorned every surface of the room and rose petals were strewn across the floor leading a path to the bedroom.

Morgan looked at Jared. "You had all this done?"

Jared shrugged. "With a little help from Antoine."

"You're an incredible man, Jared Robinson, and I adore you."

"The feeling's mutual," he murmured. "Now come here, woman." He took her by the hand and led her to the bedroom where they stripped each other naked and came together in a meeting of mind, body and souls. Ecstasy soon swallowed them and they shuddered in simultaneous orgasm. Morgan suspected their rapture had created a miracle.

It proved true several weeks later when a home test showed positive and her doctor confirmed Morgan was pregnant with Jared's baby.

"Are you happy?" Morgan asked when Jared drew her into his embrace after she'd finished dressing at the doctor's office. She was shaking.

"Deliriously," Jared said, smiling down at her. "I can't

wait to have a little Morgan running around. She will be Daddy's little girl."

Morgan grinned from ear to ear. "I love you, Jared."

And she did. Loving him had enriched her and now they would have a new life to share theirs with.

It didn't get any better than this.

\* \* \* \* \*

# COMING SOON!

We really hope you enjoyed reading this book. If you're looking for more romance, be sure to head to the shops when new books are available on

## Thursday 14th May

# MILLS & BOON

## THE HEART OF ROMANCE

---

## A ROMANCE FOR EVERY KIND OF READER

---

**MODERN**

Prepare to be swept off your feet by sophisticated, sexy and seductive heroes, in some of the world's most glamourous and romantic locations, where power and passion collide.
**8 stories per month.**

**HISTORICAL**

Escape with historical heroes from time gone by. Whether your passion is for wicked Regency Rakes, muscled Vikings or rugge Highlanders, awaken the romance of the past.
**6 stories per month.**

**MEDICAL**

Set your pulse racing with dedicated, delectable doctors in the high-pressure world of medicine, where emotions run high and passion, comfort and love are the best medicine.
**6 stories per month.**

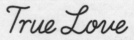

Celebrate true love with tender stories of heartfelt romance, fro the rush of falling in love to the joy a new baby can bring, and a focus on the emotional heart of a relationship.
**8 stories per month.**

Indulge in secrets and scandal, intense drama and plenty of siz hot action with powerful and passionate heroes who have it all: wealth, status, good looks...everything but the right woman.
**6 stories per month.**

**HEROES**

Experience all the excitement of a gripping thriller, with an inte romance at its heart. Resourceful, true-to-life women and strong fearless men face danger and desire - a killer combination!
**8 stories per month.**

**DARE**

Sensual love stories featuring smart, sassy heroines you'd want a best friend, and compelling intense heroes who are worthy of t
**4 stories per month.**

---

To see which titles are coming soon, please visit

## millsandboon.co.uk/nextmonth

# JOIN US ON SOCIAL MEDIA!

Stay up to date with our latest releases, author
news and gossip, special offers and discounts, and
all the behind-the-scenes action
from Mills & Boon...

 millsandboon

 millsandboonuk

millsandboon

*It might just be true love...*

# MILLS & BOON

## HEROES

### At Your Service

Experience all the excitement of a gripping thriller, with an intense romance at its heart. Resourceful, true-to-life women and strong, fearless men face danger and desire - a killer combination!

# MILLS & BOON
## MODERN
# Power and Passion

Prepare to be swept off your feet by sophisticated, sexy and seductive heroes, in some of the world's most glamourous and romantic locations, where power and passion collide.

# JOIN THE
# MILLS & BOON
# BOOKCLUB

* **FREE** delivery direct to your door

* **EXCLUSIVE** offers every month

* **EXCITING** rewards programme

50% OFF
YOUR FIRST
PARCEL

## Join today at
### Millsandboon.co.uk/Bookclub